THE
BLACK HAT
SQUAD

GHOSTED

To Bob!

Enjoy!!

Greg Herbachuk

GREG HERBACHUK

Tellwell Talent
www.tellwell.ca

ISBN
978-0-2288-4942-1 (Paperback)
978-0-2288-5924-6 (eBook)

DEDICATION

This book is dedicated to my dear deceased mother, Rose Herbachuk, who taught me to read and write my name before I started school. I know you are an angel in heaven, looking down on me. I miss you.

I would like to thank all the people at Tellwell who helped me with my book. From editing to doing the design. It made me look more professional.

ACKNOWLEDGEMENTS

I want to thank my mother, Rose Trosky Herbachuk, for teaching me to read and write and for teaching me right from wrong. I want to thank my father William Herbachuk teaching me hard-knock lessons, and I want to thank my brothers Bill and Jimmy-Ray and my sister Judy for their support. I also want to thank my best friend Bill Auger, who asked me to make him the villain in this book. My main character is based on my uncles John Tiny Trosky and Mike Trosky.

CHAPTER ONE

A middle-aged man with dark, greying hair, brown eyes, and a muscular build is disguised as a room service person, wearing a red uniform and white gloves. He knocks on the door of room 575, and in a French accent, says, "Room service."

The door opens, and a forty-five-year-old man with dark, slicked-back hair, slim build, standing at about five-foot-seven tall, and wearing a blue dress shirt and dark blue pants, yells, "Yes. Come in."

The service person looks at the bill and says, "Doctor Blackwell?"

"Yes, yes, come in. What took you so long?" Dr. Blackwell says.

"I am so sorry, sir, but with this convention on, we are swamped. You ordered a bottle of Albert Bichot Chablis 2059 and Duck à l' Orange with asparagus and rice?"

"Yes, set it down on this little table," Dr. Blackwell replies.

The service person sets everything up, opens the bottle of wine, and pours some into a glass. The doctor samples it. The service person then steps back, turns sideways, injects something into the wine bottle, and pours more wine into the doctor's glass. The doctor is thirsty and takes a big drink of the wine. "The wine has a lovely bouquet, nice and tart," the doctor says. He starts to eat his meal and then adds, "I don't feel well."

The service person leans down and takes out a vase with a lily in it from the bottom of the trolley. "This is from Lily, enjoy the rest of your life," the service person says.

The doctor looks the service person in the eyes and says, "What? Who? Why?" Blood starts pouring from his mouth and nose as he falls forward onto his dinner, bleeds all over the table, and dies.

The Ghost exits the room and leaves the trolley in the hallway. He slips into a maintenance closet and changes his clothes. He then leaves the hotel through the freight elevator and goes out through the loading dock.

CHAPTER TWO

Lieutenant John "Tiny" Trosky, a handsome thirty-year-old man with light brown hair and blue eyes, slim build, wearing a 1940s style black suit, a charcoal-coloured shirt, a white tie, and a black Stetson hat, is finishing a report on the husband and wife, who killed each other over drugs, Robert and Patty Burns. He checks the date. It is Tuesday, April 11th, 2070, and it is 1:35 p.m. He is sitting at his wooden, antique, hand-carved desk from the 1940s that belonged to Humphrey Bogart. His video-cell phone rings, "Dispatch, Lieutenant John Trosky, report to Vancouver Convention Center, room 575. Suspicious homicide."

"Acknowledged. Computer, save file# h7096. Hold and lock," he says.

He walks into the bullpen and says, "Detective Chuck Sidhu, you're with me; suspicious homicide at the Vancouver Convention Centre! Grab your hat, and let's go!"

Chuck grabs his black Stetson hat, and they take the elevator to the basement garage. They approach their beat-up, puke green police unit, with a new scrape on the driver's side.

"Shit, Chuck, we've got to find out who drove this piece of shit last. I hope it still runs and flies."

"I'll bet it was Detective Garry Cornburra!" Chuck says.

"Yeah, he is a dick; always screwing something up," John replies.

They blast out onto the street. John hits vertical, and the Pursuit xv90 sputters, hesitates, rises to 70 metres, stays up, and then slowly speeds to 100 kilometres per hour toward the Vancouver Convention Centre. John gasps, "I can't wait to get my new vehicle; this thing will kill us one day!"

They arrive quickly and take the elevator to the fifth floor and go to room 575. There is a uniformed officer at the door. Officer Silvia Estabrook says, "I don't know if you can enter the room as it could be contaminated."

John pulls out his badge and says, "I'm Lieutenant John Trosky, homicide. I'm primary on this case. Is Doctor Luci Ryan, the chief medical examiner, in there?"

"Yes, lieutenant."

"Ask her to come out here."

Officer Estabrook opens the door and calls the doctor. Dr. Luci Ryan steps out. She is gorgeous, with long red curly hair, blue eyes, five-foot-six, about 120 pounds. She is wearing a medium grey suit and a white smock.

"Hi, John, want to join the party? I've already scanned the body and the room for deadly diseases and toxic substances, and it's safe to come in," she says.

Lieutenant John Trosky and Detective Chuck Sidhu seal up their hands and shoes with a spray can of sealer.

"Recorder on, and activate yours too, Detective Sidhu," John says. "Thanks, Luci, we'll break out the champagne later. Chuck, get some uniforms to canvas the guests on this floor, and get the hotel manager to give us the security footage of this floor, hallways, entrances, and all exits."

John scans the room with his eyes. The room contains cheap hotel art, a small kitchen, a mini-fridge, an auto chef, and a small closet. He notices the lily in a vase on the table and thinks it's an unusual flower to put with lunch.

"Luci, did you do a scan of the body with your handheld x-ray scanner?" he asks.

"No, I was just checking for blood diseases and injuries," she says.

Luci pulls out her scanner and runs it over the body, and says, "Whoa, his heart is missing!" She opens Doctor Blackwell's shirt and sees no cuts. She exclaims, "What the hell? His heart is gone, but it wasn't cut out."

"Wait a minute, who is this guy?" John asks.

"I checked his prints and time of death. He is Doctor James Blackwell, a heart surgeon. He is here for a heart surgeon's conference. He is from Winnipeg, a resident doctor at Seven Oaks Hospital. His time of death is 2:32 p.m. He died quickly," Luci informs.

John checks his minicomputer. "Doctor James Blackwell, sixty-three years old, heart surgeon, his wife died of cancer five years ago. "Well, this is murder for sure. I wonder who wanted him dead? Detective Sidhu, start checking the hospital records for any patients that died under his knife. Get a warrant if you need to; hospitals are sensitive about records. Every doctor loses a patient now and then. Let's check this room for a laptop, cell phone, hotel phone, and check his clothing for any clues. Luci, who found the body?" John asks.

"The maid, a Miss Jayne Applebee, twenty-three years old, has worked here for two years, no criminal record."

"Chuck, let's get Miss Applebee's statement, but not in this room. Where is she?" John asks.

Officer Tracy Grewal took her to a breakroom on the first floor," Luci says.

"We will talk to her later; give her time to settle down. Chuck, get the Electronic Detective Division in here to check his phone and laptop history of calls and emails," John says.

CHAPTER THREE

The killer sends an email that reads: "Lily delivered." He waits a few minutes and checks his secret account to see that his fee of one million dollars has been deposited, and smiles.

Lieutenant John Trosky and Detective Sidhu check the room and personal items of Dr. Blackwell to find nothing suspicious, as Electronics Detective Randy Chan enters the room.

"Randy, my man, welcome to the party. Dive into this laptop and cell phone. The victim is Dr. James Blackwell of Winnipeg, a heart surgeon. Someone wanted him dead," John says. "Chuck, let's go talk to Miss Jayne Applebee; see what she has to say."

They enter the breakroom to see female Officer Tracey Grewal sitting with Miss Jayne Applebee, the housekeeper, a twenty-three-year-old girl with medium brown hair, brown eyes, slim build, wearing her red uniform. She is still upset; her eyes are red, and she is weeping and holding a crumpled-up tissue in her hand. "Hello, Miss Applebee. I'm Lieutenant John Trosky of the homicide squad, and this is my partner Detective Chuck Sidhu. I'm sorry you had to discover the body. It must have been very traumatic for you. Please, relax, but we must take your statement, as you were a witness. I will also have to read your rights to protect you. You are not under arrest," John says.

John proceeds to read her the revised Miranda rights. "Do you understand these rights?" he asks once finished.

"Yes, I do," she says through tears.

"Miss Appleby, tell me how you found the body and what time you found it; in your own words."

"Well, I work the fifth floor, and I went to room 575 to change the sheets and towels at 2 p.m. I knocked on the door and called out. I waited a few minutes, and when I didn't get a response, I used my master key to open the door, and that's when I saw the man slumped over his meal. I noticed all the blood and screamed! I know not to enter the room of a crime scene, so I closed the door, ran down the hall, and took the elevator to the first floor. I then told my manager what I saw, and he called the police."

John takes her hand and says, "I'm sorry we had to put you through this, but it is part of our procedures. If you need help dealing with the trauma, we can provide a consultant. We are done here now. I'll tell your boss to give you the rest of the day off and more time if you need it. Here is my card. If you think of anything else or need help, call me or Detective Chuck Sidhu."

Jayne rises and softly says, "Thank you."

John Trosky gets up and says, "Detective Sidhu, let's go see the manager and collect the security camera discs, then head back to the station."

Back at the station, they throw their black hats on the hat rack, and John turns to Chuck and says, "Detective Sidhu, call Seven Oaks Hospital. See if you can get a list of Doctor Blackwell's patients who have had heart surgery and any who have died. If they give you any grief, let me know, and we will see if we can get a warrant from Assistant Prosecuting Attorney Nikki Anders. I'm going to put my report in my office computer—file number h7099—and send a copy to Captain Tibor Fedora and Commander Carl Caputo. I'm also going to load the discs to my computer and send the images to both our home computers so that we can both study them."

CHAPTER FOUR

John goes home to his mansion, surrounded by a twenty-foot-high strengthened wall and a decorative gate, and a camera identifying his car opens the gate automatically. He goes up the driveway to the five-storey Victorian-style stone mansion, updated with large bulletproofed windows and a glass terrarium that opens to a patio on the roof. It also has a gym, a game room, a hologram room, and an indoor grotto style swimming pool with a waterfall feature. There is also a Jacuzzi, a shooting range, and two elevators that move sideways and up and down. It also has a large garage filled with several antique cars and two dragsters for 1000-foot drag racing, and a golf cart that looks like a 1957 Chevy. A security force field surrounds the home, which can be toggled off and on.

John drives up the long driveway to the house, walks up the stairs, remotes his car to the garage, and enters the house. He throws his Stetson hat onto the antique hat rack in the corner of the room. He is greeted by Thom Saunders, his best friend and house manager/butler dressed in his 1940s style black suit with a narrow white pinstripe and charcoal shirt, and a black tie. He is thirty years old with a slim, muscular build, brown eyes, and brown hair.

"Good evening, lieutenant. Catch any bad guys today?" Saunders says.

"No, and though I appreciate your quips, I keep telling you to call me John when I have no guests or police officers with me," John says.

As Chrissy, John's cat, bounds down the stairs to greet him, Saunders asks, "What would you like for dinner, and what time would you like it?"

"How about steak and lobster in an hour, and tuna for Chrissy. You and Chef Julie can join me if you are free. Did my brother Mike phone?" John says.

"Not on the house link, maybe on your office link."

"I'm anxious about the new car he is building for me. I have some work to do in my office, so I'll catch you later," John says and makes his way up the stairs to the second floor with Chrissy following. He takes off his weapon harness and his LZ250 blaster laser pistol and locks it in his vault, hidden behind a wall panel. He looks at the hotel's security discs for a while, but doesn't find anything interesting yet. He then stops working, changes into his gym clothes and puts in a workout. He then showers, changes into an old University of Manitoba T-shirt and a comfortable pair of blue jeans, and goes downstairs to the small dining room with Chrissy following behind.

John joins Thom in the dining room, and Julie enters, wearing a bright blue floral print dress with a white apron over the top. She is thirty-two years old, five-foot-six, very slim with light brown curly hair, and always hums in the kitchen as she cooks and bakes. Saunders pours the Chablis wine into the glasses as John exclaims, "*Na zdrowie!* God bless us."

"Saluda," they both reply.

John rubs his hands over his face and says, "Don't ask me about my day; it was too sad and gross to talk about."

Julie goes into the kitchen and comes back with the steak and lobster with julienned carrots and little potatoes.

"This food smells great!" John says.

Julie gives Chrissy some tuna and a saucer of milk in her little dishes by the table. John asks, "How are the chickens and ducks doing? Are there any new chicks hatched?"

"They are doing great, John. There are twenty-four new chicks in the incubator. We are also getting two dozen eggs a day! Would you like an omelette in the morning?" Julie asks, batting her eyelids and fluffing her hair.

Thom looks at Julie and says, "Does that omelette offer include me, hint, hint?"

She laughs. "Of course, Thom."

John looks at Julie and says, "Where is Savana; has she eaten yet?"

"She is in her room with her colouring books. She ate earlier," Julies says.

"How is Savana doing since the kidnapping?" John continues.

"She is recovering well, but slowly. I can't thank you enough for getting her back and catching that creep," Julie says.

"I'm just glad I could help; she is so precious, and I love you too," John says.

"Oh, John, your brother Mike called while you were in the shower. He said your new car is ready, and he wants to come over for dinner at eight tomorrow and deliver your car at the same time if that is convenient for you," Thom says.

"All right, barring any factors, let's do it. Julie, Mike loves a good thick sirloin steak with roasted little red potatoes and asparagus with a cream sauce, and Gladys loves sockeye salmon and a "Kardashian" salad. Also, can you bake some Pascha bread [Easter bread] with saffron?" John asks.

"Yes, I have all the ingredients. I can also bake an apple pie with apples from our Macintosh trees," Julie says.

John gets up and says, "Well, I have to review some discs from today. So I'll be in my office for a while. I'll call Mike about tomorrow and let you both know if he and Gladys are coming for dinner."

John calls Mike on his link. "Mike, my brotha from the same motha, how's it hanging? A big bird told me that my new car is finally ready! You can come for dinner tomorrow at eight o'clock or come earlier, and we can take the car for a blast."

Right on, brother. Gladys and I are both excited to see you. It's been a while as you've been busy busting serial killers and kidnappers. OK, we will be there at seven-thirty! See you then," Mike says.

John uses the house intercom, saying, "Julie and Thom, the dinner is on for tomorrow with Mike and Gladys. Ten-four."

CHAPTER FIVE

He turns on his computer and starts reviewing the security discs from the hotel. He checks the front desk camera, puts it on fast forward to 2:00 p.m., and searches to 2:30 p.m. He only sees couples checking in. He goes to the same time on the fifth-floor camera and sees the room service person go to room 575 at about 1:15 p.m. The service person keeps his face away from the camera, but John can see that he is about five-foot-six, average weight with dark hair, and is in his mid-thirties to early forties. The service person leaves the room at 1:34 p.m. and rolls his cart into the hall. He steps out of camera view and is gone.

John checks all the other floor cameras and can't find the service person on any of them. *This guy is a ghost,* he thinks.

He calls Detective Chuck Sidhu on his link. "Chuck, I've been reviewing the discs and found the unsub dressed as a room service person at room 575 at 1:15 p.m. Have you checked your computer yet?"

"Yes, but I missed that. What does he look like?"

"He looks like an average guy, five-foot-six with dark hair, wearing a red uniform. He left the room at 1:34 p.m. Left his cart in the hall and stepped out of camera view, and was gone, ghosted! I couldn't find him on any other cameras," John says.

"Let's call him the GHOST from now on!" Chuck says.

"Good idea, Chuck, it's better than unsub. Next, we check the morgue. I'll pick you up at seven-thirty in the morning, and we'll hit the morgue at eight. Ten-four."

John showers, watches the news, and goes to bed. Chrissy comes in and curls up beside him.

The next morning, John wakes up, looks out his bedroom window, and sees that it is a nice day. After enjoying the omelette Julie made for him and a coffee, John picks up Detective Sidhu at 7:30 a.m., and they head for the morgue.

They enter the morgue to find Dr. Luci Ryan scratching her head with Dr. Blackwell's body cut open.

"Hi, John and Chuck. I can't believe his heart is missing. I have done every test, and I cannot figure out what ate his heart. I removed his kidneys and liver, and they are normal with no toxins in them. We should get the C.D.C. and some universities like U.B.C. involved in this," Luci says.

"I concur," John says. "It's got to be some new technology or a new virus, but a virus usually attacks the whole body. At least we know what he looks like. I caught him on one of the cameras last night, but he hid his face well. Luci, you contact the C.D.C. and U.B.C., and I'll talk to Captain Tibor Fedora about getting other universities or other tech places involved in this case. Good luck, Luci, see you later." John and Chuck leave the morgue.

CHAPTER SIX

"Chuck, I think we should go talk to the captain in person. This is a delicate issue with him. He doesn't like getting any other agencies involved in anything," John says.

They head for the police station. John exclaims, "Oh, Chuck, I'm getting my new cop car tonight. It was designed and built by my brother Mike. It will have way more power than this heap and even have an auto chef in it and seat warmers. Did you get the doctor's patient records from Seven Oaks Hospital yet?"

"I contacted them by email, and they want a warrant and good cause for getting the records," Chuck says.

John turns his head and says, "Well, we will talk to the captain as soon as we get to the station."

Chuck wipes sweat from his forehead. "Hmm, maybe you should talk to him alone."

John gives Chuck a glaring look and says, "Oh, no, you don't. We are in this together. The captain isn't that scary; he can be a nice guy! Besides, we both might need to go to Winnipeg to get the doctor's records."

"Nice guy, when did that happen? He's chewed my ass several times in the past."

"Well, maybe you deserved to get your ass chewed. By the way, I know some really beautiful women in Winnipeg," John says.

They enter Captain Tibor Fedora's outer office, and his admin Sharon lets them into the inner office. "Sir, Lieutenant John Trosky and Detective Chuck Sidhu reporting. We are here to update you on the Doctor Blackwell case."

"Hello, gentlemen. Help yourselves to some of my chocolate covered almonds. It's the only half-assed health food my wife Sarah will allow me to eat," Captain Fedora says.

John and Chuck take some, to be polite.

"I read your report so far. Was his heart really missing with no cuts to his body?"

John answers, crunching on the almonds, saying, "Yes, sir, that is why we are here. Doctor Ryan doesn't have a cause of death. She and I both believe we should get the Center for Disease Control involved and some universities and tech companies you may know to figure out how something can eat a man's heart and not affect the rest of his body. Also, Detective Sidhu and I may have to go to Winnipeg to get Doctor Blackwell's patient surgery records, and they want a warrant and good cause as to why we want them. He was a heart surgeon, and they lose patients occasionally, and someone wanted him dead. We have a security camera shot of the unsub, but his face is hidden. We need to go back to the hotel and find out how he got the uniform, the room service cart, and the dinner. The kitchen/room service manager was off duty when we were there."

Captain Fedora thinks for a minute, then says, "First, I'll get Detective Randy Chan involved in researching Dr. Blackwell's background, then I'll talk to our attorneys and the police in Winnipeg. I'll also get the Electronic Detectives Division to check for any new technology on viruses or what else they can find. Meanwhile, you and Detective Sidhu head back to the hotel and report back to me. By the way, Detective Sidhu, I've been keeping my eye on you, and you are doing an excellent job. Also, this is code blue, which means no talking about the missing heart until I clear it. No reporters, John, like Jenny Olson of Channel 24. I know she has a thing for you! Dismissed."

John and Chuck head back to the hotel in their beat-up cop car. John looks at Chuck and says, "See, I told you Captain Fedora was a nice guy. He even complimented you on doing an excellent job."

Chuck smiles and replies, "You're right, it puts my mind at ease to be acknowledged in doing a good—no—an excellent job. I didn't know Jenny had a hard-on for you."

"We are just good friends, really," John says.

They enter the hotel and go to the kitchen/room service area, looking for the manager. A chubby man in his forties with salt and pepper hair about five-foot-eight, wearing a red and black uniform, approaches. "Can I help you gentlemen with something?"

"We are not gentlemen; we are cops. I'm Lieutenant John Trosky, and this is Detective Chuck Sidhu of Vancouver Homicide Division, and you are?"

"I'm Stewart Wilson, manager of the kitchen and serving staff. Oh, you are probably here about the unfortunate incident yesterday in room 575, a Doctor Blackwell succumbed mysteriously in his room."

John pulls out his video-cell phone and shows the picture of the Ghost to Stewart. "Do you know this man?"

"Yes, I hired him for the day yesterday, as we were short-staffed."

"What was his name, and do you have any photos or videos of him?"

"Yes, he said his name was John-Claude Van Damme, and we didn't have time to give him proper photo ID, but we might have some videos of him; though the cameras in the kitchen have been acting up lately," Stewart says.

"Are you serious? John-Claude Van Damme was a famous actor in the late 1990s and into the 2020s, so I doubt if it was his real name!"

"Oh, he spoke with a Parisian French accent, if that helps. I'll see if I can get any videos of him," Stewart says.

"While you do that, what staff were working with 'Jean-Claude' yesterday? I'd like to talk to someone who saw him up close. Also, do you put flowers on the trollies with the meals, like a lily, for instance?" John asks.

"We may put roses in a vase, but never Lilies. They mean death or sorrow. I'll check the schedule, but I think Michelle Torres was working that shift with him."

John turns to Chuck and says, "Do you remember a lily flower on that trolley? I don't forget things like that."

Chuck hesitates, then says, "I think you're right. I'll check my recording of the crime scene."

Stewart comes back with a short, cute, slim, dark-haired, brown-eyed girl about twenty-three years old, with a wavy, stylish hair-do, wearing a red uniform, a white shirt, and black pants.

"This is Michelle Torres. Michelle, these are homicide detectives Lieutenant John Trosky and Detective Chuck Sidhu. They want to ask you some questions about John-Claude," Stewart says.

Michelle looks shocked. "Who?"

"You know, the part-time guy I hired yesterday with the French accent," Stewart says.

"Oh, yeah. He was friendly and charming. What did he do?" she asks.

"Miss Torres, we just want to ask you a few questions about this man on record," John says to her. "Record on: The date is Wednesday, April 12th, 2070, the place is the Pacific Hotel, the time is 10:15 a.m."

John then reads her the revised Miranda rights. "Miss Torres, do you understand your Miranda rights for this interview?"

"Yes, but I'm not a suspect, am I?" she asks.

"No, I read you your rights because you are a witness to identify John-Claude. He is a suspect in a homicide. Could you describe him to a sketch artist?" John says.

"Yes, I think so. I chatted with him a bit."

"We would like you to come with us to the station and sit down with a sketch artist," John tells her.

"Sure, if it's okay with my boss, Mr. Wilson," she says.

John looks at Chuck and says, "Chuck, check to see if Rembrandt is free; he is the best. Mr. Wilson, may we take Miss Torres to the station now?"

"Go ahead; I'll find someone to cover her shift. We want this incident over as soon as possible. It's bad publicity," Stewart says.

"Rembrandt is free now. We can go," Chuck says.

They take Miss Torres to the station and meet with Jorge "Rembrandt" Garza, a thirty-one-year-old, dark-haired, olive-skinned, slim man about five-foot-ten, who looks like Antonio Banderas, wearing a black 40s style suit and fancy black and white shoes.

"Miss Michelle Torres, meet Jorge 'Rembrandt' Garza. We nicknamed him Rembrandt because he draws realistically but with panache," John says, introducing the two.

Michelle's eyes brighten, and she blurts out, "Um . . . um, very nice to meet you, I'm sure!"

"Rembrandt, take good care of Michelle and let me know when you have an image. Make sure Michelle is escorted home," John tells him.

After an hour, Michelle says, "You know, it really looks like him, but he looked funny like he was wearing a lot of makeup, or maybe one of those *Mission Impossible* latex masks, now that I think of it."

"You could be right, but you can't change the position of the eyes. You can change the eye colour. Let's take a break and go for coffee, okay?" Rembrandt says.

She smiles and says, "I'd love to, Rembrandt."

John and Chuck go back to the bullpen. John says to the room, "Everyone who is available in my office in ten minutes. Detectives Sam Slade, Eddie Bennetti, Razh Mendosa, Larry Cornburra and Randy Chan if any of you are not on a hot case, I need you in a briefing on a new homicide case."

"Lieutenant, I'm running an Op. on a Filipino gang in a few hours, and I need the time to set it up," Detective Razh Mendosa says.

"Okay, Razh, your Op. is more important. Carry on. I have to contact Rembrandt first, so, ten or fifteen minutes in my office everyone else," John says.

John goes into his office and places a call. "Rembrandt, do you have an image to send me now?"

"Yes, but Michelle—Miss Torres—thinks that he either had makeup on or a latex mask, like in *Mission Impossible*. On the other hand, we have a good enhanced full-body image. I'll send you both images now," Rembrandt says.

"Thanks for all your excellent work. Ten-four."

The images appear on John's computer, and John sends them to his giant wall screen as his team enters his office.

"Grab a seat, everyone. We have a new homicide. The file number is h7099. A Doctor J. Blackwell was murdered in the hotel in the Vancouver Convention Center at 1:32 p.m. yesterday in room 575. This part is classified code blue by the commander period, so if you like your job, you talk to no one, not even your dog! Now, we come to the 'Twilight Zone' part. The victim's heart is missing, and there are no cuts on his body. He bled out through his mouth and nose. The M.E.

can't figure this out. Doctor Luci Ryan checked for viruses, diseases, and poisons. All negative. Also, the main suspect is pictured on the wall screen. As you can see, he is a regular looking guy, has a Parisian French accent, and could have been wearing makeup or a latex mask a la *Mission Impossible*, but he is no Tom Cruise, as he is a bit chubby. He was disguised as a room service person. This is all we know about him currently. Any questions?" John says.

"This man, what kind of doctor was he and who would want him dead?" Detective Samantha Slade asks.

"He was a heart surgeon from Winnipeg, and we are trying to get a warrant for his patient surgery records. We should work both ends of this case," John responds. "Randy Chan, I want you to check the good doctor's financials and find whoever can help you with that. And dig deep; do a level-three dive. Okay, Chuck and Sam, I want you both to divide your workload. Contact the French police, Interpol, and whoever else you can think of to try and find the Ghost—as we will call him—since his name can't be John-Claude Van Damme. Detective Bennetti, I want you on the Ghost also. Try facial recognition in Canada, Europe, and Interplanetary Police. That should keep you all busy for a while. Send updates to me when you have made progress. I'm going to get our profiler Doctor Lyle Gavinchuk involved," John commands.

"Doctor Gavinchuk retired. The new profiler is Doctor Jo Weber," Sam says.

"Well, our shift is almost over. I'll see you all tomorrow at eight in the morning. Oh, Chuck, I want you to ride home with me, as I'm getting my new car tonight, and I want you to take 'old faithful' home with you. We'll meet up at work in the morning."

Chuck drops John off at home and exclaims, "I can't wait to ride in your new car. I'll drop this clunker off at maintenance in the morning."

CHAPTER SEVEN

John enters his house, throws his hat on the hat rack, and is greeted by Thom Saunders as Chrissy paws at John's pant leg. John crouches down, picks up Chrissy, and pets her.

"Lieutenant—ah, John—it's only six-thirty. You must have had an easy day today," Thom says.

"As the marines say, the only easy day was yesterday. Did Mike call, and is dinner still on for tonight?" John asks.

"Yes and yes. He is bringing your new car with all the bells on, and they are bringing their daughter Jackie as well."

"Does Julie know that Jackie is coming too?"

"Yes, she does, and she is preparing spaghetti and meatballs, her favourite."

"Great. And, of course, I want you, Julie, and Savana to join us for dinner and have the house droids serve us. You can have a nice thick steak or whatever you'd like. You all are part of the family, and Savanna and Jackie can play together. They are about the same age. Jackie is five years old, and Savana is six. Well, I'm going to work out, swim, and check my emails. I'll be down by seven-thirty to greet my guests."

Mike, Gladys, and Jackie arrive at 7:30 p.m. in John's new car! John hurries out to greet them with a big grin on his face. He blurts out, "Mike, Gladys, and little Jackie! It's great to see you! Jackie, you've grown an inch since I last saw you, and you are even more pretty."

"Hi, Uncle Tiny, I love you!" Jackie says.

John looks down at her pretty little face and curly blonde hair and says, "I love you too, Jackie. Gladys, you look ravishing in that flowery pink dress, and your hair looks great in waves!"

"Thank you, John. You look great too."

"Well, you two can go in the house and relax while Mike and I drool over my new car and go for a short ride."

The car is a deep candy blue with a sloped front nose, a streamlined body, and a small rear wing.

"Well, Mike. Let's jump in and put this unit through its paces, and you can explain all the features in it."

Mike hands John a key fob and says, "The car is coded to your voice; just say a code phrase to unlock the alarm."

"I'm going to use 'Open Sesame' as no one will think of that," John says.

"You can use the key fob or your voice to unlock the car. If you want someone else to drive the car, just tell them the phrase. Press the blue button, and the front doors will flip up like a Lamborghini, and the yellow button opens rear doors like a Tesla—gull-wing style—and your voice will fire up the hyperdrive. The hyperdrive fuels itself, but don't ask me how it works. Our R and D guys developed it, so we have the patent on it, and it's on the market already," Mike explains.

They get in and start cruising down the driveway. Mike continues his spiel. "The seats will conform to your body or any body's body and warm or cool automatically. Your voice will activate the in-dash console, the phone, the siren, all the lights, boost to one thousand pounds thrust, and turn on the force field-alarm system. The car is bullet and bombproof, and when you hit vertical, it lifts fast to about 70 feet, and small wings flip out the sides for stability. You can adjust the flying height to suit you. By the way, the colour is embedded in the composite flex-body, so no scratches or dents. The body cannot be damaged as it is made up of special polymers; that's why it is bulletproof. It also has built-in auto chefs in the front and back. Okay, we are free of traffic, so boot it and get ready to be pushed hard into the seat."

John hits full boost, and the car blasts him into his seat at 5Gs. "Wow," he shouts, "you weren't kidding! I have driven a fuel dragster with 8000 horsepower, and this equals it."

"Well, let's head back, or Gladys will kill us," Mike says.

They get back to the house, and as they walk around the car, Mike says, "John, did you notice the badges, JT8000XP. It stands for John Trosky 8000 Experimental Pursuit. The civilian model will be available in six months, minus all the cop stuff and less power, so you can catch the bad guys. Oh, I forgot the most important thing. Your car also has a tractor beam and an EMP gun, so you can slow and disable the car you are chasing."

John remotes the car to the garage, and they go into the dining room.

CHAPTER EIGHT

"Did you boys have fun?" Gladys says as John and Mike walk inside the house.

"Your husband is a genius. He put everything I wanted and things I never would have thought of in that car, and the power is unbelievable," John says. "Well, Julie, I think it's time to activate the server droids, Ann and Rob. Have Ann serve the ladies their meals first and then have Rob serve the men," John adds.

Julie activates the androids with her cell phone, and they enter the room, wearing white shirts and black pants. They serve wine for the adults and milk for the girls. Jackie looks confused and whispers to John, "Are they real people?"

"No, they are androids made to look and act like people. They don't eat, and you can program them to do just about anything, like clean your house, cook, even be a bodyguard. If something happens, they will protect all of us. They are very strong and made of strong metal inside," John explains.

"Wow, can I have one of those? Dad? Mom?" Jackie asks.

"No, you are not old enough. Maybe one day, but we have servants and a nanny for you," Gladys says.

Gladys is served a salmon steak, rice, and a "Kardashian" salad, while Mike, John, and Thom have thick sirloin steaks with roast potatoes, julienned, carrots, and broccoli. Jackie and Savana have spaghetti and meatballs, and milk. Then they all have Julie's Macintosh apple pie a la mode.

"Julie, that was an outstanding, delicious meal!" John exclaims. "I know why I pay you the big bucks! Girls, you can go play with the animals outside. We have some new baby goats and ducklings, or you can go to the game room while us adults talk."

"Come on, Jackie. You've got to see the new baby goats," Savana says, grabbing Jackie's hand. They run out toward the barn.

"Julie, maybe you should send Ann to watch over them in case they get bitten or whatever," John says.

"I'll go myself; I can show them how to feed the goats and how to be gentle with them. Besides, Ann and Robb need to do clean up in the kitchen," Julies says.

Gladys is about to leave when John turns to Mike and says, "Mike, I've been thinking about that special composite car body material. Do you think it can be adapted to make body armour? It could be made into very light clothing, like a coat or jacket and pants. If it could take a hit from a laser gun or a bullet, it could save a lot of lives."

"I never thought of that! Yes, why not? It could be a whole new company for us! I'll get my research and development guys and girls on it right away. You also are a friggin' genius," Mike says.

"I'll go fifty-fifty on this project and the company if it works out," John says.

Gladys pipes in and says, "You guys make a really great team. John, I know this is a sensitive subject, but it's been three years since Sylvia died in that car accident, and you have all this great stuff and no one to share it with. You need to start dating again and find someone to love."

John sighs. "I guess, but I'm in the middle of a murder investigation, and I don't know if I'm ready for a relationship right now. It would have to be the right person, and I would know as soon as I met her."

"Listen, John, I'm hosting a charity silent auction for the Vancouver Children's Hospital this Saturday at the Surrey Hilton ballroom, and there will be a lot of beautiful, rich women there, including some of my close friends. There will be a lot of art, sculptures, and some high-quality antique furniture for sale. I know you like good antique furniture. I also have a tip on an upcoming artist who goes by Gregg Senna. His art is going to be very valuable very soon," Gladys says.

John thinks for a second, then says, "Okay, barring circumstances of the murder variety, I'll be there. I don't have to wear a 'monkey suit,' do I?"

"No, wear one of your many black suits."

"Well, it's getting late for the girls. I'll get Jeffery to drive you home in the limo, don't worry," John says, then adds in his best *Rain Man* impression, "He's an excellent driver, ya, an excellent driver."

"You kill me with that voice. I don't know how you do all those voices. You do JFK. really well, too," Mike says.

"Next time, I'll play the piano for you and sing. I'm learning some new jazz songs. Well, let's find the girls and get you home. Gladys, you piqued my interest in that auction. I'll probably be there unless I get a 'hot case.' I'll let you know," John says.

Mike, Gladys, and Jackie leave for home, and John goes upstairs, watches the news, and then goes to bed with Chrissy curled up at his feet.

CHAPTER NINE

The next morning, John leaves for work, picks up Chuck, and accelerates rapidly toward the cop shop.

"Holy cow, John! This baby is a jewel and goes like a rocket. Did the seat just conform to my body?" Chuck asks.

John nods and says, "Yes, and it will warm or cool according to the outside temperature. It has front and rear auto chefs, and the body is bulletproof. I could go on all day about this car, but we will learn its traits as we go along. I want to meet with the new profiler, Jo Weber. I hope he is as good as the old guy, Lyle Gavinchuk. I want you to check on the status of the hospital records with the commander, and we'll meet back in my office in an hour. We may have to go to Winnipeg later."

John heads to the profiler's office in the same building but on a different floor. John enters Jo Weber's office and says to the admin, who is a lovely blond, middle-aged, slim woman named Chloe, "Hi, I'm Lieutenant John Trosky. Does Doctor Weber have a minute to talk to me?"

"Yes, go right in. There are no appointments for an hour," she replies.

John walks in and sees a tall, slim, dark-haired woman, wearing a pastel coral-coloured business suit, who looks familiar. John looks at her in shock. He fumbles his words, saying, Joanne Mallanchuk—err, Weber—is that you? God, I haven't seen you since that summer we spent in Paris at university!"

"John, you're a sight for sore eyes! You're a detective now?" she says.

"Yes, a lieutenant in homicide. You still look incredible. So I guess you're married now, any children?" John asks.

"Yes, I married an architect who designed many of the buildings in Seattle and Vancouver after the earthquake. His name is Remy Weber; maybe you've heard of him?"

"No, I've never heard of him. We sure had a great summer in Paris, seeing the sights, dancing in the night clubs, hitting the jazz clubs. I'll never forget it. I should have you both over for dinner sometime. You can meet my brother Mike, his wife Gladys, and their daughter Jackie. I have a great live-in chef, Julie, and she has a six-year-old daughter Savana. How many kids do you have?"

"I have two girls. Adele is seven, and Rose is six. By the way, why are you here today?" she asks.

"I have a bizarre case; an assassin killed a doctor from Winnipeg—a heart surgeon—and used some unknown substance to melt his heart. Like his heart is gone with no cuts to his body. I'll send you the file, but we don't have that much data except a bad photo of the killer and a sketch from a witness. Also, the killer left a lily at the crime scene, which I believe is a clue. Detective Chuck Sidhu is my partner and is working on this case with me. Right now, he is trying to get Doctor James Blackwell's surgical records from Seven Oaks Hospital in Winnipeg. Captain Fedora is also trying to put pressure on the hospital board. I want you involved in this case to get a profile on the killer. I know he will strike again, whether he is doing this for kicks or money. I want to know if Doctor Blackwell had a patient named Lily, who possibly died during an operation. Chuck and I may have to go to

Winnipeg today. I must talk to Commander Fedora. So are you interested in getting involved?"

"Yes, this is a very interesting and weird case; you couldn't pull me away with a dozen horses," she replies.

"Good, the file number is h7099. I'll send it to you, and I will tell Captain Tibor to keep you informed. See you later," John says, and then in his best Arnold Schwarzenegger voice, adds, "I'll be back."

Joanne laughs. "You've still got it, Johnny boy!"

John enters the squad room and says, "Detective Sidhu, could you come to my office, please?"

Chuck enters the office and says, "I know what you want. Captain Fedora talked to Commander Carl Caputo, and we have an appointment at 3:00 p.m. today with a Doctor Belinda Beck, the hospital administrator. I reserved your private shuttle and your pilots at your private shuttle port. We can be in Winnipeg in one hour and take a helicopter and land on the roof of the hospital, boss."

"Chuck, you make a great secretary, too, bro. Did you say, Dr. Belinda Beck?"

"Yes, and secretary? Fuck you, sir," Chuck says.

"I went to high school with Belinda, and her sister Ronnie . . . Veronica. They are both gorgeous, and I'm glad you said, sir, or I'd have to kick your ass. Well, grab your hat and let's saddle up and get the hell out of here."

CHAPTER TEN

They get on the shuttle, and John says, "Chuck, you're going to love Winnipeg; the food is great, and the women are beautiful."

They land at the shuttle port and take a helicopter to the hospital. They enter Doctor Beck's office.

"John Trosky, what are you doing here?" Belinda says when he and Chuck arrive.

"Hi, Belinda. It's good to see you. I'm now Lieutenant Trosky of the homicide squad in Vancouver, and this is my partner Detective Chuck Sidhu."

"Nice to meet you, detective," Belinda says.

"You can call me Chuck."

"Did Commander Caputo call you about Doctor James Blackwell's murder?" John asks Belinda.

"Oh, yes. Your captain said you wanted Doctor Blackwell's surgical records. I'm confused as to why you want them, but he did send me a warrant," Belinda says.

"The good doctor was assassinated with an unknown substance injected into him that dissolved his heart; there are no cuts on his body. We believe it had to do with a patient he operated on and died on the operating table. The killer left a lily on the food trolley, and I want to see his surgical records to see if someone named Lily died due to a heart operation gone wrong. I'd like to go back three to five months to start. Will you grant us access?" John asks.

"So, you just want the surgical records, John?" she asks.

"Yes, and it stays confidential unless we find the patient and the next of kin because if we find something, this could have been a contract hit on the doctor. We also have a partial photo of the killer dressed in a room service person's uniform."

"All right, I'll set you two up in a small office and get you the files," she says.

"How is your sister Ronnie? How about we take you out for dinner tonight to the best restaurant in town, money is no object, and we can catch up on old times?" John suggests.

"Sure, I'll give her a call. I'm sure she will be glad to see you and meet handsome Chuck here," Belinda says.

John and Chuck follow her to a small office and start going through the surgical files on their laptops. However, they find nothing.

"Chuck, let's go back another three months; there's got to be a Lily in here somewhere," John says.

They continue searching, and just before six o'clock, they find Lily Dupuis and her parents, Raphael and Lisa. Lily was born with a heart valve problem but died at the age of six after an operation due to bad stitches that caused her to bleed out.

"Chuck, I found her! Look at this file. Lily Dupuis, parents Raphael and Lisa, French citizens. So these people bring their little girl all the way to Winnipeg to get the best heart surgeon to repair her heart, and she dies on the table. A good recipe for revenge! We'll have to check them out when we get back," John says.

Just then, Belinda walks in and says, "Did you find anything?"

"Yes, we found Lily Dupuis, six years old. Look at this file," John says, handing Belinda the folder.

Belinda looks at the file and says, "Oh my God. She died on the table! That is tragic. You can copy that file and send it to your boss. By the way, it's almost six o'clock, and my shift is over. Are you two staying in town tonight?"

"You better believe it. I promised you dinner tonight, and we need to celebrate this big break in the case. We will pick you and Ronnie up in a limo at, say, eight o'clock? I reserved a table at the Wellington Restaurant, is that okay?"

"The Wellington Restaurant? It's very expensive. Are you sure you want to go there?" Belinda asks.

"Money is no object, Belinda."

CHAPTER ELEVEN

John and Chuck register at the Inn at the Forks in a two-bedroom suite, shower, shave, and pick up Belinda and Veronica at Belinda's three-bedroom mini-mansion in the Wellington area in a stretched limo.

Belinda has her long blond hair done in curls and ringlets down the sides and wears a low-cut, sexy, pale yellow dress with red and pink flowers printed on it and a pale yellow cashmere overcoat and candy red spike heels. Veronica wears a short, low-cut, simple black dress with spaghetti straps that shows off her ample bosom. Her black hair is done in curvy waves down to her shoulders, and she wears metallic black spike heels and a black, smooth cotton overcoat.

John and Chuck help them into the limo, and John exclaims, "Ladies, you look marvellous. I hope you are hungry. Oh, Veronica, this is my partner, Detective Chuck Sidhu."

"Nice to meet you, Chuck; you can call me Ronnie," she says.

Belinda looks bewildered. "John, how can you afford a limo and buying us dinner at the most expensive restaurant in town? Are you rich now?"

"Yes, my parents were killed in a shuttle crash several years ago and left me a lot of money, and I've invested it well and own several companies with my brother Mike, one of which built this limo we are riding in tonight, Trosky Custom Vehicles."

"You've come a long way since high school," Belinda says.

"So have you. You have a great job, and I know you were smarter than me in school. Well, here we are, ladies."

They enter the Wellington Restaurant and are surrounded by antique furniture and old English-style décor.

"I like this place already. My house is full of antique furniture. I hope the food is as good," John says.

They sit down and study the menu.

"Order what you want; money is no object. I feel adventurous tonight. I'm going to have a bison steak. I've had bison burgers before, and they were juicer than a hamburger. Chuck, I guess you don't eat red meat, so you should try the goldeye fish or the lobster or pike. Ladies, what is your pleasure?"

"I've had bison before, and it was good, but I feel like a beef tenderloin tonight, and we could have a merlot with that," Belinda says.

Chuck looks at Ronnie and asks, "What would satisfy your appetite tonight?"

"Besides you, Chuck, I think I'll have the goldeye and a sauvignon blanc," she says.

Chuck stammers, "I dig you too. I'll have the goldeye, too, and we could share a bottle of sauvignon blanc. Here comes the waitress."

They order their food.

"Is it all right if I order the wine?" John asks.

They all nod yes.

"We will have a bottle of Troubadour Merlot 2068 for the red meat and a bottle of Troubadour Sauvignon Blanc 2067 for the fish. It's from my winery."

During the meal, Belinda asks, "So, John, are you married?"

"I was, but my wife Sylvia was killed in a car accident three years ago, and I found out she was pregnant with a girl, so I haven't felt like dating since then. Also, we never caught the driver that hit her."

"I'm really sorry to hear that," Belinda says.

"I'm really sorry too," Ronnie adds.

"I didn't know about this, John. But I guess I've only been your partner for two years," Chuck says.

"Let's change the subject," John suggests. "So, Belinda, are you or Ronnie married?"

"I was, but I'm divorced now," Belinda answers. "It didn't work out. Ronnie is divorced too. We both married dirtbags who cheated on us."

"We are both single now and playing the field," Ronnie chimes in. "It's time to have some fun in our lives! So Chuck, are you married or have a girlfriend?"

"No, John keeps me very busy at work. It's a lot of work catching bad guys. We don't get many enjoyable trips like this one. Sometimes we need to go off-planet. One time, we tracked a killer all the way to Alpha One and found him in a resort, drinking gin and tonics with a girl on his lap," Chuck says.

"What's it like to go off-planet?" Ronnie asks.

"Once you get there, it's all right, but I don't like travelling in a space transpo, but some people really get off on it," Chucks replies.

"How about we go to our hotel and have a nightcap?" John suggests. "We are staying at the Inn at The Forks in a two-bedroom suite."

Belinda and Ronnie both say yes. They leave in the limo and get to the hotel quickly. As they sit in the suite, drinking more wine from the auto chef, they start to relax.

"Belinda, did you know I had a crush on you in high school?" John asks.

"Yes, your sister told me, but I don't know why you didn't do anything about it."

"I was very shy in my teenage years. I was afraid to talk to girls, but I gained confidence after a few years as a cop. I now have no problem interrogating criminals, public speaking, or firing people."

"I had a crush on you too, and still do," Belinda says, sliding next to him. They look into each other's eyes.

John says, "I'm sorry, but as much as I like you, I'm just not ready to do this. It wouldn't be fair to either one of us."

"I understand. I'm not sure either," Belinda replies.

"Well, we should take you, ladies, home as we all have to get up early tomorrow," Johan suggests.

They take Belinda and Ronnie home in the limo and go back to the hotel. The next morning, they have breakfast and go to the shuttle port and fly back to Vancouver.

CHAPTER TWELVE

They fly back, and John says, "Well, that was incredible luck finding that patient Lily. Sometimes my hunches pay off. We had a great time last night, didn't we?"

They enter the bullpen at the station, and John says, "Detective Sidhu and Detective Chan, I want both of you on finding a Mr. Raphael Dupuis. He is a French citizen in Paris or near there. Randy, I want you to dig deep, level-three, into his financials. Look for a million-dollar payout to the assassin, though we do not have an extradition treaty with France. I'm going to fill in Captain Fedora and Commander Caputo on our findings in Winnipeg. Also, check with the French National Police and Interpol to see if Mr. Dupuis has left the country."

John enters Captain Fedora's office and fills him in on the Seven Oaks Hospital and Raphael Dupuis findings. The Captain says, "So this guy is a French citizen, and you think he hired this Ghost to kill Doctor Blackwell because the good doctor killed his daughter during heart surgery?"

"Yes, and I already have Detectives Sidhu and Chan looking into his financials and his whereabouts, and I told them to check with the French police. Also, we should get

Interpol involved in finding the Ghost, as we have a video of him from the hotel," John suggests.

Captain Fedora replies, "Good idea, Lieutenant Trosky. Put that in action. You and Detective Sidhu did a good job in Winnipeg. Send your computer report to me when you get back to your office and keep me updated on your progress. Dismissed."

John goes back to the bullpen and asks, "Chuck and Randy, how is your search going?"

Chuck says, "We have an address on Raphael Dupuis in the fifth arrondissement of Paris and a cell phone number and landline, but no one answered. Nothing from the police yet."

Randy adds, "I shot the video and Rembrandt's sketch to Interpol and the national police, but we may not hear back from them until Monday."

"I'll be in my office if anyone has any questions," John says and goes into his office. John starts his murder board, putting pictures from the video of the Ghost, Doctor Blackwell face-down on the little table with the lily in front of him, little Lily herself. There is a knock on his door, and John yells, "Enter at your own risk."

Detective Samantha "Sam" Slade, a slim, five-foot-six, blond Ukrainian woman, opens the door and says, "Lieutenant Trosky, do you have a minute to talk to me?"

"Sure, Sam, and call me John. What's up?"

"I've got a case of some young girls bullying and beating up a teenage girl on school grounds. The girl, Dana Kloss, is in Vancouver General in critical condition. There is camera footage of the beating, but we need a warrant to get the footage. The school principal, a Miss Clooney, is being a bitch. We know the leader of the gang is Lila Krause. Can you help me get a warrant?"

"You bet; I hate bullies," John says. He picks up the phone, dials, and says, "This is Lieutenant John Trosky. Sarah, can I talk to A.P.A. Nikki Anders, please?"

John is immediately put on hold, and in less than a minute, Nikki picks up.

"Hi, John, how can I help you? I know you want to take me out for dinner!"

"Sure, when you dump your boyfriend. Listen, my crack detective, Samantha Slade, needs a warrant for some school footage of some girls beating the shit out of a defenceless teenage girl, Dana Kloss, who is in the hospital in serious condition. Can you find a judge and get her a warrant?"

"Yes, I hate bullies, boys or girls. Is Samantha there?"

"Yes," John replies.

"Give me her video-cell number, and I will call her for more details. I'll get her a warrant, and I won't dump my boy toy yet, but don't give up on me yet, John. Ciao baby!" Nikki hangs up.

"Thanks, John," Sam says. "She has the hots for you." She gets up.

"You're welcome, Sam. Don't hesitate to come see me anytime. We all help each other."

Sam looks at John's murder board and says, "Wow, John, what happened to that guy?"

"He was murdered, but we still don't know how, as his heart is missing, but there are no cuts on his body. We have a picture of the guy who killed him. That picture of the little girl, whose name is Lily, died on the dead doctor's operating table, and I think her father hired an assassin to kill him. By the way, I shouldn't be telling you this as the commander classified it code blue, but I trust you to not talk about it to anybody."

"My lips are sealed," she says. "Thanks for the help." She smiles and leaves.

John looks at his watch and notices his shift is over. He puts on his black hat, locks his office, and walks into the bullpen, asking Chuck, "Do you need a lift home?"

"I still have some work to finish, so I'll find my own way home. I'll take the new subway," Chuck replies.

"Okay, see you on Monday."

CHAPTER THIRTEEN

John gets into his new car and races home, thinking of riding his horse, Steely Dan.

He drives his car straight to the barn and says to his farmhand, "Autrey, please saddle up Steely Dan; I'm going to ride him down to the pond. Put the western saddle on him."

John puts on his denim outfit and straw hat from his barn office and rides out on the pasture to his private pond, where he and his wife Silvia used to go to relax and take in the fresh air and quiet. The reflection on the water puts him in a mellow mood, and he thinks to himself, *John, you've got all this and a job you love, but no one close to share it all with, so get your butt in gear and do something about it. Time waits for no one.*

John gets on his horse and rides quickly to the barn and says, "Autrey, could you cool Steely Dan off and give him some oats. I gave him a good run on the way back."

"Sure, boss, with pleasure," Autrey says.

John drives back to the house, sends the car to the garage remotely, and then enters the house. Thom is standing there and says, "Good evening, lieutenant. You must have had a really good time in Winnipeg; I got your bills. I didn't think anyone could spend that much money on a business trip."

"It's okay. It didn't come out of your paycheck. What's for dinner? And don't say mac and cheese, that joke is so old; it's rotting."

"Greek salad, lamb souvlaki, roast potatoes, and rice. I'll have my usual gruel."

"Yeah, and the pope is Jewish. I'll be upstairs. I need a shower; I smell like my horse, and don't say you agree with me," John says and makes his way upstairs, showers, and calls Gladys.

She answers, "Hi, John, how are you?"

"I'm fine. I just got back from Winnipeg on a police matter. The reason I'm calling is to ask what time that charity auction is tomorrow? And if it is a silent auction, do we need to be there earlier, as I want to buy some antique furniture and paintings and check out some of your beautiful lady friends!" he says.

"So you must have changed your mind about dating again. I'm glad you did. The silent auction starts at seven, so we should get there at six. And I'll show you the art you should invest in and introduce you to some women. I think you will like Grace Chan, she is a good friend of mine, is very beautiful, and has an excellent brain. She is the CEO of several companies, so you should have something in common there," Gladys says.

"Your limo or mine?" John asks.

"You can pick us up at five-thirty, okay?"

"Sure, it's casual dress, right?" John asks.

"Yes, wear one of your one hundred black suits."

"I only have twenty suits, and some are charcoal with pinstripes, and others are different colours."

"Wear the black suit; it goes with your hat," Gladys suggests.

John walks downstairs as Chrissy follows him to the dining room. "Chrissy, I swear, you can smell food a mile away."

Chrissy looks up at John and meows.

John sits down at the dinner table with Thom, Julie, and Savana. Chrissy sits in a chair beside him. "Julie, let's have a bottle of Troubador Chablis, chilled, of course. Are you all having Greek food too?" John asks.

"Yes, even Savana likes Greek food. She doesn't eat mac and cheese every day, but she doesn't like wine yet," Julie says.

"Mom, I'm too young to drink wine," Savana says.

"Your mom was just joking with you," John says.

They finish eating dinner, and Savana and Julie go to the kitchen. Savana likes to help her mom clean up the dishes.

"By the way, Thom," John says, "my trip to Winnipeg was fruitful. We searched the surgical records and found the father of a girl named Lily Dupuis; his name is Raphael Dupuis. We think he hired the assassin that killed Dr. Blackwell because the doctor accidentally killed his daughter when he was doing a heart operation on her. Did I tell you the killer left a lily in a vase on the dining table in the hotel room? I had a hunch about that flower because that hotel doesn't put lilies with room service dinners, but Mr. Dupuis is a French citizen, and we can't find him. Even if we find him, we can't extradite him. However, my men searching his financials."

"Too bad we can't 'extradite' him ourselves like in the old days!" Thom says.

"Yeah, that would be great, but I must do this legally all the way if I want to put him and the assassin in a cage. By the way, I'm going to a silent auction and dinner tomorrow afternoon with Mike and Gladys. Do you want to come along? Before you answer, there are going to be a lot of gorgeous women there."

"Sure, hot chicks and good food. What time do we leave?"

"We are picking up Mike and Gladys at five-thirty, so we'll leave here at five," John says. "Well, I'm going up to my office to finish my file and then hit the sack. Good night."

CHAPTER FOURTEEN

The next afternoon, John and Thom get ready to go to the auction. John puts on a black suit with a thin white pinstripe, a charcoal shirt, and a black silk tie. It's almost five o'clock, so John calls his chauffeur to bring the limo to the front door.

They get in the limo, and John says, "Jeffery, take us to Mike and Gladys's mansion and then we are going to an auction at the Surrey Hilton Ballroom."

They pick up Mike and Gladys and go to the hotel. They have appetizers and champagne and wander around. John gets a brochure and checks off the furniture he is interested in buying. He says to Gladys, "Who is this new artist I should look at, and where are his paintings?"

Gladys leads the way to an adjoining room and says, "His name is Gregg Senna, and here is his work."

John looks and says, "Wow, this set of pen and ink drawings of Miles Davis, Ray Charles, and Charles Mingus are great! I must have them. I'll put in an offer of ten thousand dollars each. The brochure said they only want five thousand dollars each. That should get them. You know how much I love jazz. I have every disc and vinyl record of Miles Davis, Ray Charles, and Charles Mingus. Where is the furniture? I have my eye on this Braunschweiger Barock-Kommode dresser for my bedroom. It's gorgeous, and only $2000. I'll bid $2500. There are also four Louie XV fauteuils for $1200. I'll bid $1600. I also see a beautiful Brarock-Komode for $1200. I'll bid $1650 for it! I also want an antique desk for my home office; that one over there is the right size, hand-carved, and from England. It's only $2000. I'll bid $5000 for it. Let's go to the auction room or wherever we're supposed to go," John says.

Gladys, Thom, and Mike lead the way to the silent auction room to see whether John won any of his bids. As they enter the room and stand around with their champagne glasses, John looks across the room and locks his gaze on a gorgeous, slim, five-foot-seven Chinese woman with light brown wavy hair down to her shoulders, wearing a short pale green dress with pink rose flowers printed on it and thin straps. John notices that she has incredible deep green eyes. They both smile, and John feels like time is suddenly standing still. He goes into a dreamlike state, and then his heart starts racing! John looks at Gladys and says, "Who is that gorgeous Chinese woman in the pink and green flowered dress?"

"Oh, that's Grace Chan. Would you like to meet her?"

John continues to stare at Grace and replies," Yes, I think I'm in love! Did you say she's a friend of yours?"

"Yes, I told you the other day that you would like her. She is a very successful businesswoman and charming."

They announce the winning bids, and John wins all his bids. He goes up to the podium to settle his bill, and Grace appears beside him and says, "Did you get the Gregg Senna pen and ink drawings?"

He looks into those incredible deep green eyes and stutters, "Um . . . hello . . . yes, I did. I also bought some beautiful German furniture, an English hand-carved desk for my home office, and four Louie XV chairs. Did you win any bids?"

"Yes, I got some vintage dresses and some modern-style paintings for my downtown office. I bought a Gregg Senna watercolour of a European courtyard last year," she says.

Gladys appears beside them and says, "Grace Chan, I would like you to meet my brother-in-law, Lieutenant John Trosky. He is a jazz fan also, and I'm sure he would like you to come to his place to see the drawings."

"Gladys, you told me about your brother-in-law, John, but you didn't tell me how handsome he is," Grace says.

"I'm glad you think so," Gladys says. "Also, this is Thom Saunders; he is John's best friend and house manager."

"Lovely to meet you, Thom," Grace says.

"We could all get together at John's modest mansion for dinner soon," Gladys suggests.

"Yes, I would like that very much. Do I call you lieutenant or John?" Grace asks.

"Call me John unless I'm arresting you," John manages to say.

She laughs and says, "You are funny!"

"Is it Miss Chan or Mrs. Chan?" John asks.

"It's miss, and call me Grace. I just love Miles Davis. You know, I'm free tomorrow afternoon and evening," Grace offers.

"Okay. Gladys, are you and Mike free for dinner tomorrow at, say, eight o'clock?" John asks.

"Sure, we can make it," Gladys says.

John says, "Make sure you bring Jackie; she can play with Savana again. They loved those baby goats. Grace, what kind of food do you like? I have a really great chef, Julie Crawchuk; Savana is her daughter."

"I like just about anything," Grace replies.

"Julie is Ukrainian, but she can cook anything, but have you ever had Ukrainian food? Perogies, cabbage rolls, garlic sausage?" John asks.

"No, but it sounds good. Oh, I've had cabbage rolls, and I loved them," Grace says.

"Great, I'll pick you up at . . . wait a minute. Do you ride horses? I have several Arabian horses and a nice mare named Adele you can ride," John suggests.

"I love horses; I have a few of my own. My favourite horse's name is Cher. You can pick me up in the afternoon at, say, two o'clock?"

"That's works for me, and Mike, Gladys, and Jackie can join us later. They have their own limo. Oh, do you need a ride home? We have my limo here. Then I will know where you live."

"Okay, I'll tell my driver not to pick me up."

They gave Grace a ride to her mansion, close to the size of John's mansion. They go up the long driveway to the front entrance and see a 1957 Chevy parked there.

"Is that your car?" John asks.

"Yes. Damn, I forgot to put it in the garage," Grace says.

John gets out and circles the car as its turquoise green and white paint gleams in the sun. He says, "Is it all original?"

"I had to change out the original motor and put in a pulse drive, which is programmed to sound like a hot-rodded 283 since they outlawed gasoline-powered motors, but I still have the original 283 cubic inch motor; restored."

John gets in the car and excitedly looks around. "You still have the stock upholstery and dash, and the clock and radio still work! Cool!" He gets out and stands back. She remotes the car to the garage, and he watches her gracefully walk into her mansion.

CHAPTER FIFTEEN

The next afternoon, John goes to pick up Grace.

They get into John's limo and pull up to John's mansion. Grace looks confused and says, "This is your modest mansion?"

John says, "I didn't say that; Gladys did, as I recall. She likes to joke around a lot." Then, in his John Wayne voice, John says, "Let's go to the barn and saddle up pilgrims."

Grace laughs and says, "Gladys told me you do all kinds of voices. That was a good John Wayne."

They take a golf cart that looks like a '57 Chevy and drive to the barn.

"Where did you get this cart?" Grace asks.

"My brother Mike built it for me because I also have a '57 Chevy, and Mike and I own a car manufacturing company and a separate company that customizes cars, bikes, golf carts, and whatever. Wait until you see my new cop car that Mike just finished."

They go into the barn to get the horses, and Autrey has already saddled them.

"This is my groom and trainer, Autrey, and this is my steel-coloured horse, Steely Dan. This light brown beauty is Adele. She was my wife's horse, and she is very gentle."

"Are you divorced?" Grace asks.

"No, my wife died in a car accident three years ago, and she was pregnant with our little girl."

"I'm very sorry; I didn't know about your wife," Grace says.

"Anyway, Sylvia named her horse after her favourite singer, Adele. Well, let's get going. I want you to see my manmade pond, and it's out in the back forty, as my dad would say," John says.

They ride out to the pond and are surprised to see a picnic basket and a blanket spread out. John opens the basket to find a bottle of chilled Troubadour Chablis and some sandwiches, fruit, and cheese.

"This is the work of Julie, my chef. How did she know we were coming out here? I know, probably Thom. Anyway, let's not let it go to waste."

John opens the bottle of wine, and they start to indulge in the portable feast. John sips his wine and says in his Michael Caine voice," So, Grace, tell me about yourself. I'm a police officer, and I need to interrogate you. Where were you born, do you have any siblings, what do you do for a living?"

Grace laughs. "How do you do all those voices?"

John continues in Michael Caine's voice, "Never mind, madam, just answer the questions."

She laughs again.

He switches back to his normal voice and says, "I don't know; my brother and I have done this since we were kids. I started imitating one of my favourite teachers, Mr. Kedziora, who was Ukrainian but sounded more Russian and was a nice guy who was stern but funny at the same time. But, seriously, tell me about your life and what hidden talents you have?"

She answers, "I grew up in Kerrisdale. My mom Shawna, who is Irish, and my Chinese dad Joseph owned a grocery store that my sister Jasmine and I worked in. I went to Point Grey High School and went to U.B.C. on a computer sciences grant. Later, I designed an app for Chinese herbs for health and a medical diagnosis app for cell phones. That alone made me 80 million dollars. Then I started a research company, a clothing company, and started my own real estate company called Chan and Associates. How about you, John? You are a police officer, and yet you have a lot of money. How did you get rich?"

"Well, to start off, my parents were billionaires. They made their money in construction and started an engineering company, but they were killed in a shuttle crash seven years ago and left my brother, my four sisters, and me their entire estate. Plus, we received a large settlement from the crash. I didn't want the money, but Mike took me aside and said that we should use this money to do some good in this world, so we started some children's charities and a research company to develop 'green' products and, being into cars, we started a company building pollution-free, high-powered cars and custom-designed cars like my cop car. To change the subject, when I first looked into those beautiful green eyes of yours yesterday, I felt something I haven't felt in years. I felt love in my heart." He then leans in and softly kisses Grace. She returns the kiss.

"I feel the same way about you. I think we have something special. I have spent so much time on my career and businesses that I have neglected my personal life," Grace says.

John and Grace start kissing passionately. John then says in Mandarin, "I love you, my lotus blossom and holder of beauty!"

"You speak Mandarin? That was a beautiful thing to say," Grace says.

Suddenly, John's watch alarm goes off. "It's a text from Julie, saying supper will be ready in forty minutes. We better get going, or she'll be mad as hell. Is this God's way of telling us to slow down?" John says.

He calls Thom on his phone and says, "Thom, tell Julie we are heading in, and send a droid to pick up this picnic basket as we are riding horses."

They head back to the house and change for dinner. John enters the dining room and finds Mike, Gladys, Jackie, Thom, Savana, and Julie sitting at the table. Grace enters the room, wearing a low-cut navy blue dress with a red floral print with her long wavy hair flowing to her shoulders, and sits next to John.

"Wow, you look beautiful, Grace. I didn't know you brought that dress with you. I guess you know everyone here except Julie and Savana and maybe Jackie?" John says.

"I've met Jackie before," Grace says.

All of a sudden, Chrissy saunters in and jumps up on Grace's lap. Grace looks down and says, "Hello, little one, and what's your name?"

"Grace, meet my cat, Chrissy. She really likes you. I've never seen her jump on someone before; she is always shy of strangers. Chrissy, meet Grace." John says, and Chrissy meows.

"Nice to meet you, Chrissy. You're beautiful, and nice to meet you, Julie and Savana. The food sure smells great in here. I'm hungry. John, what kind of wine goes with Ukrainian food?"

"Either a Chablis or a Cabernet. Do you like Riesling because some people find it too dry or bitter," John asks.

"Well, we just had some Chablis, so let's have some Cabernet. I like either one." The server droids bring in the cabbage rolls and perogies and garlic sausage and Easter bread. They all start eating.

Julie, these perogies are great. What is in them? They are like Chinese dumplings," Grace says.

"These have potatoes and cheddar cheese in them, but you can put sauerkraut or even feta cheese and spinach. Some people make dessert ones with peaches or other kinds of fruit. I can show you how to make them sometime," Julie offers.

"Yes, I would like that. I love these cabbage rolls too."

"Did you two enjoy the picnic basket I prepared for you?" Julie asks.

"Yes, we did. I guess my secret spot isn't a secret anymore, but thank you; it was just what we needed. What's for dessert?" John says.

"Chocolate mousse, anyone?" Julie asks.

"You have a moose made of chocolate?" Jackie asks.

"No, sweetheart, it's a dessert, like pudding. You will love it!" Julie says.

Everyone else agrees to have some.

They finish dinner, and Savana and Jackie go to the game room to play pinball. John says, "I'm going to give Grace the fifty-cent tour of my 'modest-mansion' and show her my newly acquired furniture."

"I think Gladys and I will go watch the girls, and I want to try out your Formula One driving simulator," Mike says.

"You have two of those side by side, don't you?" Gladys asks.

In his Sean Connery as James Bond voice, John says, "Yes, Miss Moneypenny, but don't wager any large bets with him. He is a scoundrel when it comes to competition."

Gladys and Grace both laugh, and Gladys says, "I still can't get over how you can do all those voices."

Grace says, laughing, 'Yeah, I can't get over that too."

John escorts Grace into the grand dining room, where the four Louie XV chairs are arranged in the corner, and the Brarock-Kommode side table is set up with flowers in vases and a small sculpture. Grace says, "That's a Brarock-Kommode! It's gorgeous. I love the chrome finish on it, and it's an unusual design. I didn't see that at the auction."

"Yes, when I saw it, I had to have it. I paid too much for it, but it's for the children's hospital charity. Would you like to see the companion, the dresser? It's in my bedroom; I have the Gregg Senna drawings in there as well. It feels like the old line, 'Would you like to come up to my room to see my etchings?'"

In a Southern Belle voice, Grace says, "I would love to see your etchings, sir. Bless your heart."

John laughs and says, "Apparently, I'm not the only one who can imitate voices."

"It's the only voice I can do besides fake Russian."

They take the elevator to John's bedroom, and she says, "You have an elevator in your place. I've got to get one installed."

"Yes, it also moves sideways. I'll recommend my contractor to you. Mike designed the mechanism to make it move sideways. I also have one at the rear of the house." He switches to his Mathew McConaughey voice and says, "Well, Miss Southern Belle, how do you like my etchings?"

"I love them. I hear he did one of Stevie Wonder, but I don't know if it's a rumour or not. It looks like he did these pen and inks on watercolour paper and did the background feathering with Pain's grey watercolour paint. I did some watercolours in grade school," Grace says.

John turns on a Miles Davis CD, playing "Sketches of Spain," and says in his McConaughey voice, "Would you like to dance, Miss Southern Belle? I think Miles would insist we dance to his music."

Grace kicks off her high heeled shoes, and they start slow dancing and then kiss passionately, moving around the room in a graceful motion. Suddenly, the intercom dings, and John pushes the button to answer.

"Lieutenant, you seem to have forgotten your other guests, and they are about to leave," Thom says.

"Sorry, Thom. We'll be right down." He turns to Grace and says, "Grace, can you stay here tonight?"

"I really want to stay, but you'll have to give me a ride to work tomorrow to my real estate office as I have several meetings scheduled starting at nine."

"No problem. I'll fly you there in my new cop car. Let's go say goodbye to our guests. I think they have cracked the code that we are in love by now."

"I think so too. We are all very intelligent people here. I'll leave my shoes in here; I like to be barefoot whenever possible."

"You know, I kind of have a foot fetish, and you have beautiful feet. I will gladly give you a foot massage whenever your heart desires for the rest of your life," John says.

"Sold! Let's go down and say goodbye," Grace suggests.

They go downstairs and say goodnight to Gladys, Mike, and Jackie.

"Grace, do you need a ride home?" Mike asks.

"No, John has kindly offered to take care of me tonight."

"Yes, John has always been a gentleman and a scholar. Well, you two have fun," Mike says. "Oh, John, that idea of the body armour made from that car body material is working out well. I think we will have a prototype in a week or two. We'll try it out on you first, okay? Just joking; we'll use another dummy first. Well, gang, let's get going before John gets mad. Goodnight, you two. Congratulations on recognizing each other's souls."

John and Grace go back to his bedroom and continue their romantic dance to more mellow jazz. He starts to undress her, and her dress floats to the floor, leaving her standing there in a black lace bra and panties, a garter belt, and black silk stockings. He unhooks her bra and lovingly caresses her big breasts. She unbuttons his shirt and reveals a muscled chest and abdomen. She unzips his pants, pulls them down, and pulls off his silk underwear, exposing his erect penis. He slides her silk panties off to reveal her bald vagina.

"You are the perfect woman. I like a smooth mound."

"I had my pubic hair permanently removed because I used to model lingerie and bathing suits, and the agency made all the models remove their pubic hair by shaving or waxing, which hurts when they do it. But I found out that it exposes all those nerves around my vagina, which gives me a better orgasm."

John reaches down and gently runs his fingers over her mound and says, "You mean these nerves?"

She begins to shiver with excitement as he sucks on her erect nipples. She starts to moan in pleasure and becomes wet. She shoves him back onto the bed and slides on top of him, and guides him into her pleasure place. They make love passionately for hours and finally collapse in a heap and cuddle together. Grace breathlessly says, "That was okay, but you're going to need a lot more practice."

"Any time you want to practice with me is fine. One day, we will get really good at this." They both laugh, and John turns on the remote gas fireplace and dims the lights by voice control.

"What was that music we made love to?" Grace asks.

"That is a jazz group, ironically called 'Fourplay,' as in the number four. That was Chaka Kahn and Phil Collins singing on the disc. Did you enjoy the music?"

"Very much, but I enjoyed the other part more."

Chrissy saunters into the bedroom, circles, and lays down at the bottom of the bed.

CHAPTER SIXTEEN

The next morning, they get up, shower together, and have "shower fun." Then they put on plush white robes, taken from John's hotel travels, and sit down to eat in the sitting area of his huge bedroom.

He brings out two Denver omelettes from his auto chef and two cups of his brand of real coffee, J and S Kona Gold, from his plantation in Hawaii. She says, "This coffee is ridiculously good. I suppose you own the plantation?"

"Actually, my wife Silvia and I started it, so the brand is still called S and J Kona Gold. We have other grinds, but I like this one the best. Gladys now owns Silvia's half of the business and runs it. I have no time to run all these enterprises. I also have a modest mansion in Lahaina. I have an idea! Let's take our breakfasts up to the roof. It has a polycarbonate bubble dome on it, it's heated, and it has a year-round flower garden. We can watch the beautiful sunrise."

They go up, and the sunrise is amazing. They sit at a small table for a while, enjoying the view and eating their breakfasts. John says, "We should go to Lahaina sometime if I ever get a break. Maybe we could go there between Christmas and New Year's. Since I was a kid, I always wanted to be a cop, especially a detective."

They finish their omelettes, and John puts on his black suit. Grace returns in her flowery dress and says, "I'm going to have to go home and change into my business suit as I have many important meetings today. Can you give me a ride home, or should I call my limo driver?"

"I'll drive you home in my new cop car; we can fly to your place in ten minutes, and then I can pick up Detective Sidhu."

They get in the car and fly to Grace's place. She exclaims, "Wow, this car is unbelievable, and I love the colour. Is that an auto chef in the dash?"

"Yes, would you like a coffee?"

"No, I'd probably spill it on my dress. Oh, here we are already. You can land on the driveway near the front entrance. Well, call me later John, I love you!"

"I love you too. Just remember, I'm working on a hot case, and I may have to leave town at any time, so please, don't get mad at me if that happens. I never know what is going on until I get to the office. I'll call you later or text you if I have complications. Have a great day, sweetheart."

"I understand, sometimes I have to leave town for business, so we shouldn't get mad at each other."

He watches Grace walk into the house, then motors down her driveway, flies over her front gate, and picks up Detective Sidhu.

"How was your weekend, John?" Chuck asks.

"I had a great weekend, man. I have a new girlfriend named Grace Chan. I met her at a charity auction and bought some artwork, expensive furniture, and four beautiful Louie XV chairs, and she spent the weekend at my place. We are in love, man! I haven't been this happy in years!"

"You mean *the* Grace Chan, the billionaire? She's your girlfriend?" Chuck asks.

"What do you mean *the* Grace Chan? Is she like famous or something?"

"Have you been hiding under a rock? Grace Chan is like a Rockstar in the business world."

"She told me her life story. She comes from humble beginnings; her family had a grocery store, and got into U.B.C. on a computer scholarship. I don't care if she is poor or rich; she has a heart of gold, she likes everything that I like, and I fell in love with her at first sight. I swear, I'm going to marry her; not right away, but I'm going to marry her. Mark my words, Chuck. So, how was your weekend? Did you sneak off to Winnipeg to see Ronnie?" John asks.

"No, I would like to see her again, but I can't afford to shuttle around like you do. I talked to her on the weekend, though," Chuck says.

"If we don't get stuck travelling on this damn case, you can take my shuttle next weekend. You deserve a mini holiday. I wish I could give you more time off, but we must solve this case. My Spidey Senses tell me this jerk is going to kill again soon, probably this week," John says.

"Thanks, John. I appreciate all you do for me."

They walked into the bullpen at 8 a.m., and John threw his Stetson hat on the rack and spotted Randy Chan.

"Detective Chan, did you find anything more on Mr. Raphael Dupuis's whereabouts? Anything?"

"I wondered what he did for a living and found out he is a medical and biological engineer. Get this, he was working on something called nano-bots. Apparently, these things can be injected into the bloodstream and be programmed to heal different body parts, sort of like stem cells. Well, I think he found a way to program them to pinpoint and damage the organs. He must have sent this device to the Ghost somehow," Randy Chan says.

"Well, the next step be to check Mr. Dupuis's travel records from the last few years, all shipping companies, and any other ideas you can think of. If you need help, get the captain on this."

Suddenly, John's mobile phone rings: "Dispatch, Lieutenant John Trosky, report to 2200-13th Avenue. Dead body found on the premises."

"Shit, Chuck, what did I tell you? He struck again."

CHAPTER SEVENTEEN

Sunday, 8:30 p.m., and the Ghost is busy, entertaining real estate agent Ken Leung.

He pours Ken a glass of champagne with his back turned away from him and slips some drops into his drink.

"This calls for a celebration. Have some champagne, Ken! Let's sign the papers, and you will own this place," he says.

Ken Leung signs his part, drinks the champagne, and starts to feel dizzy in a few minutes. He blacks out. When he wakes up in pain, he realizes that he is nailed to a partly-built wall of two-by-fours. "What the hell is going on?" he asks.

The Ghost says, "Mr. Pavel Romaniuk sends his regards. He apparently didn't like you screwing him out of this house." The Ghost then takes a drill with a long bit and drills into Leung's heart, leaving the bit in there. He takes a small pack of Russian stacking dolls out of his pocket and puts it in Leung's left jacket pocket as he is dying. He doesn't realize he is standing in front of a nanny-cam disguised as a teddy bear. He removes his coveralls, washes his hands, and leaves the house.

John and Chuck pull up at the house at 8:20 a.m. There are four cop cars in front of it and barricades set up at each end of the street. They seal up, turn their recorders on, and enter the house. John looks at the cop at the door and says, "Officer Brennan, were you first on the scene?"

He looks like he will vomit and says, "Yes, lieutenant, the body is in the living room."

"What time did you get here?" John asks.

"We got a call from dispatch at 7:45 a.m. from a hysterical woman, screaming to the 911 operator about a dead body, and we arrived here at 7:52 a.m. and found a Miss Karen Wong freaking out and crying. We tried to calm her down, but she kept pointing to the living room and crying."

John and Chuck enter the living room and see a body posed like Jesus with his arms spread and his hands and feet nailed to the wall. A drill bit is sticking out of his chest and a pool of blood around him.

"Holy shit, Chuck. What a way to die. It looks like he was killed by Romans, like Jesus! I'll print him and check the time of death. You go find Miss Wong, and I'll join you in a few minutes."

John gets out his gauges, fingerprints him, and checks the time of death. He finds out that he died at 8:10 p.m. on Sunday night, April 16th. His name is Ken Leung, and he is a real estate agent employed by Chan and Associates. Grace Chan CEO.

"Oh, God, Grace is going to freak out. It's a good thing she was having dinner at my place last night, not that she could ever do something like this."

He goes into the kitchen and finds Chuck comforting Karen Wong. She is no longer weeping but still shaky. John says, "Hello, Miss Wong, I'm Lieutenant John Trosky of the homicide squad. Please try to relax and tell us when you found Mr. Leung and what he was doing here last night."

"He was supposed to be in the office at seven-thirty this morning, and I was to notarize his contract on selling this house. But he didn't answer his cell phone or texts, so I drove down here and found him like that. I can't get that vision out of my mind," she says.

"Who was he meeting here?" John asks.

"He said his name was John Luc Picard, and he was a shuttle pilot for Enterprise Air."

John rolls his eyes and looks at Chuck. "Detective Sidhu, have you ever seen *Star Trek: The Next Generation?*"

"Yes, on the Nostalgia Channel. Yeah, Captain John Luc Picard of the Starship Enterprise," Chuck says.

"Sorry, Miss Wong, but he gave you a phoney name. We've come across this guy before. Did he have an accent at all?" John asks.

"Yes, he sounded like he was upper-crust British and arrogant."

"Did you see him in person?"

"No, I talked to him over the phone."

"Do you work with Grace Chan?"

She looks down at her shaking hands and says, "Well, yes, she's my boss."

"What do you want to do now? We can get you to a grief counsellor, or do you want to go to work? I can phone Grace. She is my girlfriend, and I need to talk to her anyway," John says.

"I should go back to work; we have a lot of meetings today. Is Grace really your girlfriend?" Karen asks.

"Yes, we just met on Saturday. Can you drive?"

"I don't know, maybe not in this state," she replies.

"We can get an officer to drive you and another to drive your car. Oh, and give Detective Sidhu your contact numbers in case we need to talk to you again," John says.

John phones Grace and says, "Hi, Grace. I'm sorry to bother you, but one of your employees has been murdered. Do you know a Ken Leung?"

"What? Yes, I know Ken; he's been working here for four years. He's really dead?"

"A Miss Karen Wong found him in a house that he was selling. Karen is freaked out but she insists on going back to work. Do you need her there? We can drive her and her car to your office if you need her."

"Yes, drive her here; we need some papers that she has, and I need her for the first meeting, then I'll probably send her home if I see she needs to go home and relax, but she is a very strong woman."

"We have a grief counsellor at the cop shop if she needs help later; her name is Joanne Weber, and I've known her since my college days. Oh, we will contact his next of kin, so don't contact them until we do. Well, sweetheart, I'm going to have a long day here. We're just getting started, and I've got to get the sweepers in here to tear this place apart and check if there are any cameras in here to get some video on the killer. He gave his name to Karen as John Luc Picard, shuttle plot, very funny."

"You're kidding, right? Even I know about Star Trek," Grace says.

"I'll call you much later. Love you."

"I love you too, later."

John hangs up the phone and asks Chuck, "Did anyone call the M.E., Luci Ryan, and the sweepers?"

"Luci should be here any minute, and the sweepers are delayed, but should be here within an hour."

"Chuck, a house this size should have a security room and cameras. Check for a security room, and I'll check around in the living room." John looks around and notices a stuffed teddy bear sitting on a shelf with some knickknacks. He picks it up and finds a hidden nanny-cam. He takes the camera out and sees that it is a wireless unit. "Chuck, where are you?"

"I'm in the security room near the second bedroom," Chuck replies.

John walks into the security room and says, "Look what I found, Chuck, a nanny-cam, and it's wireless, so it must be hooked up to the computer in here."

Chuck punches some buttons and finds the footage. "Scroll it back to around 8 p.m., that's when he died," John instructs.

Chuck locks onto the scene at 7:30 p.m. and says, "It looks like the Ghost spiked the drink that knocked him out. Jesus, he used a nail gun on him to nail him to the wall. Is that an industrial drill? God, he did all this while the guy was awake! I'll print some stills from this footage. This is the best footage we have of him so far. This camera has a sound option also, but it needs to be enhanced a bit. We should get Randy Chan on this for the sound."

John looks at the screen and says, "Wait a minute. What did he put in Leung's pocket? Roll the footage back. It looks like one of those Russian or Ukrainian stacking dolls. They are called matryoshka dolls. I don't want to touch the body until Luci gets here. I'll have her check his pockets. I think I hear her voice." John walks back to the living room and says, "Hi Luci, sorry about the mess in here, but I didn't do it."

"That's very funny, John. I've got to write that down. Holy shit, someone sure screwed this guy and nailed him, obviously," Luci says.

"I only touched the body to fingerprint him and get the time of death. We found some footage of the murder; it's the same guy that killed Doctor Blackwell. Do me a favour and check this guy's jacket pockets. The killer put something in there. I think it was one of those Russian stacking dolls. You know the ones that fit inside each other and get smaller and smaller? Make sure you wear gloves; he may have left prints or put poison on them. I sure as hell don't want you dying because of this kook. You're just too cute to die."

"Aww, John, I didn't know you cared, you sweetie! Now, how the hell are we going to get these nails out of the wall without damaging his hands further?"

"Maybe I can find some tools here, or we can get the firefighters in here. They do this for a living, but I'd rather have the sweepers in here first before we have too many people tramping around. You can work on him for a bit like that, can't you?"

"Yes, I can, but I want him on the table as soon as possible," Luci says.

"I'll tell you what. You start on him, and I'll get the sweepers to do this room first, as I want his fingerprints badly, then I'll get the firefighters to extract him. I know a good fireman at the local station, Captain Jim Hoglund. He is a long-time friend of mine, and he is brilliant and careful. I've seen him build a '32 Ford roadster out of pieces from different cars. I'll call him now." John switches to his Sean Connery, James Bond voice and says, "Anything to make you happy, Miss Moneypenny."

Luci looks at John, laughs, and says, "Carry on, 007. I'll be waiting on pins and needles for you."

John calls Captain Jim Hoglund on his private line and explains his dilemma.

"I'll be there in twenty minutes," Jim says.

Once Jim arrives, he and two other firefighters carefully extract the nails and release Mr. Leung off the wall in minutes. John thanks him and says, "Jim, we'll have to catch up soon. I'd like to see your new hot rod."

"Sure, Tiny. Debbie would love to see you and bring a bottle of that great Merlot from your winery. I'm building a '32 Ford coupe with a new pulse engine in it, and it's almost finished. See you later."

They leave, and Luci finds the stacking dolls in Mr. Leung's jacket pocket and gives them to John in an evidence bag. She starts to leave with the body, then turns around and says, "I'll see you guys later at the morgue."

"Chuck, did you get the video footage on a disc or download it to your laptop?" John asks.

"I did both and sent a copy to Captain Fedora," Chuck says.

"Now we must do the sad part; go and tell the family that Mr. Leung is dead. Apparently, he has a wife and two daughters. They don't live far from here, so let's go and let the sweepers finish up here. I hope they find some fingerprints or DNA."

CHAPTER EIGHTEEN

John and Chuck drive to the Leung residence and knock on the door. The door opens, and a tiny Chinese woman says, "Yes, can I help you, gentlemen?"

"I'm Lieutenant John Trosky, and this is my partner Detective Chuck Sidhu from the homicide squad. Are you Mrs. Iris Leung?"

"Yes. Homicide? Are my daughters, Zoe and Sophia all right?"

"Yes, may we come in?" John asks.

"Yes, what is going on?"

John looks sad and steps into the living room. "I think you should sit down. I'm sorry to tell you this, but your husband was murdered last night at around 8 p.m. in a house on 13th Avenue."

Mrs. Leung starts to break down and cry. "I don't understand. Ken didn't have any enemies." She starts to hyperventilate.

"Can I get you a glass of water, ma'am?" Chuck asks.

"What? Oh, yes, please. I'm sorry. I couldn't understand why he didn't come home last night. He said he had to show a house to a Mr. Picard, a shuttle pilot. It was an expensive home," she says.

"Can we call someone to stay with you? A friend, relative?" Chuck asks.

"Yes, my sister Amanda and my daughters are at school. They need to come home," Mrs. Leung says.

"We will have them picked up. We will also need to look at your husband's files on his house sales. We already have video of your husband's murderer. We know what he looks like, but he used a false name. We know that he is a hired assassin, but we don't know why he killed your husband," John says. "Does your husband have a computer in the house?" he adds.

"No, his computer is in his office, downtown at Chan and Associates," she answers.

"We can get access to his computer there, as I know Grace Chan. If you need a grief counsellor, we can arrange one for you and your daughters. I know this is a great trauma for you. Well, thank you for your time, and God bless you. We will get the killer. It's just a matter of time, Mrs. Leung. We'll be in touch."

They leave and go to Grace's office.

Once there, they announce themselves and ask her secretary Maya if Grace is busy. She buzzes Grace, and Grace enters the reception area and says," John! And detective . . .?"

"Oh, Grace Chan, meet my partner, Detective Chuck Sidhu. I forgot that you two haven't met."

"Nice to meet you, detective. Did you talk to Iris Leung?" she says.

"Yes, we just came from her house. She is not taking it well. Grace, we need to get into Ken Leung's computer to check his house sales. I think it will help us find the killer."

"Anything to help, John. His office is this way. Follow me. However, I don't know his password."

"Don't worry, Miss Chan, I have a program that can open it," Chuck says.

"Call me Grace. Have at it. I have one more meeting, then I'll get back to you," she says, then winks at John and leaves the room. She purposely wiggles her hips as she walks out of the office.

Chuck starts working on the computer, then turns to John and says, "John, you forgot to tell me how beautiful your girlfriend is!"

"I'm glad you noticed. Now, use your can opener on that computer and keep your eyes on it."

Chuck starts checking Ken Leung's files and can't find anything illegal.

"There's got to be something 'hinky' in there," John says and leaves the room to find Grace. She steps into the hallway, and John says, "Grace, I need to talk to you about Ken Leung. Let's find a room where we can talk."

"Let's go into my office over here."

They go into her office, and John asks, "Grace, how well do you know Ken Leung, and how long has he worked for you?"

"I just know him as an employee. I met his wife and daughters at functions, but I don't know him that well. He has worked here for about four years. His work seems to be more than satisfactory," Grace says.

"Does he sell anything off-planet or in other countries? It is bugging me that someone would kill him so brutally. He must have screwed someone out of a lot of money because what other motive is there? And why would the assassin kill him in that specific house? Do you know if that house was sold before?" John asks.

"No, I don't know if that house was sold before, but it was Ken's listing all along, so it should be in his files."

"Okay, I should see if Chuck has found anything in Ken's files. After we finish here, we must go back to the station and do some more digging. Do you want to get together for dinner later?"

"Just dinner?" she asks.

"And dessert, if you know what I mean. Nudge, nudge. Wink, wink," John says.

Grace answers in a southern drawl, "Yes, John, y'all talk so sweet."

"I must go see the captain and check with my squad, so I'll call you later, and we'll go for dinner. Why don't you choose the restaurant?"

"Yes, I do have a favourite restaurant. It'll be a surprise!"

"Great, I'll see you later," Grace says. "Oh, John, if you can't reach me for some reason, call my secretary Maya Yeng at this number, and she can find me or tell you if I'm in a meeting or at my other office downtown."

Chuck knocks and comes into Grace's office. "I can't find anything on the first layer of Mr. Leung's computer, Miss Chan . . . Grace. Can we take it into the station to dig deeper and get more people working on the programming?"

"Yes, just give me a receipt for it," Grace says.

John writes her a receipt, and they drive back to the police station. They enter the police station, and John says, "Chuck, let's go see Captain Fedora and get his help with digging further into this computer, but first send a copy of the files to my office and home computer."

CHAPTER NINETEEN

Chuck sends the files, and they entered Captain Fedora's office.

The captain says, "Lieutenant and detective, what can I do for you gentlemen today?"

"I didn't realize we were gentlemen, but as simple, ordinary, bumbling detectives, we need your brilliant mind to help us solve a problem we are having with the victim, Ken Leung's computer. We can't find any illegal transactions, but I know he must have screwed someone to get brutally killed the way he did. I mean, nailing him to a wall like Jesus and drilling him in the heart—that is overkill if I ever saw it," John says.

"Well, let's see what we can dig up. How many levels did you get into?" Captain Fedora says.

"I only looked at it in his office, so I got to levels one and two. We need a better program to go any deeper, like a worm or a Trojan Horse," Chuck explains.

"Let's take it into the lab and bust its cherry. I'll get Randy Chan on this too. Why don't you two take a break," the captain says.

"Okay, I have some paperwork to do," John says.

Chuck looks at Captain Fedora and says, "I'm not tired. I want in on this; to learn more tech solutions."

"Good idea, Chuck; you should never stop learning," the captain says.

John goes back to his office to sign paperwork from his Black Hat Squad Detectives from the previous day. There is a knock on the door. "Enter at your own risk," he says.

Detective Binh Tran opens the door and says, "Have you got a minute, lieutenant?"

"Detective Tran, what can I do for you?"

"My confidential informant Bui Phuong from the Vietnamese gang, the Golden Tigers, which is run by Li Pham, tells me that he has cell phone video of Li Pham ordering the killing of Sonny Chen, the leader of the Red Dragons gang, right in front of his gang. This video and the drive-by killing are in Li Pham's computer and as are his illegal financials, and Li Pham called for a meeting tonight at 10:00 p.m. So, we need a warrant to go in tonight and arrest the whole gang and confiscate all his computers and cell phones, as he has to have more than one."

It looks like you've done your homework. I'll call A.P.A. Nikki Anders right now, but I can't go with you tonight; I'm too busy with this serial assassin case."

"We have enough men to do this raid tonight," Tran says.

John calls Nikki Anders, and she says, "You'll have your warrant within the hour, John. Tell Detective Tran that I want to be there when he interrogates Li Pham. Ciao."

Detective Tran says, "Thanks, lieutenant. I've been after this asshole for three years, and this is the break we needed.

Tran starts to leave the office, but John stops him, saying, "Wait, before you go, I know you have a team but are you taking SWAT with you?"

"Yes, lieutenant. Shane Travis has planned this operation, and we are all wearing combat gear."

"That's good; make sure everyone is safe, and don't be afraid to stun or kill these bastards, but, of course, don't kill your C.I. Bui Phuong. Arrest him with the others, and separate them all," John commands.

"Copy that, sir."

CHAPTER TWENTY

At the same moment, the Ghost waits for the order for his next kill.

He thinks back to his teen years. He was born in the projects on the outskirts of Paris, surrounded by a drug slinging gang. The leader of the Royals named Remy "the Butcher" Boucher killed the Ghost's drug slinging mother and father. He came home to their grungy apartment to find his parents nailed to the floor with cocaine stuffed up their noses and spikes through their hearts. He didn't even like his parents, but he needed revenge, and he knew who did it, Remy Boucher.

He stalked Remy for a month. Learned his faults, who his friends, enemies, and gang members were and where they lived and hung out. He also learned who his girlfriend, Gabrielle Berne, was.

He snuck into Remy's place one afternoon and spiked all his liquor with a knockout drug, waited for him and his girlfriend to come home and drink and pass out. He then nailed them to the living room floor, spread-eagle. He waited until they were conscious and got out his drill and said to Remy, "You killed my parents, you piece of shit, and now I'm going to slowly kill your girlfriend while you watch, and then it's your turn. Does the name Auger mean anything to you, motherfucker? They call me 'The Auger' or the Drill. Try to relax."

"No, kill me but spare Gabby; she had nothing to do with your parents' deaths!" killing your

"Have you read the Bible? It says, 'An eye for an eye,' so I must kill her, you see. I also need you to suffer as I suffered when you killed my parents. Don't worry, I'm going to kill the rest of your gang, too, but don't tell them; I want it to be a surprise."

Then Gabby and Remy started screaming until there was silence and a lot of blood.

CHAPTER TWENTY-ONE

John Trosky looks at his watch and says, "Oh, man, it's the end of my shift, I better call Grace." He picks up his desk phone and calls Grace and says, "Hi Grace, how is your day going?"

"I'm just about finished here. How about you?" she says.

"I'm done here. What time do you want to go for dinner?" John asks.

"I had to skip lunch as I was so busy today. What time is it now?"

"It's six o'clock, and I'm getting hungry, too," he says.

"I have to go home and change first; can you pick me up at seven o'clock?" Grace asks.

"Sure, but since I don't know what restaurant we are going to, what do I wear? A suit or casual attire?"

"Casual attire. You know, a black shirt, black sweater, and black pants."

They both say goodbye.

John puts on his black Stetson hat and overcoat, as it is only seven degrees Celsius outside, steps into the bullpen, and sees Chuck. "Chuck, are you ready to go home or are you going back to work with Captain Fedora?"

"The Captain told me to go home and rest. He and Randy went home; we will continue digging tomorrow, so we can go."

John drives Chuck home and says, "See you in the morning. I have a date tonight with Grace."

"I like Grace; you two seem right for each other. You have love and respect. Well, have fun, see you tomorrow," Chuck says.

John goes home, showers, and changes into his casual attire but chooses a light blue shirt, medium blue sweater, weapon harness and blaster, dark blue blazer, dark blue slacks, and a dark blue overcoat; just to show Grace that he can wear brighter colours. He tells Thom and Julie that he is going out for dinner and to "behave themselves" tonight. Thom jokingly says, "I think we should be telling you that, but it is not our place to do that, lieutenant."

John retorts, "Yes, well, don't wait up. See you later."

He orders his limo around and goes to pick up Grace, and they park at her front door. He gets out just as she comes out of her mansion. She is wearing a dark blue dress with yellow and pink flowers printed on it, black silk stockings, and a dark blue overcoat. She looks at John and says, "I guess we are in tune with each other tonight. Blue looks good on you, John; it brings out the colour in your eyes."

"You look amazing yourself, Grace," he says.

They get into the limo, and John says, "There is a speaker button on your right, so you can tell the driver, Jeffery, where we are going."

"Oh, okay. Jeffery, go to Demetri's Greek restaurant on 10th Avenue."

"How did you know I love Greek food?" John asks.

"I've had a private detective following you around for a while. Just joking! Julie told me all the foods you like. You'll like this restaurant; it has a sliding roof that opens up on the second floor at the back of the restaurant and lots of plants for décor."

John slides closer and says in his James Bond voice, "You know what I like better, Miss Moneypenny, is you and this limo," and grabs her, kisses her hard on the mouth, and starts to slide his hand under her dress and up her thighs.

Just then, Jeffery hits the intercom button and says, "We are at Demetri's restaurant, sir."

"Darn . . ." John mutters. "Uh, thank you, Jeffery."

In Mandarin, Grace says to John, "I suppose we must save dessert for later, Mr. Bond."

John replies in Mandarin, saying, "Yes, my little lotus blossom."

They enter the restaurant and are greeted by Dimitri himself. "Welcome, Grace. I haven't seen you in a few weeks, and who is your friend?"

"This is my boyfriend Lieutenant John Trosky! We have a reservation in my name, and we want to sit upstairs under the open roof, so we can look at the stars," Grace says.

He leads them upstairs to their table and says, "Would you like some wine to start with?"

"Do you mind if I order the wine, John?" Grace asks.

"Go ahead."

"We would like a bottle of Troubador Merlot and some pita bread, tzatziki, and hummus to start."

They look at the menu, and both order lamb souvlakia with rice and roasted potatoes. John says, "Grace, this place is great, and you look beautiful in this candlelight. I love this open roof, too. We can see the stars and the moon, and yet it is warm in here."

Their food comes, and they enjoy their lamb souvlakia and tzatziki. Grace asks, "So, John, where did you grow up?"

"I grew up in Winnipeg, or as we call it Winterpeg, in a poor area. Winnipeg is very cold, it is 20 to 40 degrees below zero all winter long, and we would get 10 feet of snow some years. My dad was an unskilled labourer. I don't know how he and my mom raised six kids with so little money, but he ended up a billionaire. He and his brothers got into buying land and sold it to the railway company, then they got into developing malls and building housing. What was it like for you growing up in Vancouver?" he says.

"Well, we didn't get 10 feet of snow, but it felt cold because of the dampness. My sister Jasmine and I had fun playing in the snow when we did get some and would make snowmen. When we were teenagers, we worked in my parent's grocery store. I studied computer sciences and found I had a knack for it. I discovered that I could develop apps for simple things and went to U.B.C. on a computer grant. Later, I developed an app for pairing Chinese herbs to cures for different diseases and diagnosing diseases. That alone made me a billionaire. Once I realized that I was rich, I started a children's charity and later got into real estate. I also own a clothing manufacturing company."

They finish eating their meals, and once they are back in the limo, John says, "It's still early; do you want to come to my place for a nightcap?"

"I'd love to go to your place," Grace says.

CHAPTER TWENTY-TWO

They arrive at John's place, and Saunders greets them, saying, "Good evening, lieutenant and Miss Chan. Did you enjoy your meal?"

"Yes, it was excellent. We'll be having brandy in the parlour. Thom, is everything okay in the house?" John asks.

"Yes, and there were no calls for you."

They go into the small parlour, followed by Chrissy, and John opens a wall panel. He brings out two snifters of brandy and hands one to Grace. He then remotely lights the gas fireplace.

"Computer, play Miles Davis's 'Sketches of Spain' on low volume," John says.

They sit side by side on the couch, and Grace casually pets Chrissy as she purrs.

Then John says, "Bless you," in Polish.

"What did you just say?" Grace asks.

"I said 'bless you,' in Polish."

"How many languages do you speak?"

"Let's see, I speak Mandarin, Polish, and Ukrainian, some Russian, as it is close to Ukrainian and French, because I spent two years in Paris at the Sorbonne University and some Arabic and Urdu because I was in the army in Afghanistan with Thom. We were snipers in that crappy desert. What a waste of time that was. Those people will always be at war. They have been fighting since before Jesus. What about you? I know you speak Mandarin. Do you speak any other languages?" John says.

"I speak some French, as I deal with some companies in Quebec, and I also speak German as a good friend of mine in school, Greta, was German," Grace replies.

"You must be about the same age as me. When is your birthday? I want to buy you something expensive," John says.

"You are a sneaky interrogator. I'll show you mine if you show me yours, as they say. My birthday is April 29th, and I will be thirty-two years old. Your turn."

In his Sean Connery as James Bond voice, John says, "That's why I'm a cop, Miss Chan. I was born on July 27th, and I am twenty-nine years old, and I do love older women!"

She laughs and says, "So, I'm an older woman, eh? You'll pay for that, Mr. Bond; I know Karate and kung fu." She grabs John and starts wrestling with him, which quickly turns into sexual touching and giggling. They kiss passionately as she takes John's blazer off and says, "Do you wear a weapon all the time?"

"I have to wear a weapon all the time; it's the law, except for private property and bathtubs or swimming pools." He unhooks his weapon harness, drops it to the floor, and lifts her dress over her head. "I see you're wearing my favourite outfit, black lace undergarments, my lotus blossom," he says.

She stands there in a black lace bra, panties, garter belt, and black silk stockings as she removes John's sweater, shirt, slacks, and underwear. She gently grabs his erect penis, strokes him slowly and says, "I see you have a hidden weapon. Do you have a license for this?"

"No, are you going to punish me for that?" he asks.

"Maybe; it depends whether you are a good boy tonight," she says.

"I'll be more than good; I'll be great."

He unhooks her bra and slides her panties down, and pulls them off along with her shoes. He gently rubs the area just above her smooth vagina, making her inhale quickly and start to moan.

"I love that you removed your pubic hair," he says.

He gently rubs the area above her vagina, and she shudders and moans, "Oh, God!"

They fall back onto the big couch, and she guides him into her warm wet womanhood, and they start rocking and thrusting as he nibbles at her ear, neck, and luscious lips. He cups her beautiful big breasts and rubs her nipples with his thumbs. Grace reaches a peak and shudders and cries out as she orgasms. This triggers John, and they have a simultaneous orgasm and collapse in a heap.

"Oh my God, John, that was awesome. I think my brain melted!" Grace says.

John catches his breath and says, "Just think, with a little more practice, we can become really good at this."

Grace laughs and says in Mandarin, "Yes, grasshopper, we need to practice a lot, and when you can grasp the pebble from my hand and have an orgasm at the same time, we will have reached the ultimate level."

"Seriously, though, Grace, that is the first time I've had a simultaneous orgasm. You are a magic woman!" he says.

They fall onto the couch, and Grace asks, "John, are these bullet wounds on your back?"

"Yes, a present from Afghanistan. Thom and I and our squad entered a small village on foot, and we got ambushed by some Afghani rebels. I took two shots in the back, and Thom got grazed in his left arm. He dragged me to cover and saved my life. Then he and the squad killed all the rebels, and the medic patched me up. That's why I trust him to take care of my house and run and keep it secure. You don't know what he does behind the scenes."

They cuddle up together under a blanket and watch the fireplace burn as they sip more brandy and listen to more Miles Davis.

"I'm glad you told me that. I now have more respect for Thom. This is excellent brandy. It's better than Courvoisier. I've never heard of Artis brandy before," Grace says.

"That's because it's not on the market yet. It's from my winery. It's Gladys's idea, and she developed the taste of it. The brand is named after her grandmother, Artis, who is French and still alive and feisty at one hundred and ten years old! So, you like it? So do I. I'll tell Gladys to put it on the market tomorrow," John says.

"Well, it's getting late. Did you bring your jammies?" John asks.

"You know I don't wear jammies to bed or anything. I like to be naked, and if that is your way of asking me if I want to stay the night, the answer is yes, but you have to let me get some sleep, just some sleep, if you know what I mean," Grace says.

"Yes, in my quirky way, I was asking, and I love you naked, my lotus blossom. What time do you need to be at work?" John says.

"You can drop me off at my house at seven-thirty as I need to change. Oh, I might need to go out of town tomorrow or the next day," Grace says.

They shower together and "play" for a while, and Grace says, "I've decided not to punish you because you've been a very good boy."

They go into the drying tube and then climb into bed. Chrissy curls up at their feet, and they cuddle and fall asleep.

They get up early in the morning and go into the small dining room, followed by Chrissy.

"Julie is making us a spinach and feta cheese omelette unless you want something else?" John says.

"Good, that's my favourite omelette, that and a Denver omelette. Do you have a private eye following me around?" Grace asks jokingly.

"Maybe, there's also the internet and Facebook. You are famous, you know," John says.

He pours them both a cup of coffee.

"I am not famous; I admit to being rich, but not famous," Grace says.

Okay, if you say so, but have you ever Googled yourself?" John asks.

"Is that a euphemism for some sexual thing? I know what Google is; I use it for research. This is a different coffee; I like it too," Grace says.

"Yes, we call it Afrikaans Dark Roast; it really comes from Africa. We have a small plantation there. It's a fair-trade deal. We like to pay the workers a decent wage, and we drilled water wells in the nearby villages," John answers.

Julie enters with their omelettes and puts their plates down in front of them, saying, "Enjoy! Do you need anything else, toast or something?"

"Could I have a glass of orange juice, please, Julie?" Grace says.

"Sure, coming right up."

They start to eat their omelettes, and Julie comes back with two glasses of freshly squeezed orange juice and says, "John, you need your vitamin C too."

"Thank you, mother. How is everything going in the house? Do you need anything?" John says.

"Besides a vacation, everything is great. Savana is very happy lately, and all the grocery accounts are paid in full," Julie says.

"Spring break for Savana is coming up soon, isn't it?" John asks.

"Yes, in another two weeks, I think. Why?" Julie asks.

"Would you like to go to my place in Lahaina with Savana and anyone else you would like to invite? I'll provide all the transportation, and there is a car for you to drive. I'll also give you a few thousand bucks spending money. You deserve a good holiday."

"Are you kidding? I would love to go to Hawaii. Thank you, John. Have a great day!" Julie says.

She hurries out of the room to tell Savana the good news.

"Now I know why I love you, John; you treat ever one you know with such love and generosity," Grace says.

"Julie is like a sister to me. She does her job with love, and she went through a rough time when Savana was kidnapped," John says.

"Wait! Savana was kidnapped? When was this? Is she okay now?" Grace asks.

It was a few years ago, and I caught the guy. He didn't rape her, but he kept her tied up in a small room, and now she can't stand small spaces. He won't be bothering anyone anymore because I had to kill him. He somehow got hold of a banned antique machine gun and started a gunfight with us, and I stunned him, but he wouldn't stop shooting, so I had to kill him. Please don't talk about this to Julie. She doesn't like to be reminded of this, okay?"

Julie comes back into the room and says, "Savana is so excited about going to Hawaii that she's jumping up and down and dancing around her room."

Grace says, "Julie, that was the best omelette I have ever had. Thank you. Well, we must go now, or I'll be late for work. Have a nice day."

They get into John's car and drive to Grace's mansion, and kiss goodbye. "I'll call you later to let you know if I have to go out of town," Grace says.

"Call me on my mobile, as I'll be all over town today. I have to go to the morgue first, for example. Love you." He kisses her and watches her walk into her mansion.

CHAPTER TWENTY-THREE

He turns the car around and goes to get Chuck.

"Hi, Chuck. I hope you had a good night because our first stop is the morgue. We need to get the autopsy results on Doctor Blackwell," John says.

"I had some buddies over, and we watched the football game—the B.C. Lions beat the Calgary Stampeders 28 to 21. It was a great game, and we had a few beers," Chuck says.

They enter the morgue, and Dr. Luci Ryan is putting Dr. Blackwell's brain on the scale. She is wearing pink scrubs, a white lab coat, and a clear visor. She flips her visor up and says, "Good morning, Lieutenant Trosky and Detective Sidhu. I'm on record, so I'm being formal. I'm redoing the autopsy. So far, all Dr. Blackwell's organs are normal for a man of sixty-three years, except for his heart being dissolved, of course. His bloodwork just came in, and there is a residue of an unknown substance. It is a biological agent and is barely there, so it is very hard to diagnose."

"Chuck and I went to Winnipeg and went through Dr. Blackwell's surgical records and found the man who hired the assassin to kill him. His name is Raphael Dupuis, and Detective Chan found out that Mr. Dupuis was working on something called nano-bots that can be injected into the bloodstream and programmed to heal different organs. He must have found a way to use these nano-bots to kill, so keep that residue from his blood. It will go into evidence if we get to trial. We can't find Mr. Dupuis right now, but we have every agency looking for him, including Interpol. Well, Luci, send your report to my office computer, Detective Chan and Commander Caputo, and I will have Detective Chan send his report to you. We need to communicate better with each other. That was my fault; you should have known about the nano-bots and Dupuis. See you later. When are you going to do the autopsy on Ken Leung?" John says.

"Either later today or tomorrow. I have a few more urgent cases to do."

"Tomorrow will be fine; just email me your report when you finish doing Mr. Leung's autopsy. See you later, John says and he, and Chuck go back to the police station to type up their reports.

CHAPTER TWENTY-FOUR

In an undisclosed location, Auger thinks back to when he waited a month to stalk the next gang member, Trevor Jenkins and his girlfriend, Sheila Harris. They lived in a modest house but never cleaned it, and they hoarded stolen television sets, stereos, drills, grinders, blenders, and whatever they could get their hands on. The Auger broke into their place and hid in their basement until midnight. He crept into their bedroom and injected them with a pressure syringe of a knockout drug. He didn't have nails or a nail gun, so he tied them to a chair each, taped their mouths shut, and woke them up by slapping them around. "Surprise! I'll bet you didn't expect to see me again. Remember me? They call me the Auger now because of how I killed your asshole gang boss, Remy "the Butcher" Boucher and his slut, Gabby. Well, I butchered them and guess what? It's your turn, Trevor. But I think I should start with Sheila; she needs some new holes as hers are worn out. Your dirtbag boss shouldn't have killed my parents. Any last words? Sorry, I can't take the tape off your mouths, as this place is not soundproof." He started drilling holes in Sheila's body and finished by drilling a hole through her temple and into her brain and did the same to Trevor Jenkins. He cleaned up and left with a smile on his face. He tracked down four more Royals gang members and did the same to them.

He then went into business as a paid assassin and took "special orders," some to look like accidents or whatever suited.

CHAPTER TWENTY-FIVE

John hears a knock on his door, and Detective Razh Mendosa sticks his head in. "Lieutenant, do you have a few minutes? I have a gang problem."

John sarcastically says, "Sure, I'm just sitting here sipping my cappuccino and eating my croissant. Seriously, Detective Mendosa, how can I help you?"

"Well, my squad has solid intel that Matias Ramos, the leader of the Black Snakes, and his gang did the drive-by on the Chechen Rebels gang leader, Aysa Basayev and his right-hand man "Big" Bishr. Apparently, they wounded some other gang members last night, Sunday, April 10th, around 8:30 p.m. We believe that Aysa is dead and Bishr is badly wounded. We want to put a raid together tonight, so we need a warrant, and we would like you and Detective Sidhu and the SWAT team to come with us if possible."

"Yes, I need some real action. I'll call A.P.A. Nikki Anders right now and see if anyone else wants in on this. Like Sam Slade, who needs more training on this type of mission," John says, then picks up the phone to call Nikki Anders.

"That drive-by? Oh, you bet I'll get you a warrant if I have to kill some prick myself. Set up your plan, and I'll come with you, even if I have to stay in the communications van," she exclaims.

"You heard her, Mendosa; let's get a team together and get these fuckers."

Mendosa leaves the office, and John's mobile phone rings. "Hello, Lieutenant Trosky speaking," John says.

"Hi John, it's Grace. I just got a call from my clothing manufacturer, Graceful Images, in Toronto. Somebody screwed up badly there, so I've got to fly down this afternoon, so I'll be gone for probably two days to straighten out this mess. I'm sorry."

"That's okay, honey. I'll miss you, but I've got to run a gang-related mission tonight and interrogate them after, so it will be a long night. I'll call you later tonight when I have a break, okay?" John says.

"I'll miss you too. I'll call you later. Remember, Toronto is three hours ahead. Kiss, kiss, goodbye," Grace replies.

"I love you. Take care, honey. Goodbye."

John asks his detectives to meet in his office and explains what happened with the gangs to them. "The reason I called you all into this meeting is the fact that Detective Razh Mendosa has solid intel on Matias Ramos, the leader of the Filipino gang, the Black Snakes, and his right-hand man Luke 'Sal' Salazar. They did a drive-by on the Chechen Rebels gang leader Aysa Basayev and killed him and wounded his second in command, Big Bishr, and possibly wounded several other gang members last night. We need to put a stop to this before any more blood is spilled. So, we are going to raid the Filipino gang headquarters tonight and arrest Matias Ramos and the rest of the gang tonight with the help of Lieutenant Shane Travis, and SWAT and Detective Mendosa and our Black Hat Squad, including myself, Detectives Sidhu, Samantha Slade, Randy Chan, Eddie Bennetti, and Larry Cornburra since Bhin Tran is not available tonight. Also, I want you to know that A.P.A.

Nikki Anders will be in the communications truck to monitor this mission, and she is not to come out of there under any circumstances at all. It's too dangerous. You all will be wearing full combat gear, including helmets—no bitching and no excuses. No one gets hurt tonight, understand? Stun people, and, as a last resort, blast them to save your life. Lieutenant Travis, the floor is yours and then Mendosa," John explains.

Lieutenant Travis says, "Detective Mendosa, what time is this Filipino gang most vulnerable?"

"These guys take drugs all day long, but I would hit them at seven in the evening when they are most drowsy," Mendosa says.

"Mendosa, your men will park half a block from the clubhouse, and I will have a man across the street on the top of the building with an infrared sensor to see where all the gang members are situated. My men will hang back about one block, and we will all be in communication via mics and will hit the place at the same time. The SWAT team will go in the front door. Lieutenant Trosky's team will go in the back door, and Mendosa's men will go in the two side doors. We have photos of all the gang members, and we will all be wearing combat gear, so we don't shoot each other," Lieutenant Travis says.

"Lieutenant Travis and the SWAT team will go in first with LZ-2000 laser rifles and flashbangs. Then Detective Sidhu and I next, followed by Detective Sam Slade and Detective Randy Chan, then Detective 'Fast Eddie' Bennetti. Detective Cornburra, I want you to hold back and stay at the back door to cover our backs. There may be gang members outside that we may have missed. We will all carry LZ-265 laser pistol blasters. I want everyone to turn on their recorders. I believe the SWAT team will have flashbang grenades. Is that correct, Lieutenant Travis?" John says.

"Yes, flashbangs, blasters, and some will have laser rifles. Okay, we go at six-thirty and hit them at seven o'clock, when we get the all-clear from the communications truck. Is everyone clear on their duties?" Lieutenant Travis asks.

They answer yes, one at a time. They all go to their vehicles in the garage, and John comments, "Chuck, Sam, and Randy will ride with me in my new ride. Bennetti and Cornburra will ride together in another plain unit. We will park in the alley behind the building a half-block away and will race to the back door on Lieutenant Travis's signal."

They all leave the garage and drive to their primary positions. They wait for the signal, and John mashes the throttle to the floor and stops at the back door. They burst out of the car and rush into the building. John and Chuck turn on their recorders. John spots a Chechen Rebels gang member with wild orange and green hair, holding a blaster and stuns him with his LZ-265 pistol blaster, and the gangbanger goes down. He looks in the first room, and it's empty, so he and Chuck keep going with Sam and Randy following. Sam cuffs the wild gangbanger. They split up and check other rooms, and Sam stuns another gang member, and Randy hits the girlfriend. They were both naked but armed with homemade blasters. They put plastic cuffs on them and cover them up with bedsheets. John is looking for Matias Ramos or Sal Salazar. He and Chuck head for the second floor. "Travis, Chuck and I are heading up to the second floor; I think Ramos is up there," he says into his mic. At the same time, Lieutenant Travis and his men break down the front door, throw in a flashbang grenade, kick in the first door on the right, and stun two tattooed gang members. They cuff them and leapfrog each other, going from room to room, checking and blasting gang members until they have ten people cuffed and have cleared the bottom floor of any members. John gets to the top of the stairs and goes up to the first room. The door is closed. He whispers, "Chuck, I'll go high, and you go low." Chuck nods, and they kick the door in and start to go in. John takes two laser hits from Salazar in his right hip area and right arm, but he is left-handed and shoots Ramos right in the neck, hitting a major artery, and Ramos drops dead. Sal Salazar is crouched behind a sofa and shoots at John as Chuck stuns Sal, and Sal drops but is still alive. John drops to the floor, clutching his right side, and starts to shake as he feels the laser bite him. He is bleeding from his right arm and right hip area and feels his legs go numb.

Chuck yells, "John, you're bleeding, are you okay?" Then says into his mic, "We need a medic. John took a hit, but we killed Ramos and wounded Salazar, and we need back-up here!"

Lieutenant Travis says, "Repeat that, Detective Sidhu. Did you say Lieutenant Trosky is hit?"

"Yes, he took two hits and is bleeding and shaking. Send a medic and back-up to the second floor."

"Okay, we've cleared the building, and Detective Cornburra took a hit, but he killed the prick that blasted him. He just has a minor wound in the side, so he will be going to the hospital also," Lieutenant Travis says.

Chuck cuffs Sal Salazar, slaps him, and yells, "Wake up, fucker! You're under arrest for attempted murder on a police officer. Detective Slade, take this shithead in and book him for attempted murder on Lieutenant Trosky."

The medic comes in and patches up John's arm and puts a pressure bandage on his hip area, exclaiming, "We have to get Lieutenant Trosky to the hospital now."

Chuck says to Detective Sam Slade, "I'm going to the hospital with John in the ambulance. You can take John's car back to the station. I'll unlock the car for you. Then throw Salazar in the back seat, secure him with the rear seat force field, and drive quickly and erratically to scare the shit out of him. A.P.A. Nikki Anders wants to have a word with him."

CHAPTER TWENY-SIX

"John was going to interrogate him, but do you want to do it?" Chuck asks Sam.

"I'd love to do that with Nikki Anders. Call me from the hospital; I want to know if John is going to be all right," Sam says nervously.

"Sure, I'll call you later. You should inform Captain Fedora about John getting hurt and the arrests. He may want to be involved in the interrogation of Salazar. John may be in the hospital for a while."

Chuck gets in the ambulance and goes to the hospital with John. John wakes up dizzy and says, "Chuck, what the hell happened? I got Ramos, didn't I? Man, I feel like shit, and I can't feel my legs."

Chuck replies, "If it makes you feel any better, you killed Matias Ramos, as you took a hit, and I wounded Salazar, and he is in custody. Sam Slade and Nikki Anders are interrogating him now, so try to relax. We will be at Vancouver General in two minutes. Should I call Grace or Thom or Julie?"

"Shit, Grace is in Toronto on business. I was supposed to call her tonight. She'll kill me if I don't call her. Tell you what, call her and downplay my injuries as we don't really know how bad I am, and tell her to stay there another day. She will probably freak out, damn it, but I can't stop her if she comes back. Call Thom and Julie as well so that they know I'm in the hospital," John says.

They take John into the emergency, take x-rays and different types of scans, and take him to the operating room to sew up his arm and repair his hip. Doctor Harrison comes into the waiting room and announces, "Detective Chuck Sidhu?"

"Yes, that's me. What's the word, doc? Is he going to be okay?"

Doctor Harrison replies, "We repaired his hip with a new polymer bone fuser, and it's healing well, but he has nerve damage to his legs, which should heal on its own, but it could vary from a few days to a few weeks. He will need complete bed rest to let the hip bone fuse together. So, overall, he should heal completely."

Most of the squad is crowded around the doctor, and they all look relieved. Chuck takes out his phone and calls Thom and tells him about John's injuries.

"What can I do to help? Should I come to the hospital?" Thom asks.

"Tell Julie that he will be in here for a few days, at least, and will need some nursing when he gets home. He won't be able to walk for, well, the doctor said a few days to a few weeks, so we will need a wheelchair for now. Oh, and call Mike and Gladys, and I will call Grace. She is in Toronto, and I just know she will freak out, so I have to break the news gently. John wants me to downplay his injuries, but Grace will see right through that, so I'm going to tell her the truth and let the chips fall where they may. Oh, you should send lots of flowers. Well, I have to go now and call Grace," Chuck says.

Chuck finds a quiet corner and calls Grace, "Hi, Grace, how are things going in Toronto?"

"Fine, Chuck, but why are you calling me? Damn, John got hurt, didn't he? I could feel something was wrong all the way out here. Don't soft soap me, Chuck. How badly is he hurt?"

"Grace, John took two hits during our raid tonight. He got hit in his right arm and his right hip area. Doctor Harrison operated on him, and he is healing well but, and don't freak out; he can't feel his legs right now. The doctor said it is nerve damage from the blaster hit, but he will definitely heal from that in as little as a few days or weeks. John said for you to finish your business there before you come back," Chuck says.

"I can have my shuttle in the air in an hour. I can fix the rest of the problems in Toronto from home, and even if I couldn't fix them from home, John is way more important than losing some money. I'll be at the hospital in a few hours. Which hospital is it?" Grace says.

"The Vancouver General in the main building. They are getting a suite ready for him. Okay, Grace, I'll see you later. I'll be here unless they need me at the police station. Goodbye, and take care."

Chuck gets a call on his phone, telling him that he is needed at the police station to interrogate Sal Salazar. He has a uniformed officer drive him back to the station. Captain Fedora is standing there with A.P.A. Nikki Anders, Sam Slade, and Randy Chan. "Detective Sidhu, I've reviewed some of the discs of the raid and saw that it was a 'righteous' shoot, but there was no need for Lieutenant Trosky to get hurt that badly. You two should have thrown a flashbang in that room first," Captain Fedora says.

"You're right, captain, except we didn't have any flashbangs with us; only the SWAT team had them. Lesson learned. We will take flashbangs with us on the next raid," Chuck says.

"I'll put that in my report, and so will you. In the meantime, A.P.A. Nikki Anders wants you to sit in on Salazar's interrogation in Room Two, across the hall. I'll be in the observation room in case you have any questions," the captain says.

Nikki and Chuck enter the interrogation room and start questioning Sal Salazar.

"Recorder on, A.P.A. Nikki Anders and Detective Chuck Sidhu entering Room Two with a Mr. Sal Salazar, a suspect in the attempted murder of Lieutenant Trosky and the murder of the Chechen Rebels gang leader Aysa Basayev. Have you been read your rights, Mr. Salazar, and do you understand them?" Nikki says.

"Yes, they read me my rights just after I shot that fucking cop. I was just defending myself, see," Sal says.

Nikki rolls her eyes and says, "Yes, Mr. Salazar, but you were defending yourself with an illegal weapon. Ordinary citizens, like yourself, are not allowed to own laser blasters, let alone use them to shoot at police officers," Nikki says.

Sal sneers. "I ain't no ordinary citizen, see, I belong to a Filipino social club, and I'm vice president, see. So, I ain't no ordinary citizen," Sal says.

"You mean the social club called the Kings? I think you should call a lawyer, or we could appoint one for you," Nikki says.

"I don't want no damn lawyer; I ain't done nothing wrong, see."

Chuck pipes in, "Nothing wrong? You shot at Lieutenant Trosky and me as we entered your room."

Nikki asks, "Where were you and Mr. Ramos on the night of April 10th, at eight-thirty? That was last night in case you don't know how to read a calendar, Mr. Salazar."

"We was at a Kings club meeting with all our guys; you can ask any one of them," Sal says.

"Other officers are asking them as we speak. Let's take a break now, shall we? Would you like a soda or water, Mr. Salazar?" Nikki asks.

"I'd rather have a beer," Sal says.

Nikki rolls her eyes again and says, "Would you like a craft beer or an import?"

"No, just a Canadian beer."

"I bet you would, but we don't serve alcohol in a police station, you moron," Chuck says. "This interview is over—for now. We will have an officer bring you a Canadian cherry soda."

"A.P.A. Nikki Anders and Detective Sidhu leaving Room Two," Nikki says.

They leave the room and talk to Captain Fedora.

"Detective Chan is interviewing a Raymond Cruz. Let's go see if he got anything out of this jerk," Captain Fedora says.

The captain knocks on the door of Room Three and says, "Detective Chan, can you step out here for a minute?"

"Yes, sir. Detective Chan leaving Room Three. Stop recording," Detective Chan says.

He steps out and says, "What's up, captain?"

"Have you got anything out of Mr. Cruz, detective?" the captain asks.

"Yes, I tricked him into saying that Matias Ramos and Sal Salazar planned the hit on the Black Snake gang leader Aysa Basayev and Luke Anzorov, but Luke was only wounded, as were a few other Black Snake gang members. This guy is so stupid; he didn't even ask for a deal," Detective Chan says.

Captain Fedora replies, "Great work, Detective Chan. Nikki and Detective Sidhu, let's go finish off Mr. Salazar and get him booked for murder. Then, let's all go home; I'm tired, and it's been a long day. Before you come in tomorrow, Chuck, go check on Lieutenant Trosky to see if he is healing all right and send our well wishes and update him on our progress. You can come in an hour or so late, as you've put in a long day today."

CHAPTER TWENTY-SEVEN

Grace gets on her private shuttle and lands in Vancouver in an hour and a half and is at the hospital in another half hour.

She walks up to the reception and asks for Lieutenant Trosky's room number, and goes to his suite. She rushes into the room and takes off her dark blue overcoat, and sees John sleeping. She pulls up a chair and holds his left hand, and John wakes up, feeling groggy, "I must be in heaven; an angel is sitting beside me."

"John, are you all right? You scared the hell out of me. I could feel something was wrong when I was in Toronto," Grace asks nervously.

"The doc said I'm going to heal; my right arm is patched up. They had to rebuild my right hip with some kind of magic glue, and it hurts like hell, but my legs are numb, but that should be gone in a few days or weeks. You came back from Toronto. What day is it?" John says.

"Well, it's almost midnight on the same day as your raid, in which you failed to tell me there was going to be a gunfight. I'm just glad that you're all right. Where is Chuck? Do Thom and Julie know you are in the hospital?" Grace asks.

John replies, "I told Chuck to call you, Thom, and Julie, then I passed out. He is probably at the police station, as we had a successful raid. I killed the leader of the gang as his partner shot me with his blaster, and we arrested about a dozen gang members, so he will be busy tonight."

Just then, Thom Saunders and Julie walk into the room, and Thom says, "John, how many times have I told you to duck when someone is shooting at you? Well, it's good to see you're still alive. I called Mike and Gladys to tell them that you were in the hospital."

Julie steps up to the bed and says, "John, I was so worried about you when Chuck called and said that you were shot. Are you all right?"

"I'll be all right. I got shot in the right arm and right hip, but I can't feel my legs yet. Don't worry, okay? The doc said I'll heal soon. Thanks for the flowers, whoever sent them," John says.

Thom says, "They must be from your squad, as the florist said they couldn't deliver the flowers I ordered until tomorrow. By the way, there are a dozen cops in the lobby as they're only allowing relatives and close friends in to see you for now."

"Are Mike and Gladys on their way now?" John asks.

"I don't know if they have someone to take care of Jackie," Thom replies.

Just then, Mike and Gladys walk into the room, and Mike says, "John, I just talked to the doctor, but how are you feeling? You look like shit, but I'm glad to see you're alive."

"Nice to see you too, Mike," John says.

Gladys pipes in, saying, "You two will never change. John almost dies, and you tell him he looks like shit. John, you look fantastic for a man who's been through hell."

"Thank you both. I know Mike's humour after all these years. Who is taking care of Jackie? I hope she isn't too worried about me," John says.

"My mother is taking care of her, and she knows how to calm her down because she is worried about you. Now that we see that you are healing, we can assure her that Uncle Tiny is alive and healing. We can bring her here tomorrow, and she can give you a big hug. Well, we better get going and let you get some sleep. Goodbye," Gladys says.

Julie asks, "What can I do for you, John?"

"Just take care of Savana. I'll be all right. Well, Thom, you and Julie better get going; it's been a long day for all of us," John says.

Grace says, "I'm going to stay here tonight to keep an eye on you. Can they bring another bed in here? There's lots of room."

"I'll tell the nurse to bring in another bed," Thom says.

John says, "Oh, I forgot one of my guys got shot too, a Detective Larry Cornburra. I don't think he was hurt badly, but can you ask the nurse if he is all right?"

"Sure, I'll take care of that for you. She can let you know when she brings the bed in here. Grace, do you need anything else tonight? Clothes, maybe?" Thom asks.

"I have a suitcase with me in the car, so I'll call my chauffeur to bring it in, but thanks, Thom," Grace says.

Thom leaves, and Grace's chauffeur brings her suitcase into the room. Two nurses push a ready-made bed into the room, and pretty Head Nurse Betty says, "Lieutenant Trosky, the man you asked about, Larry Cornburra, is doing well. He was hit with a laser gun in the arm and will be released tomorrow. They want to keep him overnight just to make sure he doesn't go into shock, but most people will go into shock right after a trauma. Is there anything else we can help you with?"

John replies, "No. Grace, do you need anything else?"

"No, thank you. I'm tired and just want to go to sleep. Will you be checking on John . . . Lieutenant Trosky during the night?" Grace asks Betty.

"Yes, we will make sure he gets a good night's sleep and is not in pain."

The nurses leave, and Grace pushes her bed closer to John's so that she can hold his hand. She whispers, "Good night, sweetheart."

"Good night, my lotus blossom. I love you," John says in Mandarin and falls asleep.

In the morning, Grace wakes up and bends over John and kisses him awake. He keeps his eyes closed and says in his Sean Connery as James Bond voice, "Nurse Betty, please, my girlfriend is right here."

In her southern accent, Grace says, "Why, Mr. Bond, whatever do you think I'm going to do?" She switches to her normal voice and adds, "You know, I could kill you ten different ways, Mr. Bond."

Then they both laugh, and John says, "Oh, hi, Grace, where did Betty go?"

"I see you have your sense of humour back," Grace says, then kisses him again and adds, "Should I order us breakfast?"

"You mean from this hospital? Are you crazy?" John asks.

"Hell, no! There is a great restaurant right across the street. I can order anything on my phone from Skip the Dishes. What is your pleasure, sir? Oatmeal, porridge, bacon and eggs? I know, you love omelettes, so a Denver or maybe spinach and feta cheese?" Grace says.

"You know my heart already. Yes, I guess the spinach and feta omelette is healthier, my love, and a large coffee, real coffee, I hope?" John says.

Their meals arrive and Grace eats, and helps John eat, as she cuts his omelette up and puts cream and sugar in his coffee. He looks at Grace and says, "You make a great nurse, too, honey. Hey, this is real coffee, not that soy crap. I love you, Grace."

They finish their omelettes, and Grace gets ready to leave for work and says, "I'll see you later, John. I love you."

"Love you more. Take care, my lotus blossom," John says.

Chuck Sidhu appears at the door a few minutes later and says, "How are you feeling today, John? I have some good news for you, too."

"I'm pretty good. I had a good breakfast with Grace, but I'm still in pain in my hip. What's the good news? I could use some," John says.

"We got that idiot Salazar to admit he tried to kill you, and one of the gang members, a Raymond Cruz, admitted to hearing Matias Ramos and Sal Salazar plan the hit on Aysa Basayev and Luke Anzorov, but Anzorov survived. We booked Sal Salazar for the murder of Aysa Basayev and attempted murder of a police officer, and conspiracy to murder the whole Chechen Rebels gang. Captain Fedora told me to tell you that your shooting of Matias Ramos was 'righteous,' but next time we do a raid, we should take flashbangs with us. He thinks we should have thrown a flashbang grenade into that room before we went in. I told him that we didn't have any flashbangs with us. How long do you think you will be in the hospital?" Chuck says.

"Doctor Harrison originally said at least two days in here, but I want to see if I can get released today as the food in here will probably kill me, and I have a gourmet chef at home and can hire a nurse or whatever I need. I can heal better at home," John says.

John looks around Chuck and sees Doctor Harrison standing in the doorway. Doctor Harrison walks up to John and says, "Let's look at your hip wound." He lifts the bed covers, removes the bandage, and looks at the wound. "That skin patch is healing very fast, and there is no infection, which is what we worry about in hospitals. Lieutenant, can you feel your legs yet?"

"The pain in my hip is subsiding a bit, but I just feel some pins and needles in my legs."

"I heard you talking, and I agree with you that you would heal better at home since you can afford a private nurse, and I wish I had a gourmet chef at home. My wife is a terrible cook, but you didn't hear that from me. If you can get someone to bring you a wheelchair, you can go home as soon as you want. Just take it slow when you start to walk again," the doctor says.

The doctor leaves, and John says, "Chuck, hand me my phone, please." He dials and says, Thom, are you busy?"

"I'm never too busy for you, John. What do you need?" Thom says.

"I'm ready to get out of here. Can you get me an electric wheelchair and some fresh clothes, as they cut mine up, and as soon as possible, please," John says.

"Okay, John. I can get a wheelchair right at the hospital; they have a dealer on the first floor. I checked into it yesterday. I guess you want comfortable clothes, like your University of Manitoba T-shirt and sweatpants or jeans," Thom says.

"Yes, the T-shirt and sweatpants, as my hip is still sore. So, I'll see you in an hour?"

"Yes, an hour should be about right. Later, John."

Chuck says, "Well, I better get back to work and tell everyone the good news."

"Oh, by the way, Chuck, send your report to my home computer on the Chechen/Filipino gang case, and I'll talk to you later. Also, see if you can find out more information on Raphael Dupuis's whereabouts and see if Randy Chan has anything else on the Ghost. Also, where is my car now?" John says.

"Well, I'm driving it. I didn't want it sitting at the police station."

"You might as well keep driving it as I won't be able to drive for a while. Don't worry, you can't dent it; it has a special body on it and a force field. There is a manual built into the dash computer, and it is voice-controlled. Well, call me later at home if you have any new information."

Chuck leaves for the station.

Two hours later, Thom enters the room, driving a new electric wheelchair. "Here's your new ride, John. I want one for myself. It's fun to drive."

"That can be arranged, but I'd have to shoot you first. Help me change, and let's get out of here; you know cops are allergic to hospitals. How am I getting home in this rig?" John asks.

"We have a special taxi that can take a wheelchair. You can ride in it, or I have the limo here also. Your choice, lieutenant."

CHAPTER TWENTY-EIGHT

John gets in the wheelchair, drives to the elevator, and goes to the special taxi.

"Hey, this is fun. We need to customize this thing. I'll go in the taxi; it's easier. I'll see you at home."

They get to the mansion, and John says, "Shit, I forgot about the front stairs. We can go in through the garage and the elevator." Then he goes into the house.

"Julie couldn't come to the hospital; she had to get Savana ready for school, but she has a good meal ready for you now," Thom says.

John drives to the small dining room in his wheelchair, and Julie walks in carrying some cabbage rolls and pierogies and coffee on a tray. She is shocked to see John in the wheelchair. "John, why are you in a wheelchair? Is it going to be permanent?"

"Oh, no. This is temporary, the doctor assured me. It's nervous system trauma, and it will take a few days or weeks for the nerves to heal."

Chrissy walks into the room, jumps up onto John's lap, circles around, and sits down.

"Hi, Chrissy. I missed you too. Well, I'm starving, and that looks delicious. Why don't you join me? I better call Grace to let her know that I'm home as well," John says.

"Okay, I could eat, and Savana will be home in a few hours. She will be excited to see you. She was so worried about you. I had a hard time getting her to sleep last night," Julie says.

"I can't wait to see her. She will probably want a ride on my lap in this contraption; kids love anything they can drive."

They eat their perogies with sour cream, cabbage rolls, and garlic sausage and chat about the raid on the Filipino gang and how John got hurt. Julie clears the dishes, and John calls Grace on his mobile phone and says, "Hi, Grace. I just wanted to let you know that I am home now. The doctor said I am healing very fast. How is your day going?"

"It's going really well. I haven't had to fire anyone today, and the problem in Toronto is fixed. I scared the crap out of the woman in charge there and said if she screws up again, she is gone, and I will make her secretary the boss. Damn, I have an important call on the other line, but I'm really not that busy today, so I will see you later at about five o'clock. Love you," Grace says.

John says, "I love you too; see you at five."

John takes the elevator up to his room and crawls into his king-size gel bed. Chrissy jumps up on the bed and snuggles in beside him. He pets her and then falls asleep. Later, he is woken up by Savana running into his room, followed by Julie. Savana whispers, "John, are you okay?"

John opens his eyes and says, "What? Oh, hi, Savana. You know that you aren't related to me, but you and your mom are like family to me, so you can call me Uncle Tiny like Jackie does. I'm a little hurt, but I'm going to be okay."

"I was so worried about you last night I could hardly sleep. Are your boo-boos healing?"

John laughs and says, "Yes, sweetheart, my boo-boos are healing, but I can't walk very well right now."

"I'll help you to walk again; my mother taught me how to walk. I can hold your hands and show you."

John holds back the tears and thinks how children are so innocent and always think positive. *What a sweet little girl. Lesson learned; I must think positive, and I'll walk again,* John thinks.

Julie is on the verge of tears, then says, "Um, Mike, Gladys, and Jackie are here, John. Should I tell them to come up here, or do you want to come downstairs?"

"Tell them to come up here. I'm still a bit tired," John replies.

Savana jumps up on the bed, pets Chrissy, and says, "Uncle Tiny, Chrissy can help you heal because cats are magic, the Egyptians said so on the TV."

"You know, I agree with you because once I had a really bad chest cold and Chrissy would jump up on my stomach and pat my chest with her paws, and I would feel better," John says.

"Cool," Savana replies.

Mike, Gladys, and Jackie enter the room, and Jackie exclaims, "Uncle Tiny, are you okay? You look tired," and jumps on the bed.

John looks at her and says, "Yes, I'm all right, but I am kind of tired. I'm very happy to see you."

Mike asks, "I heard you got hit twice with a laser pistol in the arm and hip. Is that right? You know that armoured clothing we were talking about? Well, we have a prototype coat in testing right now. We still need to see how much laser power it will deflect. We could possibly have one ready by the time you get back to work."

"Yes, I got hit in my right arm near the shoulder, which is nothing really, but I got hit in the hip right to the bone and in the abdomen. The worst thing is that it messed up my nerves going to my legs, so I feel numb sometimes, or I feel pins and needles in my legs. But the doc said it should go away on its own within a week or two."

Gladys is busy putting a large vase of pink roses on John's new sideboard that he bought at the auction and says, "I brought you some flowers to cheer you up, Uncle Tiny," and chuckles.

John looks at Mike and says, "I wish I would have had that coat last night. What are we going to call it? You know, we could make pants, and who knows what else with this material. If someone could help me out of this bed and into that wheelchair, I would like to go downstairs."

Mike and Gladys help him into the wheelchair, and they take the elevator downstairs. They start to go to the dining room when Grace comes in the front door and sees John in the wheelchair. He looks puzzled. "Where did you get a wheelchair so fast? I can't believe you're home already. Hi, everybody." She bends down and kisses John. "I love you, and I'm ready for a glass of wine."

"Let's go into the dining room and have a glass," John says.

Julie asks, "Shall I open the Merlot or something else?"

John looks around and says, "Fine with me unless someone wants something else, but maybe Jackie and Savana want milk?"

Jackie says, "Wine is yucky. I want milk."

"Me too," Savana says. "Are we going to eat too? Because I would like mac and cheese, please."

"Me too," Jackie says.

"Sure, I can make mac and cheese, girls. What does everyone else want?" Julie asks.

They all look at each other, and John replies, "Since we didn't really plan this, what can you make quickly?"

"How about an Asian beef and pork stir fry? I can get the androids to help cut up the vegetables, and it won't take long," Julie says.

"Sounds like a great idea. Is it all right with everyone else? Grace, do you like Chinese food?" John asks.

Grace pokes John and says, "You are really funny tonight, John. Of course, I do, I'm Chinese, in case you didn't notice."

"You're Chinese, I didn't notice. I thought you were Canadian," John jokes.

She punches him in the arm and says, "You're going to get it tonight, John."

"I hope so, but I'm very fragile, so take it easy," he says.

They both laugh, and John says, "Julie, tell Thom to join us for dinner if he wants to." John then turns to Mike and says, "So, Mike, have you thought of what we should call this laser proof coat?"

"I don't know yet. We need to toss some names around," Mike says.

"You have a laser proof coat? Why didn't you wear that last night, John?" Grace asks.

Mike says, "We are still testing it and have no production yet, but think of the lives we will save."

"Do you have a manufacturer lined up to do this?" Grace asks.

Mike says, "No, but we are almost finished testing the armoured material."

"Mike, did you know that I own a clothing manufacturing company? That's where I was yesterday, in Toronto. I also have a branch in Winnipeg. I would love to go into business with you if my company could make this coat and maybe pants or vests or whatever," Grace says.

Mike asks, "What do you think, John?"

"I would love to do that. We could all make money and save lives at the same time, and I mean that, Grace and Mike.

Grace, what do you think we should call this armoured clothing line?" John says.

She thinks for a minute and then says, "Let's see, words impact you in different ways. I'm thinking Ironclad, but that's too close to Iron Man—can you say lawsuit? The chemical name of this material would be too confusing, but when I'm around John, I feel safe because he can handle himself. He feels like a bodyguard, so how about Bodyguard Clothing?"

Mike and John simultaneously answer, "Yes!"

Mike says, "Grace, you must have studied psychology and language. That name is genius! The only thing we need now is a chemical company to produce the material. Our research and development department has made small batches of this material. The body of John's new car is made of a stiffer version of this stuff. Once we get going on this, the sky is the limit, but the first customers we need to sell it to are the police and military. We could start with making coats for John's squad. So, first, we stand John up against a wall and shoot at him."

John frowns and says, "That's very funny, Mike. How about we flip for it? I'm just joking, too. We have droids we can shoot at, but we should put extra sensors on them to detect things like heat and pressure and electrical shock, etcetera."

"I wouldn't put it past you to shoot at each other; you were probably wild brats when you were young kids," Grace says.

Julie brings the Chinese food in, and it looks and smells great. "Thom has a date tonight, so he won't be joining us," she says.

The droids come in to help with serving the food to Jackie and Savana. They start eating, and Grace says to Mike, "I should meet with your R and D people to see what chemicals and machinery we need to manufacture this material."

"Yes, I'll call you and set up a meet this week as I don't know your schedule," Mike says.

"Great. Julie, you are a great cook; this smells great and is delicious!" Grace says.

"Thank you, Grace. I have to give credit to my mom and grandmother for teaching me how to cook Ukrainian food and Canadian food, but I did go to a good culinary school," Julie says.

Jackie looks at John and says, "Uncle Tiny, can I try some of your Chinese food? You aren't eating very much."

"The food is really good, but the drugs they gave me are making me drowsy and killing my appetite. Here, Jackie, take my plate. I think I need a nap. I'll wheel up to my room."

"I'm finished eating. I'll go with you to help you to bed. I did some volunteer nursing in my twenties, so I'll lift you safely," Grace says.

They leave the room together and go to John's bedroom. Grace helps John into bed and checks the bandage on his hip. "John, this bandage needs changing. Do you have a first-aid kit here?"

"There should be one in the bathroom."

"I almost forgot, I have some Chinese herbal ointment for your wound, some herbs that will help your immune system, and some tea that will help you sleep. It's in my huge purse on that couch. I'll go make some tea in your auto chef and get the first-aid kit."

Grace comes back with the tea in a cup, some ointment, and a big first-aid kit, and says, "You could patch up a whole platoon with this kit." She has him drink the tea mixture, then changes his bandage, puts the ointment on his wound, and closes the bedroom door. She then strips off her business suit and slides into bed with him naked. "I just want to cuddle with you and make sure you are all right," she says.

"That's an excellent idea. I'm glad you're here to keep me safe," John says.

They fall asleep together.

Downstairs, Mike says, "Well, Gladys, I guess Grace put John to bed. We better get going, it's getting late, and we have to put Jackie to bed."

They say goodbye to Julie and Savana and go home.

CHAPTER TWENTY-NINE

The next morning, John wakes up at seven o'clock. Grace is fresh out of the shower and leaning over him, naked and lifting the covers. In his Sean Connery voice, John says, "Miss Moneypenny, if you want something, you just need to ask."

"Mr. Bond, I was just checking your state of health, and I see you are functioning at full capacity and that your wound is healing miraculously! Seriously, John, look at this wound, the Chinese ointment I put on you worked so well; your wound has closed right up, and you can hardly see a scar."

He sits up, looks down at his hip, and says, "Wow, that is amazing, and it doesn't hurt. Maybe you can do something for my 'full capacity' problem, seeing as we are both naked."

She says, "Just lay back, Mr. Bond, and let me do my best to cure your problem."

She then climbs on top of him and "rocks his world" until they are both satiated. He says, "I'm cured; now, can you help me into the shower and put a stool or something in here for me to sit on?"

She gets a stool, sets him on it, soaps them both up, and he gets an erection again.

"Mr. Bond, you naughty boy. I don't think you are cured yet; I'm going to have to do a bit more work on you."

She soaps him up and strokes him, and they do some carefully scripted moves in the shower.

Once showered, they dress and go down to the dining room.

Julie comes in and says, "Good morning, John. Grace, what would you like for breakfast? Omelettes again?"

John answers, "Yes, for me. Grace, what would you like?"

"I'll have the spinach and feta cheese omelette, if it's no trouble, Julie."

"No trouble at all. I have both ingredients, and I'll bring you coffees."

"Oh, Julie. I put some Chinese immunity tea in the auto chef in John's room, and it is working really well for him. Does it transfer to the one down here?" Grace asks.

Julie says, "It should, as they are all hooked together. There are some auto chefs in some of the other rooms too."

Just then, Chrissy comes into the room and jumps up on Graces' lap and meows. John stares at Chrissy and says, "It looks like Chrissy likes you better than me now. Chrissy, you traitor."

"She is just checking me out to see if I'm good enough for you," Grace says.

"I think she's checking you out to see if I'm good enough for you, sweetheart," John says.

Thom enters the dining room and says, "Good morning, everyone. John, Captain Fedora called, and he wants to talk to you about an Interpol special agent, Holly Morgan, who wants to come and see you about the Ghost case. He hopes you are well, but he thinks this could be a break in the case. He wants your permission for her to come to your place."

"Thanks, Thom. This could be the break we need in this. I'll call him after breakfast. Sit down and have breakfast with us."

"Okay. I'll just go tell Julie to make me a Denver omelette." He goes into the kitchen.

Grace says to John, "I forgot to get Mike's phone number and to give him mine last night so that we can meet with the R and D people about making the fabric for Bodyguard Clothing."

"He should still be at home; give me your phone, and I'll dial his number so that it will be in your phone." He dials, and Mike answers. In an East Indian accent, John says, "Mr. Mike Trosky, would you like to buy some of my humble sawdust? You don't have to swear, Mr. Mike Trosky!"

John puts the phone on speaker, and Mike says in his East Indian accent, "Your humble accent needs more work, Mr. Humble John Trosky, who's phone this is, and why are you calling me?"

"It's Grace's humble phone, and she wants to talk to you. Here's Grace."

"Hi, Mike. I apologize for my humble and injured partner, but I rudely didn't get your phone number last night, as I was so concerned about John. I'll give you my office and personal cell numbers so that we can meet with your R and D guys soon," Grace says.

"Okay, I'll give you my office number, and we can meet tomorrow if you are clear."

"Tomorrow around one o'clock would be good for me. Maybe you should pick me up as I don't know where your R and D place is," Grace says.

"Sounds good. I'll pick you up tomorrow, just before one o'clock, and tell East Indian John that I don't want any of his crappy sawdust. His last batch had mould in it. Bye, see you tomorrow," Mike says and hangs up.

Thom and Julie come back in, and they all eat breakfast with Savana, who has her Cheerios.

"Thom, I'm going to need you to help me around the house today, you know, like when I have to use the bathroom, as I still can't walk. I've also been thinking; we don't have proper access for handicapped people entering the house at the front door. We should get a crew to install a ramp, or, I know, let's install a small covered elevator beside the front steps," John suggests.

"Yes, an elevator would be faster to install. I know a great contractor who can do that. I'll get right on that."

"Well, I have to go to work now, so I'll call you later, John," Grace says.

"I'll have Jeffery drive you to work. You spend a lot of time here now; I think you should bring some clothes here. There's lots of room in my wife's old walk-in closet," John says.

"Okay. Goodbye, everyone," she says and bends over and kisses John goodbye. John drives his wheelchair to his office and calls Captain Fedora.

"Good morning, captain. I hear you wanted to talk to me about this Interpol agent, Holly Morgan. Has she got some information that we don't have?"

"Yes, she believes this Ghost guy is the same person who has killed several people over the years, in Paris and other countries, by a similar method. She wants to exchange information."

"This could be the big break we need. When can she come over to my place?" John asks.

Captain Fedora replies, "I can send her over right now if you are up to it."

"I'm fine. I'll need Detective Sidhu here too. He can drive her here in my car, and maybe you should come too, sir. I don't know how much we can tell her, legally."

"Good point, John. I better come too. We'll be there in an hour, okay?"

"One hour is fine. I'll be in my office reviewing the case files. See you later, captain."

CHAPTER THIRTY

An hour later, Captain Fedora, Chuck Sidhu, and a five-foot-four slim, beautiful blonde walk into John's office, escorted by Thom Saunders.

"Interpol Special Agent Holly Morgan, meet Lieutenant John Trosky, head of the Black Hat Squad, the homicide squad," Captain fedora announces.

"I'm glad to meet you, Special Agent Morgan. I hope we can be of benefit to each other," John says.

With a French accent, Agent Morgan says, "Pleased to meet you, Lieutenant Trosky. I believe we may help each other's case."

John replies in French, "I look forward to working with you. What would you like me to call you, Agent Morgan?"

"You speak French really well. I'm surprised, lieutenant," she says.

John switches back to English and says, "You may call me John. Yes, I spent two years in Paris, but we should speak English for everyone's benefit."

"To save time, just call me Holly. Maybe later, we may speak French. I miss speaking French when I'm in another country. Well, anyway, I have a lot of information you probably don't have. We believe this man you call the Ghost may be a man called William Auger, a French citizen. We believe his parents were drug addicts and were killed by their dealer Remy "the Butcher" Boucher when William was eighteen years old. Boucher was the leader of a gang called the Royals. One month later, this Remy Boucher and his girlfriend, Gabrielle Berne, were killed in a ritualistic way. They were nailed to their bedroom floor, like Jesus Christ, and then drilled all over their bodies, including their temples. I know you have a similar crime. Is that true, John?"

John looks at Captain Fedora, and Fedora nods to signal John to agree.

"Yes, we have a person in the morgue right now, a Mr. Ken Leung, who was killed in that fashion, though he was nailed to a wall in an empty house that was for sale. We also have this man on camera at two different crime scenes, though we think he was heavily disguised. He also poisoned Doctor Blackwell in a downtown hotel with a biological agent that dissolved his heart. We also have his voice on tape from a nanny-cam he didn't know was on when he killed Mr. Leung."

Holly says, "We believe Mr. Auger killed every member of the Royals gang in a period of six months, as they were killed in the same fashion with nails and a drill. He even killed all their girlfriends. In fact, we think he killed the girlfriends first, probably to make the men suffer more, but we couldn't get any proof. We also have a voiceprint of him and a juvenile and early adult file on him, but the pictures of him are twenty-five years old when he was a skinny runt. He should be about forty-one years old now. As he now does designer kills and travels under different identities and even off-planet, we haven't been able to capture him. We have been checking his passports, and we believe he is still in Vancouver."

Chuck adds, "I was at Ken Leung's autopsy, and everything was pretty obvious. He was nailed to a wall and was drugged with a common knockout drug you can buy anywhere. We should compare the voiceprints at the lab and exchange files with you by computer."

John drives his wheelchair out from behind his desk, and Holly looks shocked and says, *"Mon Dieu!* They didn't tell me you were disabled, *Monsieur* John!"

"Don't worry, Holly; it's only temporary. I was shot with a laser pistol on a gang raid a few days ago. It blasted my nerves. The doctor said I will be back to normal in a few days or weeks, but I am healing fast. My girlfriend, Grace Chan, is Chinese, and she gave me some magic ancient Chinese tea and ointment to help me heal, and it is working quickly. We still have a lot to talk about, and it is getting near lunchtime. I'll get my chef Julie to make us something for lunch. He wheels to the intercom and says, "Julie, what can you make four people for lunch, that's quick?"

"Do you want something light or heavier? We have lots of eggs from our chickens. I have hard-boiled eggs. I could make egg salad sandwiches, which I know you love, or I can make omelettes, or both. I also have some cold chicken meat."

John says, "I'll have an egg salad sandwich on white bread. What would you like guys? Holly?"

"I would love a spinach and feta omelette if you have the ingredients," Holly says.

"We do; that's my favourite omelette. Captain Fedora?" John asks.

"I'll have the same omelette."

"Chuck, how about you?" John asks.

"I'll have the egg salad sandwich on whole-wheat bread."

"Have you got that, Julie? Oh, and send Thom up here; I need help with the bathroom. We will be down in about a half-hour. Is that enough time, Julie?"

"Yes, that should be fine. I guess you don't want any wine. Do you want me to make a pot of your wonderful Afrikaans coffee?" Julie asks.

"That will be perfect, and put some of that Chinese herb that Grace gave you in my coffee. She said that it's all right to do so. You think of everything, Julie. See you later," John says.

They go down to the dining room in a half-hour, and Captain Fedora observes, "I love the wood panelling in here, and there is a lot of natural light. John, how can you afford a palace like this on your salary?"

"I don't. My parents died and left me this place. It's really too big for me, but I promised them that I would keep it in the family. Besides, they left me a few billion dollars to keep it up. That's one reason why I pay my own way and use my private shuttle when I travel for police business. Besides, my shuttle is faster and more comfortable for me, Detective Sidhu, and anyone else who tags along. Right, Chuck?"

"I've never complained about anything you do. You are the man, John," Chuck says.

"I like to use my private shuttle, especially if I go to another planet. Oh, here's Julie with our lunch. Julie, this is Special Agent Holly Morgan from Interpol and Captain Tibor Fedora. Everyone, meet Julie, the best chef in Vancouver," John says.

Captain Fedora says, "John, where on Earth do you get this coffee? I haven't tasted anything this good in years!"

John says, "I own a plantation in Africa with my brother and his wife. We have several blends. I'll get you some. Julie, see that Captain Fedora and Agent Holly get some when they leave. Chuck, do you still have some, or do you need more?"

"I could use more. Thank you, John," Chuck says.

"Oh, Holly, you could help us with something else. We know the name of the person who hired Mr. Auger. His name is Rafael Dupuis. He lived in the fifth arrondissement in Paris, and he is a biological scientist who invented these nano-bots that can be injected into the human body. They were designed to cure diseases, but he changed them to kill. Apparently, this is what killed Doctor Blackwell. These nano-bots dissolved his heart. Our problem is that we can't find Rafael Dupuis. We know that he left the country, but we don't know where he went. With all your resources, you can probably locate him," John says.

"Yes, I will start a trace on Mr. Rafael Dupuis immediately. I will start with shovelling . . . I mean, digging into his financial records and credit cards and check the facial recognition records at the shuttle ports. I should get the video and voice recording from you and give you mine. Can we do that here or at the station?" Holly asks.

"We can do that here. Let's go back to my office and use my computer," John says.

Back in John's office, John turns on his computer, and Holly turns on her laptop, and they exchange video and written files. The voice recordings match exactly. "We also have an eyewitness who saw Mr. Auger at the first crime scene where he disguised himself as a room service person; it's in my report," John says. "The eyewitness sat down with our sketch artist, and we got a good likeness of him. We might get a facial recognition shot from the video of him from the Ken Leung killing. I would like to know who hired him for that job and why they decided to kill a real estate agent who seems harmless. Oh, I just remembered, we found some Ukrainian or Russian stacking dolls in Mr. Leung's jacket pocket, which makes me wonder if he financially screwed a Russian or Ukrainian client."

"That sounds to me like a good reason to kill him. Did you research Mr. Leung's financial records?" Holly asks.

Captain Fedora answers, "I have my best Electronic Detectives looking into Mr. Leung's financials. On the surface, he looks clean, but we are now looking for off-shore and off-planet hidden accounts. So, maybe something will pop up. Well, I think we have covered everything we can, for now, so we should get back to the shop. Thanks for the coffee, John. Take all the time you need to heal."

"It was nice meeting you, John. I will pray for you to heal quickly," Holly says and then bends over and kisses him on both cheeks, saying in French, "Take care, and I'll see you again, John."

Chuck adds, "I'll let you know if we get any more breaks in the case. Thanks for the coffee. Your car is working great, by the way."

They leave and start working on the facial recognition once they arrive back at the station.

CHAPTER THIRTY-ONE

Thom walks into John's office and says, "John, are you busy?"

"No, I just finished my meeting. Why?"

"I rigged something up for you in the gym. Follow me; this will help you, I promise."

They go to the gym on the first floor, and Thom says, "See this exercise machine? I rigged an electric motor to it and straps for your feet to keep your muscles going again. They used a machine like this on me in the hospital when I got hurt in Afghanistan, and it worked. Let's try it for, say, an hour and see how you feel."

"I'm game for anything at this point. If this works, I'll call you a genius," John says.

Thom helps John onto the machine that looks like a stationary bicycle with a motor attached to it. He starts the motor, and John begins to pedal.

An hour later, still pedalling, John says to Thom, "Thom, I'm starting to have some feelings in my legs!" John gets off the bike, and Thom brings him a bottle of water. John then showers and finds that he is a bit steadier on his feet but knows he still needs more healing. He limps to his wheelchair and goes back to his office.

CHAPTER THIRTY-TWO

William Auger thinks back to his first paid assassination. He was working in a bar in Paris. His friends knew that he killed the Royals gang leader and the rest of the gang. The gendarme couldn't prove it but suspected him because he had the biggest motive to kill them. His friend Jean-Claude introduced him to a rich businessman named Gaston Bisset, who asked him to kill a man named Jean-Luc Roux, who had raped his fifteen-year-old daughter Cosette and got away with it, as his family was rich and had several sleazy lawyers.

"I'll pay you a million dollars to kill this bastard, but it has to look like an accident, so no one comes looking for either one of us. Can you do that?" he asked.

"How do I know that this story is true? You could be setting me up?" Auger said.

Gaston pulled out a clipping from a local French newspaper and showed him the article on Jean-Luc Roux being found not guilty in his trial. Gaston then said, "Now, do you believe me?"

"Yes, I believe you now. For a million dollars, I'd kill his whole family."

"No, I don't want his whole family killed. That would be too suspicious."

"How about a car accident? If he doesn't drive, I could run him over with a stolen car. I hate rich pricks who rape young girls and get away with it. I'll kill him the way you want, but if I had it my way, I'd use my drill on him. Okay, I'll set up an off-shore account and have you transfer half the payment upfront and the rest when he is dead. Do you agree with those terms, Mr. Gaston?"

"Yes, when can you do this?"

"Give me a few days to stalk him, and I'll text you a code sentence, such as 'landscaping job is done,'" Auger said.

"That sounds great."

For the following two weeks, Auger followed Jean-Luc around and memorized his routine, noting that he'd drive his fancy sports car to a nightclub every night and would leave with a young girl each time, except on Wednesdays.

Auger hacked into Jean-Luc car's main computer and synced it to an enhanced handheld remote control for a remote-controlled toy car. The sports car had electric steering, brakes, and transmission. Jean-Luc Roux came out of the nightclub by himself on a Wednesday and drove up onto Avenue Henri Martin freeway, followed by Auger, holding the remote control. They were travelling at 125 kilometres per hour when Jean-Luc accelerated to nearly 300 kilometres and was coming up on a sharp curve. Auger pushed the throttle joystick forward, cutting off the brakes, and locked the steering. Jean-Luc hit the guard rail at 315 kilometres per hour, his car flipped up and over the rail of the elevated road, landed upside down, and burst into flames, leaving Jean-Luc for dead.

Auger texted Bisset, saying that he had completed the landscaping job.

The next morning, Auger checked his account and found the last payment of the million dollars in it. He smiled and thought, *This is the way to make big money.*

CHAPTER THIRTY-THREE

John is at his desk sending an update on the two murders to the psychologist Joanne Weber when Jenny Olson, the reporter, calls him on his cell phone.

"Hello, John, I heard that you were shot in that Chechen gang raid. Are you all right?" she asks.

"It's so sweet of you to call, Jenny. Is that you at my gate?"

"Yes, may I talk to you?"

"Sure, why didn't you just press the intercom button? Press the button and drive up to the house, and Thom will meet you at the door. I hope you don't have a camera person with you since you know that I don't allow cameras in my house."

"I don't have a camera person with me, John."

She drives up to the door, and Thom lets her in and shows her to John's office. Jenny enters the room with her long curly red hair flowing down past her shoulders. She is wearing a pale green overcoat, an above-the-knee green dress with yellow flowers printed on it that shows off her long legs, and bright yellow high heeled shoes. John wheels around his desk to greet her, and she says, "My God, I heard you got shot in the arm. Why are you in a wheelchair? I'm so sorry you are hurt that badly."

"It's only temporary nerve damage as I also got shot in the right hip area. Here, I'll stand up as I want to hug you."

John stands up, and they exchange a warm hug. Chrissy enters the room as Jenny removes her coat and drops it on the couch. "Is this your cat? She is beautiful."

"Yes, Chrissy, this is Jenny."

Jenny sits down in the office chair, and Chrissy jumps up on her lap, licks her hand, and looks up at her, meowing. John says, "She likes you; you passed the test. If Chrissy likes you, you are good people. I've missed you all these years, even though I see you on TV all the time on *Crime Beat* on Channel 24. How can I help you, Jenny?"

"Maybe I shouldn't have come, but my boss asked me to talk to you about the two murders you are working on involving a Doctor Blackwell and a Mr. Ken Leung, the real estate agent. There is no connection between them, and we can't figure out why they were killed."

"All I can reveal to you right now is that they were both murdered in bizarre ways, and I mean really bizarre, by the same person. I personally think this guy is a hired assassin, but we don't have enough proof yet." John replies.

"Why do you think it is an assassin doing this?"

"We have a strong lead and have him on video, but he was disguised. We are also working with an Interpol agent. Jenny, you can write this in your notebook but do not audio or video record this. When we put this all together and arrest this guy, I will personally give you an exclusive interview, okay?"

"Okay, John. I agree."

"Also, if anyone leaks the suspects' names, don't publicize it, as we don't want the murderer to know that we are onto him. Furthermore, don't pay anyone from my department for leaks, or I will never discuss anything with you ever again. I still care about you, but I mean that. I can't do my job properly with leaks in my department. If I find someone leaking information, I will fire them or transfer them to the Yukon unless I want it leaked. On a softer note, when I'm back on my feet, hopefully within a week, I'm going to throw a big party with lots of food and a band, and I plan on playing my piano as well. You and your boyfriend are invited."

"Thanks for the invite. My boyfriend is also a musician. His name is Rick Sumner, and he plays a mean guitar, jazz, blues, or rock."

"Good, bring him along, and we will jam."

John stands up and hugs Jenny when Grace walks into his office and says, "Hi John, I hope I'm not interrupting anything!"

John breaks away and says, "Hi, honey. Grace, this an old friend of mine, Jenny Olson; she is a TV reporter. Jenny, this is my girlfriend Grace Chan."

Jenny says, "Oh, hi, Grace. That wasn't what it probably looked like. I was talking to John about the two terrible murders. I wanted to get some more information on them. My boss Rupert Coombes sent me here, but you see, John and I dated in high school a million years ago, and I haven't seen him in all those years. I have a boyfriend, in case you are wondering. Sit down, John, and rest your legs."

"Well, I'm glad you cleared that up, even though I trust John; he knows that I've studied several Martial Arts, and I know ten ways to kill him. I'm just kidding," Grace says. She bends over and gives John a long sensual kiss and says, "That's better. I'm glad to meet you, Jenny. I watch your show *Crime Beat* on Channel 24 every day. By the way, the second victim, Ken Leung, worked for me at my real estate company, and we are devastated by his death. Please don't bother his widow and daughters. They are taking it very hard. Well, I need to take a shower. Are you staying for dinner, Jenny?" Grace says.

"No, I have to tape a show in thirty minutes, so I'll see myself out. Nice to meet you, Grace, and take care, John."

Chrissy leaves the room to look for someone to feed her. Jenny says to John, "I'll pray for you to heal. Goodbye."

She leaves the house and goes to her studio to tape her show.

CHAPTER THIRTY-FOUR

Grace comes back into John's office, and he says to her, "Grace, come with me; I want to show you something." She follows him to the gym, and he shows her the exercise machine. "Thom rigged up this machine so that I can get my leg strength up again, and it is really helping me. I'm starting to feel my legs again, and I can stand up for short periods of time."

"That's great news, John; I'm proud of you," she says.

"I want to show you a few other rooms. This is the hollo room. Watch this." John goes to a panel in the wall by the door and says, "Computer, engage nightclub scenario with the Fourplay band." The room goes into waves and turns into a nightclub with low light and several people wandering around. Fourplay starts to play "Between the Sheets" with Chaka Khan singing the lyrics.

Grace has a shocked look on her face and says, "Wow, how did you do that?"

"It's just a program. I could bring in any celebrity or musical band in here. I could even sit in with them and play the piano and sing. I could change this into a beach with ocean waves against the shore. If you don't want to travel to a meeting, we could beam people into this room, and it's like they are really here. We just need their GPS coordinates to get them here." John takes Grace's hand and wheels to the piano and says, "It's time I showed you my skills." He sits at the piano, puts on sunglasses and says to the band, "'Higher Ground,' boys," and starts to sing "Higher Ground" in his Stevie Wonder voice and plays the piano. Grace stands beside him, looking shocked. He pulls her down beside him onto the piano bench and sings to her. She grins and sways to the music and looks straight into his eyes with love and admiration. He finishes playing and says, "Thanks, boys. Great harmonies." He turns and looks at Grace and says, "Any requests, ma'am?"

"I'm in shock, John. I knew you did voices, but I didn't know you could sing in them."

"I'll do two more for you," then sings Elton John's "Tiny Dancer" and plays the piano in Elton's style. Then he sings "Imagine" in John Lennon's voice, and then says, "I hope we passed the audition." He then says in his normal voice, "What say we hit the beach with no people around?" John reprograms the room into a beach scene with a blanket. They take off their clothes and lie on the blanket with a fake sun shining down on them.

"John, I can't believe you can do all these things. I suppose you can cook too, eh?"

"Actually, I can cook some pretty good meals. My sainted mother taught me to cook when I was a teenager, as my parents both worked and my brother and I could feed our sisters. I'll tell you what. When Julie goes on holidays, I will cook you some of my special meals and some Polish meals."

They get dressed and go down to the dining room in search of food. Julie walks in and says, "Are you two lovely people in search of food? It is dinnertime, and I made a rack of lamb just for you with roasted potatoes and asparagus. Would you like some wine or coffee?"

"I better stick with Grace's ancient magic Chinese tea. Grace, what does your heart desire?"

"John, I need some wine, a glass of Merlot."

They start eating, and John says, "This is excellent lamb. Where is Savana?"

"She ate already. She is in her room doing her homework, which is mostly colouring in her books. She is starting to draw, which is really cute," Julie says.

"Are you going to eat with us?" John asks.

"Yes, if you want me to. Thom is riding the perimeter of the property, checking the fences and the cameras, in case you were wondering," she says.

Julie gets her meal and comes back into the dining room.

John says, "Grace, I think I'll go with you tomorrow to see the R and D people as I have no important things to do on the two murder cases right now. I have Chuck Sidhu, Randy Chan, and Interpol Special Agent Holly Morgan researching the cases and the assassin. Do you need to go home for a change of clothes?"

"No, I had my driver bring some clothes in and put them in the closet this afternoon, but John, are you up to going out tomorrow?" Grace says.

"Yes, I can walk with a cane now. I had one in the closet, as I've been hurt before, and I have more feeling in my legs. I'll call Mike and tell him that we will pick him up in my limo, all right?"

"Okay, I might have a company that can make this fabric, depending on what we learn tomorrow. It's in Winnipeg, and I own part of it," Grace says.

John calls Mike and arranges to pick him up in the morning. They finish eating, and John says, "Grace would you like to watch a movie? I have another room that is a home theatre with a huge screen as big as a local theatre."

"Yes. I love old movies in black and white or Kungfu movies or movies where they blow up a lot of stuff," Grace says.

"You are my dream girl. That's what I like too."

They get into the elevator, go to the third floor to the home theatre room, and sit side by side on a comfy couch. John says, "Put your feet on my lap. I promised you a foot rub, and I have yet to do it."

"Well, you have been busy and hurt, but I'm glad you are a man of your word," she says. John starts massaging her feet, and she says, "Oh my God, that feels so good. That's almost as good as sex, and notice I said almost."

"How about a Jason Bourne movie? I liked the first movie the best because it was more of a mystery, being a cop and all," John says.

"Yes, I liked the first one best also. Put it on and keep rubbing my feet, Honorable John."

They watch the movie and then go to John's bedroom. Grace rubs more Chinese Magic ointment on his hip. Chrissy joins them in bed, and they go to sleep because they are tired.

The next morning, they wake up early. John gets out of bed to feed Chrissy her salmon dish, and she trots after him to his auto chef and he gets two cups of coffee. He walks back to the bed when he notices that he is now walking normally and without any pain. He puts the coffee cups down on the side table and says, "Grace, look! I can walk normally without pain or numbness."

She looks up with a groggy look on her face and says, "What did you say, John?"

He spins around and says, "Look, Grace, I can walk normally without any pain or numbness. Your magic ointment works miracles! I love you, sweetheart. You get the first cup of coffee."

He hands her the coffee cup. She takes it and says, "Is that all I get?" and wiggles her eyebrows.

In Mandarin, John says, "What else would you like, my lotus blossom? Give me a hint. I don't know what you are talking about."

She pulls the covers back, exposes her naked body, and in Mandarin says, "Does this give you any hint, Honorable John?" He takes the coffee cup from her, puts it on the side table, jumps on top of her, and starts kissing her with abandon. They make mad love as Chrissy watches them from the couch with a puzzled look on her face. They shower together and dress for the meeting, and then go down to the dining room for their Julie omelettes.

CHAPTER THIRTY-FIVE

John calls the chauffeur and says, "Jeffery, let's take the flying limo to Mike's house and then to our R and D shop in Richmond as the traffic is jammed today. There is an accident in the Massey tunnel. Put the limo behind the house for takeoff."

They go out to the flying luxury helicopter/limo combination behind the house. They fly to Mike's mansion on a huge 27-acre lot in Surrey not far from John's mansion and fly to east Richmond near Number Six Road and land on the roof of the Trosky Research and Development building. They meet with Larry Browning, the manager and head researcher. He introduces himself to Grace and says hello to Mike and John. They get down to business over good coffee, and he explains how their polymer/liquid chemical-based laser, knife proof, and bulletproof material is made and what industrial machines they will need to mass-produce it and what thread they will need to sew it together. Larry already created an overcoat in black material like cotton with a silk-like liner for John to try on. The overcoat is certified laser, knife, and bulletproof, and two others, one that looks like leather and the other like cashmere.

Larry says, "Your initial outlay should be about six hundred thousand dollars for the machines and the special chemicals, not counting a four thousand square foot building to contain all of this and, of course, sewing machines and staff."

"Does that include the chemicals? Where do we get the basic chemicals?" Grace asks.

"Yes, that includes the basic chemicals, and we found two sources in B.C. and two in Winnipeg to get them," Larry says.

"We can do this, but how long do you think we can get our first product out on the market? I have a seven thousand square foot building in Winnipeg already making clothes, and there is an empty wing to make the material in. How long would it take to get the machines to convert the chemicals to clothing material?" Grace asks.

"There are machines available that the Formula One teams use to make carbon fibre for bodies that are easily converted to suit your needs. They are in Germany, but you can get them here in a week or less. Don't you own a transport company, Grace?" Larry asks.

"Yes, I do, and if I can buy the machines in a day, I can have them here the next day. My transporters are fast."

"I think you could get your product out to market in about a month or less, depending on your staff. I can help you train your staff to make the chemicals and make the cloth if Mike wants me to do that, but you should keep your best workers on salary so that you don't lose them," Larry says.

"John and Mike, can you put money into this and get this going? We should form a new company together. I will get rid of my partners in Winnipeg and retool the company but will keep my workers who do the patterns, cutting, and sewing," Grace says.

"You know that I'm in for sure, and my squad gets the first coats, and you get one too. I need to keep you safe," John says.

"I'm in all the way. I'll help you set up the factory, as I also have a construction company, and Larry can help train your staff. Also, I know about overruns, and I think we should put an account together with one million dollars in it or more, and if we don't use it all, we just split it and take our shares out. We should get our lawyers involved to protect ourselves, and we need to patent this material. So, are we going to call the company Bodyguard Clothing? That's what you wanted to call it, right Grace, John?" Mike asks.

They both agree.

John says, "I just thought of one thing. Grace, do you own that building, or are you renting it?"

"I own it by myself, none of my partners have money in it, but I will have to buy them out, but they only have one hundred thousand dollars in the business altogether, and our sales have been down lately. I won't have trouble buying them out, especially since we may have to shut down for a month," Grace says.

"If we are going to be equal partners in this business, Mike and I should put in more money since you own the building. Did you want us to own part of the building, or do you want to own it yourself?" John asks.

"Good point, John. You both can buy into it if you want, then we will have equal shares in the company. We can work out the details of that later, along with the cost of the machinery, chemicals, construction, and all the salaries, etcetera. Well, Larry, can you get those overcoats for us to try on, and then we will leave you to your work?" Grace asks.

They try on their new coats, and Grace says, "This looks and feels like really expensive material. It feels like cashmere, and it fits. How did you know my size?"

John says, "I have spies everywhere. Actually, I have a scanner built into my front door that analyzes and records everything, including the sizes and types of weapons someone is carrying. This coat really feels like cotton and moves like a regular coat."

Mike says, "This coat really like leather, but lighter, and the lining looks and feels like silk. Well, let's go for lunch, wearing our new coats and celebrate our new partnership and enterprise. I'm buying! Where should we go?"

"Somewhere we could land a helicopter/limo would be nice," John says.

"There is a new building downtown with a restaurant on top called The Lookout, and we can land on the roof or in the parking lot. It's near the area where the Trump Tower fell during the 2025 earthquake and tsunami, collapsing half the high-rises in Vancouver—the poorly built ones—and where some of the land washed away. Anyway, the food is great there. They have everything from East Indian to French to Greek," Grace says.

Sounds great. I feel like East Indian food. I could use some spicy food right now," John says.

"Yes, I feel like something different, and let's land on the roof. Jeffery, land on the roof of The Lookout, will you?" Mike orders.

"Good, I won't know what I want until we get inside and smell the food. I know the chef, Dominic, he's a diva, but he's an excellent chef. I could have him make me something new," Grace says.

They enter the restaurant and are seated at a table near the giant windows. The waiter comes to their table and asks for their order. John says, "We will start with a bottle of Champagne as we are celebrating a new venture, and we would like menus, please." John looks out the window and says, "What a great view of the city! You can see Stanley Park from here. It took them a long time to rebuild the city after the earthquake, and I'm glad they restricted the number of high-rises to be built, as they would have crumbled again.

They are an eyesore and jam too many people in one area. I lived in one for a while on the eleventh floor, and I hated it."

The waiter comes back with the Champagne and menus and pours some Champagne into Grace's glass. She samples it and replies, "It is excellent! Could you tell Dominic that Grace Chan would like a word with him?"

"Yes, ma'am. I'll go tell him."

They peruse their menus, and Dominic comes up to the table and, in a French accent, says, "Miss Chan, so lovely to see you again. What may I do for you?"

"I can't decide what I want to eat. Do you have any suggestions or a new dish you have invented?" Grace asks.

"I just received some swordfish today, and I have it simmering in a special cream sauce. I also have some bison steaks in a barbeque-type sauce that I created," Dominic says.

"I've never had swordfish. I'll have that, Dominic."

John says, "I was going to have some chicken tikka, but that swordfish sounds tempting. I'll have that too, and a bowl of mulligatawny soup."

"I'll have the bison steak. I haven't had that since I left Winnipeg," Mike says.

Dominic says, "The bison steak comes with roasted little red potatoes and asparagus. Does that suit you, sir, or would you like another vegetable or rice?"

"That's fine, and call me Mike, and this is my brother Lieutenant John Trosky. He and Grace are a couple now."

"I'm happy to meet you, Mr. Mike and Mr. Lieutenant John Trosky. I've known Grace for a long time. You are a very lucky man."

"I see that you have key lime pie. Bring us three of those, please," John says.

Grace and Mike both say, "Yes, key lime pie. How did you know?"

"Who doesn't like key lime pie?" John says.

"Yes, I will go now to prepare your meals; it won't be too long. Enjoy!" Dominic says.

John lifts his glass and says, "A toast to a new adventure into a business that will save lives and injuries and make us some money in the process."

They all say, bless you, and Mike says, "Grace, John and I can transfer one million dollars each to your account with our phones right now so that you can order those machines. We'll put our heads together on the factory's refitting and get our lawyers to draft a contract for our new business. We also need to open a business bank account. Once we get some coats made, we can sell them to the police and the military and possibly to some wealthy, paranoid people. We should start designing pants and whatever else you can think of to market."

"I'll help out where I can, but I'll have to go back to work tomorrow. I can't let this case go stale, and I think Chuck and Randy and agent Morgan will have found something to follow up on. Here is our food. Let's talk about something else," John says.

"Please, excuse me, I need to go to the ladies' room," Grace says.

She leaves, and John says, "I'm glad she went to the ladies' room. I wanted to talk to you alone. Grace's birthday is on July 29th; it's a Saturday. You know that '57 Chevy golf cart you built for me? Can you build one for Grace by her birthday and paint it turquoise and white? Her eyes lit up when she saw mine. I'm also going to propose to her on her birthday. We'll have a big party for her, and I'm going to buy her a ring when I get the chance."

"I'll not only build it for you, but it will be a present from Gladys and me!" Mike says.

In a low voice, John tells Mike, "I want to keep this quiet as long as possible."

Grace returns to the table, and the waiter brings the swordfish and the mulligatawny soup, and John says, "Waiter, could you bring me an order of naan bread? I forgot to order it."

Grace and John start eating their swordfish, and Grace exclaims, "This is really good; the swordfish has a subtle taste, but the cream sauce makes it taste fantastic."

John points his fork at her and says, "You hit it right on the nose, Grace. I agree."

Mike says, "This bison steak is really juicy, and the barbecue sauce makes it really special. He put something else in the barbecue sauce, maybe turmeric and spicy pepper. I'll have to bring Gladys here at some point. I'm glad we came here today, Grace. Do you have any other favourite restaurants I can check out?"

"I'm glad you like this one. I'll get my secretary Maya Yeng to send you a list. She usually makes my reservations," Grace says.

John tastes the mulligatawny soup and says, "Grace, you have to try this soup," and spoons some into her mouth.

She tastes it and says, "That is spicy, but it's really good. What's in it?"

John replies, "I've had it before; it has lentils, apples, carrots, ginger, garlic, red jalapeno peppers, and coconut milk in it. If you want some more, I'll have the waiter bring a small bowl."

"I'd love some more, and a small bowl would be perfect."

John calls the waiter over and orders a small bowl of soup.

John says, "Grace, dip the naan flatbread into the soup."

CHAPTER THIRTY-SIX

Suddenly, John's phone rings. His ring tone is "Superstition" by Stevie Wonder. He says, "Sorry, I have to take this; it's the commander." He steps away from the table and answers the call, saying, "Lieutenant Trosky speaking. Hello, Commander Caputo. Yes, I'm feeling better. I was going to come back to work tomorrow. You want me to go to Paris tomorrow? Oh, you have a lead on Rafael Dupuis? Okay, I'll take Detective Sidhu and Agent Morgan with me. I can use my own transport. It will be a lot faster. Thank you, sir. Yes, I'm having lunch with my girlfriend Grace and my brother Mike. I'd better get back to them. Goodbye, sir."

John goes back to the table, sits down, and says, "That was Commander Caputo; I have to go to Paris tomorrow with Detective Chuck Sidhu and Agent Holly Morgan. A Detective Marie-Helene Brodeur has a lead on a suspect in Doctor Blackwell's murder. I'm sorry, Grace and Mike, but I have to go. At least I can take my own transport, so it will be a fast trip. I hope I will only be there for a day, but I won't know until I get there."

"Well, John, it is your job, and it's important, but I'll miss you even if it's for a day," Grace says.

"I agree, your job is more important, and Grace and I have a lot of preliminary work to do. I'm going to get Gladys to help me organize the design and construction of the building in Winnipeg and look into the building and electrical permits. She has done that before," Mike says.

"Waiter, we'll take that key lime pie to go," John says.

They finish their meals, and Grace says, "I need to freshen up, excuse me."

John says to Mike, "I'm glad we are alone. About Grace's birthday on Saturday, I'm going to propose to her, and I'm going to have to scramble to put it all together. I'll get Thom to do most of the organizing and get Julie and a caterer involved. You can invite your R and D guys and the Trosky Auto staff and anyone else I'm forgetting. I'm going to buy her an engagement ring when I'm in Paris and maybe a few antique cars. Maybe Gladys can help some, but I want her to help with redoing Grace's building. Do any of your guys play an instrument? I plan to jam with the band, and anyone else is welcome to join in."

They fly to Mike's place and then to John's place. Thom and Chrissy greet them at the door, and John says, "Thom, I have to fly to Paris tomorrow. Can you pack me a bag for two days? I may only be there for a day. I see the outdoor elevator is finished. I won't need it, but we should keep it in case we get disabled visitors. I should have thought of that years ago. I mean, we've seen our guys get half blown up in Afghanistan."

Thom says, "I'll see to the packing, and I'm glad we are keeping the elevator."

John and Grace go up to the glass terrarium room and have coffee and key lime pie. John says, "This is really great pie. That was a great meal. So, Grace, do you want to stay here while I'm gone, or do you have things to do at home? Does your mother live with you or your sister? It's funny that I don't know much about your living situation. I guess because I want you here so much. If you have things to attend to, I should give you the freedom to do that."

"John, you are a very kind and loving person, and I enjoy being with you every day, but you are right, I have been neglecting some of my duties at home. I live with my mom and dad, but they are still young and can take care of themselves, and they have servants who can cook and clean for them. My mother is funny about servants; she will clean up before the cleaning lady cleans the room, but my house has twelve rooms to clean, so there must be some rooms for the cleaning lady to do. Sometimes, we have friends or relatives drop in for a visit. My mom can't do it all. She also argues with the chef all the time; she would rather cook for herself. So, when you go away tomorrow, I'll go home and see my parents, and I need to work out of my home office to get the Bodyguard Clothing business going. Let me tell you, I would rather eat glass than talk to a lawyer."

"Damn, we have something in common, and let me tell you, criminal lawyers are the worst. They would sell out their grandmothers to get a win." They both laugh. John adds, "Didn't you say you had a sister growing up?"

"Yes, I have a sister, Jasmine, but she is married to David Travers, who is also in real estate. They have two daughters, Fawn, who is four years old and Megan five years old. They are precious little darlings. You will have to meet them sometime."

"Yes, I can't wait to meet your whole family," John says.

CHAPTER THIRTY-SEVEN

"I have an idea, why don't we ride the horses out to the pond to work off all this food we've eaten. Do you have blue jeans here?" John says.

"Yes, and yes, I do have a change of casual clothes here. Let's go!" Grace says.

They change and ride Steely Dan and Adele down to the pond, wearing their cowboy outfits and their new laser proof coats. They sit on a bench overlooking the pond and enjoy the sounds of the birds and the horses chewing the grass, and talk about nothing special, as they are nervous about having to be apart but want to be calm about it. They get back on the horses and head back to the barn. They are halfway there when Steely Dan starts limping, and John yells, "Grace, hold up, Steely Dan has thrown a shoe! We need to walk back to the barn. Darn, I left my phone at home. Do you have yours on you?"

"Yes . . . no, I must have left it in my purse at the house."

John says, "So, we can't call Autrey, meaning we'll have to walk home, or you can ride ahead and get him to bring the farm truck and horse trailer."

"I don't mind walking, but will it hurt him to walk?" Grace asks.

"I think we are about a half-hour from the barn. He'll be okay for that distance."

"Let's walk then. We can build up an appetite for dinner."

"Yes, I think Julie is cooking a beef roast for dinner with roasted potatoes and carrots. I'll walk for that alone."

They walk to the barn and find Autrey repairing some bridles. John tells him about Steely Dan, and in his southern drawl, Autrey says, "Don't worry, y'all, I'll fire up the blacksmith shop and put new shoes on him. He'll be good as new."

They get in the '57 Chevy golf cart and drive back to the house. Grace says, "Autrey is quite a character; where on Earth did you find him?"

"Would you believe I found him at a rodeo in Cloverdale? I was looking for a ranch hand, and I saw this guy limping around. Apparently, he had fallen off a mad bull called Diablo, and he needed a job to get his leg fixed. He told me he was from El Paso, Texas, and from his drawl, I believed him, so I took him to Peace Arch Hospital and got my doctor to fix his broken leg. He is so tough; he was walking around with a broken leg. Can you believe that? I was so impressed with him that I paid his hospital bill, told him not to pay me back, and gave him a permanent job. He has been here ever since. You should see the room I had built for him above the barn. It's like a suite at the Hilton! I love the old guy."

They drive back to the house and enter the dining room. Julie and Savana are sitting there with Julie, helping Savana with her homework. Savana says, "Hi Uncle Tiny and Grace. Did you have a nice ride out to the pond?"

"We did until Steely Dan threw a shoe, and we had to walk him to the barn," John says.

"Is he going to be all right?" she asks.

Grace says, "Don't worry, Savana. Autrey is making him new horseshoes as we speak. He'll be fine. My horse Cher has thrown shoes before, and she is fine."

"You have a horse named Cher, that is so cool!" Savana says.

John walks over to a cabinet and gets a bottle of Troubadour Cabernet red wine, pours some for Grace and himself, and says, "Julie, that roast smells terrific. Is it going to be ready soon?"

"It should be ready in fifteen or twenty minutes. We are done with Savana's homework now. If you are really hungry, I can fix you a quick Greek salad with cucumbers and feta cheese and tomatoes," Julie says.

"I'm hungry. How about you, Grace?" John says.

"Yes, I'm hungry too after that walk, and I love Greek salad. How about you, Savana? Do you like Greek salad and roast beef?"

"Yes, but I'm only little, and I eat small meals, and I do get tired of mac and cheese sometimes. My mom says I have to 'variety' my diet. Is that the right word?" Savana says.

"It's close; you say 'vary' my diet. I know English is a complicated language. When I was a little girl, my parents taught me to speak Mandarin before English."

"What is Mandarin?" Savana asks.

"It's what Chinese people speak, and some speak Cantonese."

"So, are you Chinese?" Savana asks.

Grace looks at John, then at Savana, and says, "Yes, I'm Chinese, couldn't you tell that I'm Chinese?"

"I don't know; I just think you are very pretty, and I like you, and Uncle Tiny loves you. That's all I need to know."

"Out of the mouths of babes. That is so sweet, Savana," John says.

"I like you too, Savana, and you are sweet," Grace says.

Just then, Chrissy saunters into the room, looks around, and jumps on Grace's lap and lovingly pats Grace's face. "Hi,

Chrissy. I love you too. We are getting to be good friends. Should I feed her, John? I don't know where her food is."

John takes a sip of wine and says, "Her food is in the kitchen, but she loves beef roast, and it's okay to feed her at the table, but not on the table, just not all the time. But her favourite food is salmon. She goes crazy over it. I once put a tin of it on the back porch when she was way out in the field, and she came running like her life depended on it. You can feed her some roast when we eat. She will wait; she can smell it."

Julie enters carrying four bowls of salad and sits down to eat with them. John says, "By the way, Julie, I have to go to Paris tomorrow for a day or two, so you will be on your own, except for Thom, and Grace will be staying at her place with her parents. Also, we, that is Grace, Mike, and I, have started a new company called Bodyguard Clothing, making laser proof and bulletproof clothing, so we will be busy with several meetings to get this company going and producing some product. We already have laser proof coats in the closet. By the way, where is Thom? He usually joins us for dinner."

"He said that he packed a bag for your trip and he has a dinner date with his new girlfriend, Bridgette. He is a very private person. It took me two weeks to get her name out of him. I think he met her at a farmer's market. I'll pry the rest out of him soon," Julie says.

"Tell him that I suggested he bring her here for dinner. Ask him what kind of food she likes, and you can cook something gourmet for them and have some of our great wine," John says.

"That's a great idea, John. I will subtly suggest that," Julie says. She goes out to the kitchen and brings in the roast beef dinners with the serving droids.

Grace says, "That smells so good, I can smell the garlic, and I love garlic."

"I love garlic too; my mother used to load it up into the roast every Sunday," John says.

Chrissy starts meowing and jumps up on Grace's lap. She cuts some meat up and says, "Don't worry, Chrissy, I'll feed you, but you have to wait for it to cool." Chrissy meows and walks around to John and looks up and meows again.

"Don't meow at me, Chrissy, you'll just have to wait until the meat cools. Grace wasn't being mean. Go drink your milk first and go back to Grace, okay?" John says.

Chrissy looks indignant and walks into the corner and drinks her milk. Grace puts some roast on a small plate and blows on it, and puts it on the floor beside her chair. Chrissy sniffs, turns her head, trots over, and attacks the roast like it was a mouse. Grace looks down at Chrissy and then at John and says, "I think she still loves me," and sips her wine.

CHAPTER THIRTY-EIGHT

They finish eating dinner and go up to John's bedroom and turn on the 62-inch television mounted to the far wall. John takes Grace's feet in his lap and starts massaging them as they watch the news. The news comes on, and the announcer says, *"This is Fritz Berger of Channel 45 with the latest news. Sources from the Vancouver police tell us that Lieutenant John Trosky of the Black Hat Squad has been stalled in his investigation into the bizarre murders of a Doctor J. Blackwell of Winnipeg and a Mr. Ken Leung, a real estate agent of Vancouver. Lieutenant Trosky could not be reached for comment in the last week. In other news . . ."*

John turns down the TV and says angrily, "That jerk has the brains of a mosquito. I was in the hospital having a serious operation and recuperating at home. Not to mention that the commander issued a 'code blue' on this, which is a complete media blackout. What the hell am I supposed to do now?"

"Aren't you friends with Jenny Olson?" Grace asks.

"Yes, but I'm not allowed to give her any detailed information."

"Yes, but anyone with a brain could find out that you are going to Paris tomorrow, quote, in search of more information with an Interpol Agent. Hint, hint."

John smiles and says, "Grace, you are a genius!"

"I know that, and now you know it. What are you waiting for? Call her; play your cards, John."

John picks up his phone, calls Jenny, and transfers the call to the wall screen, "Hello, Jenny, I hope I'm not disturbing you, but your esteemed colleague Fritz Berger just dissed me on live TV, and I am not a happy camper. He said my investigation into the two murders is, quote, stalled, and he couldn't reach me. Screw him sideways."

Jenny quips, "No, thank you; I hate that bastard. He has stolen more stories from me than you can shake a stick at. So, how can I help you if you can't talk to me?"

"Well, as my brilliant girlfriend Grace just said to me, someone with a brain can find out that my partner Detective Sidhu, Agent Holly Morgan of Interpol, and I are flying to Paris tomorrow in my private shuttle in search of more information from an unidentified source. Are you writing this down, Jenny?"

"Thank you, mister unidentified source. I guess I owe you a favour now. Wait a minute, are you massaging Grace's feet?" she asks.

"Yes, I promised her I would massage her feet every day, as she wears those damn high heels that kill her feet."

"I have got to get a new boyfriend; Rick never does that for me," Jenny says.

"Actually, you technically owe Grace and me a favour. I'll have more exciting news for you in a few weeks, and I promise you an exclusive interview when I catch this bastard. Sleep well, Jenny. Goodnight." John hangs up the phone and says to Grace, "Well, Grace, let's go to bed and rock ourselves to sleep." He then says to the room, "Fireplace on. Computer, play the Art Pepper Plays the Blues album on low volume." He then reaches over and slowly removes Grace's clothing as she removes his. When they are naked, he asks, "Miss, would you like to dance?"

"I hardly know you, but I like dancing. They start dancing and rubbing against each other.

"John smile and says, "Let's hit the bed; I can't stand the wait any longer. I'm hungry for you, my lotus blossom. They fall into bed and ravage each other. John feels his head is about to explode and ejaculates into her, and she orgasms at the same moment and screams. They exhaust each other and fall on their backs. John exclaims, "Wow! When I have an orgasm, it feels like an electrical charge goes up my spine and explodes inside my brain."

"I feel an explosion in my brain, but it multiplies," she says.

"I really am going to miss you tomorrow," John says.

"Me too," she says, and they fall asleep in each other's arms.

They get up in the morning, shower together, have breakfast, and John grabs his black hat and coat and packed bag. He says, "Grace, do you need a ride home?"

"No, my driver is on his way here, and I need him to drive me to my office after."

John kisses her goodbye, goes out to the limo, and leaves to pick up Detective Sidhu and Agent Holly Morgan.

CHAPTER THIRTY-NINE

They go to his private shuttle port and leave at 7 a.m. Vancouver time. After a three-hour flight at warp speed, they arrive in Paris at 7 p.m. Paris time. They hire a private limo, and Holly says to the driver, "We need to go to 11 Rue de Saussaies, the police headquarters.

They go to the police station and find Detective Marie-Helene Brodeur in her office and introduce themselves. Holly smiles and says, "Hello, Detective Brodeur. It's good to see you again. I'm sorry we are so late, but with the time difference and a headwind, we couldn't get here sooner."

Detective Brodeur says. "This is about Mr. Raphael Dupuis, whom you think hired an assassin to kill a Doctor J. Blackwell. His lawyer, a Mr. Granger, is giving us a hard time. Mr. Dupuis is staying at the Claretta Hotel, and we can't bring him in for questioning until tomorrow morning. We got your facial recognition program and found him at the shuttle port and hotel a few days ago. We realize that this doctor was responsible for the accidental death of his daughter Lily, which is a questionable reason to connect him to the assassin, but the fact that Mr. Dupuis ran from Vancouver to Paris is suspicious."

John says, "The fact that the doctor died of a dissolved heart caused by these nano-bots that Mr. Dupuis invented is reason enough for a warrant to bring him in for questioning. Don't you think?"

"I agree with you, but his lawyer was blocking this, but I got a Judge to sign a warrant a few hours ago. You can return tomorrow morning at 9 a.m., and we can question him together. Do you have a hotel at which to stay?"

"Yes, I arranged a suite at the Grand Belair Hotel. I heard it was good."

"You picked the most expensive hotel in Paris, lieutenant; I hope you can afford it."

In French, he says, "Don't worry; I will manage it. We will see you in the morning, Detective Brodeur. Goodnight."

"You speak very good French, lieutenant. Goodnight."

Chuck says, "John, I'm glad you speak French. I think she likes you now."

John and Chuck go to the hotel and check into their suite. They unpack their bags, and John says, "I want to call Grace, and then we'll call room service and discuss tomorrow's strategy." John then picks up the phone and calls Grace. "Hi, sweetheart. How is your day going, and what time is it there?"

"Hi, yourself, Mr. world traveller. I ordered the specialty machines, and the guy wanted to raise the price, but as I am a good negotiator, I got him to drop his price, as I pointed out to him that when this company really gets going, we will need more machines. They also sell the chemicals, which I got him to sell to us at wholesale plus ten percent. They are shipping the works today through my transport company, which saves him money but is cheaper for us to use my company. How is your end going?"

"Well, I forgot about the time difference. It's nine hours ahead here, so it is seven at night, and we can't interrogate this guy until tomorrow morning. Chuck and I are stuck in this luxury hotel and have to eat this fancy French cuisine tonight, so it is awful."

"I feel so sorry for you as I eat my tuna sandwich for lunch and chase it down with bottled water. Mike, Larry Browning, and I will have to interview people to run the machines to make the chemicals and the cloth, and I have put my best designers and seamstresses on retainer and a bonus so they can get a bit of a holiday. Well, I've got a lot of work to do today, so I have to say goodbye. I love you, John. I mean, Mr. James Bond. Good luck tomorrow."

"Goodbye, Grace. I love you, and I hope to be back tomorrow, but we'll have to see how everything works out." He hangs up and asks Chuck, "What do you feel like eating? They probably have everything here."

Chuck says, "How about a steak dinner and a bottle of Merlot wine? Do they have your brand here?"

"Good idea, Chuck. Yes, they do have Troubadour wine here; that's why I picked this hotel. I know Mr. Dumont, the guy who owns this hotel and made a deal with him to carry my wines. You know, I used to live in Paris in my college days. That's why I can speak French and German."

John picks up the house phone and orders room service in French. John says, "I was thinking that for tomorrow's interrogation, I want you to start off playing good cop, appeal to his father side. After all, this doctor killed his daughter, and you sympathize with him. Then I hit him with the nano-bots. He invented them, but how did the killer get hold of them? Holly can hammer at him too. By the way, while I'm here, I'm going to buy an engagement ring for Grace because the moment I laid eyes on her, I knew I was going to marry her. I know a great jeweller here, and I want a big pink diamond as they are rare, and it is her favourite colour. This is a secret, for now, so please not a word to anyone, especially Grace. If I can't find that diamond ring here, we are flying to Belgium."

Their food arrives, and the porter opens the Merlot wine and pours it into John's glass. He tastes it, and they dig into their steaks. John says, "I hope you like your steak rare because that's what I ordered. I love to see the blood run out, then you know it's juicy. You know, Chuck, we can't extradite Dupuis, as Canada can send criminals back to France, but France won't send people back to Canada. I don't know what idiot made that deal, but he must have no brains. Dupuis must have hired Mr. Auger in France. I just don't know much about the laws governing the internet. Did you or Randy ever find Dupuis's hidden bank account?"

"We got stalled there; whoever did the money transfer for the hit bounced it around several countries, and then it disappeared. I think Randy and Captain Fedora are still working on that. Maybe they will find a different angle. I'll text Randy and tell him to send us any progress on the case. What about the Ken Leung case? I know he worked for Grace, but she couldn't keep track of everything this guy was into. You said those stacking dolls were either Russian or Ukrainian, right? It must be an oligarch of some kind. Who else has that kind of money? Leung must have shafted one of those oligarchs, and probably with the house he was killed in. I don't think Auger picked that house at random. Do you?"

"Your brain is really cranking tonight. You are probably right about the house, as Auger does things for a reason. Also, we forgot about the nanny-cam. It was equipped with sound, but the sound was too low, and he said something to Mr. Leung just before he killed him. We've got to get the sound guys working on that. Send Captain Fedora a text on digging deeper into Leung's finances and cleaning up the sound on the nanny-cam. It's still daytime there. Well, I'm going to have a shower and hit the sack."

CHAPTER FORTY

They get up early in the morning, eat breakfast, and head to the police station. They connect with Detective Marie-Helene Brodeur as Agent Holly Morgan enters the bullpen. Detective Brodeur says, "Agent Morgan, you can observe from the other room, but only Lieutenant Trosky, Detective Sidhu, and I can interrogate Mr. Dupuis with his slimy lawyer."

John says, "I would like Detective Sidhu to start. He is good at playing good cop and will soften Mr. Dupuis up. Then I will hit him with the hard facts, and you can scare the shit out of him."

She laughs and says, "Sounds good to me."

They enter the interview room and read him his rights. Chuck starts, "Mr. Dupuis, we are sorry to hear about the death of your daughter during her heart operation. It was a tragic accident."

Mr. Dupuis snarls and says, "It was not an accident. That bastard killed her, the same as shooting her in the head."

Chuck says, "I understand; if I had a child who died like that, I would be devastated and extremely angry, but I would have sued the doctor and not killed him."

Dupuis says, "I didn't kill him. I was in Paris when he was killed."

John breaks in and says, "You are a famous scientist and biologist. Is that correct, Mr. Dupuis?"

"Yes, I am."

"And you recently invented these nano-bots that can restore health to diseased organs. Is that correct, sir?"

"Yes, it is my greatest invention, and I'm proud of it. It might have saved my daughter Lily, but it is not approved by the FDA and is still in the testing stage in our laboratory."

"Is this laboratory secure, and how many people have access to it?" John asks.

It is very secure. I'm the only person who can experiment with it. Two other people help me in the lab, but the substance never leaves the lab."

Detective Brodeur says, "These detectives showed me a lab report that shows that some of your nano-bot residue and pressure syringe marks were found in the body of Doctor Blackwell, and they have a video of a Mr. Auger disguised as a room service person going into the doctor's room just before he was killed."

John pushes into Mr. Dupuis's face and says, "So, how did Mr. Auger get enough of these nano-bots to kill Doctor Blackwell? Also, how did he get a program to cause these nano-bots to kill instead of curing him?"

Mr. Dupuis's lawyer, Mr. Norman Granger, says, "Don't answer that, Mr. Dupuis. I would like to take a break to confer with my client, please."

Detective Brodeur says, "How much time would you like to confer with your client, Mr. Granger?"

"I would like two hours, as I need to bring in another lawyer who is more experienced in this area."

"All right, but your client stays here in a cell until you are back. Is this okay with you, Lieutenant Trosky?"

John takes Detective Brodeur aside and says, "It's fine with me. In fact, I want to do a bit of shopping while I'm here for some jewellery for my girlfriend. You can call me on my mobile if I'm delayed. I'm going to Chopard House; it's not far from here."

"You must really love your girlfriend. That is the most expensive jeweller in Paris."

"Yes, I know *Monsieur* Karl-Friedrich Scheifele. He and I both collect vintage cars, and he knew my father. I'll be back as soon as I can. You and Detective Chuck Sidhu can put your heads together and see what else you can come up with. I don't know what else to hit Mr. Dupuis with. If you think of anything, let me know. I have to go now."

CHAPTER FORTY-ONE

John leaves to go to the Chopard House and finds *Monsieur* Scheifele.

John says in French, "Karl, it's been years since I've laid eyes on you, but you haven't aged a bit." They hug, and Karl kisses him on both cheeks and says, "I'm so sorry to hear about your parents' unfortunate accident, and you are looking for hmm? Ah, you are in love. I see it in your eyes. What is her name?"

"Her name is Grace Chan, and she is the reason I'm here. She doesn't know it yet, but I'm going to marry her because I know that she loves me."

You mean, *the* Grace Chan, the billionaire real estate mogul, Chinese herbal internet app. inventor, and clothing manufacturer Grace Chan?

"When you put it that way, I don't feel worthy of her, but yes, and I want to buy her an engagement ring with a quality pink diamond in it and matching earrings. I know her ring size. So, what do you have that is special and that I could take home today or tomorrow?"

Karl says, "I have a collection called Happy Hearts that I think you will love, and I will give you a special price on. There are two styles of the ring, and we match the earrings to the ring. Let me show you the two styles."

They walk over to the glass counter, and Karl pulls out the ring displays and says, "You can have a simple ring in the shape of a heart with an 8 or 10-carat diamond in the center or the same pink diamond surrounded by several small half-carat diamonds around the inside of the open heart. What do you think she would prefer, John?"

"Yes, I think she would like the round shaped pink 10-carat diamond surrounded by the small white diamonds and the pink diamond earrings, of course. This ring looks like her size. Can you engrave it today?" John asks.

"Yes, what do you want to be engraved on it?"

"How about, 'Grace, you are my heart. Love, John.' Will that fit?"

"It's a bit long. How about 'Grace and John entwined hearts'? I think it is more elegant and more heartfelt."

"Yes, that is perfect. Now, the price, and can I have the package this afternoon?"

"With the 10-carat pink diamond and the earrings, I should charge you 1.4 million dollars, but I can sell them for 1.2 million dollars with taxes," Karl says.

"Great, I'll be back around five o'clock. Is that good for you?"

"Yes, and let me know if you want to go for dinner—on me."

"Thank you, Karl. In the meantime, you can design wedding rings for Grace and me, but mine must not be as shiny as hers, but close to her design if possible. I'll be back later. I must go back to the police station now. I would love to go for dinner and talk cars with you."

John goes back to the police station and enters Detective Brodeur's office. She and Chuck are in the middle of a serious discussion.

"Well, how is it going, detectives?" John asks.

Detective Brodeur says, "We are in trouble. This new lawyer they brought in is trouble. I know her, Miss Francine Cier. She is a hellcat in court. Let's go back into the interrogation room and try to battle her.

They enter the room, and Detective Brodeur says, "Record on. Let the record show that I Detective Marie-Helen Brodeur, Lieutenant John Trosky, Detective Chuck Sidhu of the Canadian Vancouver homicide squad, and suspect Mr. Rafael Dupuis and his lawyers Miss Francine Cier and Mr. Norman Granger have entered the room and are on video. The date is Saturday, April 22nd, 2070." Detective Brodeur continues, "Mr. Dupuis, you are still under oath."

Francine Cier says, "As far as I'm concerned, this interview is over. You have absolutely established no financial, verbal, or electronic connection between my client and this mysterious Mr. Auger. Mr. Dupuis is a biological scientist working on these nano-bots, which is not a crime, and you haven't proven reasonable doubt enough to search his lab, which is a classified secret government-funded lab. So, I want my client released right now unless you are going to charge him with something."

Detective Brodeur states, "You are correct, Miss Cier; we don't have proof enough right now, but we have enough suspicion to keep digging into Mr. Dupuis's financials, and we will get him sometime. Interview over. You may leave, Mr. Dupuis. Recorder off."

They all leave the interview room, and John says, "I know this guy hired Mr. Auger to kill Doctor Blackwell. We need to keep digging into his financials. Our electronics detectives couldn't find the end of the money transfer. Maybe your servers can find the last part of the transfer. Chuck can give you the start of the search, and you can contact Captain Fedora to help you with the case. Chuck, give Detective Brodeur the information, then we have to go to see Mr. Scheifele about some jewellery and have dinner with him."

CHAPTER FORTY-TWO

John and Chuck go to Chopard House jewellery and are greeted by Karl-Friedrich Scheifele.

"John, you are just in time to see your finished ring and earrings. I will go and retrieve them, and who is your friend?"

"This is my partner Detective Chuck Sidhu of my Black Hat Squad."

Karl says, "Lovely to meet you."

"Glad to meet you also," Chuck says.

Karl goes to the back room and comes back with the engagement ring and earrings in small pink velvet boxes and puts them on the glass counter to show John and Chuck. John exclaims, "Grace is going to love these pieces and the pink boxes. This is an excellent design and exquisite workmanship."

"Wow. John, I've never seen anything like this. I didn't know pink diamonds even existed!" Chuck says.

John gives Karl his bank account transfer number and says, "This is well worth the money."

"I'll just take care of this, and dinner is on me tonight at the best restaurant in Paris, La Parisienne, and that includes *Monsieur* Chuck. Then I will take you to see my car collection. Actually, I have a few of my antique cars for sale if one of them catches your eye," Karl says.

John replies, "This is turning out to be a good day as my police business took a bad turn today. We have to go back to the Grand Belair Hotel to change and call my girlfriend to tell her I won't be back until tomorrow. What time are we having dinner, Karl?"

"I'll pick you up in my white limousine at, say, eight o'clock. Is that appropriate for you?"

"That is very appropriate for us. We will see you there, and thank you for making this beautiful jewellery. She has to marry me now, and you are invited to the wedding next summer, sometime in June, I hope. We will see you later, Karl."

They get back to the hotel, and John calls Grace. "Hi, Grace, how are you?"

"I'm tired, but I'm busy building our empire. The machines are here, and Larry, Mike, and I have already hired some employees to run the machines. It's only ten o'clock here, but my brain is fried already. How is your thing going?"

"We tried to nail Mr. Dupuis with hiring the assassin, but his female lawyer, Miss Francine Cier, pointed out that we don't have enough evidence for a search warrant for his lab and have no digital connection to the assassin, Mr. Auger, so it was a bust. If I'm ever in deep trouble, I'm hiring her. She is a brilliant lawyer. Anyway, Chuck and I are having dinner with an old friend of the family, Karl-Friedrich Scheifele, who owns a jewellery store and has a great antique car collection. Do you want me to buy you a car? He has some for sale?"

"No, but you can bring me an order of coq au vin."

"I will be back tomorrow, or would it be today? This time change has me confused, but I know that Vancouver is nine hours behind. Anyway, we'll be leaving here tomorrow morning at 8 a.m. on my private shuttle. I'm trying to remember how long the flight was coming here."

"I think it was three or four hours. You called me at ten in the morning when you got there. Anyway, I guess I'll see you tomorrow morning. I better get back to work; my phone is going to explode in a minute. I love you, *Monsieur* John. Take care of my man."

"You mean, Chuck. Okay, I love him too," John says.

"I mean you, stupid. I'm going to kick your ass when you get back, Mr. James Bond."

John replies in Mandarin, "I love you too, my lotus blossom, and I will kiss your ass."

"I said 'kick,' but if that's what you want, you can kiss my ass and other female parts, Mr. Bond. Goodbye."

CHAPTER FORTY-THREE

John gets an idea and calls the French police station. "Detective Brodeur, we can't let Mr. Dupuis get away with this. I have an idea. Mr. Dupuis said he had two lab assistants; maybe you could put someone undercover to follow these two people around and find out what bar they hang out in and make friends with one of them, and maybe one is a woman. Anyway, get close to them and see if you can get some information from one of them. A lot of people hate their boss. Maybe get one of them to bug his phone or office, whatever."

"That is a great idea! I will arrange for that mission to happen and keep you informed. Thank you for calling. Are you going to be in town much longer?" she asks.

"No, I have to get back to Vancouver and work on the other murder of Mr. Ken Leung. I think Mr. Auger is still in Vancouver and will kill again, and my hunches are usually right. Well, I must go; I have a dinner date with an old family friend at La Parisienne. I'll keep in touch. Goodbye."

Karl picks them up in his long white limo, and they go to the restaurant. They are seated at a window with a beautiful view of Paris and the Eifel Tower. John says to Karl, "So, Karl, what is the specialty here?"

"They make the best coq au vin here and confit de canard. Also, beef bourguignon. I, myself, prefer the coq au vin. They also serve Troubadour wines. They have an excellent Cabernet."

John says, "Yes, I prefer it myself as I own the winery."

"You own Troubadour? I did not know that. You have excellent taste."

The owner comes over and says, "Good evening, *Monsieur* Scheifele and gentlemen. Would you like a menu or perhaps some wine to start with?"

"Good evening, Marcel, please bring us a bottle of Troubadour Cabernet. I would like you to meet Lieutenant John Trosky, who happens to own Troubadour, and this is his friend Detective Chuck Sidhu of the Canadian police. Please bring us some menus," Karl says.

Marcel brings the wine and menus and pours the wine. Chuck looks at the prices on the menu and thinks, *I'm glad this guy is buying. Seventy-five francs for a steak!*

John says, "I'll have the coq au vin and chocolate mousse for dessert."

Chuck says, "I'll have the beef bourguignon and the chocolate mousse also."

Karl says in French, "I'll have the confit de canard and a dessert wine later. Thank you, Marcel."

Marcel serves dinner, and Karl says, "John, have you ever seen a 1935 Delahaye designed by Jean-Fracous? I have a beautiful, fully restored blue metallic roadster that I would sell to you and some antique 1900s race cars you might be interested in."

"A 1935 Delahaye, now you've got my attention. Is your collection near here?" John asks.

Karl says, "Yes, it is only a few kilometres from here."

They finish dinner later and go to Karl's warehouse and look at his antique cars. John spots the 1935 Delahaye under a spotlight, a gleaming candy blue metallic swoopy-looking roadster and falls in love with the car. He blurts out, "This is not a car; it is a work of art. It's like a moving sculpture, and the colour is perfect for this car. Any other colour wouldn't suit it. How much do you want for it, Karl?"

"I had it appraised for eight hundred thousand dollars by an American appraiser, but since you are practically family, I will sell it to you for seven hundred thousand Canadian dollars and two cases of your Troubadour Merlot wine, do we have a deal, John?"

John replies, "Yes, but I'll throw in two cases of Merlot and two cases of my Chablis. I know you will love it. Deal?"

"It's a deal. Now, I also have a few 1900-era Alfa Romeos that are restored, and you can actually race them."

They walk through the warehouse, and Karl points out a 1907 Alfa Romeo race car driven by a famous driver from that era. Karl says, "Now, this car is a lot less money. I can sell it to you for four hundred thousand Canadian dollars."

"I want to buy something for my girlfriend. Something safe, old, and classy. What is that in the corner with a tarp on it?" John says.

"That would be the perfect car for her. It was used in the James Bond movie *Goldfinger,* and it's bulletproof. I can give you a good deal on it."

They take the tarp off the car, and it's a Rolls Royce. John exclaims, "Are you kidding? This is perfect; I'll take it."

Karl adds, "You can drive these two cars around the compound right now to make sure they run properly."

"I'll take this Alfa Romeo too. I don't own anything from this era at all. Chuck, let's go for a ride."

"Yes, boss. I've never ridden in anything this old ever!"

They drive the cars around with big grins on their faces. Then John pays Karl for the cars and arranges for all three to be shipped to his mansion. He then arranges for the cases of wine to be shipped to Karl's place.

They go back to the hotel, and John calls Thom to tell him to expect the three antique cars. He tells Thom to put them in the garage and have his mechanic check them over for damage and safety concerns. He also asks him to polish them up.

They then go to sleep and fly back to Vancouver in the morning.

CHAPTER FORTY-FOUR

They leave at 7 a.m. to get back at 10 a.m.

Once they land, they go straight to the office and report to Captain Fedora. John tells him about the lawyer blocking the warrant and his idea of telling Detective Brodeur to send in an undercover operative or two to make friends with the lab assistants to see if they can get some incriminating evidence against Raphael Dupuis. Then John says, "I also want to talk about the Ken Leung case. Have the lab boys enhanced the sound from the nanny-cam? I think Auger told Ken who paid him to kill him and why. Also, I think Mr. Leung shafted someone out of a large amount of money, possibly someone Russian, because of the stacking dolls. I also think it had something to do with that house. I mean, of all the places Auger could have killed him, why that house? He could have mugged him, sniped him, or run him over with a car or truck. Auger was a sniper in the French army, with medals for shooting and silent killing. We should also look into where Auger bought those stacking dolls to see if they are Russian or Ukrainian. Not many places sell them. It could point us to a Russian oligarch. I don't know about Chuck, but I would like some time off today to get over the shuttle-lag and the time difference, just for the rest of the day. I feel fuzzy and tired, and I'll think better tomorrow. I also have a feeling Mr. Auger is not finished here. I think he is still in Vancouver waiting for orders to kill. You know, if we get too close to him, he could come after me or any of us. I hope he stays away from Grace."

"Great ideas, John. I wouldn't worry about him coming after us just yet as he loves to kill for money. So, get the hell out of here, and I'll see you tomorrow at eight sharp, and say hello to Grace for me if you happen to see her," Captain Fedora says.

CHAPTER FORTY-FIVE

John leaves the office, and it is near noon, so he goes to Grace's office in the limo and walks in, holding a big package. In Mandarin, he says, "I'm looking for a Miss Lotus Blossom."

Grace looks at him, jumps up, and in Mandarin, says, "That is me, Mr.?"

In his Sean Connery voice, John says, "Bond, James Bond, Miss Lotus Blossom? I have a package for you from Paris, France."

He hands her the package, and continuing in his Bond voice, he says, "You said to bring you some coq au vin. Are you hungry, my dear? Do you have a lunchroom? I brought enough for you and me and your secretary, Maya."

Grace catches her breath and says, "John, I can't believe you did this; I was just kidding."

He looks at her lovingly and says, "I wanted to surprise you and I hope you like it. The food in Paris costs a fortune. You have to take out a mortgage to have dinner there."

Grace calls Maya, and they go into the lunchroom. Maya says, "You brought this from Paris, France today?"

"Yes, I'm just following orders from Grace. Whatever she wants, I get it, as long as it's legal. I am a police officer, after all. The coq au vin is still pretty fresh. The flight only took three hours, and we kept it fresh in my private shuttle, so enjoy! I feel like we should have a waiter here serving this.

They dig into their meals, and Grace says, "John, I love you even more. This is delicious, and that isn't a good enough word for it.

"Yes, this is the best meal I've ever had. Thank you, John. Do you have a brother I can marry?" Maya says.

John laughs and says, "Yes, but unfortunately, he is married to a beautiful woman and has a daughter. Sorry, Maya. I'll see if I can hook you up with a billionaire if it's money that you want. Oh, Grace, my boss gave me the rest of the day off, but I know how busy you are, so maybe I can help you with the new business."

"John, I hate to say this, but you look tired. I can't think of anything for you to do right now; you should go home and rest. You're going to need your energy when I get there after work, Mr. Bond, James Bond," Grace says.

"Yes, that's an excellent idea, Miss Lotus Blossom."

"Who is James Bond?" Maya asks.

"He is a character from a series of old spy movies from the early 20th century, who was handsome, a gentleman, and deadly to the bad guys," Grace says.

"Oh, I see; this is a code name you two use when you want to have fun," Maya says.

"I do feel what they used to call jet-lagged, but really, it's the time difference. Okay, I'll see you later, Grace," John says.

John goes home and realizes that Grace's birthday is on Saturday, April 29th, and today is Saturday, the 22^{nd,} and he hasn't organized a party for her yet. He enters the mansion and is greeted by Thom and Chrissy. He says excitedly, "Thom, I have screwed up. It's Grace's birthday next Saturday, and I need you to organize a party, and I'm going to propose to her that same day. I need you to email everyone in my squad and all my close friends and get an orchestra, or we can do a hologram band, but I'd rather have a real band, plus I need someone to decorate the main ballroom in pink and green pastel colours, nothing too garish. I'll get Julie on the food. She will need a caterer to help her, and I'll call her sister Jasmine Travers and her parents. We'll start the party at eight o'clock, and the band will start at nine o'clock so that people can dance. I'll call Grace's secretary Maya and get her to email all of Grace's friends and employees. This is getting to be a lot of people, but it is a big deal, and I want everyone to have a good time. You can bring your new girlfriend that you are so secretive about. Is her name Brigitte, or did I hear that wrong?"

Thom says, "Yes, her name is Brigitte, and I like her a lot, but it's not serious yet, but I would like to bring her. I'll take care of everything else. Oh, we should hire extra help for valet parking and security. The caterers will have their own servers; some might be androids, so they won't steal anything."

John talks to Julie about the party. She replies, "You are going to propose to Grace, that is great! I love her. I have a good friend, Natalie, who has a catering business and her chef, Rolf, is really good—no—excellent. It's called All Nations Organic Catering. I went to a dinner party she catered, and it was fantastic. We could have chicken, fish, beef, bison, lamb, curried dishes, vegetarian, Ukrainian, light appetizers, and smaller meals for the children. Maybe wraps?"

John thinks for a moment and then says, "Maybe we should simplify the menu so that it won't be too heavy. Otherwise, people won't feel like dancing."

Julie replies, "I'll have her put a menu together for your approval. What about kids? Are kids welcome?"

"God, you think of everything. Yes, kids are very welcome. I want kids here. They are so cute when they get dancing around," John says.

"I'll have Natalie put an adult menu and a kid's menu together," Julie says.

"What about a birthday cake? It would be great to have one shaped like a 1957 Chevy like her car. It must be green on the bottom and white on top with 'Happy Birthday Grace' written on it. Have the hood and trunk made of chocolate cake, the fenders made of vanilla cake, and the roof made of lemon cake and a crunchy base," John says.

"I'll get Natalie started on designing that cake; I know she has built some incredible cakes for other people more extensive than that, like a whole street scene, so I know she can handle a car cake."

"I also want a big band that can play songs from the 1940s to the present day and a lot of 1970s music like Stevie Wonder, Jimmy Buffet, Ray Charles, and some later stuff like Steely Dan. I'll get Thom to search for a band like that. Hopefully, he can find one in time for the party. I'll tell him to pay them double what they get for a gig and free food. I also want to sit in with them and have some friends play with them, like Jenny Olson's boyfriend, Rick Sumner. He plays in a band and is an excellent guitar player. Well, I have to phone Grace's secretary, Grace's sister Jasmine, her parents Shana and Joseph, and I also have to call Mike."

John goes to his office and makes all the calls to Maya, Jasmine, Grace's parents, and Mike. He tells Mike about the birthday party for Grace and that he is going to propose to her. He tells Mike to invite all his R and D people, the dealership staff, and all the mechanics from Trosky Custom Vehicles.

"That's great, John. Grace is the right woman for you. She will keep you out of trouble, and she has a brilliant mind. Everyone seems to like her, and Gladys, Jackie, and I like her too," Mike says.

"Thank you for saying that. I fell in love with her as soon as I met her at the charity auction, so I have Gladys to thank for introducing her to me," John says.

"Gladys is beside me and says that she wants to help decorate the ballroom, order some flowers, and just help to organize the party," Mike says.

"Tell her that I would really appreciate her doing that. Well, take care. I have to go. Goodbye."

Thom enters the room and says, "Hi, John. I've been working on getting a band, and I've narrowed it down to five bands, but I'm leaning toward a band called the Centurions Big Band. The band leader, Duke Mingus, plays a mean guitar. They have a horn section and a great female lead singer called Roxy, and three women background singers. They can play everything from Sinatra to Jimmy Buffet to blues and jazz."

"Do they have a YouTube video or demo tape, and are they available for Saturday?" John asks.

"Yes, they have a YouTube video. We can look at it now if you like. Yes, they are available for Saturday, and a practice for Friday if you want to sit in with them."

"Okay, let's look at it now," John says.

They look at a video of them playing a jazz version of Ella Fitzgerald's version of "A Tisket a Tasket" with Roxy singing the lead. John says, "Wow, they are great. Do you agree, Thom?"

"You bet, John; I'll book them."

"Pay them double what they get, and tell them I want to sit in with them on Friday."

Thom says, "I'll call them right now. I'm working on the security also. It will be in place for Saturday. I'll hire some of the guys from our old regiment. I'll also get a valet service together."

Grace arrives at John's place and rushes into his office. He is checking his files on his computer to see if they found anything on Ken Leung's accounts. She walks up to him, grabs him out of the chair, and drags him into the bedroom, saying, I missed you, Mr. Bond, James Bond, and you owe me an ass-kissing."

In his Bond voice, John says, "I don't know who you are, miss, and I don't know what you are talking about."

She starts taking her clothes off and says, "Maybe this will refresh your memory." She finishes stripping, then takes his clothes off, and says, "Now, I remember you; I never forget a body like yours, but I still don't know your name." She throws him on the bed, jumps on him, looks down, and says, "Your little friend down there seems to remember me."

"Colonel Wai Lin, is that you?" John says.

She grabs his manhood and says, "No, guess again, and if you get my name wrong, your friend won't be entering the tunnel of love."

"Now, I remember; it's Grace, isn't it? I'm sorry, I have jet lag, Miss Grace." Then he cups her breasts and starts kissing her, and his friend enters her tunnel of love. After wildly making up for lost time for a half-hour, they fall onto their backs, breathing heavily. In his Bond voice, John says, "How could I ever forget your name, Miss Moneypenny?" They both laugh, and Grace punches him in the arm. "By the way, Grace, what are you doing on Saturday?"

"I have to go Winnipeg to check on the refitting of my building. Why would you ask that, John?"

"Do you have to go that day? Can't you go on Monday?"

"Well, maybe I could, but I'd need a really good reason to stay here."

He starts to talk and sputters, and she says, "You should see the look on your face, John. I got you! I know it's my birthday and that you are having a party for me here."

"All right, who told you? I swore everyone to secrecy."

"Well, John, when you use my secretary to email everyone in my employ, you should tell her that I'm on that list."

"Wow, you really had me going there for a minute. But you will love me when you find out what else I brought you back from Paris, and I'm not telling no matter how hard you beg or what sexual favours you offer me. Damn, I shouldn't have said that last part; that is my kryptonite."

"Don't worry, John, some things should be kept secret, like birthday gifts or Christmas gifts. Sex is my kryptonite also. Oops, I shouldn't have said that. Have mercy, Mr. Bond, James Bond."

"I love the way you say that; it's like you've seen *Tomorrow Never Dies,*" John says.

"I have seen it; that's why I say it that way. When I'm a year older, will you still love me?" she asks.

"I told you before; I love older women. And don't hit me again; it hurts. That's my wounded arm, so hit the other one. Oh, I owe you a foot rub or two, I guess since I couldn't do it from Paris."

"I'm glad you have a foot fetish. My aching feet thank you."

"I never thought of it as a foot fetish as I took a course in reflexology years ago, but you do have cute feet. He starts massaging her feet as they sit on the couch naked. Chrissy saunters in, looks up at them, and meows. John says, "It must be dinnertime. Let's go down for dinner and see what Julie has for us. Please don't let on that you know about the party. A lot of people, including Julie, are working hard on this because they love you."

"My lips are sealed."

They go down for dinner and see Julie and Savana setting the table. Julie says, "Oh, I'm glad you are here; I was just going to call you."

John says, "Hi, Julie and Savana, what have you prepared for dinner tonight?"

"I've prepared a small salad with Savana's help and spaghetti with meatballs and garlic bread."

"I helped my mom make the salad and put garlic butter on the bread, and I helped set the table," Savana says.

"Yes, she's been a good girl. Would you like some wine with dinner?"

"Yes, I think a Cabernet would go good with the spaghetti. Is that okay with you, Grace?" John asks.

"Yes, that sounds perfect."

"I'll go get the wine," John says. He goes into the kitchen and brings back the wine, and pours it into their glasses. Julie brings in the food, and they start eating.

"John tells me he is having a party here on Saturday," Grace says.

John almost chokes on his food and starts to talk, but Grace continues, "To celebrate his recovery from his wounds. Do you need any help with anything?"

John says, "Grace, you're too busy with all your businesses and our new clothing company. I don't want to stress you out. Besides, we have everything covered between me, Julie, and Thom. Thom will get a live band that plays old big band tunes from the 1940s, like Frank Sinatra, Aretha Franklin, Glenn Miller, and the Dorsey Brothers, and I just may sit in with them at the piano. You haven't heard me play the piano yet, have you?" Chrissy enters the room, looking for food dropped by Savana. She then jumps up on Grace's lap, and John says, "Traitor. Well, Grace, I guess she is your cat now."

"I think she just wants my last meatball, and yours are all gone," Grace says.

"She just ate, but if you give it to her, put the plate on the floor; I don't want her to get used to eating on the table, especially in front of company. My mother would be horrified at any animal on the table, and she loved cats."

"My mother is the same way. Did you hear that, Chrissy? No eating on the table," Grace says and puts her plate on the floor. Chrissy jumps on it, eats the meatball, and licks the plate. She then jumps up on John's lap, and John says, "I take it back, Chrissy; I know you still love me because my plate is empty. I love you too. Oh, Julie, where is Thom?" John asks.

"He is either on the phone or on the computer, trying to find a band and other stuff for the party," Julie says.

"Good, make sure he doesn't starve to death, so save him some spaghetti."

CHAPTER FORTY-SIX

"Okay, Grace, do you want to try to beat me at a video game or go down and shoot some blasters?" John asks.

"I want to beat you in a video car racing game, and when I beat you, you will play the piano as my reward," Grace says.

They go to the game room and start the Gran Turismo game on an arcade-style gaming machine with a steering wheel and racing seat.

"I always play as Ayrton Senna; you can play as whoever you want," John says.

"I'll play as myself; can I do that?" she asks.

"Sure, but I'll pick the track. Spa is really good and fast, while some of the others are harder, like Nürburgring. It's very long and frustrating. In real life, a lot of drivers were killed there."

She says, "I do love a spa day."

"You do have a sense of humour, graceful one. Now, we pick cars. GT cars are the most fun and easy to handle. Let's use Porsche GT3s," John says.

They start the race. Grace accelerates ahead of John but goes too fast around the first right-hand turn, and John gets ahead of her. He blasts up the long hill up to 190 mph and slows for the S-turns, but she catches up to him. He punches it through the short straight and into the next S-turns and slows down, but not enough. He goes off the track as Grace passes him and goes up through the next straight and into more S-turns. John catches up to her as they approach the final S-turn onto the straightaway, but she beats him by three-thousandths of a second.

"That was fun. Do you want to do that again?" she asks.

"How about a ten-lap race? I'm used to a longer race," John says.

"Another time. You promised me you would play the piano for me, and then I can reward you with kinky sex," she says.

"How can I refuse that? Let's go to the main ballroom where the piano is on the stage."

They go and sit down at the piano, and John says, "Do you remember The Beatles?"

She says, "Is that the group Paul McCartney was in last century?"

"Yes, they recorded a vinyl album called *Rubber Soul* and did a song called 'Drive my Car.' You can join in on the harmonies if you want."

John starts to play and sing in McCartney's voice. Grace joins in on the chorus, and she sounds really good!

"Wow, you are a great singer, Grace!"

They finish, and Grace says, "This is fun; we make a great team."

"We should do this at the party," John suggests.

"I don't know about that. It's one thing to do this on our own, but in front of a bunch of people, no."

"Yes, but we'll be drunk before we sing, and you are great. I have played in front of a crowd before, and once I was relaxed, I felt like a Rock Star. Okay, I won't pressure you, but I plan on playing the piano with the band, and if I see you are getting into it, I'm going to drag you up on stage." He switches to his

John Lennon voice and sings "Imagine," and Grace joins in again.

John laughs and says, "Let's face it, Grace, you've got the bug now; I don't think I'm going to have to do much dragging."

CHAPTER FORTY-SEVEN

Bill Auger finally gets a call on his encrypted satellite phone, and it is Pavel Romaniuk.

"Mr. Auger, I have another job for you. You know Abel Zalinski, the Ukrainian oligarch?"

Bill says, "Yes, I'm vaguely familiar with him. He lives in Vancouver in one of those ugly high-rises, so?"

"He is encroaching into my territory, my casinos. I want you to kill his daughter Carol."

Bill says, "I didn't know he had a daughter. Where does she work?"

Pavel laughs and says, "Work? She is only six years old."

"Pavel, have you ever seen the movie *The Transporter*?"

"Yes, what's that got to do with anything?"

"The main character played by Jason Statham had rules like no names, exact weight of package, etcetera. Well, I have rules also. My number one rule is that I don't kill children, and if you try to kill this girl or hire someone else to kill her, I will kill you. Understand? I don't want anything to do with you anymore," Bill says.

"You will regret this, and I will have her killed. Screw you," Pavel says and cuts off the phone.

Bill looks at the phone and says, "Screw you too. Now, I have to kill you for free. If this bastard wants me to kill children, he is going to suffer for even asking me."

CHAPTER FORTY-EIGHT

John says, "I'm going to check with Thom to see if he got that band, and then let's go to bed."

He calls Thom on the intercom, and Thom says, "Yes, I finally got the Centurions Big Band booked for Saturday. They can play anything from Duke Ellington, Frank Sinatra, the Beatles, the Beach Boys, Jimmy Buffet—you name it. The band leader is named Duke Mingus. We saw the video, and they are really good, but they are expensive."

"Don't even tell me; money is no object. Just hire them at double their price and give them a bonus if they really shine at the party. Tell them that I'm going to jam with them on piano and possibly Grace if I can drag her on stage, and that is non-negotiable. Also, tell them that we have a huge ballroom and a stage for them and a great Bose sound system unless they want to bring their own."

"Okay, boss. It's as good as done. I also have the security and valet parking set up. All the security guys are ex-military and vetted. You might know some of them."

"Thanks, Thom, you're doing a great job. Is your girlfriend coming? I'd really like to meet her."

"Yes, she is coming. She is obsessed as to what to wear."

Grace pipes in and says, "Just tell her to wear a nice dress. Some people will dress formally, but semi-formal is fine. We just want everyone to have a good time to celebrate John's recovery and to be comfortable."

"Thank you, Grace, for clarifying that. I forgot about the dress code. I just thought it was formal. Well, if that's all, then have a good night," Thom says.

John and Grace both say goodnight and then head to John's bedroom for some passionate love-making.

CHAPTER FORTY-NINE

Bill Auger is still angry but has switched to assassin-planning mode. He calls an associate and tells him to warn Abel Zalinski that Pavel Romaniuk has put a hit on his daughter Carol and to keep her in the house or somewhere safe. He also finds out that Pavel Romaniuk is in Vancouver and gets his address. He goes to his storage unit and retrieves his special combination sniper rifle. He goes to Pavel's mansion and sets up on the rise about one hundred yards from his mansion, and waits.

CHAPTER FIFTY

John says to Grace, "Sweetheart, have you ever been to Graceland?"

"What? No, I haven't been to Graceland. Why?"

"Do you have your black lace undies here? I have a surprise for you if you do. Let's do a little role-playing, okay?"

"Yes, I have my black lace undies here. Oh, I think I know where this is going. Let's go change."

John comes out dressed in an Elvis-style white jumpsuit and oversized sunglasses, and she is dressed like Priscilla. "Elvis, where have you been? I've been waiting for you all day," Grace says.

"Sorry, Priscilla, darlin'. I was in the studio recording, and then I got stuck signing autographs. I'll make it up to you." John then starts to sing "Love Me Tender" to her as he lifts her dress over her head and takes the white silk scarf from around his neck, and drapes it around her neck. He undoes his jumpsuit and unhooks her black lace bra. He fondles her big luscious breasts as he continues singing. She reaches out and pulls his jumpsuit all the way down. He kicks his white shoes off and steps out of the jumpsuit. He pulls her panties down and off and breathlessly says, "Keep the garter belt and silk stockings on." He sings toward her crouch, and it becomes a humming vibration as he places his mouth right against her sensitive parts and keeps singing.

"Elvis, I hope you are getting the words right . . . Oh my God! I think I'm going to cum! Oh my God." She then starts vibrating and has the most intense orgasm she ever had. She then collapses onto John. He grabs her, and they fall back onto his bed, and John says, "Did you enjoy that, darlin'? I tried my best to make it up to you."

She catches her breath and says, "Oh my God, John. That was earth-shattering. I've never had such a powerful orgasm in my life. Where did you learn to do that? You have to do that again."

"I just thought of it now and wondered if it would work." He then crawls on top of her, and they have another orgasm. A bit later, they shower, go to bed, and cuddle as Chrissy comes in and jumps up on the bed, circles, and curls up at their feet.

CHAPTER FIFTY-ONE

Saturday night, at around ten o'clock, Bill Auger sees Pavel Romaniuk leave his mansion and walk to his limo with his bodyguards. Auger raises his rifle, sights Pavel's neck, and fires a tiny dart into his neck. The tiny dart contains a combination of the malaria virus and a very slow-acting poison that causes extreme pain, hallucinations and ends in a heart attack.

"Take that, you child killer. Rot in hell!" Bill Auger says.

Pavel feels a sting in his neck and believes a bee had stung him. He goes to a casino and drinks and gambles. In the middle of a game of Blackjack, he starts getting confused and loses four hundred thousand dollars in one hand. Then he continues to lose until he is down one million dollars. He's sweaty and begins to feel nauseated, then pukes on the Blackjack table. His bodyguard Frank says, "Boss, are you okay? I think we should take you to a hospital; you don't look so good."

"You know I hate hospitals; just take me home. I probably got food poisoning from this dump," Pavel says.

Frank loads him into the limo and takes him home. Pavel develops a fever, then chills, and he starts hallucinating. His wife Stella puts cold cloths on his forehead and gives him a painkiller. He starts feeling more pain, like his head will explode, and punches his wife in the stomach. She yells to Frank to get in the bedroom and runs out. She calls an ambulance as Frank tries to calm him down.

"Frank, give me a shot of heroin; the pain is killing me. Frank opens Pavel's safe and gets a shot of heroin. He ties him off and shoots it into his arm. The shot dulls the pain, and he says, "No ambulance, Frank. Pay them and send them away."

Frank goes out and pays off the ambulance attendants a bonus of one thousand dollars, telling them it was a false alarm. Pavel falls asleep. He wakes up several hours later, sweating and screaming. He jumps out of bed and runs to the bathroom, and vomits blood. His wife Stella comes in and tries to talk him into going to the hospital.

"I hate hospitals; they kill you in there. Give me some painkillers, Stella." She hauls him back to bed and gives him some strong painkillers, and puts cold compresses on his forehead and chest. He falls asleep again. He wakes up at four o'clock in the morning, sweating, and sneaks outside as it is cold out and he wants to cool down. He runs into the bushes and collapses.

An hour later, Frank finds him and brings him back into the house and puts him back in bed.

CHAPTER FIFTY-TWO

Grace and John wake up on Sunday morning, make love in the shower, and then go down for breakfast. Julie greets them with a pot of coffee as Savana walks in, followed by Chrissy.

"Good morning, Uncle Tiny and Grace. I've just been playing with Chrissy. I've been trying to teach her to fetch, but she doesn't seem interested in it," Savana says.

John says, "That's because she is a cat. Dogs will fetch, but cats won't; that's just the way they are. I had a dog when I was a little boy. His name was Buddy, and he would fetch and run into the lake, but cats don't like water."

"Oh, I didn't know that. Mom, can I have pancakes and eggs?" Savana says.

"Yes, dear, you can have pancakes," Julie says.

"That's a great idea. I'll have pancakes too, and bacon and eggs," Grace says.

"I'll have the same as Grace," John says.

They finish their breakfast, and John says, "Grace, let's take the horses out for some exercise and get some fresh air."

"Good idea, John. I've been in my stuffy office all week."

They go upstairs to change, and John's phone rings. He looks and sees that it's Chuck Sidhu. He answers, "Hi, Chuck, what's up?"

"Randy Chan just called me and said he got the audio cleaned up from the nanny-cam from Ken Leung's murder scene. We can hear Bill Auger, saying that Pavel Romaniuk sent him. The captain is working on a warrant, and he wants us to go to Romaniuk's mansion tomorrow and bring him in. We meet at 8 a.m. in the main conference room."

"Finally, a break in the case. Okay, I'll pick you up in the morning," John says.

He meets up with Grace outside and says, "Grace, we caught a break in Ken Leung's murder. The nanny-cam picked up the killer saying this guy Pavel Romaniuk hired him to kill Ken. We are going to get a warrant and pick him up tomorrow morning."

"That's great, John. His wife and daughters will be relieved to know who killed him and why he was killed. Let's go riding."

They ride out to the pond and sit on the bench next to the pond. John says, "You know, Grace, tomorrow and probably most of the week, I'm going to be busy with this case. We have the killer on video saying Pavel sent him to kill Ken, but we don't know why, and my team will have a lot of work to do."

"I know what you're going to say; you and I won't see much of each other this week. Well, I think it gives me a chance to go to Winnipeg and supervise the conversion of the Bodyguard Clothing building and start training the staff," Grace says.

John replies, "That's a great idea, and we can have the hordes of people work on your 'surprise' party sooner than if you were around, not that I don't want you around. When we put our heads together, we make a great team and get things done. No wonder I love you. So, when are you coming back, Friday night?" John asks.

"Yes, Friday afternoon or evening. I wouldn't want to miss my birthday party after all the trouble you went through. I'll call you during the week and let you know how things are progressing. I want to start designing some fashionable

Bodyguard Clothing. We can start making coats for your squad soon, but you need to get me their sizes and what type of fabric they want. Maybe they can all look like leather so that it looks like a uniform."

"Okay, I'll get their sizes and their preferences for fabric type. Let's go back to the barn. I feel like brushing Steely Dan. It's a soothing thing to do; it's like a meditation. Do you want to brush Adele?"

"Yes, I like grooming my horse sometimes," Grace says.

They ride back to the barn, and Autrey takes off the saddles and rubs them with saddle soap. John and Grace start brushing the horses, and the horses whine softly, as they are enjoying the brushing and the attention. John says, "Sometimes, I like to feed them myself. Once in a while, I give them oats with a splash of brandy. They love it!"

"You're kidding, right?" Grace says.

"No, I'm serious. An old cowboy named Roy told me about this years ago. He said it makes their coats shinier too," John says.

"Then I think I'll try that with Cher and Sonny sometime."

"I knew you had a horse named Cher, but you have one named Sonny also?"

"Well, someone has to keep Cher happy, and he is a stallion," Grace says.

"I'll 'stallion' you in a minute," John says, then grabs Grace and kisses her hard on the mouth.

"Oh, no, I'm not doing it in a barn; it's cold in here. Let's put Steely Dan and Adele in their stalls and go back to the house. Let's use the hollo room, and you can program it to your delight, John."

"You get the best ideas, Grace. How about a beach that's nice and warm? We could even get a tan?"

They go into the hollo room, and John programs a beach scene at a shore with no other people, a bar, and a blanket.

"We can strip down and get a tan from these special lights, and no one will bother us. Do you want a Mai-tai, a Chi-Chi, tequila sunrise or a margarita and some Jimmy Buffet?" John asks.

"Yes, let's have some margaritas, and I love Jimmy Buffet. Can you sing like Jimmy Buffet?" Grace asks.

"Yes, but first, let's have an android bartender mix our drinks. Computer, bring in an android bartender and play Jimmy Buffet's 'Margaritaville.' Now, we can drink and refresh my memory of the lyrics and dance naked. The bartender doesn't care if we are naked."

They sip their drinks and move to the music, then they get up and dance naked to the music. They swivel their hips and dance and sway to the music, then John says, "Computer, replay 'Margaritaville' without Jimmy Buffet." John sings along to the music in Jimmy's voice and sings to Grace as they dance.

She looks up at him and says, "You are incredible," and pulls him down to the blanket. They start to make love as he continues to sing to her.

He stops singing and increases his thrusting into her, and she thrusts back at him until they both have a super-strong simultaneous orgasm and yell, "Oh my God!"

They roll apart, breathing heavily and sweating, and John says, "I love you, Grace. That was incredible!"

"Ditto," she says, and they laugh.

"Let's hit the shower and change for dinner; it must be dinnertime by now."

"Yes, I think we worked up an appetite, I'm starving," Grace says.

They pick up their clothes, and John says, "Computer, end and save program."

CHAPTER FIFTY-THREE

They shower and go down for dinner. Julie and Thom are sitting at the table drinking coffee as Grace and John enter the dining room.

John says, "Hi, Thom and Julie, what's for dinner?"

Julie answers, "A beef roast with extra garlic in it, and carrots, broccoli, and mashed potatoes. Where did you guys get such a suntan?" Julie says.

"In the hollo room. John programmed a beach scene, and you can get a nice tan from the special lights without burning."

"John, can Savanna and I use that room before we go to Hawaii? It will save us from getting sunburned," Julie says.

John says, "Sure, but I will have to make one adjustment to the program, so let me know when you want to use it."

"Great. The roast is ready, but I want it to cool for ten minutes before I carve it," Julie says.

Just then, Savana walks in, carrying Chrissy and crying, "Chrissy hurt herself; I think she stepped on something sharp and cut her left front paw."

Grace says, "Bring her to me. I used to work for a veterinarian. John, do you have a first-aid kit and a healing wand? She has a small cut on her paw. We just need to clean the cut, disinfect it, and use a healing wand to seal the wound."

Thom gets up and says, "I'll get the kit and wand; I know where they are. Don't worry, Savana, Chrissy will be okay." He leaves and comes back with the kit, and Grace fixes Chrissy's cut paw. Savana sits beside Grace and watches her work on Chrissy and is amazed as the cut closes when she uses the wand.

"That wand thing is magic. Thank you, Grace," Savana says.

Grace hands Chrissy back to her, saying, "See, she's good as new. Give her a bowl of milk to settle her down."

Savana gives Chrissy a bowl of milk, and Julie comes in with the roast and vegetables and goes back for the mashed potatoes. "Savana, go wash your hands and have some dinner, sweetheart," Julie says.

Everyone starts to dig in, and Chrissy starts begging for food from Grace. Julie says, "Grace, this time, I thought ahead and cooled off some roast for Chrissy. I'll go get her plate."

John looks at Julie and says, "Grace and I will have coffee, as we indulged a bit in Margaritaville in the hollo room. By the way, Julie, Grace is going to Winnipeg tomorrow for most of the week to set up the new company, but she will be back by Friday, and I'm going to be busy with this murder case most of the week, so my hours are going to be erratic."

Julie thinks for a moment, then says, "Maybe I could make you something I can serve quickly, like a casserole or spaghetti, something like that."

"That's a great idea, spaghetti and meatballs is my favourite, and you could do casseroles too."

Grace says, "John, I'm going to go home after dinner. I have to pack my clothes and get my notes and drafts for the building plans together, and I may take my secretary with me, so I have calls to make."

"Well, you gotta do what you gotta do. I have notes to make myself. I'll walk you to the door and have Jeffery drive you home. I'll call you during the week and get those coat sizes and fabric types to you from my squad," John says.

They share one more passionate kiss, and Grace leaves. John goes upstairs to his office to make notes on the Pavel case. He goes to bed, and Chrissy curls up beside him.

He has a restless night, but he gets up in the morning, has breakfast, and picks up Chuck on the way to the station.

CHAPTER FIFTY-FOUR

John says, "Chuck, Randy Chan called me yesterday and said that he cleaned up the audio, and the killer said that Pavel Romaniuk sends his regards."

They walk into the bullpen, and John says, "I have a few announcements to make that you will like, squad. You are all getting new laser, knife, and bulletproof coats that my company is making at no cost to you because after taking that hit with a blaster, I want my squad to be safe. I need your sizes. We can make these coats look like leather, cotton, wool, or cashmere. Email your sizes to my computer and your preference of choice of material and colour. I don't want us looking like an SS squad. They will be ready in a few weeks. The factory is being built as we speak. Also, I am having a dinner and dance party on Saturday as it's my girlfriend Grace Chan's birthday. A sit-down dinner starts at eight o'clock and dancing at nine o'clock. Presents are optional, as I know all your salaries. I just want you all to show up and have a good time. The dress code is casual, no monkey suits, okay? Also, we are carrying out a search warrant on Pavel Romaniuk's mansion today. We know he hired the man who killed Ken Leung. I want everyone who doesn't have a hot case in on this. Let's meet in my office in five minutes."

Chuck Sidhu, Randy Chan, Eddie Bennetti, and Larry Cornburra come into the office, and John tells everyone their jobs. The captain sends him the warrant on his computer, and he prints it out. His desk phone rings, and he puts it on speaker. "Dispatch, Lieutenant John Trosky. Suspicious death and possible hazmat situation at 3315 Riverside Drive."

"Shit, that's Pavel Romaniuk's address. Don't tell me he's dead. Well, we have to go down there anyway. Wait, I want to call Luci Ryan first and see if she is there and if it is a hazmat situation." John dials Luci and says, "Hello, Doctor Ryan, it's John Trosky. Are you at Pavel Romaniuk's residence?"

"Yes, and he is dead. I've scanned his bedroom for viruses, and it is clear. It looks like malaria or poison. He bled through his nose and mouth, and he looks like he saw the devil."

"What do you mean by the devil?"

"I mean, the look on his face. He looks like he died of fright or extreme pain. It's safe for you to come in. I just need to test his blood to see what kind of poison killed him. Come join the party and bring your friends. Ten-four."

CHAPTER FIFTY-FIVE

John puts on his black Stetson hat, and he and the squad rush down to the scene of the crime.

John and Chuck turn on their recorders and enter the mansion. John tells everyone else to record their interviews and the scene. John enters the bedroom with Chuck and says, "Hi, Luci, are you sure it's safe in here? Oh, God, there's so much blood."

"It's safe, but not for this guy. Do you see what I mean about him seeing the devil?" Luci says.

"Yes, he looks like he could scare the devil with that look on his face," John says and leans over the body. He notices something and says, "Luci, do you have an LED penlight on you?"

She replies, "Yes, here, why?"

"There is something on the side of his neck. See this?"

She looks with the penlight and says, "You have great vision. It looks like a small puncture like someone injected him or maybe hit him with a dart. He must have a bodyguard, being an oligarch and all." She adds, "There is a guy named Frank who looks like he could bench press a Prius. I bet he is the main bodyguard."

"I should go interview him. Let me know when you have the bloodwork results. Do you have a time of death?" John asks.

"Yes, 7:15 a.m. today, Monday the 24th of April, though I think he suffered most of the night before he died."

John asks, "So, you think he contracted this disease possibly yesterday or the day before?"

"It's hard to say at this point. I'll need to do more tests. Maybe his bodyguard noticed something unusual."

John thinks and says, "Okay, Chuck, you are the sensitive one. You go interview his wife Stella, and I'll go interview Frank the bodyguard."

John finds Frank in the living room and says, "Frank, what is your last name?"

"Frank Mannetti?"

"Mr. Mannetti, I'm Lieutenant John Trosky of the Vancouver homicide squad, and I'm going to read you your rights as a witness in my investigation, okay?"

Frank looks puzzled and says, "Yes, I'm not under arrest, am I?"

"No, I just told you that you are a witness." John then reads him his right. "How long have you worked for Mr. Pavel Romaniuk?"

"About four years as a bodyguard and a driver."

"When did you notice Mr. Romaniuk get sick?"

"Saturday night, the 22nd, at about ten o'clock. I drove him to the casino, and he was playing Blackjack and drinking. Then he threw up on the table, which really pissed off the dealer. That shit is really hard to clean off a velvet cloth covering."

"Do you think he got food poisoning?"

"No, he didn't eat anything, and he never drank any booze unless he saw it poured from a sealed bottle."

John continues, "Did you see anybody put something in his drink at any time?"

"No, and I watched him play cards the entire time. He is a shitty player, and he lost a lot of money that night."

"When you were leaving the mansion, did you notice anything unusual happen on the way to the limo?"

"No . . . wait a minute, I remember he slapped at his neck like a mosquito had bitten him, but it's too cold out for bugs this time of year, so I thought that was weird," Frank says.

"Which side of his neck did he slap, the right side or the left?" John asks.

Frank thinks for a moment, then says, "The right side because he turned right to get in the left side of the car. The left side of the car was close to the house, and he was always afraid of getting shot."

"So, what happened when he got home? Did he get sicker?" John asks.

"Yes, he started sweating and got a headache. He seemed to get a lot sicker and was in a lot of pain. I don't want to get in trouble here, but I sort of gave him an injection of a heavy painkiller, if you know what I mean," Frank says.

"Look, I'm not here to bust anyone for drugs. I'm just trying to figure out a timeline for when and how he got sick and what killed him."

In the opulent living room, containing old wood panelling, red velvet curtains, expensive sculptures, and old paintings, Chuck interviews Stella Romaniuk.

She is sitting on an antique red and gold couch that would cost a year of Chuck's salary. She is crying and repeating, "Why did he die? I don't understand."

"Mrs. Romaniuk, I'm Detective Chuck Sidhu of the Vancouver homicide squad, and we are trying to figure out what happened to your husband. Why he got sick and died. I'm now going to interview you on record as a witness, so I must read you your rights." He reads her the revised Miranda rights and says, "Tell me what happened when your husband returned home from the casino. Was he sick?"

"Yes, he looked pale and was sweating a lot. I put him to bed and put cold cloths on his forehead as he had a fever. I called an ambulance, but he refused to go to the hospital, and he had Frank send the ambulance away. He even ran outside to cool off, but Frank found him and brought him back. Frank gave him a shot of something from his safe, and it knocked him out for a while. He later woke up screaming, and I ran in and gave him some painkillers. He still refused to go to the hospital. I should have pushed harder; maybe they could have saved him. I feel guilty about that, but he was a very stubborn man," she says.

"You shouldn't feel guilty about that; it was his decision not to go to the hospital. The medical examiner will do an autopsy on him today and check his blood for toxins. Did your husband have any enemies or someone who would want to hurt him?" Chuck asks.

"My husband was no angel, but he didn't tell me anything about his business dealings, and I didn't want to know about his business, so I don't know who would want him dead. Frank might know something about his business, but you would have to ask him."

"Did your husband have a computer or a cell phone?" Chuck asks.

"Pavel wouldn't know how to operate a computer; he was old school, but he had a cell phone. It's probably in his room."

"I'll check on that later. So, who found him deceased this morning, and what time was that?" "I found him. We sleep in separate bedrooms because he keeps long hours and I like to go to bed early. He is usually up by seven-thirty or eight o'clock, and I knew he was sick, so I went to check on him just after eight o'clock and saw all the blood around his head and screamed. Then Frank came rushing in, checked for a pulse, and said he was dead. Then he called 911," she says.

CHAPTER FIFTY-SIX

John says, "Who found Pavel deceased this morning, and what time was it?"

Frank says, "Stella found him; I think it was just after eight o'clock. I heard her screaming in his bedroom and ran in to see what was wrong. That's when I saw blood all around his head. He had bled from his nose and mouth. I figured he was dead, but I checked for a pulse anyway. Nothing, and he was cold. I tried to calm Stella down and then took her into the living room and called 911. Then some cops—err—police officers came, then some medical chick doctor came, and then you guys."

"Okay, Frank, let's go outside. I want you to show me where you and Mr. Romaniuk were standing by the limo when he slapped at his neck," John says.

They go outside and stand by the limo, and John asks, "Is this exactly where the car was parked?"

"Yes, see the tire marks? It's where I park it all the time," Frank says.

"And Mr. Romaniuk was standing at the left rear door. I want you to stand exactly how he was standing."

Frank stands in the spot and turns a bit to the left. "He was standing exactly like this, right here."

John continues, "Don't move," and he stands by Frank. He then looks to the corner of the yard and sees some bushes there. He pulls out his video-cell phone and calls Randy Chan. "Randy, where are you?"

"I'm in Mr. Romaniuk's bedroom. I have his cell phone, but he doesn't have a computer."

"Come out the front door and over to me by the limo. I need you out here," John says.

Randy comes out, and John says, "Does your blaster have a laser light on it?"

"Yes, it does."

"Stand behind me and point it over Frank's shoulder toward that corner of the yard, but put your safety on. Does your scope read the distance?" John asks.

"Yes, let's see; it's reading 102.5 yards," Randy says.

"Let's go look over by those bushes for some disturbance. Frank, go back in the house and send one of the photographers to us by those bushes. I think we are going to find some footprints out there."

John and Randy walk to the bushes in the corner of the lot and start searching for any signs of disturbance. John says, "Let's turn our recorders on." John goes in behind the bushes and spots some footprints and broken branches. "Randy, look at this. I want you to record this area too. Oh, here's the photographer. What is your name, officer?"

"I'm Officer Mat Fraser, part of the CSI team. What do you want me to photograph, lieutenant?"

"I want you to photograph these footprints and these broken branches."

"Okay, I need to put my ruler down beside the footprints to get the shoe size, and the pattern can tell us what brand they are." He then takes pictures of the prints and says, "This broken branch here is thick enough to possibly get some fingerprints from. We should get Officer Dianne West out here. She is the best fingerprint person we have."

They get Officer West to the bush, and she looks at the branch and says, "I think the best way to get any prints off this branch is to cut it off and put it into the Krazy Glue fumigation chamber in the lab. I'll put it in a paper bag to transport it. Let's take this other branch too."

"Okay, I want to video you cutting those branches off and putting them in the paper evidence bags," John says and starts filming. "Okay, Mat and Randy, let's backtrack through this bush to see if we can find out where he came in."

They follow the footprints to an opening of a small dirt lot and find tire tracks. John looks at Mat and says, "Well, look at this. Tire tracks and footprints. Photograph these, Mat. Do you have a ruler?"

"I never leave home without it, like my . . ."

John pipes in, saying, "American Express Card. Funny."

Mat looks at the tire tracks and checks his hand-held comp. "Lieutenant, these tire tracks were made by an SUV, a Toyota or a Nissan. "You should get some people to canvas the area."

"Yes, carry on, I'm going back in the house to talk to Detective Sidhu and to search Mr. Romaniuk's office. Randy, come back inside the house when you're finished here; I'll need your help searching the office. I think Mr. Romaniuk has a hidden record book somewhere as he doesn't have a computer."

John goes back inside the house and meets up with Chuck Sidhu. He tells Chuck about the evidence they found in the bushes. John says, "I'm now sure that he was shot with a small dart that infected him from someone hiding in those bushes. Maybe it was the assassin, but why would he kill him? Pavel paid him off unless someone paid him to kill Pavel, or maybe he wanted Pavel silenced himself. How was your interview with Stella? Did you learn anything new?"

"She said he got sick on Saturday night after going to the casino, and she was worried enough to send for an ambulance, but Pavel had Frank send it away. It might have saved his life if they could counteract the poison that was in him. He got really sick; he was in a lot of pain and was vomiting. She put cold cloths on him and gave him a few painkillers," Chuck says.

"Yes, and Frank told me he gave him a shot of, quote, a heavy painkiller, unquote, from the safe. Probably heroin. We should open his safe since we have a warrant. We could get Frank Mannetti to open it. If he refuses, I'll scare him with charging him with injecting Pavel with a harmful drug and sending the ambulance away that could have saved his life." Chuck continues, "Stella was the one who found him dead just after eight o'clock this morning. She also said that he was hallucinating and even ran outside once, but Frank found him and brought him back inside. That's about it."

John says, "Let's get Randy and search Pavel's office and bedroom. And get Frank and see if we can get him to open the safe, and ask him if he knows whether Pavel has more than one safe. Pavel is one sneaky bastard."

Chuck goes and brings Randy and Frank into Pavel's office. John says to him, "Frank, I want you to open Pavel's safe. We have a warrant to search this entire house, including any and all safes and compartments."

"Okay, but you said you weren't interested in drugs," Frank says.

"What we are interested in, Frank, are any ledgers Pavel kept pertaining to his business, and whether he has more than one safe," John says.

"This is the only safe I know of; maybe he has more, I don't know."

Frank opens the safe, and John walks over and says, "My recorder is still on; is yours still on, Chuck?"

"Yes."

John finds a big old-fashioned ledger, heroin, cocaine, a stack of hundred-dollar bills, and some stocks and bonds. John exclaims, "As Dirty Harry would say, 'Frank, you made my day!'"

"I don't know anyone named Dirty Harry," Frank says.

John laughs and says, "Never mind, Frank, you can go and check on Stella."

John takes the ledger out of the safe and opens it up, and says, "This thing is written partly in code and probably under shell companies. Randy, see if you can make any sense of this ledger, maybe coordinate it with his cell phone."

"I checked his cell phone, and it's a satellite phone, and it is encrypted, but we should be able to crack it. I'll have to take it to the station to do that. We have some programs there that may work to crack it," Randy says.

"Okay, Randy, take this ledger and the phone back to the station and send Detective Bennetti in here to help us search for another safe or anything else that will help us with this case."

John, Chuck, and Eddie Bennetti go into Pavel's bedroom and search for a hidden compartment or safe. They look behind paintings, check floorboards, and behind couches. John studies the room, looking for anything odd or out of place. He notices one wall is expensive wood panelling and has Russian staking dolls and hand-painted Russian Easter eggs on a glassed-in shelf, hanging on the wall. He says to Chuck, "That's funny; I wouldn't think Pavel would be the type of guy to collect Russian stacking dolls and hand-painted eggs."

"Yes, he doesn't have a sentimental bone in his body," Chuck says.

John runs his hands around the frame of the shelf and finds a button underneath the shelf on the right side. The shelf unlatches and swivels out to the left to reveal a hidden safe with a digital keypad. "Bingo, guys. Look what I found. Do we have any EDD guys here, Chuck?"

"Yes, the new guy, Detective Brad Walinchuk," Chuck says.

"Get him in here, Chuck, and ask him if he can crack a safe."

Chuck brings Detective Walinchuk into the room. He is about five-foot-ten, has blond hair, blue eyes, is slim, and wears glasses with blue plastic frames. He is holding a small black box in his hand. "Lieutenant Trosky, I'm Detective Brad Walinchuk. Did you want me to crack a safe, or was Detective Sidhu joking with me?"

"No, we are not joking. Come over here and check out this safe and see if you can crack it. And please, call me John." He walks over to the safe and says, "It's a Brinkman 6000, and this device I have can crack it in five minutes or less. It's a cheap safe." He puts the digital device on the safe door, as it has a magnet on it, and punches some buttons on it. He stands back and watches the digital readout run through its program. In two minutes, it beeps and unlocks the safe. Brad says, "She's open, John. She was a cheap date."

"Thanks, Brad. I owe you! Now, let's see what's in this safe. Here's a bunch of papers and a second ledger, more stocks, and a lot more money," John says. He takes the papers out and gives some to Chuck, Eddie, and Brad. "He was a smart bastard; almost everything is in his wife's name except an import/export company near the Vancouver docks called Rovel Imports, parts of his first and last names spelled backward, smart. First, let's get that photographer Detective Mat Fraser in here to photograph all these documents, and Detective Walinchuk and I will dig into the financials for Rovel Imports to see if it is a legitimate company. I'll bet he is smuggling drugs or even people. Check all these other companies too. Get Randy to help you, but Rovel is top priority."

Mat Fraser comes in and photographs all the documents, including a three-million-dollar life insurance policy on Pavel. When he finishes, John says, "I'm going to talk to Stella; Chuck come with me and bring those papers, except for the Rovel documents and the ledger. We are confiscating those until we find out if it is legit."

They go into the living room and see Stella sitting there. John approaches her and says, "Misses Romaniuk, did you know your husband had a hidden safe in his bedroom?"

"No, I didn't. What was in there?"

He hands her the papers and says, "His life insurance policy is worth three million dollars, and most of his companies are in your name. These are stocks, and there is a pile of cash in there; it looks like about fifty thousand dollars. So, you don't have to worry about money. The safe is hidden behind that shelf with his collection of Russian stacking dolls and hand-painted eggs. Here is the combination; it spells out Stella. We should have guessed that, but we used a digital device to get into it. I'll show you where the hidden button is to release the hinged shelf."

She looks at the papers and says, "He owned all these companies and put them in my name. Why?"

"My guess is that if anything happened to him, it would save you a lot of trouble getting control of the companies. If I were you, I would get a good lawyer and an accountant to check out these businesses and sell them if you don't want them. We are keeping some documents on an import/export company he owned by the docks; there are some answers we need to know on that, and it was the only business he had in his name, so it may not be a legitimate business. You don't have to worry about that as your name is not attached to that business. I hate to tell you this right now, but we think your husband hired an assassin to kill a real estate agent last week. We can't prosecute your husband since he is deceased, but we are trying to find this assassin and how your husband contacted him. So, we are confiscating his satellite phone and his ledgers. There are two of them. I'm sorry to have to deliver this news, but at least you can put your mind at ease about being financially sound. I also must tell you that I think this assassin murdered your husband, but we won't know for sure until we get his bloodwork and autopsy results. Frank thinks your husband was shot with a poisoned dart as he was getting into the limo on Saturday, but like I said, we need to wait for the autopsy, so I will let you know what we find. Well, we need to get back to the station. The medical examiner has taken Pavel's body away, and as soon as the CSI people are finished here, you can have the bedroom cleaned up. Well, goodbye, Misses Romaniuk. If you have any questions, here is my card."

John checks his Apple watch and says, "Man, it's two o'clock already. Chuck and Eddie, let's stop for lunch at the Retro Diner for a cheeseburger and a real chocolate milkshake and then hit the station."

They get in John's car and blast down to the diner. They get served by a cute blond waitress, flirt with her, eat their cheeseburgers, fries, and shakes, and then walk over to the police station across the street. John says, "Chuck, we need to check into this so-called import/export company by the docks. It smells of probably importing drugs and smuggling people into the country. Start on that now, and dig into their finances. I also need to see Luci Ryan about the toxicity results and whether she found a dart in Pavel's neck. I need to add to my murder board. John goes into his office and adds Pavel's picture to the murder board, and draws an arrow to Bill Auger's picture. He also adds Frank's picture. He sits at his desk and is about to write up his report when he thinks of Grace and calls her on his videophone. He punches in her number, and she appears on the screen, wearing a hard hat. John says, "Hi, Grace, I like your new cute hat and vest.

"Oh, I'm glad you like it. It's my new look as a construction foreman or forewoman, I guess. We are almost finished with the Bodyguard Clothing building's new wing, where the chemical mixing machines are located. Do you want me to wear this outfit in one of your sexual fantasy sessions?"

"Hmm, I was going to say no, but okay, then you can boss me around and take advantage of me. So, yes."

"You are sick, but I would enjoy bossing you around, but no whips and leather, okay?" she says.

"By the way, I can email you the coat sizes and cloth preferences from my squad, but I don't have your email address, and I've been really busy as someone killed Pavel Romaniuk on the weekend, so I've been at his house most of the day."

"Isn't he the one who hired the assassin?" Grace asks.

"Yes, and I think the assassin killed him, but I don't know why."

"Weird. I'm sending you my email address now. Darn . . . someone is yelling for me. Oh, the machines are installed, so Mike's R and D guy Larry Browning can start training men to run them. I've got to run. I love you, John. Take care."

John replies to Grace in Mandarin, saying, "Goodbye, my lotus blossom. I love you."

John dictates his report to his computer and goes to see Luci Ryan. He enters Luci's medium-sized office and notices a big poster of Lucy from Charlie Brown standing behind a wooden lemonade stand with a sign that reads: THE DOCTOR IS IN.

"I absolutely love your poster. That is your type of humour!" John says.

"Yes, Lucy is my hero; she never gives up and has a good sense of humour."

"Have you got the toxicity report back from the lab for old Pavel, and did you dig anything out of his neck?" John asks.

"Yes, I dug this tiny dart out of his neck, and he has a malaria virus and a very nasty poison mixture in his blood. Some of it is from a type of snake only found in Africa, and it has been modified. He must have been in extreme pain when he died. He also had heroin in his system and some over-the-counter painkillers in him. Tell the cleaners to burn those bed sheets and the mattress; they are a biohazard. Also, was there blood in the limo? And call the casino and tell them to decontaminate that table he threw up on."

CHAPTER FIFTY-SEVEN

"Take this dart and put it in the evidence locker and record me giving it to you," Luci says.

"Smile for the camera, Luci. You have a cute smile. By the way, are you coming to my party on Saturday? It's a secret, but the party is for Grace's birthday, and I'm going to have a live band, and you can bring a plus one."

"I wouldn't miss it for the world, John. What time does it start?"

"A sit-down dinner starts at eight o'clock and dancing at nine. Save me a dance, okay? Do you know if they got any fingerprints off those branches?"

"I don't know. You will have to talk to Diane West."

John calls the casino and tells them to decontaminate the blackjack table. He then calls Frank Mannetti and tells him to burn the mattress and get a hazmat team to clean Pavel's bedroom. He then goes to see Diane West.

"Hi, Lieutenant Trosky. I don't have very good news for you. I tried the Ethly2-cyanoacrylate fumigation chamber, commonly known as Krazy Glue, and tried a black light, but there were no fingerprints. He wore leather gloves, but Detective Mat Fraser sent me some pictures of some boot prints, size nine and a common brand, but the treads have some cuts and distinguishing marks on them, so if you find the boots, we can match them. I'm afraid that's all I can do for you now."

"Thanks, Diane, you can call me John, and I want to invite you to a party on Saturday I'm throwing for my girlfriend Grace Chan's birthday if you are not busy. You can bring someone too, and it starts at eight o'clock."

"That sounds great; I'll be there. I don't have a boyfriend right now, but I'll be there. What is your address?"

John smiles and gives her his address. "You can bring one of your girlfriends or whoever. I want lots of people there. You can meet some of my family and my squad."

"I'll bring my girlfriend, Tamie."

"Great, I'll see you there if not sooner if something breaks on the case. I want to get this guy. He has killed three people here and more in Paris over the years. Well, I've got to go see the captain and give him my report. See you later, Diane."

He goes to see Captain Fedora and tells him about the interviews, the ledgers he found, and Pavel's import/export shady business, Rovel Imports. John says, "Chuck is looking into Rovel Imports, but you are welcome to join the party, captain. I wonder if Pavel hooked up with the Mafia; I hear that they control the docks again. Speaking of parties, did my major-domo, Thom Saunders, send you an email about the party I'm throwing for my girlfriend's birthday on Saturday?"

Captain Fedora says, "Yes, I got an email from him. My wife and I will be there. However, he didn't say it was a birthday party. He said it was a celebration for you recovering from the hit you took in the line of duty."

"I told him to do that because I'm keeping it a secret from Grace. I want it to be a surprise, and I'm going to propose to her that night."

Captain Fedora looks at John and says, "It's about time you got married again, John. I hope she makes you as happy as my wife has made me and that she will keep you in line, not that you need much of that. You are doing a great job, except for getting shot, of course."

"About that, captain; see this coat I'm wearing, it is a special coat my brother and I invented. It is laser, knife, and bulletproof. It's been tested, and my brother Mike and my girlfriend Grace, and I formed a company to design and manufacture these coats and other clothes, and I'm giving everyone in my squad a coat within a week or two as soon as they are ready. So, no more hospitals for me or anyone else who has one."

"I would like one of these coats myself. What do they cost?" the captain asks.

"Grace is going to do the math on that, but I will get you one for free as I value your life too. What is your size, and do you want the black leather look? We are going to make some in cloth and in different colours too. Grace is in Winnipeg, getting the factory together and designing clothes as she has owned another clothing company for several years. I would like to get these coats in every police station in Canada for a start, and maybe the military. After that, who knows?"

Captain Fedora says, "If this test phase works, I'll help you get these coats into law enforcement for sure, John."

John goes back to his office, sends his report to Commander Caputo, and sends him an invite to the party just in case he didn't get one. He gets EDD to check the nearest traffic cameras at the time of the shooting and gets some people on checking neighbourhood cameras around the time Pavel was hit and a few hours before.

John arrives home by six o'clock. Thom and Chrissy greet him at the front door as he throws his hat on the coat rack and hangs up his new Bodyguard coat. Chrissy paws at his pant leg and meows. He picks up Chrissy and pets her as Thom says, "Good evening, lieutenant. I guess you had a full day as

I saw on the news that the Russian oligarch Pavel Romaniuk died suspiciously this morning, and you are a tad late coming home. The plans for the party are coming together nicely. Oh, the band called, and they want to set up on Friday evening and rehearse to get the sound right. They want to know if you want to sit in with them?"

"That is a great idea; tell them Friday evening is good, and unless I'm stuck on a case, I would really like to practice with them. Have you eaten, Thom?"

"No, I wasn't hungry."

"Let's go eat. You too, Chrissy. Let's see what Julie has prepared for dinner."

They go into the dining room and see Julie and Savana sitting there.

"Hi, John and Thom. I guess you are hungry. I cooked a beef roast with mashed potatoes and asparagus and julienned carrots, and I cooled some pieces of beef for Chrissy," Julie says.

"Hi, Uncle Tiny and Thom and Chrissy. Isn't it a nice day today? I played with the baby chicks for a while today; they are so cute, and they climbed all over me and made me giggle!" Savana says.

Chrissy jumps up on Savana's lap, sits down, and looks up at her as if to say, "What do you want?" Savana says, "Hi Chrissy, sit down," and pets her. Chrissy sits and starts purring softly. Julie comes back in with the dinner plates and puts them on the table. She goes out again and comes back with a bowl of milk and a small plate of beef for Chrissy. Chrissy abandons Savana for her dinner like she was shot out of a cannon.

They all start eating their roast beef dinners.

John looks at Julie and says, "Julie, you are an artist in the kitchen; this looks and smells delicious! Thom, is the security set up yet?"

He replies, "It is mostly together. I've hired some ex-soldiers from our unit, and I'm working on two others who are experts in computers to man the control center."

"I have to call Mike and see if he finished building Grace's '57 Chevy golf cart and when he is going to deliver it. I also need the Rolls-Royce detailed and waxed for Saturday."

John goes to his home office and calls his brother, "Hi Mike, how's it going?"

"To what do I owe this privilege, John? Do you need money, or do you want someone killed?"

"Very funny, my dear brother. I have plenty of money, and I don't need anyone killed, so I won't have to arrest you. I just wanted to know when you will finish the golf cart for Grace and when you will deliver it?"

"Oh, it should be finished on Wednesday, and I can bring it to you that evening."

"Good, and we will have a great party. Thom found a really great band. I'm going to play the piano, and Grace and I are going to sing with them."

"Great, I can't wait. Well, I'll see you on Wednesday. I've got to go have dinner. Bye, John."

"Great, I'll see you on Wednesday. Ciao."

John calls his mechanic, Ringo, and tells him to detail and wax the Rolls Royce. He then updates his digital murder board on his wall screen, adding the photos of the boot prints near the mansion to the photos of Doctor Blackwell, Ken Leung, and Pavel Romaniuk. He also adds the results of the toxicity report on Pavel Romaniuk.

CHAPTER FIFTY-EIGHT

He looks at his watch and sees that it is 6:45 p.m., meaning it's 8:45 p.m. in Winnipeg. He calls Grace on his videophone, and she answers. She is sitting at a desk in her hotel suite, drinking a glass of white wine and drawing something. "Hi John, you look tired. Are you okay?"

"It's been a long day, doing interviews with Pavel Romaniuk's wife and his bodyguard slash chauffeur. Anyway, what are you drawing, or is that a colouring book?"

"You are hilarious, John. Actually, I'm drawing new designs for some higher-end designer clothes for Bodyguard Clothing for women and pants and vests for men. I just had a thought; do you or Mike have a patent on this fabric? We should patent this clothing fabric so that nobody steals it."

"I believe Mike has a patent on the car body formula, but I'll ask him about it and the clothing formula. By the way, my captain and my commander want coats too. I'm buying them for them, and Commander Caputo said he will help us get contracts for other police units and possibly the military, so that would be big money. I'll email you their sizes. They both want the leather look."

"That's great. Now I know I'm not wasting my time here. You know, I will bring back some colouring books for the girls, hopefully, something about Winnipeg and some about animals as they both love them."

"That's a great idea. What brand of wine are you drinking there?" John asks.

"I'm not fussy; it's called Troubador. It's okay wine for a Chardonnay," Grace says.

"Now, you are being funny."

"I knew that would get to you. I happen to be very intimate friends with the guy who owns the winery."

"Really, is he good in bed?"

"Oh, he is fantastic. I've never had better, but he is kind of kinky for a cop."

"I'd like to meet him sometime."

"That's easy; just look in the mirror."

They both laugh, and John says, "That's why I love you so much. It's only been one day, and I miss you already."

"I love you too and miss you. Well, I'll say goodnight. I want to get these designs finished tonight, and hopefully, we can get those coats made by Friday, but I don't want to rush this. It's too important for us; we want quality in everything we do. Goodnight, John, and sleep well. Love you."

"Bye, love you too, my lotus blossom."

John watches the news, and the old Seinfeld shows, then gets in bed and says, "Computer, turn on the fireplace and dim the lights to ten percent and then off." Chrissy jumps into bed with him and curls up beside him and goes to sleep.

Several hours later, he has a nightmare about getting ambushed in the village in Afghanistan. He is on foot, entering the village with a hand laser gun in his holster and a laser sniper rifle in his hand. Sergeant Thom Saunders is behind him as his spotter. They get to the middle of the village. John looks around and says, "Thom, I don't like this; it's too quiet. Keep your eyes peeled for the snipers that shoot from the rooftops." They take one step into the open, and John yells, "Ambush," as he spots an Afghani on the roof. He turns but is hit in the back with two bullets as the Afghanis are still using AK 47 antique automatic rifles that shoot bullets. Thom shoots the Afghani on the roof right in the head and takes a bullet in his left arm. He grabs John and drags him behind a wall of the nearest hut, as the rest of the squad opens fire with their laser rifles on the rest of the Afghanis. Thom throws John over his shoulder and carries him back to another hut near the village entrance, yelling for a medic. John feels the pain from his nightmare and sits up, screaming, "Help, medic!" He scares Chrissy as she jumps out of bed and jumps on the couch across the room. John is sweating and shaking like a leaf. He looks around, confused at his surroundings. He sees Chrissy and says to her, "I'm sorry to scare you, Chrissy, I had a bad dream." He then says, "Computer, turn lights on fifteen percent, and tell me the time."

The computer answers, "Good morning, lieutenant. It is seven o'clock, and the temperature outdoors is ten degrees Celsius." John decides that he might as well get up and have a good hot shower. He showers, dresses, and goes down to the dining room and greets Julie and Thom as Chrissy follows behind him, hoping for a meal too.

"John, you look tired. Did you sleep all right last night?" Thom asks.

"No, for the first time in years, I had a nightmare about that ambush in Afghanistan when we got shot. I could actually feel the bullets hit me in the dream, which woke me up. I'm still grateful to you for saving my life that day."

"I had to save you; I didn't know how to get back to the base."

"And if I believed that, you could sell me the Lion's Gate Bridge."

They both laugh, and Julie says, "I guess it's good that you two can joke about almost getting killed. What do you two want for breakfast?"

"I want a Denver omelette as I think I'm going to have another long day on this case," John says.

Just then, Savana walks into the room, picks up Chrissy, and says, "Mom, I'm hungry. Can I have pancakes?"

Julie replies, "Yes, dear, and what do you want, Thom?"

"I want a spinach and feta cheese omelette, please, Miss Julie."

"Thom, how can you eat spinach? It's gross, and what's feta cheese?"

"When you are older, you might like spinach. It will make you strong like Popeye, and feta cheese is a white cheese that comes from goat milk, and you like goats, don't you?"

"I like goats. I didn't know they gave milk, and I don't want to look like Popeye. He has weird arms and smokes a pipe. What does feta cheese taste like?" Savana says.

"It's hard to explain. I'll let you taste some when your mom brings my omelette, okay?"

"Well, okay, but I don't have to like it," she says.

"You don't have to like it; just try it, okay?"

Julie brings in their meals and gets some salmon for Chrissy so that she won't bother anyone, begging for food. They start eating, and Thom says to Savana, "Before you eat your pancakes, I want you to taste this feta cheese."

He gives her some of his omelette with feta cheese and spinach. She eats it, hesitates, and says, "I like this; it's different, it's . . . I don't know the word for it."

"I think the word you're looking for is sharp or tart. Also, there was spinach in there, but you probably couldn't taste it as it doesn't have much taste."

"Yes, tart. I've had old cheese, and they call it tart. There was spinach in there? I couldn't taste it. Could I try another little piece?"

"Sure, I thought you would like it, and it's good for you."

John finishes his omelette and says, "Well, I have to pick up Chuck and get to work. It's going to be another long day. See you all later."

CHAPTER FIFTY-NINE

John puts on his hat and coat and remotes his car to the front door with the heater on, climbs in, and flies to Chuck's place. Chuck gets in the car and says, "It's nice to get into a nice warm car. I've been trying to dig deeper into Rovel Imports, and he has a legit account, but the money going in and out doesn't add up, and I'm stuck, lieutenant. Any ideas?"

"Do we know Pavel's mother's name?"

"No. Why does that matter?"

"I've come across this before. Some of these scumbags have a hidden account under their mother's name or a combination of her name and his name, so check into his family background—mother, stepfather, sister, brother, cousin—whatever. When we get to the station, you work on that, and I will get the traffic cams with Randy Chan and maybe Captain Fedora."

They get to the station, and John sends some officers out to check residential security cameras. John tells Randy Chan to grab his laptop computer and come into his office, and they coordinate looking at traffic camera footage a few hours before Pavel was hit with the poisoned dart close to the area where they found the tire tracks and the footprints.

"This would be easier if we knew what kind of car we are looking for. I'm going to call Detective Mat Fraser and see if he knows what cars use those tires," John says.

He calls Mat and asks him about the tires. "Hi, lieutenant. Yes, I checked into that, and those tires are only sold on mostly 2069 Toyotas and Mazda SUV models built in Canada," Mat says.

"Thanks, Mat. That narrows it down quite a bit. Did you hear that, Randy? Toyotas and Mazda SUVs from 2069 have those tires. We could check licence registrations, but there would be thousands of them. I haven't seen an SUV on my footage so far as in that area, most people drive luxury cars or limousines like Pavel's. Let's work on this until lunchtime and go out for lunch. We will need a good break by then. I also have Chuck Sidhu working on Pavel's background. I want to know things like what is his mother's maiden name. I know he has hidden accounts somewhere."

They work on viewing footage until noon, and then John gets Chuck, and they all go to the Retro Diner for lunch. Margarette, their cute, young, mixed-race waitress, with light brown skin, medium-length dark wavy hair, and a slim but very feminine body, approaches and says, "Hello, lieutenant and detective. What can I pleasure you with today, sexy gentlemen?"

John says, "You know, Margarette, if I didn't love you so much, I might have to arrest you and put you in handcuffs for sexual harassment."

"Handcuffs again? I would like that," she says.

John laughs. "Right now, you can pleasure me with a cheeseburger, fries, and a chocolate shake. I'm really sorry to say that I have a girlfriend now. Maybe Detective Chuck Sidhu here would like you to pleasure him."

"I would be most grateful if you did, and I would enjoy a cheeseburger, fries, a strawberry shake, and your phone number," Chuck says.

Margarette writes in her order book and wiggles her eyebrows. "Okay, Chuck, how about Friday night? You can take me out for dinner to a real restaurant. I'll put in your orders, and," she rips off a page from her book and hands it to Chuck, "here is my phone number. I work until five o'clock. Call me tonight, sweetie."

Chuck smiles. "Lieutenant, did that just happen?"

"Stick with me, kid, and you'll go places. Seriously, though, Margarette is a sweet young girl, and she has a heart of gold. She just flirts with me, but we've never been intimate. I love her attitude. She volunteers at a shelter in her spare time. That shows you what kind of person she is. If you connect well, bring her to my party on Saturday. Now, to change the subject, I hope we nail this assassin soon. I don't want any more people getting murdered, even if they are scumbags like Pavel Romaniuk. What else do you think we can do to catch this guy?"

Chuck answers, "First, we need to check with the officers who are canvasing Pavel's area to see if they have any footage that can help us. We also need to crack the encrypted code in Pavel's satellite phone, find the assassin's phone number, and then try to triangulate his signal to see where he lives. We are pretty sure of his name, but he uses so many aliases. And so many of them are lame, I mean Jean- Luc Picard? Give me a break."

Margarette brings their food and has a big smile for Chuck and says to him, "I had the chef put extra sauce and cheese in yours, Chuck. See you later; I have a lot of tables today."

John smiles again and says, "I think she likes you, and your ideas are right on about this case. When we go back to the office, we should contact the field officers about the house security camera footage."

They finish their meals, and Randy reaches for his wallet, and John says, "It's okay, I'm buying lunch." He leaves Margarete a tip that is more than the price of their lunch.

CHAPTER SIXTY

They go back to John's office. He calls Captain Fedora and says, "Captain, have you heard from the officers canvasing Pavel's neighbourhood?"

The captain replies, "Yes, Officer Shannon O'Leary emailed me and sent some footage of a few houses in the area, and one across the street from the empty lot where you found the tire tracks and the footprints. I'll send the email and videos to you right now. I separated the videos, and the first one I labelled Ghost 101 has a silver Toyota SUV in it with some mud on the car and the licence plate, but I cleaned it up and checked the registration. It came up registered to a shell company called Central Security Incorporated, and the address is in city hall. This guy is really a joker . . . CSI. Really! But I found a post office box in Vancouver at 710 Granville street."

John says, "We should go there and ask who picks up mail there, and get a warrant for their surveillance footage if they have any cameras. We can show them a picture of Bill Auger on my phone and maybe print one out."

John starts printing out a few pictures of Mr. Auger when his videophone rings. It is Detective Sam Slade calling. "Lieutenant Trosky, I hate to bother you, but I have a woman here who said she is your sister, Judy Trosky. She was attacked in an alley by three men in the west end near her flower shop called Forget Me Nots. She knocked out two of them and killed one."

"Judy, my baby sister? Is she okay?" John exclaims.

"She suffered a few cuts and bruises, but I think she has a broken arm. The medics aren't here yet."

"Give me your location, and I'll be there in a flash."

"We are in Ackery's Alley between Smythe Street and Robson. Thanks, John."

"Randy, my sister has been attacked downtown. I have to go. You'll have to check out the post office box, take someone with you if you want. I'll tag you later. I'll probably be at the hospital." John grabs his black Stetson hat and goes into the bullpen and says, "Chuck, we've got an emergency; grab your hat and let's go. My sister has been attacked."

They get in John's cop car and fly downtown to Ackery's Alley and see two cop cars, an ambulance, and Judy's van with her shop logo on it. Sam Slade is with Judy as the medic works on Judy's right arm. John says, "Judy, what happened?"

"I was driving down this lane, taking a shortcut to my other flower shop, when I saw that guy in the blue jacket lying face down in the middle of the alley. I stopped to see if I could help him, and as I knelt beside him to turn him over, he slashed at me with that big Crocodile Dundee knife over there. I rolled back and kicked it out of his hand. We both got up, and I gave him a roundhouse kick in the head, and he went down out cold. At the same time, those two other dirtbags jumped out from behind a dumpster and attacked me. One had a big steel pipe, and the other one had a knife. The one with the knife slashed me in the side, and I grabbed his wrist, snapped it back, and broke it. Then I punched him in the nose and broke his nose at the same time. He went down, screaming and cursing. I'm glad I took that Krav Maga course from that

Israeli guy last year. Oh, so then the guy with the pipe swung at me, so I backed up, but he hit me, and I think he broke my arm. That made me mad and scared at the same time, so I semi-crouched and kicked at him, trying to hit his lung area, but I hit his throat, and I guess it crushed his windpipe, and he died. I didn't mean to kill him, honest, but when you are fighting for your life, things happen so fast."

"Detective Slade, did you take her statement and read her the revised Miranda rights?" John asks.

"Yes, I did. I really don't understand why these guys attacked her."

"Well, Judy is gay. Judy, were you carrying any money for the bank?"

"No, I wasn't."

John looks around and says, "Is that a video camera on your dash?"

"Yes, it was still on and would have recorded the whole incident," Judy says.

"Detective, check that camera; it should have a chip in it. Have her van transported to the CSI guys. Did you check these guys' IDs?" John asks.

"Yes, they all seem to be German and have swastikas tattooed to their arms and chests. The first attacker is Fritz Holz, number two is Hans Schrecker, and the dead one is Gunter Schmitt. They must belong to a white supremacist group. I'll do a more thorough search on these guys when I get back to the station."

"I'll get the medics to take Judy to the Vancouver General Hospital and follow her in my car. She will have to stay in the hospital overnight or longer. I want you to put an officer on her door just to be safe. Judy, do you have your phone on you? You should call Lois and tell her what happened."

"I left my phone in the van."

Chuck says, "I'll get it for you." Chuck gets her phone, comes back, and hands it to Judy, saying, "By the way, I'm Detective Chuck Sidhu, and I'm glad to meet you under the circumstances. Don't worry, John and Sam will get these jerks to confess to assault and battery and lock them up. We will dig into their lives, and if they are part of some gang or organization, we will shut them down."

John says, "Sam, get the medics to check these guys, patch them up, and arrest them for assault. If they belong to a neo-Nazi group, then this becomes a hate crime. Chuck, I'm going to the hospital. Why don't you ride back to the station with an officer and run these scumbags and see if they belong to a gang or whatever. I just want to get her settled; I'll come back to the station after. It will take a while to get them booked. Wait until I get back to interrogate them. See you later. Let's see, it's three o'clock now. I'll probably be there in an hour."

John flies his car to the Vancouver General Hospital, goes to the front desk, asks for Judy's whereabouts, flashes his badge, and tells the administrator that he is her brother. She tells him that she is in surgery to repair her broken right arm. He goes to the waiting room and thinks that it is about five-fifteen in Winnipeg, so he calls Grace on his videophone and says, "Hi, Grace, how is your day going?"

"It's going great. We already made some fabric with the new machines, and they work really fast. Larry brought in an assistant to run the machines, and he will be heading back to Vancouver in a few days as Mike needs him back in R and D for another project. I'm going to work for at least a few more hours, and we should have the coats finished for your squad by Thursday or Friday, so you can give them out at the party. How is your day going? Did you get the assassin yet?" Grace says.

"No, but we got a few more clues and a post office box that we think is his. But I have a more important issue right now. I'm at the hospital."

"Don't tell me you got hurt again," Grace says.

"Calm down, honey. It's my sister, Judy, who is in here. You haven't met her yet. She was attacked in an alley in the west end by three guys. Too bad the guys didn't know that my sister is a badass chick. She subdued two of them and killed the third one, but the last guy broke her arm, and the first one cut her but not badly. They are repairing her broken arm right now. I think they attacked her because she is gay, as they had swastikas tattooed on their arms and chests. They patched these scumbags up, and they are being booked as we speak. I'm going back to the station later to help interrogate them with Detective Samantha Slade as she caught the case. Actually, I really can't interrogate them as she is my sister, and Sam caught the case, but I can observe her questioning them. Chuck is doing the research on them now. They must belong to some white supremacist group. One good thing was that she has a dash-cam in her van that caught the whole incident, and it has a chip in it. So, she is not in trouble. If these jerks try to pull something, I have a team of lawyers that will eat them for lunch. Oh, here's Detective Slade; I have to go see what's going on. I love you and can't wait to see you again. Don't work too hard. Goodbye, sweetie."

"I love you too. Give my love to your sister; I hope she is okay. Goodbye, love."

Sam says, "They repaired your sister's arm and the cut on her side, and they are bringing her out now. She will have to stay in the hospital for a day or two."

"I'll arrange for a suite for her. Probably the same one I was in. Is her girlfriend Lois here yet?" John says.

"Yes, and she is hovering around her like a mother hen around her chicks. She is freaked out. There she is now."

"Hi, Lois. I was just about the get a suite for Judy," John says.

"I've already arranged one. I did it online just now. The doctors say she is going to be all right," Lois says.

"I'm glad you're here. We have those jerks in custody, and I have to get back to the station to help with the interrogation strategy. You know, I can't be involved with this case directly, but I can help Detective Sam Slade here with the strategy. We both need to get to the station, and I will be back later. Sam, give Lois your card in case she has any questions."

CHAPTER SIXTY-ONE

Sam and John leave the hospital and go back to the station. They enter the bullpen, and Chuck approaches them. "Lieutenant and detective, I found some information on Fritz Holz, who is in Room One, and his buddy, Hans Schrecker, who is in Room Two. They belong to a group called White Supreme Brothers, and they have attacked gays, blacks, middle eastern, and rich people. They are known to the police, but they usually get away from the crime scene, so few arrests have been made. They have a clubhouse downtown in one of the damaged high-rises that only has a few floors left standing."

John thinks for a moment, then says, "Okay Sam, you and Chuck interrogate Fritz Holz in Room One, and I'll watch from the observation room to see if you can get him to roll on the other so-called 'Brothers.' Sam, I know you can be bad cop and threaten him with this. He and his buddy just committed a hate crime and attempted murder on a gay civilian, and that is a federal offence, which means big time in a federal penitentiary. We can bring in the Canadian Security Intelligence Service, CSIS. Sam, here is another trick that Captain Fedora taught me; take his file and grab a bunch of random files to make him think you have more information on him than you do, and that will scare the shit out of him.

Chuck, I think you should play bad cop too. There is no reason to play good cop. These guys are complete assholes. Also, I don't want any good deals for either one of them, maybe less jail time, but they are not getting off. If they give us enough info, we can get a warrant to bust their clubhouse. Go make me proud, guys."

Sam and Chuck enter Room One, and Sam says, "Record on, Detectives Slade and Sidhu entering Room One to question Fritz Holz. It is Monday, April 24th, 5 p.m." She reads him the revised Miranda rights and then says, "Mr. Holz, do you understand your rights as read to you?"

"Yes, but I don't understand why I'm here. That woman attacked my friends and me and killed my buddy. She was crazy."

"Is that right? Maybe we should arrest her after she gets out of the hospital?" Sam says.

"Yes, you should," he says.

Sam leans in and says, "There is only one problem, asshole. She had a dash-cam in her van that caught the whole incident on video and you gentlemen attacked her to start with, and with her being gay, you are looking at big time in a maximum penitentiary because it is now a hate crime. Your buddy Hans is also in the other interview room shaking in his boots, as you should be. Now, if you help us and tell us who your fearless leader in your lovely boy's club is, we can talk to the assistant prosecuting attorney and get you a deal. Myself, I would rather throw you in a cage with a big guy named Brutus, and maybe he can turn you gay. Would you like that? See these files here; this is just a peek at your Supreme White Brothers organization that we know about. I see that you even have a website and a lot of followers. I didn't know there were that many sick people in the world. Do you have pictures of Hitler in your little clubhouse? What we have now are some names of people in the upper part of your boys' club, a Franz

Buckholts, a Raymond James—that doesn't sound German— and a girl named Sherry Fitsimmons. I thought all you guys were German. What we want is some dirt on what else they are doing, like selling drugs, prostitution, or whatever. You can't run an organization without an income, can you?"

"I ain't tellin' you nothin' 'bout our shit. Screw you, bitch. I ain't no snitch," he says.

Sam opens another file, smiles, and looks up at Fritz. "Oh, I see you have a little brother, Alfred, doing time in that new maximum penitentiary they built up north in Hundred Mile for attempted murder."

"You leave my little brother alone; he had nothin' to do with our club."

"We don't want to hurt your brother, but if you help us out, I think the A.P.A. would cut a deal to cut his sentence down and move him to a more comfortable prison."

Chuck says, "Yes, I think she would go for that. I would take that if I were you because you are in deep shit, my friend. If you don't deal, CSIS will get involved, and they are a federal organization, so they are like Canada's FBI, and they will definitely throw you in a max prison. I guess you shitheads didn't know that attacking a gay person is a hate crime and a federal crime."

Fritz thinks it over, then says, "Okay, I'll tell you what I know about the organization."

Sam says, "We need it in writing too. You can write, can you?"

"Yes, bitch, I can fucking write. Franz Buckholts runs the drug ring—mostly heroin—with Sherry Fitzsimons, and Raymond 'Rayman' James runs a protection racket. That is all I know."

Sam says, "That's all we need; I'll call the A.P.A. Nikki Anders right now. Write all that down now. Chuck, stay with him. Detective Sam Slade is leaving the interview."

She leaves the room, and John comes out of the observation room and says, "Sam, you are a genius; you don't need my help. That brother thing was genius because you saw that he wasn't going to go for the first deal, and even scumbags have a soft spot for family. We can now get a search warrant to go into their clubhouse. You should get Nikki down here to get a warrant. Oh, we need the clubhouse address. In the meantime, you can interview Hans and see if he will spill. Does he have a brother or sister?"

"I'll check on that and see how it goes."

"Actually, we just need him to admit to the attack on my sister. I'm going back to the hospital to check on her and make sure there is a cop at her door. We should plan the raid with SWAT and do it tomorrow. I don't want another incident like the last raid. As my grandfather used to say, you don't get bit by the same dog twice."

"I like that. Can I use it sometime?" Sam asks.

"Sure, that's what sayings are for. See you tomorrow. Text me if you get a warrant."

CHAPTER SIXTY-TWO

John goes back to the hospital to check on Judy. He goes to her room and sees that she is in bed and Lois is sitting beside her. He says, "Hi, Lois, how is my baby sister?"

"She is still groggy and in pain."

"I have good news; we have these Neo-Nazi jerks in jail, and one of them gave us all the dirt we need to bust their whole organization," John says. "Judy, one jerk tried to say that you attacked them, but your dash-cam doesn't lie. Detective Sam Slade will interrogate the second attacker, a Mr. Hans Schrecker, to get him to confess to attacking you. We already have him on video, but a confession will seal the deal when we prosecute him. The assistant prosecuting attorney, Nikki Anders, is already on board, and she is giving us a warrant to search their clubhouse for drugs. We are going to do a raid on them tomorrow with SWAT. We want to plan this out carefully since I was hurt in the last raid, as you know. Do you need anything?"

Judy replies, "No, I just want to get out of here as soon as possible. The doctor wants me to stay here for two days, but maybe I can get out tomorrow afternoon. I'd rather be at home; we have servant droids programmed to do anything, including nursing, cooking, and bodyguarding."

"I don't blame you; the food in here is disgusting. When I was in here, my girlfriend Grace had a great idea. There is a good restaurant across the street that makes a really good breakfast, and they deliver through Skip the Dishes. They also have good coffee. If you are feeling better, you both should come to my party on Saturday. I don't know if Thom called or emailed you about it. We sent invites saying it was a celebration for my healing from the shot I took in that raid, but it is actually a birthday party for my girlfriend Grace Chan, and I'm going to propose to her the same night."

"I'll have to see how I feel, but I would like to be there when my big brother proposes because I know you will be really nervous," Judy says.

"I know you will get a kick out of that, so I will count on you. I know your sense of humour. Oh, presents are optional, as I'm giving her a very expensive car, and Mike has a surprise for her too. Mike, Gladys, and Jackie are coming too. I want the kids to have fun. Dinner is at eight and dancing at nine o'clock. Well, I must get back to the shop to see how Sam is doing with your case, so, don't worry, just heal. See you later. Bye."

John flies back to the shop and sees Sam. She says, "I'm glad you came back; I was just about to interview shithead number two, Hans Schrecker. I have an idea how to get him to spill. I'm going to get him mad and tell him that his buddy said it was his idea to attack your sister."

John says, "Good, I think that will work. This guy isn't the sharpest knife in the drawer. Is Nikki Anders here yet? And where is Chuck? I want him in there too."

Chuck is standing behind John and says, "I'm right here, John, and ready to rock."

Sam says, "Nikki is in the observation room. You can join her. You want a coffee?"

"I'll get one from my auto chef in my office, but thanks for offering. Don't start without me. Give me two minutes, okay?"

"Sure, two minutes. I'll go read him his rights and then stare at him with fire in my eyes for two minutes."

She enters the room with Chuck and triggers the recorder, and reads Hans his rights. She puts her files down, opens them up, shakes her head, and stares at him. "Hans, you have been a bad boy. You have a record as long as your arm—assault, battery, robbery, drug possession, and rape, of course. All the main food groups. Wow, did you really kill your dog when you were twelve years old? And a neighbour's cat the next year? Jesus!"

"You're not supposed to know about that, and it's not true," he says.

"Well, your parents and juvie seemed to think you did. We can unseal juvie records when you commit a serious crime like attacking an innocent gay civilian."

Hans says, "You got it backward; she attacked us, just ask Fritz."

Sam says, "Oh, I believe you. A five-foot-three woman, weighing a buck twenty, unarmed by the way, attacked three big bruisers like you. Why would she do that, I wonder, eh?"

"Well, she didn't see Gunter and me; we were . . . smoking behind a big dumpster, and she attacked me first."

Sam says, "Look, you lying piece of shit. You would prostitute your dear mother for a nickel."

He turns red, stands up, and yells, "You leave my mother out of this, you bitch."

"You know that the woman you attacked and who kicked the shit out of you had a dash-cam in her van, and we have the video of you pricks attacking her, and . . . breaking news . . . two witnesses have come forward who also captured the incident on their phones," Sam says.

Chuck adds, "Your pal in the next room also said that it was your idea to attack her. He cut a deal."

Hans yells, "What? It was his idea to attack her, and he knew she was a lesbian. He was following her for days."

Sam says, "Thank you for admitting that. You are under arrest for attempted murder and a federal crime of attacking a gay person, which is a hate crime. You better get a lawyer, or we will provide you with the worst public defender we can find, one who came last in his class. Record end," Sam says, then looks at Chuck and says, "We're out of here."

Nikki Anders and John come out of the observation room, and Nikki says, "You both did a great job in there. Sam, you really know how to make a guy mad and lose his cool. I can now put these bastards in a cage for a long time, and if they get out, they will need walkers. John, the search warrant is on your desk and on your computer. When are you going to do the raid?"

"I'm going to assemble my team with SWAT in the morning to plan this out carefully. I don't want a repeat of the last raid, and I'm going to try out my new laser proof coat that my brother invented. It's been tested in his lab, but I want to see how it works in real situations. My brother Mike, my girlfriend Grace Chan, and I started a new company making these coats. The company is called Bodyguard Clothing, and Grace is in Winnipeg right now putting these coats together. I'm going to give them to all my team on Saturday at my girlfriend's birthday party. I'd like to delay this raid, but it's time-sensitive. We have to do it tomorrow in case they decide to move. I'll get SWAT to go in first, and we all carry smoke and flash grenades."

Nikki says, "You have laser proof coats? When you get going, I want one. I don't care what they cost."

John says, "Grace is going to figure out the cost, and she can design it to look fashionable and to look like leather, cotton, wool, or cashmere and in any colour you want. She just needs to know your size, of course. She already owns a high-end clothing company. She is known as a great designer. I'll give you her email address, but give her a few days as she is swamped putting this company together right now. She is training people to run the fabric machines and how to cut and sew the material. You should come to the birthday party I've put together for her on Saturday at eight o'clock, and I will properly introduce her to you. Do you know where I live?"

"Lieutenant, I not only know where you live, I know your shoe size," she says.

John adds, "Nikki, you are scary but beautiful."

She smiles and says, "You think I'm beautiful? Wow."

John continues, "Yes, everyone here thinks you are beautiful and scary. That's why they like you. Well, Chuck and I have a few things to do, and then I'm going home. See you later. Are you coming to the raid tomorrow? We are assembling in the main conference room at eight o'clock and will move out in an hour or so when I'm sure everyone knows their part."

She says, "I wouldn't miss it for the world. Can I ride in the EDD van again?"

"We have a seat with your name embroidered on it now. See you in the morning, Nikki. Chuck, let's go into my office."

They go in the office, and John says, "Back to the Auger case, I want to know his mother's maiden name. I want to try something. God, all these other cases are getting in our way of the main case."

Chuck researches Bill Auger's parents and says, "John, look at this; his father's first name was Jacque, and the first name of his mother was Sabine, and she was born a Basque. I'm going to get the computer to check for businesses with those names or a combination of them. This guy is smart. I'll bet he has a residence under a company name, and possibly his SUV is registered under the same company. I'm going to let the computer run all night to come up with different combinations and to check the DMV records for a Toyota SUV under any of those combinations."

John looks at Chuck and his watch and says, "Wow, it is six o'clock. It's past shift; we should get home. The meeting is at eight o'clock in the morning, but I want to get here at seven-thirty to talk to Lieutenant Shane Travis, so I'll pick you up at seven-fifteen and fly here at warp speed. Cool with you, Chuck?"

In a Scottish accent, he replies, "Aye, captain. I think we can achieve warp speed with the new dylethium crystals."

"Hey, that was really good; I'm not the only one who can imitate voices. Let's go, Scotty before the Klingons get here."

CHAPTER SIXTY-THREE

They fly home, and John is greeted by Thom and Chrissy as she winds between his legs and looks up at him, and meows.

"Good evening, John. Julie still has some roast beef left, and Savana has eaten already, but Julie and I haven't," Thom says.

"Good evening, Thom and Chrissy," John says. He picks up Chrissy, pets her, and starts to carry her upstairs. "I'm just going to give Grace a call, and then I'll be down for dinner. Can you open a bottle of Troubadour Cabernet and let it breathe? I'll be down in about a half-hour."

He goes up to his office and calls Grace as Chrissy settles in on his lap. "Hi, Grace, how goes the battle in Winnipeg?"

"Hi, John, it's going pretty good. I've got two women working with me, cutting and sewing material for your coats, Susan and Joy. They worked with me before and enjoyed the holidays I sent them on, so they are working hard and fast to get these coats done. They want to work overtime, so all the coats will be ready by Friday, and I can bring them back with me on my transport. That will include your captain's and commander's coats. That should make you happy."

"What will make me really happy is seeing you again, in the flesh, so to speak. Do you have a coat made for Chuck Sidhu yet?"

"Yes, with his name sewed inside. Why do you ask?"

"Well, I hesitate to tell you this, but we are going to raid and arrest the whole Supreme White Brothers group who attacked my sister tomorrow. I have my Bodyguard coat, but I wish Chuck had one for tomorrow. Before you start to worry about me, we will plan this better and let the SWAT team go in first with flash and stun grenades, and my squad will go in last. Could you ship his coat overnight to the police station? We will be planning this for an hour or more before we go near their so-called clubhouse," John says.

"In that case, I will ship it as soon as I get off the phone."

"Thank you. We will also have our first paying customer. Assistant Prosecuting Attorney Nikki Anders wants you to design her a one-of-a-kind, Bodyguard coat in her own choice of colour, and she doesn't care what it will cost. She wears wild colours, so it should be interesting for you, but I told her not to bother you for a few days as you are swamped putting the factory together. You will meet her at your birthday party. I've invited half the people on the planet. I've been playing salesman, and Captain Fedora and Commander Caputo are on board to get these coats on cops in house and in all the police stations in Vancouver, and who knows what's next?"

"John, that's great! You've been working your butt off, solving crimes and promoting our business. I'm going to owe you something, in the flesh, as you put it, when I get back. I love you. By the way, we, Detective Sam Slade and I arrested and charged the scumbags that beat up my sister, and they are going to do hard time in a penitentiary up north. It was Sam's case, so she did most of the work. She is a badass in the interrogation room. She worked this guy so much that he got so mad he didn't realize he just confessed to the crime. She doesn't know it, but I'm putting her up for a commendation. I wish I could give her a raise. Oh, Thom is doing a great job on the party. We have security in place and the band. The band will be here on Friday evening, and I'm going to jam with them for a while. And Julie got a great catering company. It's going to be a great party, sweetie. Oh, Julie is buzzing me; she's got dinner waiting. Well, I better go. I love you. Take care."

"I love you too, Mr. Bond, James Bond. Bye."

John goes down and joins Thom and Julie for dinner. Chrissy follows him to the dining room and circles Julie and meows. She gets her some salmon and a bowl of goat's milk, and she gobbles both down. John says, "Hi, gang, I just talked to Grace, and she already made some of the coats and is sending one for Chuck Sidhu tonight as we are going to do a raid on the White Supreme Brothers clubhouse tomorrow, and we are going in armed, and I want him protected too. This time, I'm getting the SWAT team to go in first. Actually, Sam Slade should go in before me as this started out as her case. We are going to have extra cops go in with us in combat gear, and we are going to use flash and stun grenades."

They start to eat their meals, and Thom says, "John, pretty well everything is set for the party. My buddies are doing the security and some of our old army squad. The band is set, the cars are detailed, and Mike brought the '57 Chevy golf cart here already. You've got to go see it in the garage; it's beautiful!"

Julie adds, "The catering is in place; my girlfriend Natalie is setting up the menu. She is going to have some light chicken dishes with just a few vegetables and a little rice, as we want people to dance and not be too full, also some beef, swordfish, salmon, and vegetarian dishes, and some East Indian and Persian dishes, and that big '57 Chevy cake, of course."

"Yes, tell her to do that and make some cupcakes for the kids; they love cupcakes, and they are less messy."

They finish eating, and Julie says, "I'll call her right now."

"Thom, if you are not busy, I'd like to go to the hollo range and practice some shooting tonight as that raid is tomorrow."

Thom says, "I'm in, let's go, boss."

They go to the range and practice hitting moving targets. Then John says, "You don't have to do this if you don't want to, and you might think I'm crazy, but I want to put my Bodyguard coat on, and I want you to shoot me with a laser pistol on low and then medium when I tell you. Hit me mid-body, okay? And Grace never ever hears about this."

"I don't know. If this goes wrong, she will kill me," Thom says.

"Look, Mike has already tested this coat, and I want to go into that raid tomorrow with confidence. I'll record a waiver on video if you want. Come on, Thom, I need you to do this. How about I hang the coat up on a droid first and check it out?"

"Okay, we'll do it that way first."

John puts the coat on the droid, and Thom shoots it, and the droid moves a bit from the hit. They check it out, and there is no mark at all on it, and the droid sensors record no hit or heat. John then puts the coat on and stands ten feet away. Thom then shoots at him mid-body as he cringes.

"Come here and look. I could feel the hit a bit but no heat at all," John says.

Thom comes over and looks at the coat and is stunned to find no damage. "That is amazing, John. Are you ready for the next step?"

"Fire away, Thom." Thom cranks up the laser to the middle setting and fires again. John feels the hit a bit more but doesn't feel any heat at all and says, "Okay, Thom, do it on full blast."

"Are you sure, John?"

"Yes, shoot away!" Thom cringes again and shoots full blast. He hits John in the same spot.

"Are you okay?" Thom asks.

"John laughs out loud and says, "I'm great, and I hardly felt the hit, and there was no heat at all. We have just made the world safer for cops, soldiers, and civilians. I'm going to get Grace to make pants and vests and maybe helmets. We will make a lot of money on this, but I don't even care about the money. I don't want people to go through the pain and paralysis that I had to endure, and I was lucky to recover. A lot of people have never recovered from a hit from a laser. I still don't want you to tell Grace that we did this. I will tell her myself when the time is right, but she is too stressed right now. Grace is sending a coat for Chuck Sidhu tonight, so he will have one for the bust tomorrow, and she is going to have all the coats for the squad ready for Saturday. I'm going to give them out at the party. I'll get her to make you a coat too, for free, of course. She still has to figure out a price for them to cover costs and make a reasonable profit. That is entirely up to her as I haven't a clue about the clothing business, and she has run one for several years."

"I'll pay for my own if you want. I want to customize it. I'm so impressed with this demonstration tonight. I should get one for Brigette too; she is a beautiful soul. Wait until you meet her. I'm bringing her here on Saturday," Thom says.

"I'm looking forward to meeting her. If you picked her out, I'm sure she is lovely and a good person. I wish we had these coats in Afghanistan; we would have had a hell of an advantage. Well, I'm going up to my office to make some notes on this and the cases I'm working on. Goodnight, Thom. See you in the morning."

John goes up to his office and updates his files on the Auger case and the White Supreme Brothers Organization, and Sam Slade's handling of the case. He puts in a commendation for Detective Samantha Slade in a detailed account of her impressive ingenuity in handling his sister's case and how she got both suspects to confess and reveal important details of the Supreme White Brothers organization so they could get a search warrant for their clubhouse and he emails the commendation to Commander Caputo, Captain Tibor Fedora, and Police Chief Emily Carter. He looks at the time on his computer and sees that it is close to midnight, feels tired, and goes to bed. Chrissy is sitting on the couch and jumps into the bed, and curls up beside him. He tells the computer to turn on the fireplace and turn off the lights and pets Chrissy until she purrs and falls asleep. He has pleasant dreams about him and Grace lying on a beach, but near dawn, he has a nightmare about entering the Afghan village and feeling that something is off and then getting shot in the back. He jolts up, sweating. This time, he doesn't scream or yell, but it still scares Chrissy, and she jumps off the bed and onto the couch and stares at him with a puzzled look on her little face. He looks at her and says, "I'm sorry, Chrissy. I don't know why this is happening to me." He gets up, has a long hot shower, turns the shower to a cold setting, gets out, and towels off. He gets a coffee from his auto chef and looks at the time. It is 6:35 a.m. on Tuesday, April 25th. He turns on the TV news to see if there is anything on the Supreme White Brothers that leaked. No news is good news. He says, "Chrissy, let's go see if Julie has some food for us." As soon as Chrissy hears the word food, she jumps off the couch and runs after John, and they go down to the dining room.

Julie and Savana are sitting there, and Savana is eating her Corn Flakes, and Julie is drinking coffee and eating a bagel with cream cheese. Savana gets excited and calls Chrissy to her. Julie looks at John and says, "Hi John, you're up early. Are you okay? You look tired."

"I had a bad dream last night; I'm starting to get flashback dreams about the war. I don't know why; maybe I just miss Grace so much. For some reason, I feel safe around her.

Anyway, Chrissy and I are hungry. I need a big breakfast as it's going to be a long day today. We have to do a raid and bust on those dirtbags. Anyway, can you make me an omelette with a side of bacon? Can you make an extra piece for Chrissy because I just know she will bug me until I give her a piece?"

"Okay, I'll give Chrissy some of her special organic cat food. She actually likes it, and I'll cook some extra bacon," Julie says.

"Mom, could I have a piece of bacon, please?" Savana says.

"Sure, honey. Do you want one piece or two?"

"Two pieces, please. I'll give part of the second piece to Chrissy."

Julie brings in their breakfasts, and John talks to Savana about school. She gives half of her second piece of bacon to Chrissy and smiles. "You are welcome, Chrissy." Chrissy rubs against Savana's legs.

"Well, I have to go pick up Detective Sidhu, see you later," John says.

CHAPTER SIXTY-FOUR

John flies to Chuck's place and says, "Morning, Chuck. It's a nice day for a raid; we are going to kick some ass."

They go into the station, and Trudy, the desk sergeant, says, "Lieutenant Trosky, there is a special delivery package here for you. We checked it for explosives and viruses, and it's okay."

John jokingly says, "Oh good; it's from my girlfriend. I guess she doesn't hate me yet. Thanks, Trudy, have a joy, joy day!"

"You saw *Demolition Man* too. Do you want to have VR sex with me later, John?" she says.

"I'd like to, but my girlfriend would kill us both, other than that, yes."

He takes the package, goes into the bullpen, and hands the package to Chuck. "Happy birthday, Chuck."

"It's not my birthday, John."

"Just open it up, detective."

Chuck opens it up and says, "You bought me a coat. Why?"

"Don't you remember I told you that the whole squad is getting laser, knife, and bulletproof coats? Well, I'm giving you one early as we may get shot at today, and I want your butt protected because it's too much trouble to train another sidekick, and I love you, man. Don't cry, okay?"

Chuck puts it on and says, "It fits perfectly, and there are extra pockets inside and a gold-coloured liner. Hey, my name is in here too! Thanks, John."

"Okay, squad, you are all getting your own coats on Saturday at the birthday party for my girlfriend Grace Chan. She is making your coats as we speak in Winnipeg. Let's assemble in the main conference room with Lieutenant Shane Travis and his SWAT team to plan this operation. I can't express this enough. SWAT goes in first, and everyone stays safe. Chuck and I will go in after them because we have the laser proof coats, except for Randy, who will be in the van, then everyone else goes in. Lieutenant Travis will brief us on the operation. Also, A.P.A. Nikki Anders will be in the EDD van, monitoring us, and Detective Sam Slade will be directing us and warning us of threats. Detective Chan will be running the infra-red scope mounted to the van's roof, but he will be inside the van with Detective Slade. Also, Detectives Tran and Cornburra are on other assignments, so we will be using some uniformed officers."

They go into the conference room. Lieutenant Travis stands at the head of the table beside a whiteboard and says, "It is 8 a.m. on April 25th, 2070. Good morning, all. In case you don't know me, I'm Lieutenant Shane Travis, the head of SWAT, and this is my second-in-command Sergeant Amell Lebedinsky. We are going to go in first through the front door. This is a schematic of the Supreme White Brothers' building. The front door is north, and this door is on the south side. It's a four-storey building. Two of my other crew will breach the south door, and we will throw in stun grenades and wait a few minutes after we throw them. Actually, before all this, Detectives Sam Slade and Detective Bennetti will be on coms, and Detective Chan will be using an infra-red scope to tell us where everyone is inside. Then we go in, and Lieutenant Trosky and Detective Sidhu will follow us and then we can start stunning them with our laser pistols and rifles. We will have some men across the street on rooftops with scoped laser rifles in case any scumbags get away. We will also have some uniformed officers helping us as back-up, and they will be stationed outside in case anyone rabbits. Everyone will check their coms before we enter the building and turn on all their recorders. We will be in constant touch with EDD in their van parked across the street, monitoring with infra-red scopes. The lead uniformed officer will be Audley Barnes. The only thing we are certain of is the fearless leader is named Dieter Stein. This is his photo from their website. He will probably be on the top floor. Our snipers will confirm that when we get there. They are setting up ahead of us with stealth. Everyone check that your weapons are charged and working. Okay, it's now nine o'clock. Let's saddle up and hit these guys. Try not to kill anyone unless they shoot at you and you are in extreme danger. I want you wearing helmets and protective gear."

John and Chuck put on helmets with the word POLICE painted on them. They slip on Police signs over their coats. They drive down to the clubhouse, and John and Chuck's team pull up to the back door as SWAT breaches the front door and throws in a stun grenade. Lieutenant Travis yells, "SWAT, everyone on the floor now!" No one shoots, and the members hit the floor, and SWAT cuffs them as one SWAT officer stays to cover them. Two SWAT members and John and Chuck breach the back door and head up to the second floor. The two SWAT team members go in the first two rooms and drop some shooters as John and Chuck leap-frog them and go ahead. Some members start shooting at them this time, and John and Chuck both take a hit mid-body, and the shooter is shocked to see that they didn't go down. He freezes, and John yells, "Police, on the ground now!" The guy shoots again, and John shoots back with his laser pistol on low setting, and the guy drops to the floor shuddering and drops his weapon. Chuck picks up the shooter's weapon. Another guy comes out of a room a few feet ahead of them and shoots at them, and Chuck shoots him, and he drops down. They pick up the weapons and stick them in the pockets inside their coats. They handcuff the two perps and then head up the stairs to the third floor. Just as they get to the third floor, a guy with a laser pistol shoots John in the chest at arm's length, but John tackles him, punches him hard in the face, and breaks his nose. He swings at John and can't believe John is still alive. John rears back and punches him in the side of the head, hoping to knock him out. The guy, probably on drugs, punches John in the cheek, and John rolls away, and Chuck shoots the guy twice to put him out of commission. "Take that, shithead. John, are you okay?" Chuck asks.

"I'm all right. Shit, what the hell was that guy on? He just wouldn't go down. That punch in the head should have knocked him out. I've done it before on bigger guys than him."

John's coms clicks on, and Sam Slade exclaims, "There are three more people on that floor, so be careful. Back-up is coming to you. Out."

They crouch down and slowly move forward, and a naked girl jumps out from a room just four feet in front of them and shoots at Chuck. He fakes being hit and falls as John blasts the girl in the stomach, and she goes down unconscious. John zip ties her hands behind her back and says, "Chuck, that was a good trick; you distracted her as she watched you go down and gave me a clear shot at her. Too bad; she is a good looking girl, just in with the wrong crowd."

They check her pulse and then go into her room, get a blanket, and cover her up. They then turn a corner and move two rooms ahead, as the first and second are empty. Suddenly, another girl jumps out of the room behind them with a crossbow aimed toward John. A zapping noise rings out, and the girl twitches and squeezes the trigger. The arrow flies into the wall beside John, and she drops to the floor. Standing there is Officer Audley Barnes holding his laser pistol. He crouches down and checks the girl's pulse and handcuffs her and, in a slight Jamaican accent, says, "Lieutenant, man, are you okay?"

"Yes, thanks to you. Is that a crossbow? Jesus, what kind of crazy people are we dealing with? What is your name, officer?" John asks.

"My name is Officer Audley Barnes, sir."

"I'm glad to meet you, Audley Barnes. I think you just saved my life. I don't know if my coat would have stopped that damn arrow. It will stop a knife, bullet, and laser, but an arrow? We don't come across many arrows since the natives made peace. Follow us and watch our backs again." John then whispers into his coms, "Sam, we need someone up here to watch the girl that Officer Barns just neutralized and to collect her crossbow. We don't know if they have any more damn arrows."

"Remember, there is one more person on your floor," Sam says.

"Let's go find them. I've got an idea; Audley, go in that last room and get that office chair with the wheels on it."

Audley goes, gets the chair, and says, "How did you know there was a chair in there?"

"It caught the corner of my eye, and I remember details instantly. Anyway, Audley, I want you to push this chair ahead of Chuck and us, and I will blast anyone who pops out of a room. When you push the chair, hit the floor as fast as possible to give us a shot, and if you have a shot, take it. Audley gives the chair a hard, fast push and falls on the floor. Another member pops out of the room ahead and turns toward the chair to his right, and shoots at it with an old revolver. He turns quickly and shoots John in the chest, and John staggers back a bit. He shoots the guy in the neck, and he drops to the floor, shuddering from the jolt and drops his gun. Audley scrambles and picks up the gun. He looks at it, and having never seen one before, says, "Lieutenant, what is this thing?"

"It is an antique revolver that shoots bullets, looks like a Colt 45. They were banned years ago, finally, after several hundred teenage kids were killed in school shootings with guns and automatic rifles. Give me that gun, and I'll show you how to take the bullets out of it. This asshole just added ten years onto his sentence," John says.

At the same time, the SWAT team makes its way up the opposite staircase and gets to the fourth floor. Lieutenant Shane Travis throws a stun grenade and a smoke grenade ahead of him and waits for the rooms to empty. His team shoots at the members who are coughing but are shooting back at them. The SWAT team's vests stop most of the laser blasts, but two of his men get hit in the arm, and one takes a hit in the leg. Lieutenant Travis and his sidekick drop Dieter Stein and three more members and zip cuffs them. He calls EDD and says, "Send three medics up here; three of my men took a hit. The top floor is clear now. We've got the leader and three of his members in cuffs."

John comes on the radio and says, "We've cleared our end and have seven people in cuffs, and most are still unconscious. Send some back-up officers to gather them up. They are disarmed and stunned. Detectives Sidhu and I are okay. Our Bodyguard coats protected us from the laser blasts."

John, Chuck, Officer Audley Barnes, and the SWAT team gather in front of the building by the EDD truck and see Nikki Anders, Sam Slade, and Randy Chan. John says, "Detective Slade, you and your team did a great job warning us and keeping injuries to a minimum." John turns to Lieutenant Travis and says, "Who has that crossbow?"

Lieutenant Travis says, "Sergeant Amell Lebedinsky took it in for evidence. Why?"

"I'd like to borrow it in a day or two to experiment on my Bodyguard coat to see if it will stop an arrow. I'll put it on a droid, of course," John says.

Lieutenant Travis says, "I think that can be arranged, and I'm interested in getting some of those coats for my team."

"I've been talking to the captain and commander about that very thing. I want the higher-ups to pay for them. I'm spending my own money to give them to my squad, but I need to start selling them. I'd also like to sell them to the military."

John, Chuck, and Audley help load all the prisoners into several police vans and haul them to the station and into booking and jail cells. They drive back to the station and write up their reports as the prisoners are being booked, and John sends his report to the commander, captain, and Police Chief Emily Carter. John calls Nikki Anders and Sam Slade into his office and says, "Detective Slade, since this started out as your case, I would like you to interview Dieter Stein with A.P.A. Nikki Anders and delegate other detectives to interrogate all the other members. Detective Sidhu and I will help as we interacted with some of the members of this idiot outfit. Since they are being booked now, I think we should take a lunch break now. It's going to be a long day. Let's go across the street to the Retro Diner and talk strategy."

They go to the diner and order their food. Sam Slade says, "This is a neat place; I love these old diners. Is the food good here?"

"Yes, I usually have a cheeseburger, but they serve breakfast all day. They make good omelettes, and they have beef dips, salads, and old-fashioned milkshakes," John says.

Margarette comes to their table and smiles. "Good afternoon, detectives and ladies. What can I pleasure you with today? I know John will want a cheeseburger, fries, and a chocolate shake, right?"

"Yes, Margarette, are you psychic?"

"I'm more psycho, right, Chuck?"

Chuck says, "As A.P.A. Nikki Anders here would advise me to say, I plead the fifth on that because I like you and value my life. And I'll have a spinach and feta cheese omelette, please."

Nikki says, "I'll have the same as John, and my psychic ability tells me that our Chuck Sidhu has a girlfriend!"

Sam says, "I'll try your beef dip and a vanilla shake, please, and Chuck, I'm telling the whole squad that you have a girlfriend!"

Chuck says, "Margarette, see what I have to put up with every day?"

Margarette laughs and says, "Oh, poor, Chuck. Wait until I get my hands on you."

Chuck replies, "I can hardly wait."

Margarette pats Chuck on the back, smiles, and leaves to get their food.

John says, "Okay, now, Sam, I really want to interrogate that girl who shot at me with a crossbow. She is some piece of work, and I want to know where she got hold of a crossbow. Is it a sport or an illegal weapon?"

Nikki thinks for a moment and then says, "It may not be illegal to own one, but it certainly is illegal to use it as a weapon."

John adds, "I'll have to find out her name. There was also a guy with a Colt 45 shooting at us."

Margarette brings their food, and they eat with smiles on their faces. When they are about to leave, John says, "I'm buying today."

Nikki says, "If you don't mind, John, I would like to buy. The food was really good, and the 'entertainment' was worth it."

"Okay, but I want to leave her a big tip."

"Deal."

CHAPTER SIXTY-FIVE

They go back to the bullpen, and Chuck says, "I'll get that crazy girl's name for you and Mr. Colt 45, and we'll go scare the shit out of them, boss."

He goes to the booking desk and talks to Sergeant Trudy Falchuk.

Trudy says, "Let's see. Oh, Miss High and Mighty, I don't think she's potty-trained either. Here it is, her name is Laura Baudner. Christ, she shot at you with a crossbow? Is this a typo, Chuck?"

"Hell, no! She actually shot at John, and thank God Officer Audley Barnes blasted her a millisecond before because John would be dead right now. We need to know the name of the jerk with the Colt 45 also. He is in deep shit, and we are going to nail him today."

Trudy continues, "Yes, here it is; his name is Bruno Mueller. We put him in a separate cage just because he had a gun. After this, he may be known as Bruno on Mars."

"Good joke, Trudy. Can I use that?"

"Yes, but you have to give me credit, okay?"

Chuck replies, "Sure, and I'll put it in my report. Sergeant Trudy said . . . yada, yada, yada."

"That's funny, Chuck. Have a joy, joy day! I'll send those two assholes up to you, excellent detectives."

John and Chuck enter the interview room. "Record on. Hello, Miss Baudner. I didn't recognize you without your crossbow. I'm going to read you your rights before you start lying to me. Now, I'm just wondering, why did you try to kill me with a crossbow? I also want to know where you got it," John says.

She answers, "At a crossbow store, and I thought you were a prowler and were going to kill me."

Chuck says, "So, I guess you didn't hear all these cops and SWAT breaking down your doors, yelling police, and blasters firing on all floors?"

John adds, "I also had my back to you and was wearing a police helmet and gear. I'm lucky that Officer Barnes stunned you, or you would be looking at killing a police officer and serving a life sentence in a max prison. Also, we all had our body cameras on at the time. I'm wasting my time with you; I'm formally charging you with attempted murder on a police officer and belonging to a hate group. You should get yourself a lawyer."

John and Chuck leave the room, and John says, "Officer, take this woman back to a cage. She can call a lawyer if she wants one."

They go into Room Two and read Bruno Mueller his rights and recorded the interrogation. John says, "Well, Mr. Mueller, you are in deep shit. You shot me in the chest with an illegal weapon. Where does one get a Colt 45 these days, in a museum?"

He says, "It was my grandfather's. He left it to me in his will."

John retorts, "Wasn't that sweet of him. I guess no one told you that those types of guns were banned way back in 2025, and you can't get a licence to own one, never mind firing it at someone."

Bruno says, "See, I didn't know that, and how come you're not dead? I shot you right in the chest."

John says, "Ignorance is no excuse in the eyes of the law, and I can do magic like Harry Potter."

Bruno says, "Harry who?"

"Never mind. Bruno Mueller, I'm charging you with the attempted murder of a police officer and being registered to a hate group. Thank you for your confession of shooting me in the chest. You should get yourself a lawyer."

At the same time, Detective Sam Slade and Lieutenant Shane Travis are interrogating Dieter Stein in Room Four with A.P.A. Nikki Anders in the observation room. Sam glares and says, "Mr. Stein, we have read you your rights, and we are charging you with operating a drug ring, a protection ring, selling weapons, slavery, and the attempted murder of Lieutenant Travis here. We have you on video shooting at Lieutenant Travis. Also, you are charged with being the leader of a hate group. What do you have to say for yourself?"

He says, "I have nothing to say to you, and I want to call my lawyer."

Sam says, "We don't need to waste time talking to you; we have all the evidence we need. We just wanted you to know what charges you are facing. Lieutenant Travis and Detective Samantha Slade leaving interview room four. Record off."

They leave the room, and Nikki steps out of the observation room and says, "We've got him cold, and I can freeze his accounts because he made all his money illegally. We've statements from some of his members. I'll have him in a cage off-planet for life. Good work, people. Sam, you don't need to interview the rest of the members. The rest of the gang are open and shut cases and are all being charged with the attempted murder of police officers and belonging to a hate group. Well, we all have a pile of paperwork to do. See you later."

John says to Chuck, "Can you get the paperwork started? I want to go talk to Joanne Weber about Mr. Auger to see if she has a profile on him and what she thinks he will do next."

CHAPTER SIXTY-SIX

John calls Joanne's admin to see if she has time to see him. She tells him she has an open slot immediately. He says he will be right there. Her office is in the same building but on a different floor. He enters her office and says, "Hello, Joanne, how are you today?"

"I'm fine. It's slow today, and I was just studying your file on Mr. Auger. He is a curious subject. According to the Interpol agent, Holly Morgan, she believes he performed several revenge killings. His parents died of a drug overdose supplied by a French gang called the Royals, and all the gang members were murdered in a ritualistic fashion within a month and a half of each other. They were nailed to the floor like Jesus and then killed with a cordless drill. Your Ken Leung was killed in the same way. The first set of killings was revenge killings, but the Leung killing was a paid killing, paid for by Mr. Pavel Romaniuk, as caught on the nanny-cam. Then he killed Pavel Romaniuk with a deadly virus and some vicious poison that caused him to suffer for two days. Why would he kill the man who hired him? He didn't kill the man who hired him for the first kill on Doctor Blackwell. I can understand the Doctor Blackwell killing since the man killed Mr. Dupuis's daughter, even if it was accidental. You could say that was a revenge killing, even if he got paid for it. With his psyche, he probably would have done it for free, but he already was an established assassin in France. I bet there are other murders he committed that we don't know about yet."

John says, "I agree with you fully about his mental state. We are getting close to finding him. We found out what kind of vehicle he drives, and we found a post office box he uses, and we are staking it out. I hope to find him before he kills again because there is no way we can tell who he will kill next. I think he killed Pavel because Pavel betrayed him or pissed him off somehow. I mean, the way he killed Pavel was overkill. He really wanted him to suffer. He could have killed him with a sniper rifle instead of using a dart gun. You can add the information about the vehicle. It's a newer Toyota SUV, I think. I also wanted to talk to you about a private matter, off the record, okay?"

"Sure, is something bothering you, John?"

"Yes, I don't know if you knew that I did a tour in Afghanistan. I was shot there and almost died, and my buddy Thom Saunders saved my butt. Well, I started having nightmares, reliving that scene over again. I have never had these nightmares before, so why are they happening to me now? Even when my wife Silvia was killed three years ago, I was very depressed and sad for years, but I never had nightmares."

"Sometimes people who have post-traumatic stress are delayed in getting it. Did something traumatic happen to you lately?"

"You know, I've been very happy lately, but I did get shot with a blaster last week on a raid, but I didn't feel any real trauma from that. I was just worried because I was disabled. My legs were paralyzed for just a few days, but I was surrounded by friends, and my girlfriend flew back from Toronto to be by my side. I felt fairly safe, even though I was hurt. By the way, this Saturday, I'm having a birthday party for my girlfriend

Grace, and you are welcome to come and bring your husband and daughters. There is a sit-down dinner at eight o'clock and dancing at nine, and I know you love to dance. I've hired a band that plays all kinds of music."

Joanne says, "You had me at dinner and dancing." She adds, "I would like you to come back again; you may have PTSD, and it takes time to get over it. Some of the things that help are meditation and things like Tai Chi. The more you can put yourself in a calming mood, the faster you will heal. It is a mental problem, after all. You need to talk more about it also, and I can help you to get over it."

"I will, I promise. And I may need more help on this Auger case," John says.

CHAPTER SIXTY-SEVEN

John goes back to the bullpen and asks, "Chuck, is there any progress on finding Mr. Auger's address or company name or any sighting of him at the post office?"

Chuck replies, "We finally found a Toyota SUV licence plate SABER ONE, registered to a Saber House of Fashion Inc. at 789 Granville Street, and they have a warehouse in the waterfront area. Warehouse 49632. We checked, and the Granville address is now a vacant lot. The building was destroyed in the earthquake."

John says, "Let's take the EDD van and check it out with infra-red. Who is available?"

"Detective Randy Chan is available."

John yells, "Randy, let's go, we have a lead on Mr. Auger's address, and we need the EDD van and you to run the infra-red equipment."

"All right, I'll grab my hat, and let's go!"

They grab the van and go down to the docks to find warehouse 49632. Randy works the equipment and says, "There are seven people in there, boss. What now?"

John answers, "His SUV is around the corner, out of sight. Let's drive around back and put a tracker on his vehicle and maybe hack into his vehicle's computer and track his GPS system. Can you do that, Randy?"

He says, "Does a bear shit in the woods? Of course, I can do it."

John says, "Okay, meanwhile, I'll sneak over and put a tracker on his car. My brother Mike designed it; it's undetectable because it puts out a very low frequency." John puts on workman's coveralls and a baseball cap and slowly walks over to Auger's car and puts the tracker under the rear bumper, and returns to the van. He asks, "Randy is it working?"

"Yes, and I hacked into his computer, so we have two ways of tracking him. Now, we can find out where he lives. You know, John, the infra-red can pick up speech through the walls, even if they are brick, but we need someone at line-of-sight to the building, and we can record it, so we need one or two more men in the warehouse across from Auger's warehouse."

"I'll call Sam to ask Lieutenant Shane Travis if he has two spare guys who are trained to use infra-red equipment. We can track Auger from miles away, but we need to stay fairly close to see if he lives in an apartment and if he has an alarm for trackers in his car."

John calls Sam, and Sam replies, "Travis said he doesn't have any spare men."

"Okay, are Bennetti and Tran around?"

"Bennetti is here, but not Tran. However, Cornburra is available," Sam says.

"Send Bennetti and Cornburra close to warehouse 49632 at the docks. Actually, we are two blocks south-west of the warehouse now. Auger is here, and we put a tracker on his Toyota SUV, but we need them to sit on him and tail him to see where he lives. We need Randy to stay with the van. It's a white van with the words KNIGHT AND DAY PLUMBING on the side. Bennetti and Cornburra need to meet with Randy in the van to make sure they are on the same page. Sit a block away. Bye," John says.

CHAPTER SIXTY-EIGHT

John asks, "Any action, Randy?"

"No, he is still in there. Detectives Bennetti and Cornburra are set up across the street in a warehouse, but Auger is mostly talking French. I turned on the translator, but it is not perfect, though Detective Bennetti speaks French. You can listen to the recording later, but he is mostly talking business. You know I can track him from anywhere in the city, and Bennetti and Cornburra can follow him," Randy says.

"What we really need to do is hack into all his phones and emails. Once we find out where he lives, we can set up nearby and hack into his electronics or possibly bug his apartment and his office. There must be a way to do it legally. We need to know who he is going to kill next so that we can set a trap for him. Well, Randy, keep an eye on him. I'll hang here for a while, then I have to go to my office and write a progress report."

CHAPTER SIXTY-NINE

John waits an hour, then goes to his office and phones Grace on his videophone. "Hi, Grace. Have you gone crazy yet?"

"I'm getting there. Actually, I'm having lots of fun now! I've got all your squad's coats finished, and I designed a coat for myself; it's more high fashion. It looks like smooth combed cotton and is a very pale green with pink accents. It has pink slits at the pockets and a pink collar, epilates, buttons, and silk lining. I've already shipped your squad's coats to your house and have made Susan Wells the manager and Joy Nolan the head seamstress. We have five seamstresses so far and will add more later."

"I was wondering; if this material is knife proof, how do you sew it?" John asks.

"It isn't knife proof until it is activated by spraying a polymer coating on it and pulsing low electricity through it. We are starting to design and make pants, vests, and skirts. I'm going to come home on Friday as things are running well here, and I need to check on my other businesses and attack my boyfriend until he begs for mercy."

"Boy, I feel sorry for him as I know you know Kung Fu and other deadly attacks."

"You can hide, Mr. Bond, James Bond, but I will find you," she says.

John replies in Mandarin, saying, "I certainly hope so, my lotus blossom. I'll have the whips and leather ready for you." He switches to English and adds, "Oh, did you get some presents for Savana and Jackie yet?"

"Yes, I got them a dozen colouring books each and two cute little stuffed bison that talk."

"That's great. Can I play with them too?"

She grins and says, "No, but you can play with me."

"It's a deal. Well, I have to go. There is one more jerk to put in jail, and someone is knocking at my door. Love you. See you on Friday."

CHAPTER SEVENTY

"Whoever is knocking, come in," John says.

Sam Slade opens the door and says, "John, I was just interrogating Raymond James, one of the Supreme assholes, who was running the protection racket, and he finally told me the names of some of the stores he was, so-called, protecting. They are all on Commercial Drive in Little Italy. I was thinking that we blast down there and get some statements from some of the merchants since he is in jail now and can't hurt them. We could take his mug shot and arrest report with us."

"Sam, I have too much paperwork to do. Take Audley Barnes with you and fly down to Commercial Drive and talk to all the merchants to assure them that they are safe. You can take my new car. Also, I want you to train Officer Audley Barnes to be a detective. He has shown a lot of potential besides saving my life in that raid. Which reminds me, I put you in for a commendation. If it wasn't for you, we wouldn't have all this evidence against Raymond James to add to his sentence. Now, go! I'll see you later.

"Wow. Thanks, John!" she says.

CHAPTER SEVENTY-ONE

John goes into his office and spends a few hours typing his report, sending copies to the captain, commander, and A.P.A. Nikki Anders. He goes to the evidence room and checks out the crossbow and the steel arrow, and puts it in a cardboard box, then he goes home.

Thom and Chrissy greet him at the door. John pets Chrissy and says, "Hi, Thom. Come with me; we have a little project to do."

"Okay, boss. What's in the box?"

"Our project."

They get in the elevator and go down to the shooting range. John pulls out the crossbow and takes off his coat, and puts it on a special droid with sensors on it. Thom frowns and says, "Is that a crossbow?"

"Yes, and I'm going to shoot it at that droid, and I want you to record it with your phone." John sets up with the crossbow and shoots the droid in the heart area. The arrow hits the coat and bounces off, and falls on the floor. John yells, "All right, the coat stopped it. They check the sensor readings and find very little force was registered, while Thom records everything. John excitedly says, "I can't believe how well this coat material is working. I'm going to shoot it six more times to make sure it will take multiple hits."

"I know that look in your eye, John. You want to wear the coat while I shoot it, don't you, you crazy bastard?"

John smiles. "You read my mind. Look, we know it works; I just want to know what it feels like. If I'm going to sell these coats, I want to be able to tell everyone what it feels like to be hit by any kind of weapon and how safe it is, okay? So, set my recorder up and shoot me in the back like that crazy bitch was going to do. Then I can show it to the police chief, commander, and captain, and I will even show it to Grace. Of course, I will show her the droid tests first so that she doesn't go ballistic on me, and she will have more confidence in the product. She told me that she is starting to design pants, vests, designer dresses. You know scarves would also be a good idea to protect our necks. Later, I want to design helmets. We could make a fortune selling to the military, police, and SWAT."

They set up, and Thom shoots John in the center of his back. John doesn't flinch and laughs, "It felt like a tickle. Let's check for any marks in the material." They check the coat over, and there isn't a scratch on it anywhere. John adds, "If I were Sam Slade, I would be doing a happy dance right now. Let's go have some supper. We should celebrate with a steak and maybe lobster if Julie has any."

They take the elevator upstairs and find Julie, Savana, and Chrissy in the dining room. John and Thom are smiling ear to ear. Julie says, "You two look like the cat that ate the canary. What is going on, boys?"

John replies, "We just did a test on the Bodyguard coat and found that it will stop a crossbow arrow with no injuries and not a scratch on the material. Before you freak out, we tested it on a special droid. This is going to help us sell more coats to the police and maybe the military. We want to celebrate. Do you have any steaks and maybe a lobster or two, Julie?"

Julie answers, "Yes, we have porterhouse, T-bone, filet minion, New York steak, and we just happen to have had some lobster flown in for Grace's party."

John says, "Great, filet minion sounds good with roast potatoes and asparagus or some kind of vegetable, and we could each have a lobster, including you, Julie. Thom, what kind of steak do you want?"

"Filet minion for me too and lobster."

"Let's have a bottle of Cabernet to start with. I'll get it. What do you want, Savana?" John asks.

"I'll have a steak with no bone if someone would cut it up for me and a glass of chocolate almond milk," she says.

"I'll cut it up for you. Do you want to try some of my lobster? It's really good, and you should try new foods. I think a whole one would be too much food for you," John says.

"Okay, Uncle Tiny, I'll try some. I liked the spinach and feta cheese omelette Thom made me try. If I don't like the lobster, I'll give it to Chrissy; she seems to like all kinds of seafood."

John gets the bottle of wine, opens it, and lets it breathe for several minutes. Julie brings in the steak and lobster meals. John pours the wine and cuts Savana's steak for her, and prepares some lobster for her. "Savana, you can dip the lobster in the melted butter with garlic in it," John says. He watches as she dips the lobster in the garlic butter and chews on it.

She has a neutral look on her face, and then she smiles. "I like this lobster stuff; can I have some more?"

"Sure, I'll give you some more and a little for Chrissy." Chrissy is sitting down, looking up at Savana and John, swivelling her little head back and forth. John gives Savana more lobster and another small plate for Savana to give to Chrissy. Savana gives the plate of lobster to Chrissy, and she gobbles it up like she hadn't eaten in months.

Thom shakes his head and says, "John, you must have a golden tongue to get Savanna to eat all these different foods, and they are good for her. So many kids are really fussy about what they eat and end up with a bad diet and health problems."

John shrugs, "I do what I can." He then looks at his watch and says, "I want to give Mike a call and send him the video of the crossbow experiment." He goes to his office and sends the video to Mike and then calls him. "Did you get my video?"

"Yes. What the heck was that all about, a crossbow? John, you are one crazy bastard. I hope you tried it on a droid first."

"Of course, I tried it on a droid first, one with sensors on it. A crazy girl tried to kill me with a crossbow during a raid, and she missed, so I wanted to know if the coat would stop an arrow, and it does. The arrow hit the coat and bounced off like the coat was rubber, and I didn't feel any heavy hit. This will help us sell more coats. Grace is now designing pants and vests, and I've been spreading the word to my captain and commander, who will probably help us sell these coats to the police, SWAT and later, to the military. Also, the police chief is a woman, and she is coming to the party, so she will probably want a coat too."

"That's great, John. You are a great salesman. I put the '57 Chevy golf cart in your garage, which is starting to look like a museum. That Rolls Royce looks incredible, even the interior looks hardly worn, and it looks like it is bulletproof. Does it have an alarm in it?"

John thinks for a minute, then says, "I don't know. I haven't had the time to even look at it. I'll ask my mechanic Ringo to check it out. He has been detailing and polishing it this week. I should have him put in an electric shock burglar alarm like James Bond had on that Audi. Oh, Grace is coming back on Friday to take care of her other businesses, and I'll see her Friday evening. She made herself another coat, which is more colourful and a fancier design because she wants to sell some coats to women that are custom-designed and I already have a customer for her, A.P.A. Nikki Anders, who is all excited and isn't shy about spending money. She probably has a lot of wealthy friends who will want one too. You know what women are like around clothes. They dress up for us, but we would rather have them naked."

Mike laughs and says, "You are right about that, brother. Well, I have some paperwork to do myself, so thanks for calling and updating me on Bodyguard Clothing. It looks like our investment is going to pay off. I should get Gladys to tell her friends about the designer coats. Oh, damn, we never made her a coat."

"Well, Mike, she can talk to Grace on Saturday, and they can design a coat together. Well, I've got a report to write, so I'll see you on Saturday. Bye."

"Okay, so long, John."

John starts up his computer as Chrissy wanders into his office and makes herself at home on his couch, lays down, and stares at him. He looks at her and says, "Hi, Chrissy, make yourself at home. Too bad you can't type; you could save me a lot of work." She meows and goes to sleep.

John types in Wednesday, April 26th, 2070, file #7011, and updates his report and home murder board, and slides it back into a slot in the wall. He doesn't want the children to see the slaughtered bodies and blood as it would surely give them nightmares. He opens a panel in the wall and pours himself a glass of Artis Cognac, and watches the news with Jenny Olson on Channel 24. He then watches a half-hour comedy show and finishes his Cognac, and goes to bed. Chrissy curls up beside him and purrs. He goes to sleep, thinking about seeing Grace again.

Near dawn, he has the same nightmare about getting shot in Afghanistan and wakes up sweating and looking around. Chrissy wakes up but doesn't jump off the bed. Instead, she rubs her head against him and puts her paw on his arm and cheek and meows quietly to show she cares about him. He looks at Chrissy and says, "Thank you, Chrissy. I know you care about me, and I love you too. I have to get help for these nightmares, but I don't know what will really help me. I'll ask Grace if she knows Tai Chi."

He checks the time and remembers that it is Thursday, April 27th, and he will see Grace tomorrow. He takes a hot shower, changes the temperature to cold, towels off, and gets dressed in comfortable clothes; an old University of Manitoba T-shirt and sweatpants.

CHAPTER SEVENTY-TWO

He grabs a coffee from his auto chef and starts to plan his day in his mind. He must check on his team's progress on finding Auger's next target and deal with whatever else comes up at the station. He exercises for a half-hour and then goes down for breakfast with Chrissy following behind him.

Julie and Thom are sitting at the table drinking coffee and talking about the party arrangements. John sits down and says, "Good morning, all. I was talking to Grace last night, and she will be here tomorrow evening. How many people are coming to the party? Do you have a count yet?"

Thom replies, "I've gotten 234 RSVPs, and that includes all your squad and Mike and Grace's people. Does that line up with the catering, Julie?"

"Yes, and Natalie and her chef Rolf are already preparing a lot of the food in their kitchen, and I've made a lot of the seating arrangements," she says.

"Speaking of food, Julie, I think I'll have scrambled eggs, little homemade potatoes, and three slices of bacon, no toast, okay?"

"Thom, how about you?" she asks.

"I'll have a Denver omelette and rye toast, please, Miss Julie."

John looks at Julie and asks, "Where is Savana? Is she okay?"

"She's still getting dressed and brushing her teeth. She will be down any minute."

Just then, Savana enters the room and says, "Are these clothes okay, mom?" She is wearing a pink sweater, blue blouse, and green pants.

Julie looks her over and says, "You sure are colourful, but your sweater is inside out. Come here, and I'll fix it, but you did a good job otherwise. What do you want for breakfast, dear?"

"I'll have some Corn Flakes and toast with peanut butter, please, mom. Here, Chrissy." She pats her lap, and Chrissy jumps up. She pets her, and Chrissy sits down and purrs.

"Savana, Grace is coming back tomorrow and I think she is bringing you a surprise present from Winnipeg."

"Really, what is it?"

"I don't know, and even if I did, I couldn't tell you because it's a surprise."

"Well, I will be happy to see her anyway because I really like her and she healed Chrissy, so she must be nice. You should marry her, Uncle Tiny, then she could be my auntie."

John says, "I just might do that, just to make you happy. You never know."

Savana's eyes open wide, and she blurts out, "You would do that for me?"

John smiles and says, "Remember that Saturday is Grace's birthday and we are having a big party for her. What are you going to wear?"

"I don't know; mom will probably pick out a nice dress for me with flowers on it."

John thinks and says, "You know; you should make her a birthday present."

She frowns. "I don't know how to make a present."

"Sure you do. You can draw her a picture with crayons. She told me that she would rather have a handmade present that is done with love than an expensive present that someone spent two minutes buying. She can hang your drawing in her office or on our fridge here. She loves you. She told me so and crossed her heart."

Savana smiles. "Okay, I'll draw her the best picture I ever drew of you and her, so she will feel like part of our family."

They eat, Julie feeds Chrissy, and John leaves for work.

CHAPTER SEVENTY-THREE

John calls Chuck and says, "I'll pick you up on the way to work so that we can touch base."

In the car, Chuck says, "I want to thank you for introducing me to Margarette. She is the opposite of me in personality. She is very loving in bed, yet is serious about her life path and wants to help people. She volunteers at a soup kitchen at a homeless shelter twice a week and brings left-over food from the restaurant. In my off time, I want to help her. Like you said, she has a heart of gold and yet she can be sassy and sexy."

John looks over at Chuck and says, "Well, I'm glad I could help, and I hope you two stay happy together. Where is this shelter? I don't have time to volunteer since I have all these companies to run, and I'm putting a lot of time into Bodyguard Clothing. I want to protect as many people as possible with this technology. It's not just about the money Grace, Mike, and I can make on this. Also, Grace can have fun designing fashionable laser proof clothing, as fashion is where her heart is. Anyway, I want to make a donation to this shelter anonymously. So, I want you to find out how much money they need, and I'll give a little more than that through one of my companies. Well, here we are. Let's see how much shit is flying today."

They enter the bullpen, and John spots Randy and asks, "How is the Auger mission going? You, Chuck, and I should go into my office and discuss this."

They go into the office, and John asks, "Anyone want a coffee? I'm having one. I have the Afrikaans brand in my auto chef."

Chuck says, "Sure, I take mine black."

Randy says, "I'll have mine with cream and two sugars, please."

John gets the coffees and asks Randy, "Well, where are we with Auger?"

Randy looks at his notes and says, "Well, John, we have surveillance on him and found his home address. It is 1542 West 23rd Avenue in Shaunessy. There is a lot of construction going on in that area, so we got a van with a sign on it that says CAPUTO CONSTRUCTION, a good Italian name, and I think the captain will get a kick out of it. We have an infra-red microphone on him, and we hacked into his Wi-Fi and his cell phone. So, we just wait for the call or email."

John's phone rings. "Dispatch, Lieutenant John Trosky. Robbery in progress at the Retro Diner. You are the closest one to the scene. Waitress being held at knifepoint." John looks at Chuck and says, "Shit, I hope it's not Margarette. Let's get over there fast. Okay, Randy, you go in the west door, and I'll go in the east door, slowly. We are just customers. We take our back-up ankle weapons just in case. We act scared. I'll try to distract him, and you zap him in the leg or the back so that he doesn't cut her. Let's go! Chuck, you go in through the kitchen, and if you have a shot, take it. Recorders on."

They cross the road to the diner. John goes in first and sees a skinny little guy who looks like a junkie, holding Margarette with a knife against her neck and making her open the cash register. He looks at the guy and frowns. "What is going on here?"

The guy says, "Shut up and sit down."

John cowers and sits down at a table. In a trembling voice, he says, "Okay, just don't hurt me; I have a wife, three kids, and a dog."

While John is distracting him, Randy comes in and quickly moves behind the counter. He distracts the guy as Chuck blasts him through the kitchen divider, and he falls on the ground. He tries to get up as he is on PCP, and John jumps over the counter and pulls Margarette away and shouts, "Chuck, blast him again; he's on drugs!" Chuck blasts him again on the medium setting, and the guy drops the knife and passes out. John cuffs the guy and calls for back-up. John flips the guy over and takes his picture with his phone as Chuck goes and cradles Margarette in his arms.

"Are you hurt?"

She is shaking and is scared. "No, thank God you guys showed up, or I would be dead."

John takes the guy's prints with his device and says, "His name is George Bodner, goes by 'Brutus.' That's a good fuckin' joke. This little tweaker is Brutus? Maybe he was ten years ago. He has a record as long as your arm and a bunch of aliases. "Margarette, are you okay?" John goes over to her and sits down across from her in a booth. Chuck takes his coat off and wraps it around her. John quietly says, "Let's take you across the street and get your statement. We will have to shut this place down while the CSI guys go over the scene. We'll get this asshole booked for robbery, and I'm going for attempted murder so that we can put him in a cage off-planet, and you will never see him again. He has no fuckin' brains trying to rob a place across from a cop shop, and cops are in here all the time. Randy, get those officers to haul him into an interrogation room, and I'll be right there."

John, Randy, and Margarette go across the street to the cop shop. Chuck stays back to fill in the CSI crew on what happened and makes notes in his hand-held digital notebook. John goes into the interrogation room and says, "Recorder on," and reads George Bodner his rights. He has a thick paper file on him and slams it down on the table. "Well, George, or should I call you Brutus?"

"Call me Brutus, you damn asshole cop. You ruined my day; I was going to have enough dough for a good hit. I'm going to sue you for shooting me with a blaster."

"Well, you'll have to take that up with Detective Sidhu, as he is the one who shot you while you held a knife to that innocent waitress's throat. I would bring Detective Sidhu in here, but he is busy with the CSI people right now. The waitress that you tried to kill is a good friend of mine. You must be pretty stupid to try to rob a diner right across the street from a cop shop."

"What cop shop?"

"Oh, you didn't notice the huge sign above our doors that said Vancouver Police Department? I don't know why I'm wasting my time on you. We have you on our three recorders committing this crime, you scumbag, and with your record—robbery, assault and battery, and grand theft auto—we have a solid case against you. Not to mention the statement from the waitress you tried to kill. You are screwed. I'd liked to lock the door on your cage myself, but I don't want to go off-planet to Titus Two, where you will spend a shitload of time. Though, I hear the sex life is great in there, as the guards bet on how long a guy will last until he is buggered. But it's not that bad, as I hear they give you a large jar of Vaseline with your supplies and clothes. You admitted to the robbery, and we have you on record holding a knife to the waitress's throat, you prick. You are under arrest. Lieutenant John Trosky leaving Room One. Record off."

He leaves the room and sees A.P.A. Nikki Anders leaving the observation room. "You did a good job in there, John. Slam dunk."

"He wasn't much of a challenge. We caught him with his knife to Margarette's throat, and Chuck got the satisfaction of blasting his ass. We should do a drug test on him as he was high as a kite, and he is starting to shake."

"Okay, I'll have him taken to the infirmary," she says. "Officer Blake, take Mr. Bodner to the infirmary and have them do a drug test on him and keep him cuffed."

John goes to find Margarette and Chuck. They are at Chuck's cubicle. John walks up and hugs Margarette and says, "Let's all go into my office and talk about this."

They go into John's office, and he says, "Margarette, did you give your statement?"

In a trembling voice, she says, "Yes, I gave it to Chuck, and Samantha was there too." If you need any counselling after such a traumatic event, we can supply you with one. Don't take this too lightly. I have recently started having terrible dreams about my service in Afghanistan. I can recommend Joanne Webber, she is our resident counsellor, and she is a very kind and sensitive person. I'll give you her number. She is in this building, so she isn't far away, okay?"

"John, can I see her now? I'm very upset. In fact, I'm freaking out," she says.

John calls Joanne, "Joanne, how is your schedule today? I have a friend who was just robbed at knifepoint, my good friend Margarette."

"You mean Margarette, the waitress from the Retro Diner? She is a lovely girl. Bring her to my office right now. I will move some appointments around as I am not very busy today. This has to be a very private moment for us. I'll call you when we are finished," Joanne says.

John escorts Margarette to Joanne's office, and Joanne hugs John and Margarette. She says, "You know that John and I are old friends, and you can trust me to keep everything you say to me as confident; it is the law. I know you will get over this quickly from what I've seen of you as you are a very strong woman and have a great sense of humour, which is a great asset. Okay, John, you should leave now so that us girls can talk. She is in good hands with me. I'll call you when we are finished, and you can escort her home."

"I'll have Detective Chuck Sidhu take her home, and I think she should take a few days off. Do you agree, Joanne?"

"Yes, she should, and I will subscribe a mild soother. Now, get out, John, or I'll kick your ass."

"Yes, ma'am." John goes back to the bullpen and says, "Detective Sidhu, when Joanne Weber is finished with Margarette, she will tag you, and I want you to take the rest of the day off and take care of her at her place until she is comfortable and settled.

CHAPTER SEVENTY-FOUR

John enters the bullpen and asks, "Where are we with Mr. Auger?"

Randy says, "Lieutenant, we just caught a break. He got an email from a Chad Harris, an internet billionaire, to put a hit on a Trevor Wallace, another billionaire who owns the Looking Glass search engine. The hit is paying him six million dollars—three million upfront in his off-shore account, and three million when the guy is dead. So, he might rabbit after this. Looking Glass is like Google, only more advanced, and it has a Dark Web embedded in it. We must move fast, as he wants him and his wife Alice killed tonight in his loft at 1321 Herron Street."

John says, "Shit, that doesn't give us much time. Call Shane Travis of SWAT and get everyone available in my office asap. I want pictures of Trevor Wallace and his wife. Make sure to get Sam Slade in here and a makeup artist. There she is. Sam, come with me into my office and drop whatever you are doing."

She starts walking fast and replies, "Sure, lieutenant, coming. What's going on?"

"We are going to hit Mr. Auger this evening. First, I need some pictures or video of Trevor Wallace and his wife, Alice."

"Let me do that; I know all the websites they will be on." She gets on John's computer and finds a video of them at a gala with close-up pictures.

John looks at them and says, "Good, he is about my height, and she is a pretty blonde. Are you up to taking her place? I want to set a trap for our assassin."

"Are you kidding? I live for this shit," Sam says.

John looks at her carefully and says, "Hmm, we need to get you into a dress and redo your hair. I have a makeup artist and wardrobe person coming in. We'll also put you in regular flat shoes with pointed steel toes in case you need to kick some ass."

"And you need to slick your hair back. Your suit is fine," she says.

"Yes, and I'll want to keep my laser proof coat on in case he decides to shoot me," John says.

His squad comes in, and he announces, "Everyone, take a seat and grab some coffee if you need it from my auto chef."

Sam says, "I'll program a big pot of coffee."

John adds, "I want to call Chuck; he will be pissed if he misses this."

John calls Chuck and says, "I hate to interrupt whatever you are doing, Chuck, but we are going after Mr. Auger this evening, and I just know you want to be a part of this. Does Margarette have anyone to stay with her for a while?"

Chuck replies, "Yes, I'll call her sister Emily; she lives close by."

"We are starting a meeting in fifteen or twenty minutes as soon as SWAT gets here. I'm getting the board ready, so hurry. This Trevor is a rich guy, so I'm going to get Commander Caputo to call him and fill him in on our mission and get Trevor and Alice to a safe place. They can go out the back entrance and into a ghost cop car, like now."

He calls the commander and tells him about the plan, and Caputo says, "I'll call him and pick them up in my own limo around the back door, right now."

The SWAT team and Chuck arrive together, as do the makeup people, and they start working on Sam first, as John is explaining the mission. He and Sam will take Trevor and Alice's place and Chuck will play their butler. John shows a schematic of Trevor's apartment, the surrounding apartments, and the entrances in the front and back of Trevor's loft. John says, "We also found out that Chad Harris, who hired Auger, wants him to kill Trevor and Alice with the nano-bots in a pressure syringe, and he will have two of them. I'd like to take him alive, but if things get out of hand, don't hesitate to end his life." He then adds, "Lieutenant Travis, can you set up your men across the street at the front and back in an apartment or on a roof?"

"Give me the best picture of him, and I'll do it. We better get going now. See you later, guys," Lieutenant Travis says.

The makeup people magically change John's appearance to look just like Trevor. Sam looks at him and says, "John, you look incredibly like Trevor."

He retorts, "And, you could pass for Alice."

They dress Chuck in the butler's get-up, and they all get in the limo, go to Trevor Wallace's loft, and make themselves comfortable. John asks, "What is there to drink?"

Sam replies, "They have Pepsi, want one?"

John says, "Sure, I like Pepsi but not Coke."

Chuck sets up four hidden cameras in all the rooms and sets up his computer to monitor and record them. John looks at all the cameras and the computer and says, "Okay, let's turn on the television and more lights in other rooms."

Sam finds some iced tea and gives Chuck a Pepsi. She checks her weapon strapped to her thigh. John looks at her and checks his blaster and his ankle mini-blaster, and the knife in his boot. They are all wearing earbud coms and checking in with Shane Travis and SWAT. John says, "Travis, any sign of our friend, the Pale Rider?"

Travis answers, "No Pale Rider or his horse, out."

The evening comes, and everyone is getting nervous. A brown UPS truck then pulls up, and a chubby man in a uniform gets out with a package. Travis says, "Looks like our friend is here dressed as a UPS driver."

John says, "Great, we will let him in."

Auger presses the intercom button for the loft and says, "Package for Mr. Trevor Wallace."

John gives him a hard time, saying, "I didn't order any packages; you must have the wrong address."

Auger retorts, "It says Mr. Trevor Wallace, urgent from the Looking Glass company."

John signals Sam and Chuck and replies, "Well, okay. Come up to the loft."

Sam stands on one side of the door and Chuck stays back at the corner of the next room with his blaster in his hand. John puts on his Bodyguard coat and opens the door for Mr. Auger, and says, "This better be important; my wife and I were just going to the opera."

Auger drops the package and stabs John in the stomach with the syringe. John grabs him, pulls him into the room, flips him over his head, and then turns and punches him in the face. Sam shoots at Auger to no effect and is puzzled. John and Auger both get to their feet and wrestle across the room, punching and kicking each other and rolling around the floor. Chuck comes out and tries to shoot Auger, but they are moving too fast. John reaches for his knife and cuts Auger's left hand. Auger rolls away, gets up, grabs a crystal vase, smashes it against a table, and comes at John. "Fuck, you aren't Trevor Wallace. What the hell is going on?"

John smirks. "I'm a cop, and you are under arrest, shit for brains."

Auger slices at him, and the coat doesn't get cut, so he goes for his neck, and John drops to the floor and kicks him in the chest. Auger reaches into his pocket and pulls out another pressure syringe. John grabs his wrist, twists it, hears it snap, and points it toward Auger. They struggle, and Chuck shoots Auger on medium in the neck. He jerks and stabs himself in the neck. His eyes open wide, and he cries, "Oh no!" He rolls over, and blood pours out of his mouth, nose, and ears, and he dies.

John gets up and says, "Shit, I wanted this fucker alive. I know he killed way more people than we know about, damn!" He then adds, "Anyway, we finally got the bastard. Good work, Sam and Chuck! He almost killed me; he was a strong bastard. Thank God for this coat. He couldn't believe the coat didn't slice; I saw it in his eyes."

Travis rushes into the loft, saying, "Lieutenant, you got him! I'll call Luci Ryan and the CSI guys for you. I want a look myself; I never did see what this guy really looked like."

John says, "Hey, I never thought of that. Sam and Chuck, come here. John reaches down and looks hard at his face. "Sam, does that look like a latex mask to you?"

She bends down and grabs a corner of the mask under his jaw, and peels it off. It's a *Mission Impossible* type of mask. The guy's face is skinnier, his stomach is padded, and he is wearing a combat vest. John says, "He looks a bit like his teenage picture. I'll bet if we check Bill Auger's aliases over the years, we will find many more people he killed. You two take his picture right now for facial recognition. I need to get a hold of Holly Morgan and maybe get her back here, but first, have her check her records and Interpol's facial recognition files. Chuck and Sam, grab the cameras and the computer, and we'll head back to the office."

Shane Travis and Luci Ryan come in. "Luci and Travis, come over here and meet Bill Auger. I didn't mean to kill him, but we were wrestling, and he accidentally stabbed himself with that syringe. It has those nano-bots in it, and he died instantly. Shit, I wanted to interrogate him and then put him in a cage. Well, Luci, you take over and send me your report. I have to get back to the office."

John and Chuck enter the bullpen, and he tells Chuck to write his report and copy the videos of the fight to the computer and send them to the captain, commander, and Police Chief Carter. John then calls Holly Morgan. She answers and says, "Hello, Lieutenant Trosky. What's new?"

"I finally caught Bill Auger today and killed him by accident in a tussle. I'm sending you a photo of him undisguised to your computer. I really wanted to take him alive, but he was going to kill me. I wanted to interrogate him as I have a hunch that he killed a lot more people in Europe."

"That is shocking. I do not know what to say, *Monsieur* John," she says.

John replies, "I was thinking; why don't you put his real picture through your facial recognition program and see what comes up. Also, we now have his DNA. If you find out anything, call me. Maybe you could come to my girlfriend Grace's birthday party on Saturday. The dinner is at eight o'clock, and the band starts at nine."

She says, "I'll check into the facial recognition, and we need his DNA profile. I will come to your party; it sounds like fun! I'll call or text you."

John dictates his report to his laptop and is partway through when Holly calls him back and says, "John, we dug deep on Bill Claude Auger. He had a juvenile file for auto theft, assault, and an adult file on home invasion, robbery, and assault. We also found some older pictures of him. My boss is sending me to Vancouver tomorrow by shuttle, so I will see you there. We need your paperwork to close this file, and we need a copy of his DNA and a printed photo of his body."

"Okay, Holly, I'll see you tomorrow. Do you need a lift from the shuttle port? I could send my limo for you."

"That would be great. I will see you tomorrow around noon. Ciao"

CHAPTER SEVENTY-FIVE

John finishes his report and sends a copy to all his bosses. He steps into the bullpen and says, "Chuck, are you still driving my old car?"

"Yes, Captain Fedora had the mechanics repair everything on it and told me that it's my ride now," Chuck says.

"Good, I'm going to stop by Ken Leung's wife's place and tell her we caught her husband's killer."

"Okay, I think I will go see Mrs. Romaniuk and Paul and tell them about Auger. Then, I'm going home."

John goes to the captain's office and stands in front of his desk. The captain says, "Hi, John, have a seat. I got your report. Well, I talked to Commander Caputo and Chief Carter, and they thank you for getting Mr. Auger. He has no relatives, so I think we should get his funds, but we will let the lawyers work on that. Case closed."

John says, "Interpol Agent Holly Morgan is flying in tomorrow. She found some background information on him and other crimes he committed in Europe. She has proof that he was Bill Auger. She and I will get together and share information so that the Europeans can close more cases and tell the relatives of the people he assassinated there."

Captain Fedora says, "Sure, you do that, but leave me out of it as much as you can. I'm so busy lately that my wife said she is going to file a missing person's report on me."

John laughs. "I'd like to meet your wife; she sounds a lot like my girlfriend."

Captain Fedora retorts, "No, you don't want to meet her. I'm just kidding. We are looking forward to your party on Saturday. It's not super formal, is it?"

"No, it's as Grace would say, casual semi-dress-up. No monkey suits, and don't worry, I'll handle the press on this. I owe Jenny Olson an exclusive. I'll call her on the way home. I'm exhausted; it's been a long day. See you, boss."

John gets in his cop car, puts it on autopilot, and calls Jenny Olson. He fills her in on Bill Auger's death." She is shocked and excited and wants more details. He says, "Look, Jenny, I just gave you the jump on this. No other reporter knows about this, and I've had a long bloody day. Come to my home tomorrow at . . . what time is good for you?"

"How about nine o'clock? And I'll bring my camera operator, Willow, she is really good."

"Of course, we will do an interview for one hour unless we are interrupted by another murder, okay? Tomorrow at nine. Ciao, *bambino*."

CHAPTER SEVENTY-SIX

John gets home, enters the house, and neither Thom nor Chrissy are there. He is puzzled but tired, so he heads up to his bedroom and starts toward his bed. As he approaches, he sees a large lump in there, so he pulls out his pistol blaster, pulls back the covers, and there is Grace, naked and half-asleep. "Someone has been sleeping in my bed and ate my porridge," John says.

She wakes up a bit sleepy and says, "What? Oh, John!" She grabs him and pulls him into bed, and kisses him fiercely. She replies with a gravelly voice, "Damn, I wanted to surprise you and fell asleep, and I didn't eat your porridge; that was a small golden-haired girl. Put your blaster away and get those clothes off. Hey, is that blood on you?"

"Yes, but most of it is not mine. I'll fill you in, but I really need a shower. Want to join me, little girl?"

She looks at him with fire in her eyes and says, "Yes, Mr. Bond, James Bond, but please be gentle, it's my first time."

He drags her along as he strips and smiles. "Yes, and it doesn't rain in Indianapolis in the summertime."

"What?" she asks.

"It was in a song called "Little Green Apples" by Roger Miller from 1968, so you wouldn't know it," he says.

"You know the weirdest shit. So, who's blood is this that I'm scrubbing off your penis?"

John looks down and says, "Is that what you're doing? Well, I have good news for you; the assassin, Bill Auger, is dead. I accidentally killed him earlier today."

"How do you accidentally kill somebody? Did he fall off a building or something?"

"Well, we found out he was going to kill an internet billionaire named Trevor Wallace and his wife, Alice."

"I know Alice; I designed some clothes for her. Wow!"

"So, the makeup people made me up like him and made Sam Slade look like Alice and Chuck was the butler. Auger was dressed as a UPS driver with a package. Oh, you're getting me too horny; it's my turn to soap you up, dear. Where was I? Oh, I was wearing my Bodyguard coat, and he dropped the package and stabbed me with a syringe full of nano- bots, and the syringe didn't penetrate the coat, and he froze. I then punched him in the face, and we wrestled for a while. Then he pulled out another syringe, and I broke his wrist just as Chuck shot him and he accidentally stabbed himself, bled all over, and died."

"Holy shit!" Grace says.

"Enough of this. One of us owes the other one some wild sex. I am so fuzzy that I can't remember who."

Grace grabs his penis and says, "I'll start, Mr. Bond, James Bond." She shoves him against the shower wall, and they make frantic, passionate love until they collapse.

They step into the new drying tube that John had installed during the week, and they stagger to the bed and fall in. Chrissy is sitting on the couch and jumps on the bed, and curls up beside John. John turns to Grace and says, "Oh, I should tell you that I stopped by Mrs. Leung's place and told her that we caught her husband's killer. I felt bad because her daughters were there and were crying heavily. Oh, I'm being interviewed by Jenny Olson on Channel 24 tomorrow. I can only tell her about Bill Auger and the circumstances surrounding his death, like the fight I had with him. I should get Thom to sit in, in case I screw up. Do you know where he is? He wasn't there when I came home."

"Yes, he is probably romancing his girlfriend, Brigette. Now, go to sleep, please," Grace says.

CHAPTER SEVENTY-SEVEN

John wakes up with a start at 3:35 a.m., yelling, "Ambush! Get down! Thom, I'm hit!"

Grace grabs him and says, "John, what's happening? Is someone in the house?"

He says breathlessly, "No, since you left town, I've been having flashback dreams about the ambush in Afghanistan, and I don't know what to do. I even talked to Joanne Weber, our psychologist, about it. I really thought it was because I missed you so much."

She cuddles him in her arms and says, "It's okay; I'm here. Go back to sleep, and we'll talk about this later. I'll show you an old Chinese treatment."

They wake up at seven o'clock, and she looks at him and says, "How are you feeling this morning?"

"A little better, but I wish these nightmares would stop."

She rolls over on top of him and rubs her naked body on him. He says, "Is this part of the ancient Chinese treatment you told me about?"

"No, but it is a start."

"Well, it's helping so far."

They make love passionately until they are exhausted as Chrissy watches from the foot of the bed. John says, "I think

Chrissy is starting to like watching us make love. Last time, she ran away."

Grace looks at Chrissy and says, "I think she is smiling. Can cats smile? Let's put on some sweats and go to the hollo room. I want to show you the real Ancient Chinese secret."

They get dressed and go to the hollo room. She says, "Can you program a room full of sand and a circular campfire or a quiet fountain?"

"I can do a campfire and vent it so that it won't hurt us," John says.

"Okay, you sit across from me. Have you ever meditated?"

"No, but the army taught us to sleep on command and stare at the horizon for hours, but we were looking for any enemies."

"Okay, I want you to look at the fire and empty your mind. Just see the fire and focus all your attention on it. We will do this for half an hour today. Feel the fire warm you and comfort you, so nothing can hurt you."

They do it for exactly half an hour, and Grace looks at John. "Well, how do you feel now? Tell me the truth as I have other methods we can try."

"I feel really good. Was I supposed to see an eagle?"

"You saw an eagle? That is your spirit animal. That is very powerful! Native people do sweat lodges, and if you see an animal in there, especially if it is white, that is your spirit animal. You can call on it when you are in despair. I can see that your aura is changing already."

John asks, "What is an aura?"

"It is your natural energy field around you, and you can change it by meditating, being kind to people, saving someone's life—all kinds of ways. Auras are different colours, from black to white to gold, depending on your energy and attitude. Some people can feel that energy. Have you ever met someone and didn't like them for no reason at all?"

"Yes, I work with criminals all the time."

"Yes, but you must have met, say, some cops you didn't like. How did you feel about this Cornburra cop when you met him?"

"Yes, I hated the guy right off the bat, so I'm glad he is going to the Internal Affairs Department, so I can hate him even more."

"How did you feel about me when we met at the auction?"

John answers, "Well, sometimes I have self-confidence problems, but when I looked into those beautiful green eyes of yours, my heart started pumping a mile a minute. Then when you came up and started talking to me, I couldn't believe it, and I started stuttering, but I had to recover so that you wouldn't think I was a moron. It was love at first sight, which I always thought was a myth."

She counters, "Well, I had to work up the nerve to walk up to talk to you because you were so handsome and well dressed, and I could feel your good energy. If I hadn't known Gladys, I might not have come up to you."

John adds, "It was meant to be, as Gladys was hell-bent on me getting out and dating again that day. I went through that auction and picked out the best thing in there! I don't know if you know it, but I have a photographic memory," John says.

"Okay, what was I wearing that day?"

"You were wearing a pale green dress with pink flowers on it and darker metallic green high-heeled shoes, which I don't know how you women wear without breaking your ankles, but they make your legs look incredible. You also had on a gold expensive wrist unit that was probably worth two thousand dollars, and you had two antique gold berets in your hair."

"You do have an incredible memory. I'm impressed," Grace says.

"And, for the record, Miss Lotus Blossom, I didn't know you were rich because that doesn't matter to me. I would have pursued you if you were Cinderella in rags. Now, let's go eat breakfast. We are both going to have a long day today and tomorrow."

Innocently batting her eyelashes, she says, "What's on tomorrow?"

He points his finger at her and says, "Don't pull that Goldilocks bullshit on me, Miss Chan, birthday girl."

They go down to the dining room, followed by Chrissy, who meets them in the hallway. Julie and Thom are sitting at the table with a big carafe of coffee and a tray of cups. Savana is eating a bowl of Cheerios with fresh bananas. She smiles. "Hi Uncle Tiny and Grace, you're back early from Winnipeg!"

Grace says, "Oh, I brought you back a surprise; finish your cereal, and I'll be right back."

CHAPTER SEVENTY-EIGHT

Grace comes back with a large bag and sets it on the table. "Are you finished with your cereal, Savana?"

She answers, "Almost, two more spoonsful. What did you get me?"

"Wait until you finish, and don't hurry."

Savana finishes, and Grace slowly pulls out a cute little stuffed bison toy. "He is a stuffed toy bison, and you have to name him and tell him your name, then he talks to you, and you can talk to him."

She says, "Cool, let me hold him. I'll call him Billy the Bison, yeah, Billy. Thank you, Grace." She hugs Grace.

"I also brought you some colouring books with princesses in them and different animals and new crayons. I also brought some things for Jackie, so you don't have to share if you don't want to."

Julie says, "Thank you, Grace; you didn't have to do that. Just for that, I'll make you both a surprise omelette. What about you, Thom?"

"I'll have the same; I'm curious as to what your brilliant mind comes up with," Thom says.

Savana runs into her room with all her gifts, hugging Billy the Bison. John exclaims, "Oh, Thom, we caught the assassin, Bill Auger, last night, and me and Chuck killed him."

"Details, John, details."

John fills Thom and Grace in on the details of the killing. Then Julie comes in with three omelettes with three kinds of cheese, spinach, mushrooms, onions, and Canadian bacon. "This should keep you fed for most of the day, kids," Julie says.

Thom says, "Wow, you're not kidding, Julie. By the way, John, the band is coming at seven-thirty to set up, and you can sit in with them at eight-thirty. They will leave their instruments here overnight, so I think we should have some of our security guys stay here tonight and guard 24/7."

John replies, "Security, yes, good idea, and I will sit in with the band, and Grace might join me."

Grace replies, "Well, maybe."

They enjoy their omelettes, and Grace looks at Julie and says, "That omelette was incredible, Julie; I'm stuffed. Well, we better be leaving for work, right, John?"

"Actually, Jenny is coming here to interview me at nine o'clock. Thom, I want you to sit in off-camera to make sure I don't make any mistakes," John says.

"Sure, I can do that."

John and Grace go and change clothes. He says, "I'll get Jeffery to drive you to work in the limo."

"Don't you have to give Chuck a ride to work?" Grace asks.

"No, Captain Fedora had my old car repaired and gave it to Chuck yesterday, though, we will probably ride together sometimes, just to catch up." He continues, "Oh, I guess I didn't tell you about Chuck's new girlfriend, Margarette. She is a waitress at the Retro Diner across from the cop shop. When do you think you will be home?"

She kisses him and says, "I would guess around five-thirty or six."

In Mandarin, John says, "My humble self will gaze upon your lovely body, my lotus blossom, at the approximate hour, and will miss your honourable self."

She answers in Mandarin, "Thank you, Mr. Bond, James Bond, and I will miss your honourable body too. Goodbye."

CHAPTER SEVENTY-NINE

Jenny Olson greets John, saying, "It must be nice to have banker's hours."

He retorts, "Sorry, it takes a long time to satisfy my girlfriend."

"John, you are so full of shit, your eyes should be brown. Wait, you weren't kidding, right?"

He just smiles and says, "Let's just get this done, okay? And there are some things about this we both can't talk about, or we both could go to jail, as it is code red, and you damn well know what that means. Let's do this in my office. This mission ends at Bill Auger, period. Understood, Jenny?"

"Yes, John."

"Jenny, this is my good friend and majordomo, Thom, who is going to sit in with us off-camera, for my sake."

Jenny, John, and Thom go into John's office with her camerawoman, Willow. John says sternly, "Remember, this is just about Bill Auger. We just talk about the attack in the loft, nothing else. I like you, Jenny, but if you try any bullshit about more evidence than I want out there, I'm stopping the interview and confiscating the video chip or disc."

They go into the office and get wired for sound, and sit in the comfortable couches. Jenny starts the interview, "This is Jenny Olson, reporter for Channel 24 in Lieutenant John Trosky's home office. Let's get started. Lieutenant Trosky, you have been tracking this assassin you initially called the Ghost, as he seemed to disappear after every killing, starting with Doctor Blackwell, a heart surgeon from Winnipeg, who died very mysteriously. Do you know what killed him, lieutenant?"

"Yes, we do. He was injected with poison, but that is top secret and very hard to reproduce, and if I told you what it was, we both would go to jail, and I'm not kidding. Yes, he killed two more people, and I don't want to discuss that as it would just cause more trauma to the families left behind. And to save time, I thought we were here to discuss how we caught him yesterday. I don't mean to be harsh with you, Jenny. In fact, I trust you more than any other reporter; that is why you are here today, so ask me about how we caught the assassin yesterday, okay?"

She says, "All right, let's do that. You start, lieutenant."

John then goes into the details of the events leading to Bill Aguer's death and concludes, saying, "That is all we are allowed to say at this point. Thank you for your patience, Jenny. My girlfriend Grace Chan and I watch your show all the time and respect your honest reporting."

"Thank you, lieutenant, for your time. This is Jenny Olson reporting."

They get their microphones unhooked, and Jenny walks them out. John smiles and says, "I'll see you tomorrow."

She frowns. "Tomorrow? What's tomorrow?"

"You sound like Grace. It's her birthday tomorrow. She said that to me this morning, but she was pulling my leg, and I called her on it."

John flies to the station to talk to Sam. "Let's go into my office; I need to talk to you," John says.

She cringes and says, "Did I do something wrong, lieutenant?"

He answers, "No, but remember how I told you to start training Audley Barnes? Give him some grunt work and paperwork to start. I put in the papers for your commendation. So, we will have a ceremony when it comes through in a week or two. You have done exceptional work and need to be rewarded for it. So, go get Audley now, and get him working. Take care, I'll see you on Saturday at the party. Put your dancing shoes on and call me John when we are having a private conversation like this."

"Thanks, John."

John calls A.P.A. Nikki Anders and says, "Hi, Nikki, how are you doing today?"

Nikki says, "Hi, John. I'm busy, but I have some time. What's up?"

"Well, you know we killed Mr. Auger already, but we also have proof that Chad Harris, the billionaire software company owner, hired Auger to kill Trevor Wallace and paid him three million dollars upfront to assassinate him. He paid Auger through an off-shore account, so we need a warrant to legally search all his electronics, phone—everything-as soon as possible before he gets rid of it all."

She asks, "How did you get this information on the hiring?"

"One of my tech guys was monitoring his email through his Wi-Fi, sitting outside Auger's house."

She replies, "Sounds good. I'll call my favourite judge right now and send you a warrant by email. You can get a team together right now and use SWAT as he probably has many bodyguards. Bye."

CHAPTER EIGHTY

John goes into the bullpen and says, "Anyone not on a hot case, please assemble in my office; we have another arrest to make today. I'll call SWAT myself."

Chuck, Randy, Sam, Bin Tran, and Audley Barnes enter John's office and sit around his big table. Lieutenant Shane Travis of SWAT comes in with a few of his team. John starts, "We found out who hired Mr. Auger to assassinate Trevor Wallace and his wife; his name is Chad Harris, another tech billionaire. He lives in a mansion, of course, in southeast Surrey on acreage. We just had a drone fly over his house, and he has six civilians in there and at least six bodyguards that we know of. I would love to storm the place, but let's put our heads together and see if there is a better way to go in there. Any suggestions, anyone? Here are pictures of his mansion. As you can see, it has high brick walls and wrought iron gates and gates at the rear for deliveries."

Chuck says, "I don't think he would fall for a delivery."

Sam says, "I've got an idea; how about we stage a police chase in front of the mansion. They are chasing a school bus full of migrants, and the migrants are armed and disguised cops, like Audley here, and the bus crashes through the gates and hits that tree over there, just hard enough to bend the front end. We put fake blood on them and have an ambulance pull up to pull the bodyguards away from the house, and SWAT can enter through the rear gate and secure the house. Just a thought."

John looks at everyone and says, "And that was just a thought? Anyone see any flaws in that?"

Shane Travis says, "That is a great plan. John, can we have her on our team?"

"No way! You are not stealing my best people, Shane," John says.

Shane says, "I would like to add one thing; I want two of my men in that ambulance, trained medics, of course."

John says, "Okay, can we go in one hour?

Shane answers, "I'd say, closer to two hours. We have a fake school bus, but I want to brace the front end so that we can use it again sometime, okay?"

John says, "Good, we go in two hours. I want to use my own car, and Sam, you can organize the 'immigrants' with Chuck and the makeup people."

They get everything set and leave in two hours and drive to Chad Harris's mansion. Shane Travis sets up the truck a block away, and one of his men is monitoring the estate with a drone and gets on the coms. "We are set to go; most of the civilians are in the swimming pool."

The accident is performed perfectly. The bus hits the tree, and the cop car pulls into the driveway. They run to the bus, and the guards come running too. The main cop, a Sergeant Johnson, yells to the estate guards to help the injured, and they run over and drop their rifle blasters and start helping the driver and passengers. The ambulance shows up, and the fake medics go over to the bus as SWAT goes into the rear of the house. They see five naked girls and one guy running around the pool. Shane Travis yells, "All right, everyone, get some clothes on and come into the main living room. In the chaos, the cops and fake medics grab the guards and cuff them. Some of the cops grab the guards' weapons and head for the front door of the mansion. John is sitting in his car with Sam. Suddenly, the roof of the house opens, and a red flying car emerges and hovers and then starts flying to the north.

John yells, "Sam, do up your safety belt and hang on; we are going to chase this bastard down. Computer, lights, and sirens."

They start to follow Chad Harris as they fly across the farms and vineyards of South Surrey as Chad flies low, trying to lose John and Sam. He circles back and then flies over the Oak Street bridge, going about 150 miles per hour, weaves right over to Marine Drive, and turns left up Cambie Street past Queen Elisabeth Park, going north. John orders, "Computer, turn on the police radio to channel nine. This is Lieutenant John Trosky in pursuit of a red XLS4000 going north on Cambie Street. I need back-up. I can catch him and force him to land, hopefully near the police station. Ten-four." John hits the boost and gets about 15 feet from Chad's car, and says, "Computer, engage the tractor beam to lock on red XLS4000. The tractor beam engages, and John engages the EMP, which slows the car down to 40 miles per hour and steers the cars right to the police parking lot and lands it. He locks the doors to Chad's car. Three other police cars surround Chad's car, and the police surround the car with their laser pistols drawn as John releases the door locks and walks up to Chad, pointing his pistol at Chad. Sam goes to the passenger door, and John shouts, "You are under arrest for dangerous flying, attempted escape from the police, and, oh, hiring an assassin to kill Mr. Trevor Wallace and his wife, Alice. No rabbit hole for you, sir. Cuff him and book him, officers; I'll be in there in a few minutes."

Sam says, "John, that was a wild ride. I didn't know your car had a tractor beam; that was so cool."

"It was my brother Mike's idea. I didn't think I would ever use it, but you never know. I'm going to park my car, and I'll meet you in the bullpen." John adds, "Sam, your idea worked like a charm; I have a great recall memory, but your beautiful brain comes up with great scenarios that I would never think of. I'm going to put in my report that you came up with this idea and recommend that you should be elevated to the next grade of detective and have a pay raise."

"Thank you, John. I'm glad you appreciate my work. I don't think of myself as someone special. I just enjoy doing my job, and thoughts like today just come to me. My dad was in the military, so maybe that's where I get my strategy from."

John says, "You're probably right. What time is it?"

"It's three-thirty. Why?"

"Well, we've got this guy nailed, but I'm curious about why he wanted to kill Trevor Wallace. Should we go interrogate him?" he asks.

"Sure. We've got nothing to lose, and I'm curious too."

They enter Room One, read Chad Harris his rights, and John says, "Well, Mr. Harris, you've had an exciting and interesting day today. I really enjoyed our flying car chase, and that was some car accident at your house earlier today. I'm just curious as to why you hired Mr. Auger to kill Trevor Harris and his wife. Was it for revenge, financial gain, or something else?"

Harris says, "I don't know what you are talking about. I don't know any Mr. Auger."

"Well, if you didn't know him, then why did you transfer three million dollars into his account?"

"How did you . . . um? I don't know what you are talking about."

"We know a lot more than you think," John replies.

Sam says, "Well, we'll just have to talk to your friends and employees if we really want to know."

"John says, "You better call your lawyer; we have better things to do than waste our time with you. Lieutenant John Trosky and Detective Sam Slade leaving Room One."

CHAPTER EIGHTY-ONE

As they enter the bullpen, John says, "I'm going to dictate my report and go home early; I have to practice with the band and go over the security with Thom. You can go. See you tomorrow, bye."

John goes home and enters chaos in his house. The Centurion Band is unpacking and setting up their instruments on the stage. Thom is watching them, and Chrissy is hiding under a dining table. John coaxes Chrissy to come out and picks her up and says, "It's okay, Chrissy, these men and women are musicians, and they are our friends, and I'm going to play piano with them."

The main beautiful black singer named Roxy comes up to John and says, "What a beautiful cat. What's her name? Can I hold her?"

John says, "Her name is Chrissy, and she's a bit scared right now, but you can try."

She picks up Chrissy and says, "Hi, Chrissy, you are beautiful." Chrissy likes her and starts purring and licking her hand.

"She really likes you. What is your name?" John says.

"My name is Roxy, and I've been singing with this band for nine years."

John says, "Good, my name is John Trosky, and I like the really old songs from the Ella Fitzgerald, Duke Ellington, Frank Sinatra era, and the seventies era, like Steely Dan, Jimmy Buffet, Chicago, Fleetwood Mac. You know, lots of dance music. I also like reggae music and funk music like Herbie Hancock and Earth, Wind and Fire. I want people to have a good time and dance a lot. I want to start off playing the piano with my girlfriend Grace Chan, singing a duet of the Beatles song 'Baby You Can Drive My Car,' and then a duet of Ray Charles' 'Hit the Road Jack.' Are you the band leader?"

"No, that tall black guy, Duke Mingus, is the bandleader and excellent trumpet player. He can play Chris Botti songs, Louie Armstrong, and a lot of other stuff. Let's go meet him."

They go over to Duke, and Roxy says, "Duke, this is John Trosky, and it is his girlfriend Grace's birthday party."

John says, "This is a surprise, but I'm going to propose to Grace tonight, and I'm also giving her the special Rolls-Royce from the James Bond movie *Goldfinger*. My brother Mike is giving her a golf cart shaped like a '57 Chevy. I want to start out by singing a duet with Grace. Roxy, can you sing 'Goldfinger' as we drive the Rolls into the ballroom?"

"Sure, that would be perfect."

John adds, "After I propose on stage to her, I want you to play 'Margaritaville,' as we are going on a vacation to Hawaii, okay?"

John looks over as Grace enters the ballroom and walks over to John and Roxy. She says, "I heard the music and wandered in here. Wow, this is a big band, and who is this lovely lady?"

John answers, "Grace, meet Roxy."

"Hi Grace, wait a minute; I recognize you. You're Grace Chan. I've seen your ads on TV for your real estate company and your clothing line! I wear some of your dresses. Nice to meet you, Grace. Oh, this is Duke Mingus, the bandleader of The Centurions, and that's 'Captain' Kirk on drums, Slide Murphy on lead guitar, Shirley, Paula, Maddie, and Jade are my back-up singers, Uncle Don on electronic keyboards, Slick Slim Dorsett, Walker Evans, and Miles Reeds of the horn section, and Junior Watts on big bass. So, I hear you sing also."

"Well, I sing a bit. I was in a choir in church and school, but I'm not that good."

"Well, I'd like to hear you and John do your version of that Beatle's song. What song was it, John?"

"'Baby You Can Drive My Car.'"

Grace says, "Now?"

John replies, "Come on, Grace; I'll start, and you can jump in on the duet parts. We have to practice with the band, and the more you sing, the more relaxed you'll be, right, Roxy?"

"Yes, when I first started, I was very nervous, but then I began to relax."

John sits down at the piano, "Grace, sit down beside me, and you will be more relaxed. After we do this a few times, you will learn to love it; I guarantee it."

John starts playing and singing, and the band joins in. Grace starts to relax, and John smiles at her when she starts singing, and they sing it three times. Roxy comes over and says, "Grace, I thought you said you weren't that good. You were great!"

"You really think so, or are you trying to make me feel better?" Grace says.

Duke pipes in, saying, "She is serious, Grace; you really are that good. You were on key and on time all the way through, and you have a very compelling voice. I'd like to hear you two sing the Ray Charles' song."

John and Grace look at each other and start singing. They finish, and Duke says, "Can I suggest that the background singers join you in the chorus?"

Grace nods, and John says, "Sounds like a great idea! Ray Charles always did that song with his background singers, the Raylettes."

They sing it twice more with the background singers.

"Well, that was great. I'm hungry, so we are going for dinner. You can keep rehearsing. When I close this room, it is soundproof, so make all the noise you want. You can hook into my Bose house sound system if you want. It is the best system made, and it's built into every wall; it will blow your minds! Just plug into the connectors at the back of the stage; they are all marked," John says.

"Thanks, John, I'll do that," Duke says.

John adds, "I'll send a man in here to help you. He can work the stage lighting for you also; his name is Alfredo. See you later. Do you guys and gals want snacks and drinks because I have my own chef, and she is great?" Duke looks around, and people are nodding yes, so he says, "Yes, that would be greatly appreciated, thanks!"

John and Grace go in for dinner, and Julie, Thom, and Savana are sitting at the table. Everyone is eating different dishes, including appetizers, fish, chicken, beef, lobster, and crab cakes.

Grace says, "Julie, you sure must have been busy today, cooking all this stuff."

She answers, "No, this is us trying out my friend Natalie's catering food. What would you two like for dinner?"

Grace replies, "That lobster would go down nice right now with some rice and veggies."

John says, "I'll have the same, and I just promised the band some snacks, so can you send them a bunch of appetizers and maybe some small sandwiches, you know, light food. Also, please bring them some beers and some white wine for the ladies? There are twelve people in the band and probably a few 'roadies' and the lighting guy, Alfredo."

Julie answers, "No problem, John."

Grace says, "Hi Savana, what are you eating that Chrissy is also interested in?"

Savana looks down at Chrissy and says, "Um, it's some kind of wrap with chicken in it, and I'll give Chrissy the bottom part of it because she already ate some real salmon, not the canned stuff, and she really liked it. Thank you for Billy the Bison, Grace. He is fun. He said my name and is teaching me to count and stuff. He can even say Chrissy, and that confuses her. She tilts her head and looks at him, and paws at him. I started colouring the princess colouring books, and I'm staying inside the lines and everything. Here, Chrissy, you can eat this now. Mom, can I have some of that Napoleon ice cream?"

Julie looks puzzled. "What do you mean, Napoleon ice cream?"

Savana answers, "You know, the one with chocolate, vanilla, and strawberry in the same box?"

"Oh, Savana, it's called Neapolitan ice cream; that's a big word for a little girl. Yes, I'll get you some, dear." Julie retrieves her ice cream and, with the androids, takes the snacks and beers and wine to the ballroom for the band as Slide Murphy is cranking out some Santana guitar licks from "Black Magic Woman." They hook into John's Bose stereo system, and the sound is great.

Thom is telling John that he has all the security in place and the valet parking set up. Just then, Mike, Gladys, and Jackie enter the dining room, and Mike says, "Hi, gang. What's happening?"

Jackie runs over to Savana and hugs her. "Hi, Savana, I missed you this week."

Grace pipes in, saying, "Jackie, I brought you some presents from Winnipeg. I'll be right back with them." She comes back and gives Jackie a stuffed bison and some colouring books with princesses and animals like those she brought Savana.

Jackie says, "Thanks, Grace. I'm going to call my bison, Bobbie the Bison. Hi, Bobbie, my name is Jackie, and I'm your new friend."

Bobbie replies, "Nice to meet you, Jackie; I can teach you things like counting numbers and playing new games."

Jackie's eyes go wide open, and she says, "Wow! Thank you, Grace. I love him."

The girls then excuse themselves and run into Savana's room to play a game with their new toys.

Julie says, "Mike, Gladys, and Jackie, do you want to try some of the food we are going to serve tomorrow?"

Mike replies, "I could eat anytime."

Gladys and Jackie eat some light food, and Mike tries some of the crab cakes.

Grace says, "Mike, I have all the Bodyguard coats here for John's squad and have some orders for some custom-designed coats, vests, and pants in different colours. John has been talking to his captain, commander, and the police chief about selling protective gear to the regular police in Vancouver and possibly all across Canada!"

Mike says, "That is great news, Grace. My brother is no slacker."

John says, "One more minor thing; we caught the assassin and Chuck, and I killed him."

Mike says, "Minor, are you kidding? You worked your butt off to catch that guy!"

John adds, "Yes, well, I wanted to take him alive, but as I was wrestling with him, things went sideways, and he accidentally killed himself." John looks at Grace and says, "Let's change the subject. Did you get your sister Jasmine's kids anything from Winnipeg?"

She looks at John and says, "Of course, I got them something. Megan, who is five, likes horses, so I got her a black stallion that talks and dances and jumps around. Fawn, who is four, loves kittens, so I got her a grey tabby that jumps and talks and cuddles and will follow her around. She will love, Chrissy! I also got them some colouring and simple educational books, like A B C's and learning colours. I really think kids should learn from books and not from computers at that age."

Gladys and Mike look around and listen. "It's too quiet; we better check on the girls, and we should get going home. Tomorrow is a big day for you both, and it will be a great party!" They go get Jackie, who is almost asleep, and Mike carries her to the car.

CHAPTER EIGHTY-TWO

John and Grace go upstairs and turn on the fireplace and some mellow jazz music. John massages her beautiful feet, she sighs, and then they get undressed and slide into bed. They are both tired and fall asleep.

Suddenly, in the middle of the night, John stirs and starts mumbling, "No, stop, it's a trap, get back," and jerks in his sleep.

Grace wakes up and grabs John's arm, " John, are you having that nightmare again? It's okay, honey, I'm right here." She cuddles up to him and rubs his back, like comforting a baby.

He says, "I'm okay. What time is it?"

"It's four-fifteen. Go back to sleep. We should sleep-in today; it's going to be a long and exciting day."

They fall asleep again, and at ten o'clock, John leans over and puts his hand on her breast and whispers in Mandarin, "Happy Birthday, Grace. Even though you are older, I still love you, sweetheart."

She opens her eyes and says, "Thank you, Mr. Bond, James Bond. I'll give you one hour to get your hand off my breast, and where is my birthday present?"

He pulls her toward him and lifts the covers. "Well, it's in two parts. Here is the first part, but you will have to wait a while for the second part." He starts rubbing his hands all over her body and kisses her passionately. They make love like they haven't seen each other for a year while Chrissy watches from the couch. They take a break and start making love in the shower again. John says, "Maybe we should have breakfast up here or on the roof as Julie may be really busy with Natalie, the caterer?"

Grace replies, "Maybe call her on the intercom. What about Savana? What could we have up here?"

John checks the auto chef with Grace and sees that it is stocked with pancakes, omelettes, bacon, and scrambled eggs. He says, "We could eat up here, but I guess we should check on Savana, Julie, and Thom. He calls Julie on the intercom and asks her about Savana and Thom and if she is really busy."

"Good morning, John and Grace. The caterers won't be here for another hour, and Savana and Thom are here at the dining room table, waiting for you."

They go downstairs and enter the dining room. The three of them surprise Grace by singing Happy Birthday to her, and John joins in as Julie has made her a giant omelette with candles on it! Grace is shocked and touched at the sight, and tears leak from her eyes. Savana runs up and hugs Grace. "Happy Birthday, Grace. I love you."

Julie says, "I hope you are in the mood for an omelette; it has everything in it. There is enough for all of us. It was a last-minute thought."

Thom gets up and hugs her too. "Happy Birthday, Grace."

Chrissy has followed them in and sits on Grace's lap, looks up at her, meows several times, and pats her face gently. Grace stares down at Chrissy. "Thank you, Chrissy. You can have some omelette too. I swear she understands everything we say to her, and she loves us. Well, let's eat, I'm starving."

Julie says, "You have to make a wish and blow out the candles first."

Grace thinks for a minute, then blows out the candles. Julie cuts up the omelette and serves everyone, even Chrissy, who seems to like the eggs and cheese. As they are eating, Savana stares at Grace for a long time, tilts her head, and finally blurts out, "I don't understand it, Grace, you don't look any older than yesterday."

Everyone laughs, and John says, "Yeah, Grace, you don't look any older at all."

She elbows John hard in the ribs and says, "You're going to get it later, Johnny boy. Savana, it doesn't work like that. People grow older gradually; you can't see a change in someone in one day. Just like you could be six to eight inches taller in a year. You don't grow that much in one day, but thank you for saying that I don't look any older."

John says, "I'm sorry, Grace, I just couldn't pass that up. I'll tell you what, to make up for that remark, let's take the horses out for a ride, and I'll bring my phone this time. In fact, I'll call Autrey now to saddle up the horses." He calls Autrey, and they go and change into jeans and heavy clothing and coats. They get in the '57 Chevy golf cart and go to the barn and get on Steely Dan and Adele and ride to the pond.

Grace studies John and says, "I'm getting worried about your nightmares. We need to work on that through meditation, and I want to try something else today. I also think you should talk to Joanne Webber about what else we can do about this. You know that I love you, and I want to help you in any way I can. I want you to be happy. We are in this together."

John replies, "You are right, Grace, and Joanne is coming to the party tonight, so I will make an appointment with her. I don't know why this is happening again, but you comfort me more than you realize and, I can't say it enough, but I love you."

They sit by the pond for a while and then ride Steely Dan and Adele back to the barn and get Autrey to unsaddle and brush them.

CHAPTER EIGHTY-THREE

John lets Grace drive his '57 Chevy golf cart back to the mansion.

I love this thing; I've got to get one for myself," she says.

John holds back a smile and says, "I'll see what I can do about that, Grace."

They enter the house, and Thom is standing beside a portable armoire. John says, "Grace, did you make a coat for Thom?"

"Yes, as he is your best friend and in charge of your security. It's leather, and it's in the other closet against the wall."

"Good. Okay, Thom, we need a plan for the party."

"Yes, John, I figured that I could show your squad their coats, and they could try them on. They can hang them back in this armoire and collect them on their way out," Thom says.

Grace says, "Did you notice there is a coat in the other closet for you?"

"No, I thought there was an extra in there. Thank you, Grace," Thom says.

John smiles at him and says, "Good because I want you to enjoy yourself with your girlfriend, but I also want you to check security around the house with a security droid out there programmed to look for anything suspicious. I want two guys in the security room at all times, looking at the monitors. Is Brigette coming tonight? We hope to meet her"

Thom says, "Yes, I'm going to pick her up at seven o'clock, and she can help me with the coats. She is a bit shy, but she loves to meet new people and is a great dancer."

Grace looks at John and says, "We should check with Julie and the caterers and then relax for a while, and then change into our party dresses."

John smiles, "I told you, I'm not wearing a dress."

They laugh and go to check out the kitchen. John says, "How goes it, Julie?"

She answers, "Things are going great. I'm glad we have droids helping; they can cut veggies super-fast and not cut themselves, they can extend themselves to reach high shelves, they have internal timers so that they don't burn any food, and they can use a finger to check the food temperature accurately and not burn themselves. We also need real cooks to finesse the look and taste of all the different foods we are doing. So, things are right on schedule to serve at eight o'clock. We also have different wine breathing already, so you two go relax. And John, the cake will be here soon, and Grace, you are not allowed to see it yet. It is a big surprise. Your mind will be blown."

John and Grace leave the kitchen, and Grace says, "Let's go into the meditation room for a while. Chrissy, you can come too."

Once in the meditation room, Grace says, "John, I have to go get my kit. You might call it a medicine bundle. Take your shirt off and lay face down on that massage table and program some nice mellow Chinese music." She comes back with a small rough leather bag and takes out some acupuncture needles and some Chinese special herbs. She says quietly, "Relax, John, I'm going to stick some acupuncture needles in your back; they are really thin, so they don't hurt. I'm going to put some herbs on the tops of them first and then light them on fire. I'm not kidding about the fire; it won't burn you. It will balance your chi, which is your body's main energy. I'm telling you this so that you won't freak out. It is very important that you relax and breathe slowly; trust me. This won't take that long."

She performs the treatment on him for about twenty minutes. He doesn't feel her insert or remove the needles, but he can smell the herbs. He is so relaxed that he almost falls asleep. He stirs and turns his head to face her. "Those herbs smell like cannabis. What are they?"

Grace replies, "They are pretty rare. I don't know the names of the mixture in English, and even if I tell you in Mandarin, you probably won't know."

She tells him the names in Mandarin, and he says, "No, I've never heard of them. Are we done now?"

"Yes, we should change for the party now."

He stands up and puts his shirt on, and sees Chrissy lying on a chair, almost asleep. John says, "Looks like Chrissy got some benefit out of that too, and I feel really good right now. Come on, Chrissy, let's go."

CHAPTER EIGHTY-FOUR

They go to John's room and change. John puts on a pastel green suit, an off-white and green-tinted shirt, a white tie, and a green belt. Grace comes out of the walk-in closet he had built for her, and she is wearing a low-cut pastel green dress with white Hibiscus type flowers on it. The dress stops at the mid-thigh area. They look at each other, and both say, "Wow!" at the same time.

John says, "I don't know if you are psychic, or I am, or we both are, but, damn, I love you, girl."

They go downstairs, and Thom is standing by the front door, talking to a cute, slim, pretty girl with brown wavy hair down to her shoulders, about twenty-six years old, and smiling at Thom with a gleam in her pretty whiskey-coloured eyes. Her arm is hooked in his. She is wearing a soft blue silk dress with lavender and white flowers printed on it that clings to her slim waist.

Grace and John approach them and look at Thom and Brigette. "This must be the beautiful, and, I must say, angelic, Brigette you have been raving about, Thom. Glad to meet you, Brigette," John says.

Brigette replies in a slight French accent, "I am Brigette Lauren and I am so happy to meet you also, lieutenant and Miss Grace." Thom turns red in the face.

John says, "Please, call me John. I keep telling Thom not to call me lieutenant."

Grace says, "I'm very happy to meet you, Bridgette, and I love your dress; it really suits your personality. I hear you and Thom met at a farmer's market, is that correct?

She smiles. "Yes, I run a stall for my family's organic farm in Surrey. My family owns one hundred acres of farmland, and we grow all kinds of organic vegetables and have some fruit trees."

In French, John says, "I detect a slight French accent in your voice, and I'm glad we've been eating your organic food."

She answers in French, "You speak very good French. Where did you learn to speak French?"

"I spent three years in college in Paris, and I was there two weeks ago on a case."

Grace adds, "I speak some French, as I deal with clients in Quebec, but their French is a bit different. I design and manufacture mostly women's clothing; that's why I love your dress!"

Brigette says, "Thank you, and I just realized that you are Grace Chan; I love your clothes."

"What size do you wear? I'll bet you are a four or four and a half. I would love to design a dress for you," Grace says.

She replies, "Yes, I wear a size four, but for casual or work clothes, I like a four and a half. I would love for you to make me a dress!"

Thom says, "Grace, I would like you to make her a custom Bodyguard coat, and I'll pay for it."

"Okay, Brigette, let's exchange phone numbers, and we will get together next week and design something together!" They exchange numbers and emails, and Grace says, "Oh, look, my sister Jasmine is here with her husband David and their daughters Megan and Fawn. Let's go over to them, and I'll introduce you all to them."

They all are introduced to each other, and Jasmine says, "Happy Birthday, big sister. We brought you a present; it's in the room where they put the presents. There is a lot in there."

David, Megan, and Fawn also wish her a Happy Birthday. John says, "I'm glad you could make it. Megan and Fawn, my brother Mike and his wife Gladys have a daughter your age, Jackie, and my live-in chef Julie has a daughter, Savana. After dinner, you can all dance and play together."

Grace looks down and says, "Girls, I have a surprise for you that I brought back from Winnipeg; some toys and books that I will give to you later. I have them hidden, so be nice, and you will get them after dinner."

In unison, they say, "Thank you, Auntie Grace."

Megan asks, "What kind of toys?"

Grace replies, "You will see later; they are cute, and you can talk to them, but that's all the hints you are getting, okay?"

In unison, they answer, "Okay."

John says, "Excuse us, my squad is here, and we have to go talk to them."

Chuck and Margarette come in the door, and John and Grace greet them warmly. Then Randy Chan enters with his date Tasha Silver, a cute, slim girl with long blond curly hair, wearing a short red dress. John says, "Welcome to the party, Randy. Who is your friend?"

Randy says, "John and Grace, this is Tasha Silver, my new flame."

Thom says, "Brigette, why don't you stay here and get to know Grace's sister and her family; I have to help John give his squad their Bodyguard coats. I'll be right back." He goes with Grace and John, and they hand out coats to Sam Slade, Randy Chan, Bin Tran, Razh Mendosa, and Eddie Bennetti, who arrives with a beautiful, tall, built, blonde woman, wearing a low-cut body-hugging bright red dress slit up the right side to her thigh. She is a famous fashion model. He introduces her as just Brandi.

She asks Eddie, "Why is your Lieutenant giving you a coat; you have six or eight coats already?"

He answers, "This is a special coat, Brandi; it's knife, laser, and bulletproof, and it is hand-made by John, Grace, and Mike's company Bodyguard Clothing. John has already taken two hits with a laser and a knife and didn't get a scratch on him."

"You're kidding; I want one. Do they make them for ordinary people like me?" she asks.

Grace answers, "Yes, well, I think you are more than ordinary, but I can custom-design one for you in several different fabrics and colours for about fifteen hundred dollars. You will feel safe and warm in it."

Brandi says, "Really? When can we do this?"

"Next week. We can exchange contacts and set up a time."

Brandi's eyes go wide, and she says, "Great, I should have some free days next week."

John says, "People, you can leave your coats in this armoire and take them when you leave. Oh, Captain Fedora and his wife Gale are here, and Commander Caputo and his wife Nellie just arrived. Here they come."

John introduces them to Grace, Brandi, Eddie Benetti, Brigette, and Thom and shows the commander and the captain their new coats. They are extremely pleased with them and, of course, their wives want a new coat and exchange contacts with Grace.

Police Chief Emily Carter and her husband Patrick Carter enter and walk up to John and Grace. John introduces Emily and Patrick Carter to Grace. Emily is wearing a modest but lovely black dress with yellow, pink, and green flowers printed on it, and Patrick is wearing a black suit with a charcoal shirt and maroon tie. Grace says, "Chief Carter, I love your dress, and your husband looks dashing tonight."

She replies, "Thank you. This dress is one of your designs, and I want to talk to you about designing a coat for me. And Happy Birthday, by the way."

Grace says, "I thought that dress looked familiar. Yes, we should get together next week and design your coat. John, it looks like Larry Browning, your R and D people, mechanics from your dealership and custom shop, and some female staff are here. Well, we should head to the big dining room as dinner should be ready very soon. We could start with some wine."

CHAPTER EIGHTY-FIVE

They go into the dining room, and John and Grace sit at the head of the table, as it is wide enough to seat two people. Mike, Jackie, and Gladys sit beside them. Across the table sit Chuck and Margarette and John's sister Judy and her partner Lois. John says, "Before we start, I want to introduce my horse trainer and all 'round cowboy, Autrey, who I met at the Cloverdale Rodeo years ago. He was bull riding that day with a broken leg. This man has my respect. Stand up, Autrey. People give him a hand."

Everyone claps loudly, and Autrey blushes. "Shucks, John, I'm just an old cowhand doon' my job."

John says, "Judy, you aren't wearing a cast on your arm. You must heal fast. Oh, Grace, this is my sister Judy and her partner, Lois. I forgot you haven't met. You were in Winnipeg when Judy was attacked."

Grace says, "Nice to meet you, Judy and Lois."

Judy says, "Nice to meet you too; we brought you a present from our gift shop that's next door to our main flower shop. I hope you like it."

Lois says, "John, you didn't tell us that Grace was so pretty!"

Grace replies, "Thank you. Oh, John, my parents just came in. I'll introduce you to them."

They walk over to her parents. "John, this is my mother Shawna Chan and my father, Joseph Chan."

John looks at Shawna and says, "I can see where Grace gets her beauty from and her beautiful green eyes."

Shawna smiles and says, "Thank you, John. You have a golden tongue; are you sure you're not Irish?"

"Actually, I'm Polish, but who knows, my ancestors did travel a lot." John switches to Mandarin. "I'm also glad to meet you, Joseph, and I must tell you that I'm in love with your daughter. She has a beautiful soul."

He answers in Mandarin, "You speak Mandarin. I like you already, and, yes, we taught Grace well."

Shawna says in Mandarin, "If I had known you speak Mandarin, I would have greeted you in Mandarin."

John asks, "Shawna, I've never met an Irish person who spoke Mandarin in my life, and I've been all over the world. Did you learn Mandarin from Joseph?"

Shawna answers, "No, I was a reporter years ago, and I spent a lot of time in Shenzhen, Beijing, and Hong Kong, where I met Joseph, and then we moved to Vancouver and had our girls. Grace, we bought you a birthday present, though, you are getting hard to shop for now; you've outgrown teddy bears and colouring books."

Grace says, "So what did you get me, Mom?"

"I should make you wait, but I have a feeling you have a room full of presents, and ours would get lost in the shuffle. We got you several pairs of sensible shoes to save your feet from those 'ankle breakers' you wear so much. You can thank me later, sweetheart."

Grace replies, "I'll thank you now, Mom. Well, we should get back to the dinner table; I'm hungry! Mom and Dad, I sat you close to us."

John smiles and says, "Grace, I flew in some Mahi-Mahi fish from Hawaii. I'm having some organic vegetables from Brigette's farm. Do you want some too? Have you had Mahi-Mahi before? It's delicious!"

"No, I haven't. What does it taste like?"

"It's so different that I can't describe it, and they cooked it in a cream sauce. Just try it, if you don't like it, you can eat something else. It is ready right now."

She answers, "Okay, I'll give it a try, John."

The servants bring their food, and Grace tries the Mahi-Mahi. She looks at John and says, "I'm sorry that I doubted you, John; this is fantastic, and the taste is hard to describe. It doesn't even taste like fish, and I like the cream sauce. Brigette, these organic carrots, cauliflower, and asparagus taste great."

"Thank you, Grace; we do our best. Julie cooks great cabbage rolls and pierogies, and I love this wine.

Thom says," It's from your winery, Troubador, is that right?"

John replies, "Yes, it is, and we have several varieties. Save some room people, there is a large cake coming later."

Luci Ryan says, "This crab cake dish is great, John. All this food smells so great! Who is your caterer?"

John replies, "She is a friend of my chef, Julie. I think her name is Natalie. I'll get Julie to give you her number if you want her. By the way, what is your husband's name? We've never met."

"John, meet Jack Ryan."

John quips, "Hi, Jack, I've seen all your movies. I'm a big fan."

Jack says, "Yes, my parents are a riot; like I've heard that a million times and before you ask, I don't work for the CIA. At least Luci doesn't get, 'Lucy, you got a lot of 'splainin' to do.' That's just too old now."

Luci says, "I've got to talk to Julie after dinner; we want to hire a caterer for Jack's birthday, and you and Grace are invited. I'll email you when it's time."

Grace looks at Jackie, and all the cute little girls sitting together and asks, "So, what are you girls eating? Jackie?"

"I'm eating these cakes made from crab. I like them, but they don't taste like cake, and I like this asparagus and the 'basmaky' rice."

Grace corrects her, "It's called Basmati rice, it's from India. Savana, what do you have on your plate?"

"I'm having lamb 'souvlaky' – something or other on a stick; it's really good!"

"It's called souvlakia, and it is Greek food. I'm glad you girls are trying different food. Megan, what do you have, dear?"

"I'm having a bison burger. It tastes just like a hamburger with French fries, and my little sister Fawn is having her favourite, mac and cheese. She doesn't eat much food yet as she's still little. If we have chicken, I have to cut it up for her. I love her, so I take care of her."

Grace says, "That's so sweet of you, Megan, to take care of your little sister."

Time goes on, and Julie and the staff wheel in a large cake that looks like a 1957 Chevy, white and green in colour and surrounded by little green and white cupcakes for the kids. Grace turns to John and says, "This was your doing, wasn't it? It's beautiful. Someone, please take my picture beside it."

Thom takes Grace's picture and a video with his pocket-sized camera as everyone sings Happy Birthday to Grace. Julie and the caterers cut up the cake and serve it. John passes Grace a cupcake with a lit candle in it "Make a wish and blow out the candle, little girl." Grace thinks for a minute and then blows out the candle. Then John and Grace eat some cake, as

Grace says, "I hate to spoil that Chevy cake; it looks so good, and it must have taken hours to make."

John finishes his cake and says, "Excuse me, Grace, I have to go to the bathroom and check something in my office, so I might as well use the bathroom up there."

CHAPTER EIGHTY-SIX

John takes Julie aside and says, "Julie, can you do me a favour and cut two pieces of cake from the trunk and send them to my auto chef in my bedroom?"

She grins and says, "Sure, John, are you planning a little two-person after-party later?"

John replies, "Yes, I am, we might need the fuel later. I have to sneak away and get the ring."

John goes to his office and locks the door behind him. He presses a piece of moulding on a panel on the wall that slides sideways to expose a deceptively old-looking safe. He presses a rivet at the top right corner of the safe that exposes a palm plate. He puts his hand on it and says, "Open Sesame, authorize Lieutenant Trosky," and the safe door pops open, and he retrieves the diamond engagement ring and earrings in a small elegant box and puts it in his suit pocket.

He goes back to the big dining room and sits next to Grace, and announces, "Speaking of birthday presents, Grace, Mike and Gladys have a present for you. Mike, would you go outside and get Grace's present? Bring it into the ballroom."

Mike leaves as people look at each other, talking softly, wondering what is going on." Grace says, "What is it, John?"

He replies, "What, and spoil the surprise? Everyone, let's make our way to the ballroom. Just follow me."

They all go to the ballroom. The huge ballroom doors open as Mike drives the '57 Chevy golf cart into the room. Grace's eyes pop wide open, and her jaw drops. She punches John in the arm and whispers, "You put him up to this, didn't you? You devil you."

"I plead the fifth, and I want a lawyer."

She runs over to Mike and hugs him. "Thank you, Mike. Gladys and Jackie, come over here for a hug. Did you build this from scratch for me? You got the colours to match my real car."

Mike says, "It was John's idea, but I'm glad I got to build it. It has a small pulse engine in it, so you never have to plug it in."

Gladys and Jackie quickly walk over to the cart and hug Grace. Grace says, "Let's take it for a quick spin outside around the house."

They all jump in and drive around the house as Grace giggles and smiles. "Now I can race John against his cart."

Mike leans over and softly says, "You know, Grace, I can tune this so that you can beat him. We need to teach him that he can't win all the time."

She says, "It's a deal, Mike."

They go back in the ballroom, and Grace goes up to John and says, "You are on for a race next week, pal. Cart to cart. Thank you for getting Mike to build it. Oh, I forgot to give Jasmine's daughters the presents I got for them in Winnipeg. I'll be right back."

John says, "I'm going to get the band started. We still have a few things to do."

Grace goes to give the girls their toys, and John turns on his cell phone and calls his mechanic. "Ringo, please bring the Rolls-Royce up to the ballroom door and stay outside with it until I call you to bring it in." John goes up on stage and talks to Roxy about singing "Goldfinger" when Grace comes back.

"Attention, ladies and germs. I want to introduce the Centurion Big Band! Grace and I will be sitting in on some songs in a bit."

Grace comes back to the ballroom, and John says, "Grace, could you come up on stage, please? I have another surprise for you." As she walks up on stage, John cues Ringo, dressed as a chauffeur, to drive the Rolls Royce into the ballroom. He then cues Roxy to start singing the theme from *Goldfinger*. Grace gives John a puzzled look and says, "John, what is going on here? Is that your car?"

He answers, "No, that is your car. Happy Birthday, and before you go down there to look at it, I want to ask you a question."

She is even more puzzled and asks, "A question? Okay, ask away."

He reaches into his coat and pulls out the fancy box, and gets down on one knee. "Grace Chan, I know this is sudden, but I love you, and I can't live without you. Will you marry me and make me the happiest man on Earth and in the galaxy?"

Tears stream from her eyes, and she says, "Yes, I will marry you, John Trosky. I love you too."

People start cheering and clapping as John latches onto Grace and lifts her up, and spins her around. He then puts the custom-made pink diamond ring on her hand and gives her the matching earrings. She has tears running down her face and wipes them away. "This is the most beautiful ring I have ever seen and with earrings to match! Where did you get them, and when did you have time?"

"When I went to Paris to interview a suspect and ran into a friend who owns the most exclusive jewellery store in Paris called Chopard House. His name is Karl Scheifele, and he and I designed your ring and earrings. There is also a wedding ring being made that interlocks with this ring. I also bought the Goldfinger Rolls Royce from him, which he didn't want to part with, so I bought two other cars from him—a 1907 Alfa Romeo race car and a 1935 Delahaye roadster in a beautiful metallic blue colour. We should take that car out for a drive soon. It is a work of art." He adds, "And we should wrap things up in the next two weeks because I want to take you, Julie, and Savana to my house in Hawaii for a little holiday. Thom can take care of the house with Brigette if he wants. He can have a holiday later at the Hawaiian house. I have a full staff at the house, so Julie won't have to cook. It's a big house. I had it designed to look like the mansion in *Magnum P.I.* that was filmed in 2019. It has its own private beach."

Grace says, "Great idea; I can use a holiday. I haven't had one in years."

The band starts playing "All You Need Is Love," and the crowd sings along. Jenny Olsen is in the crowd filming this on her hi-definition pocket phone. John announces, "Please, excuse us for a few minutes; I want to take the birthday girl slash fiancé for a ride in her new car. By the way, this is being taped by my crew, and you can download it from the cloud after the party is over as a souvenir."

CHAPTER EIGHTY-SEVEN

"We will be back soon, and I will play the piano for you, and Grace and I will sing two duets for you. If anyone else wants to join us with the band, don't be shy. Shane Travis, I know you can handle a rifle, but I hear you can play a mean bass guitar. Anyone else want to play or sing; let's blow the roof off this place! Audley Barnes, my Jamaican friend, I know you are in a reggae band, man."

John and Grace get in the back seat of the Rolls Royce, and Ringo drives them out the ballroom doors, and they circle the house on the long driveway. Grace says, "My head is spinning; I can't believe this day and all the things you've done for me!"

John touches Grace's hand and looks into her eyes. "Ever since I looked into those beautiful green eyes of yours at the auction, I fell in love with you. I can read people, and I could feel the beauty and warmth of your soul and the love and kindness in your heart. I think to have someone to touch your hand and have it mean something is pure love."

Grace has tears streaming down her eyes. "I love you too, and I feel your soul touching mine every day. I think we should go back in the house before we really start crying."

John tears up and says, "I think it's too late for that."

They hug and kiss passionately and go back to the mansion. John adds, "We should take a long ride in this car tomorrow with my chauffeur Jeffery or your chauffeur."

Grace smiles and says, "John, does that dark glass go up? Because we should christen this baby properly tomorrow."

John replies, "I like the way you think, and yes, I'm all for that!"

Grace says, "I want to check on the girls to see how they like their new toys, then we can party."

They go into Savana's bedroom, and the girls are playing and having fun. Megan says, "Thank you, Auntie Grace, this toy black stallion horse is really great!"

Fawn says, "Thank you, Auntie Grace. This toy puppy that I named Buddy is cute and is teaching me my ABC's, and it likes me and dances around."

Savana says, "Now that you and Uncle Tiny are going to get married, can we call you Auntie Grace?"

Grace answers, "I already am Megan and Fawn's aunt, as their mother is my sister, but I think of all of you girls like family, so you can all call me Auntie Grace.

Savana says, "Auntie Grace, I drew this picture of you and Uncle Tiny for your birthday. I hope you like it."

Grace looks at it and smiles with tears in her eyes. "It's beautiful. I'm going to have it framed and put it in my office. That was really sweet of you. Now, let's go into the present room and open some presents."

She opens the box of shoes from her mother. "These are actually really nice; my mom has acquired some taste."

Most of the squad enters the room, and Grace notices a blanket covering something in the corner. Sam Slade goes over and uncovers a comfortable recliner chair in grey velvet. She says, "We put our money together and bought you this sleep chair. It has a heater, a massager, a cooler, and a drink holder that flips out the side, and it sleeps two people. We felt you already had everything, so we decided on this. I hope you like it."

Grace answers, "This is great! It's perfect! Thank you!" She opens more presents and thanks everyone. "Let's move to the ballroom as John and I are going to sing some songs and then dance to the band. You can dance too. It will be lots of fun. Let's go!"

They go into the ballroom, and John sits at the piano and starts playing and singing, "With a Little Help From My Friends," sounding like Paul McCartney, with the girls in the band singing background and Shane Travis playing bass guitar. The crowd sings along.

When he finishes, Grace enters the room, and John says into the microphone, "We now have a surprise for you. Grace and I are going to sing two songs for you. Grace sits down beside him, and John starts singing "Baby You Can Drive My Car." Grace joins in, and they sing a great duet. People clap and whistle and yell. John waits until it dies down. "Now, we will sing 'Hit the Road Jack' by the honourable Ray Charles, and we want you to join in at the chorus."

They sing, and the crowd joins in, and some people start dancing. People clap wildly and yell, "Great, awesome, unreal!"

John says, "Thank you. Isn't Grace a terrific singer? I love you, honey! Eddie Bennetti, get up here! Borrow a lead guitar! Rumour has it you play like Carlos Santana. Now, we need a singer. Chuck, can you sing 'Black Magic Woman'?"

Chuck says, "Yes, lieutenant, but it would have been nice to have had a heads up on this."

He sings the song, and then Roxy steps up and says, "I would love to sing 'The Game of Love' by Carlos Santana with Eddie Bennetti playing guitar. Are you okay with that, Eddie?"

Eddie says, "Yes, I know all Santana's songs."

Eddie strums the guitar, and they start playing "Black Magic Woman." The squad is shocked at their talent. John goes up to Audley Barnes and says, "Can you sing any Bob Marley songs or Jimmy Cliff? I cleared it with the band if you want to go up there."

He says, "Yes, I know songs from both those guys, man. That would be cool!"

Chuck starts singing "Black Magic Woman" and Eddie wails on the guitar just like Carlos Santana. The crowd claps and yells, then Roxy steps up and starts singing the up-tempo song "The Game of Love" by Carlos Santana, and John and Grace start dancing with a lot of flare. Savana, Jackie, Megan, Fawn, and Joanne Webber's daughters, Rose and Adele, join them, dancing and spinning around and giggling like little girls do!

CHAPTER EIGHTY-EIGHT

John dances with Savana with her shoes on top of his and teaches her to waltz. She giggles and says, "This is fun!" He then gets Jackie and Megan and does the same thing. He then picks up Fawn and swings her around as she giggles.

Randy and Tasha are burning up the dance floor with their moves. Joanne Webber approaches John and says, "Great party, John. You owe me a dance, remember? Your fiancé Grace is beautiful and a really nice person; I talked to her a little while ago."

They start to Salsa dance to "Oyez Como VA" and look really good doing it!

John says, "Joanne, you haven't lost your moves. Your daughters are having a lot of fun too."

She says, "They sure are. Where did you get this band? They are fantastic."

"Oh, my house manager and best friend Thom Saunders found them, and some of my squad are up there singing. Eddie Bennetti is wailing on that guitar like Carlos Santana."

Grace is over dancing with Larry Browning, the head of John's R and D unit.

Jenny Olson comes over, and John introduces her to Joanne. Joanne says, "Jenny, I love your body-hugging red dress. I can't wear anything like that anymore; I've gained ten pounds over the years."

John smiles, looks her up and down, and says, "You still look fantastic. I like a voluptuous figure myself. Your . . . umm . . . upper body has filled out very nicely."

Joanne says, "Are you trying to say you like my breasts bigger?"

John replies, "Yes, I was trying to be polite."

Jenny says, "John, you promised me a dance a week ago. I like this Reggae song, so let's dance."

John says, "True, and that's my newest squad member Audley Barnes singing the Bob Marley song, 'Stir It Up.' I didn't know I had so many talented people in my squad. Some of my squad is mixing with my brother Mike's research people, and Bin Tran is getting very friendly with that cute little singer Roxy; they are making eyes at each other."

Grace comes back to John and says, "Our groups of people are becoming fast friends with each other. Who is that guy Maya is seriously talking to? He's kind of cute."

That's Jim Alberts; he's the shop foreman of our custom car dealership and a nice guy. He knows how to calm a customer down when they are really mad, and he solves their problem, whatever it is."

Grace replies, "Maya is like that too; she can calm people down quickly."

CHAPTER EIGHTY-NINE

John continues, "Well, Grace, this party is winding down, but I want one more dance with you. I'm going to get the band to play an old song that Ella Fitzgerald sang called 'Cheek to Cheek.'"

He goes and talks to the band and announces, "Well, friends, it's time to wrap this up. This is the last song, and if any of you are too loaded to drive home, we have a lot of empty rooms set up or my chauffeur or Grace's will drive you home. One of my security guys will drive your car home if needed. Thanks for coming and don't forget your Bodyguard coats."

The band starts playing and the background singer Maddie sings "Cheek to Cheek" as John and Grace do a slow waltz around the room. Grace kicks off her shoes.

"This was the best party ever, John. How can I ever thank you?" Grace says.

He replies, "I'll think of something when we get upstairs, Miss Moneypenny."

"I'm sure you will, Mr. Bond, James Bond."

They say good night to the guests, but Eddie and Brandi share a room, Thom has Brigette stay over in his room, and Rembrandt and Michelle also share a room. Chuck helps the band break down the equipment. John and Grace go up to his bedroom.

"That was a great party. I'm looking forward to our vacation in Hawaii. I'm going to ship the 1935 Delahaye roadster there so that we can enjoy the sun. If a big case comes along, I'm going to pass it on to Sam Slade," John says.

"I'm all for that, Mr. Bond, James Bond."

THE END

Made in the USA
Middletown, DE
30 July 2021

45064918R00215